MEET HIM.

MEET DEATH.

PENGUIN BOOKS

KING OF SWORDS

Praise for Nick Stone

KING OF SWORDS

'*King of Swords* rivals some of the greats of the thriller genre'
Daily Express

'Full of magic and mystery, *King of Swords* boosts Stone's
reputation as an up-and-coming master of crime'
Independent on Sunday

'With his second novel, *King of Swords*, Stone really gets into
his stride . . . This is brilliantly assured storytelling:
fast-paced, funny, frightening' *Observer*

'Stone really scores in his extraordinary portrait of a city
at boiling point, a giant Molotov cocktail of racial
tension, police corruption, voodoo and the cut-throat
trade in women and drugs' *Guardian*

'This is highly evocative writing, carrying a powerful and
original story' *Independent*

'Stone is a magnificent talent' *reviewingtheevidence.com*

'*King of Swords* delivers thrills and frights with the rocking
rhythm of a runaway train and the shock of getting a voodoo
doll and a packet of pins through the post' *Birmingham Post*

'The man who brought you the ground-breaking
Mr Clarinet has done it again, and even better than before'
Daily Sport

MR CLARINET

King of Swords

NICK STONE

PENGUIN BOOKS

PENGUIN BOOKS

Published by the Penguin Group

Penguin Books Ltd, 80 Strand, London WC2R ORL, England

Penguin Group (USA) Inc., 375 Hudson Street, New York, New York 10014, USA

Penguin Group (Canada), 90 Eglinton Avenue East, Suite 700, Toronto, Ontario, Canada M4P 2Y3
(a division of Pearson Penguin Canada Inc.)

Penguin Ireland, 25 St Stephen's Green, Dublin 2, Ireland
(a division of Penguin Books Ltd)

Penguin Group (Australia), 250 Camberwell Road, Camberwell, Victoria 3124, Australia
(a division of Pearson Australia Group Pty Ltd)

Penguin Books India Pvt Ltd, 11 Community Centre, Panchsheel Park, New Delhi – 110 017, India

Penguin Group (NZ), 67 Apollo Drive, Rosedale, North Shore 0632, New Zealand
(a division of Pearson New Zealand Ltd)

Penguin Books (South Africa) (Pty) Ltd, 24 Sturdee Avenue, Rosebank, Johannesburg 2196, South Africa

Penguin Books Ltd, Registered Offices: 80 Strand, London WC2R ORL, England

www.penguin.com

First published in Great Britain by Michael Joseph 2007
Published in Penguin Books 2008

1

Copyright © Nick Stone, 2007
All rights reserved

The moral right of the author has been asserted

Set in Monotype Garamond
Typeset by Rowland Phototypesetting Ltd, Bury St Edmunds, Suffolk
Printed in England by Clays Ltd, St Ives plc

978-0-141-02107-2

www.greenpenguin.co.uk

For Dad

I have supped full with horrors.

Macbeth, Act 5, Scene 5

PART ONE
November 1980

I

It was the last thing he needed or wanted, a dead ape at the end of his shift, but there it was – a corpse with bad timing. Larry Gibson, one of the night security guards at Primate Park, stood staring at the thing spotlighted in his torch beam – a long-stemmed cruciform of black fur lying less than twenty feet away, face up and palms open on the grassy verge in front of the wire. He didn't know which of the fifteen species of monkey advertised in the zoo's product literature this one was, and he didn't care; all he knew was that he had some decisions to make and fast.

He weighed up what to do with how much he could get away with not doing: he could sound the alarm and stick around to help when and where and if he was needed; or he could simply look the other way and ignore King Kong for the ten remaining minutes of his shift. Plus he craved sleep. Thanks to some Marine-issue bennies he'd popped on Sunday night, he'd been awake for fifty-nine hours straight; his longest ever stretch. The most he'd lasted before was forty-eight hours. It was now Wednesday morning. He'd run out of pills and all the sleep he'd cheated and skipped out on was catching up with him, ganging up in the wings, getting ready to drop on him like a sack of wet cement.

He checked his watch. 5.21 a.m. He needed to get out of here, get home, get his head down, sleep. He had another job starting at one p.m. as a supermarket supervisor. That was for alimony and child support. This gig – cash in hand and no questions asked – was for body and soul and the roof over his head. He really couldn't afford to fuck it up.

Dr Jenny Gold had been dozing with the radio on when she got the phone call from the security guard in Sector 1, nearest the front gate. Something about a dead gorilla, he'd said. She hoped to God it wasn't Bruce, their star attraction.

Jenny had been the head veterinarian at the zoo ever since it had opened, nine years before. Primate Park had been the brainchild of Harold and Henry Yik, two brothers from Hong Kong, who'd opened the place in direct competition to Miami's other primate-only zoo, Monkey Jungle. They'd reasoned that while Monkey Jungle was a very popular tourist attraction, its location – South Dade, inland and well away from the beach and hotels – meant it was only doing about 25 per cent of the business it could have done, had it been closer to the tourist dollars. So they'd built Primate Park from scratch in North Miami Beach – right next to a strip of hotels – making it bigger and, so they thought, better than the competition. At its peak they'd had twenty-eight species of monkey, ranging from the expected – chimps, dressed up in blue shorts, yellow check shirts and red sun visors, doing cute, quasi-human tricks like playing mini-golf, baseball and soccer; gorillas, who beat their chests and growled; baboons, who showed off their bright pink bald asses and bared their fangs – along with more exotic species, like dusky titi monkeys, rodent-like lemurs, and the lithe, intelligent brown-headed spider monkeys. Yet Primate Park hadn't really caught on as an alternative to Monkey Jungle. The latter had been around for close to forty years and was considered a local treasure, one of those slightly eccentric Miami landmarks, like the Ancient Spanish Monastery, South Beach's Art Deco district, Vizcaya, the Biltmore, and the giant Coppertone sign. The new zoo was seen as too cold, too clinical, too calculating. It was all wrong for the town. Miami was the kind of place where things only worked by accident, not because they were supposed to. The general public stayed away from the new zoo. The Yik brothers started talking about bulldozing Primate Park and converting it into real estate.

And then, last summer, Bruce, one of the four mountain gorillas they had, picked up the stub of a burning cigar a visitor had dropped near him and began puffing away at it, managing to blow five perfect smoke rings in the shape of the Olympic symbol every time he exhaled. Someone had taken pictures of him and sent them to a TV station, which had promptly dispatched a camera crew to the zoo. Bruce put Primate Park on the 6 o'clock news and, from that day on, in the public consciousness too. People flocked to the zoo just to see him. And they were still coming, most of them with cigars, cigarettes and pipes to toss to the gorilla, whose sole activities were now confined to chain-smoking and coughing. They'd had to move him to a separate area because his habit made him stink so much the other gorillas refused to go near him.

Jenny found it inhumane and cruel to do that to an animal, but when she'd complained to the brothers, they'd simply shown her the balance sheets. She was now looking for another job.

When she got to the control room she found the guard staring out of the thick shatterproof window.

'You the *vet*?' he asked when he saw Jenny, his voice brimming with incredulity.

Jenny was petite and youthful in appearance, which led to some people – usually horny men and old ladies – mistaking her for a teenager. She was the only thirty-six-year-old she knew who still had to carry ID to get served in a bar.

'Yeah, I'm the *vet*,' she replied tetchily. She was already in a bad mood because of the election results. Ronald Reagan, a one-time B-movie actor, had won the White House last night. It was hardly unexpected, given Carter's catastrophic handling of the Iranian hostage crisis and the economy, among other things, but she had hoped the American people wouldn't be suckered into voting for Ronnie.

'Where is it?' she asked him.

'There.' He pointed through the window.

They were one floor up, overlooking the gently sloping wide grass verge which separated the zoo's buildings from the vast man-made jungle where the monkeys lived. It was dark outside, but daylight was just beginning to break through, so she could make out a black mound in the grass, like someone had doused the ground with petrol in the shape of a large capital T and set it alight. She couldn't be sure what it was.

'How'd it get through?'

'Power on the fence musta been off. Happens more times than you'd imagine,' the guard said, looking down at her. The jungle was surrounded by a high electric fence which gave off a mild shock when touched – enough to stun any monkey who'd want to clamber up and over it.

'Let's go down and take a look,' she said.

They stopped off at the first aid room down the corridor so Jenny could pick up the medical kit and a tranquillizer gun, which she loaded with a dart. It was the biggest gun they had, the Remington RJ5, usually used to subdue lions and tigers.

'Are we goin' *outside*?' The guard sounded worried.

'That's what I meant by "taking a look". Why? Is there a problem?' She looked up at him like he really wasn't impressing her. They locked stares. She turned on the contempt.

He took the bait. 'No problem,' he said in a bassier, more authoritative tone and smiled in a way he must have thought was reassuring but in fact came over as nervous and near rictal.

'Good.' She handed him the tranq gun. 'You know how to use this, right?'

'Sure do,' he said.

'If it wakes up, shoot it anywhere but the head. You got that?' The guard nodded, smile still in exactly the same place. He was starting to make her nervous. 'And, if the power's really down on that fence, we could have company. Some monkeys may come to see what we're doing. Most of them are harmless, but watch out for the baboons. They bite. Worse than any pitbull. Their teeth'll cut clean through to the bone.'

She could tell from his eyes that fear was now doing fast laps in his head, but he was still smiling that damn smile. It was as if the lower half of his face was paralysed.

He noticed her staring at his mouth. He ran his tongue quickly under his lips. The speed had dehydrated him so much that the inside of his lips had stuck to his gums.

'So what do we do if we're . . . outnumbered?'

'Run.'

'*Run*?'

'Run.'

'Right.'

They went downstairs to the tunnel entrance, Jenny grinning wickedly behind the dumbass security guard as he timidly took each step like he was negotiating a steep rocky hill on his way to his own execution.

'I'll open the door; you go out first,' she said. 'Approach slowly.'

She handed him the tranquillizer gun and then unlocked and opened the door. He slipped off the safety catch and stepped outside.

They heard the cries of the monkeys – snarls, growls, whoops and roars, guttural and fierce; territories and young ones being protected – all underpinned by the snap and crack of branches being jumped from and to, the dense timpani of leaves and bushes being crashed through. And then there was the smell of the place: the animals, acrid and

7

heady; ammonia; fresh manure and wet hay mixed in with the jungle's humid earthiness, its blossomings and decay, things ripening, things growing, things going back into the soil.

Larry approached on tiptoe, coming in from the side as instructed. The vet shone a torch on the ape, which lay some twenty feet away, still not moving. As he got closer he saw that the beast's fur had a slight metallic green tinge to it, as if there were sequins strewn across its body.

He heard it make a sound. He stopped and listened more closely, because it had only been the faintest of noises, something that could quite easily have come from elsewhere. Then he heard it again. It was faint and painful breathing, a low moan, barely audible over the sing-song of the dawn birds now coming from the nearby trees.

'I think it's alive,' he whispered to the vet. 'Sounds hurt. Bring the light in closer.'

He stood where he was with the tranquillizer gun pointed at the prostrate animal's side, his finger on the trigger. The vet approached. The animal's moaning got a little louder as the light on it grew brighter. It didn't sound like breathing now, pained or otherwise. It was more of a whining drone, which reminded Larry of the time he'd once trapped a hornet under a whisky glass. The thing had attacked the glass with everything it had, trying to get out, flying at it, butting it, stinging it, getting angrier and angrier with every failed attempt until it had died of exhaustion.

The vet came in closer. Larry didn't move. His hands were getting wet holding the gun.

'What – the – *HELL*!' the vet shouted.

The ape woke up. It raised its head off the ground.

They stepped back. The noise grew louder, a kind of high-pitched hum came out of its mouth. Then, suddenly, with a speed belying its bulk, the animal sprang to its feet and rushed at them.

8

Larry pushed the vet away and heard her scream. The light was gone. He fired his gun. The dart must have missed because the animal kept coming straight at him with a hideous dull whistling scream, like the noise of a lathe cutting through sheet metal, amplified to an excruciatingly sharp pitch.

Larry went for his pistol, but before he could get his hand to it he was hit everywhere and from every angle by a blizzard of small hard pellets. They smashed into his hands, ears, neck, legs, arms, chest. They stung exposed flesh. They got up his nostrils and down his earholes. He opened his mouth and screamed. They shot down his throat and massed on his tongue and bounced around the inside of his cheeks.

He fell on the grass, spitting, coughing and retching, confused and giddy, still expecting to be trampled and mauled by the ape, wondering where it was and what was taking it so long.

Jenny rushed back to the control room and dialled 911. She was immediately put on hold. She looked out of the window at the security guard still spluttering his guts out on the floor. She felt sorry for him. He hadn't realized what he was looking at until it was too late.

When the operator took her call Jenny asked for two ambulances – one for the security guard who'd swallowed a mouthful of blowflies and the other for the body of the dead man those same flies had been feasting on before the guard had disturbed them.

2

'Who said this was murder?' Detective Sergeant Max Mingus asked his partner, Joe Liston, as they pulled up outside the entrance to Primate Park in Joe's green '75 Buick convertible.

'No one,' Joe replied.

'So what we doin' here?'

'Our J-O-B,' Joe said. They'd been driving to Miami Task Force headquarters when the dispatcher's call had come through. Primate Park was on the way. Max hadn't heard any of it because he'd been fast asleep, face pancaked against the window. Joe had filled him in along the way. 'We'll just keep the turf warm till the right people show up. What've we gotta rush off to? Three feet of paperwork and a bad hangover? You in some kind of hurry to get to that?'

'Good point,' Max replied. The pair were feeling the election-night drinks they'd had at the Evening Coconut the night before. The Coco – as they called it – was a downtown bar close not only to their HQ but in the heart of the Miami business community. Plainclothes cops interfaced with the after hours white-collar crowd who worked in the nearby banks, law firms, publishers, ad agencies and real estate brokers. They'd buy cops drinks and plug them for war stories, listening awed and wide-eyed like deranged children to tales of shoot-outs, serial killers and gruesome mutilations. Many an affair had started there, overworked, stressed-out execs with no lives outside their careers, finding soul mates in overworked, stressed-out cops with no lives outside *their* jobs – or vocations, as some called their work, because the money wasn't shit for the risks they took. And the bar was also great for picking up extra employment, anything from basic building security to consultancy to private investigations. Max and Joe didn't go there that often, and when they did it was strictly to drink. They didn't like talking about their jobs with strangers and therefore, between them, emanated such hostility that civilians stayed well away.

The cheers when Reagan's victory was announced on the bar's four TVs had been as deafening as the chorus of insults and boos hurled at the screens when Carter had appeared, conceding defeat with tears in his eyes. Joe had felt deeply uneasy. A lifelong registered Democrat, he'd liked and admired Jimmy Carter. He'd considered him honest and decent, and, above all, a man of principle. But every other cop in town hated Carter because of the Mariel Boatlift fiasco. Thanks to him, they said, being a cop in Miami now was a nightmare.

From 15 April until 31 October, Fidel Castro had expelled 125,000 people from Cuba to the US in flotillas of leaking boats. Although many of the refugees were dissidents with their families, Castro took the opportunity to – in his words – 'flush Cuba's toilets on America'. He'd emptied his country's streets of all winos, beggars, prostitutes and cripples, purged its prisons and mental hospitals of their most vicious and violent inmates and sent them over as well. In those six months, crime in Miami had rocketed. Homicides, armed robberies, home invasions and rapes were all way up and the cops couldn't handle it. Already understaffed and underfunded, they'd been caught completely off-guard. They'd never come face to face with this new breed of criminal – Third World poor, First World envious; nothing to lose, everything to gain; violence coming to them without thought or remorse.

Then, to make matters much worse, on 17 May Miami had been torn apart by the worst race riot since Watts. The previous December Arthur McDuffie, an unarmed black man who'd been doing stunts on his motorcycle in the early hours of the morning, had been beaten into a coma by four white officers after a high-speed chase. The officers had tried to cover up the beating by claiming it was an accident. McDuffie later died from his injuries and the officers went on trial. Despite fairly conclusive evidence of their guilt, they were acquitted by an all-white jury. The city had exploded, as its black community had decided to vent an anger stoked by years of resentment against police harassment and injustice.

And yet, despite this, Joe had put off voting until the very last moment. Reagan wasn't someone he trusted or liked the look of, and the only film of his he'd ever enjoyed had been *The Killers*, where he'd had a minor role as a hitman's victim.

Max had had no such qualms about voting for Reagan. He'd bled and breathed Republican since the day Joe had met him, ten years before, when Max was a rookie and they'd partnered up in patrol. Max had been a Nixon man then, and he still had good things to say about him, Watergate or no Watergate.

Max looked at the entrance to Primate Park.

'Who the fuck'd want to bring their kids here – except as a punishment?'

'Exactly what I thought.' Joe laughed. 'Brought my nephew Curtis here. Kid's five. He wanted to see some real monkeys. So I gave him a choice of here, which was closest, or Monkey Jungle over in South Dade. When we pulled up where we're at now, Curtis starts bawlin' and says he ain't goin' in.'

'So where d'you go?'

'Monkey Jungle.'

'He like it?'

'Nah, them monkeys scared him half to death.'

Max laughed aloud.

The gateway to Primate Park was in the shape of a

twenty-five-foot-high black roaring gorilla head. Visitors walked through a gate in the open mouth, passing under its bared pointed teeth, followed every step of the way by its enraged eyes. The high surrounding wall on either side of the entrance was also painted with monkey heads, meant to represent every species in the park, but they were angry renditions, capturing the primates at their most bestial and intimidating, savages completely beyond the reach of human temperance. How someone ever thought the design would be a crowd-puller was a mystery.

They got out of the car. Max stretched and yawned and rolled his neck while Joe got the crime-scene materials he kept in the trunk – green, powder-filled latex gloves, wooden tongue depressors, glassine evidence bags and envelopes, a Polaroid camera, and a pot of Vicks mentholated grease they'd smear on their upper lips to ward off the stench of death.

They made an odd pair, the two detectives, Jenny thought, as she watched them going about their business, talking to witnesses and inspecting the body on the grass. They couldn't have been more different. Mingus, the white one, was brusque to the point of rudeness. When he'd introduced himself and his partner, Detective Liston, she'd smelled stale booze and cigarettes on him. He looked like he'd slept in his car, if at all. His clothes – black chinos, grey sports coat, open-necked white shirt – were crumpled and hung off him like they wanted to be on someone else; he was unshaven and his close-cropped dark brown hair needed a good combing. He was squat, solid and broad, with big shoulders and little to no neck separating them from his head. He was a good-looking guy – behind the stubble and the bloodshot blue eyes – but there was an air of unpleasantness about him, a sense of a tightly coiled meanness just waiting to spring and sting. She was sure he was the kind of cop who

13

beat the crap out of suspects and gave his girlfriend – he had no wedding ring – hell at home.

Detective Liston was a well-groomed black man in a navy blue suit, light blue shirt and matching tie with a gold clip. He looked like a sales rep for a big corporation just starting his day. He asked her questions about finding the body, whether she'd seen or heard anything suspicious the previous night, what she'd been doing. He was professional, very much by the book, but he was also genuinely courteous and engaging, to the point where she wished she knew more so she could help him out. He reminded her of Earl Campbell, the running back. Same height, same build, same demeanour. Like his partner, he had no wedding ring.

'Looks like he's been dead two weeks,' Max said, undoing his shirtsleeves, folding them over the cuffs of his jacket and pushing them up to his elbows, the way he always did whenever he was inspecting a cadaver. It was just in case he needed to stick his hand into a wound to retrieve an important fragment of evidence.

'Smells like three,' Joe said, turning away from the stench, which had broken through the barrier of Vicks and gotten up his nose and into his stomach. It was as intense as it was vile, like a whole dead cow left in a dumpster in high summer. He didn't know how Max could stand to get in so close.

The body was that of a black man, naked, and in an advanced stage of decomposition. It was swollen and misshapen, pumped up with a cocktail of malign gasses emanating from the liquefying insides; the skin was stretched as tight as it could go, in places semi-transparent like gauze, allowing glimpses of the body's afterlife, the shadowy movements of the parasitical worms and insects now colonizing it.

The mouth was completely covered in a grotesque pout of busy fleshflies – told apart from common blowflies by their candy-striped black and white bodies. The eyes were long gone, as were their lids, both eaten by insects. The sockets had become two teeming nests of writhing maggots, the colour and texture of rancid butter. They were being picked off one by one by an orderly procession of metallic-green hister beetles, which were travelling in single file up from the corpse's left ear, grabbing a maggot in their jaws, pulling them out of their communal home and carrying them, wriggling fiercely, back into the right ear, in parallel descending streams. Viewed from above, it looked like the black man's squirming eye sockets were crying big shiny green tears.

Max and Joe were the only ones near the body. The paramedics were tending to the security guard who'd discovered it and swallowed a mouthful of flies for his trouble. They were explaining what stomach-pumping involved. He was talking about needing coffee. Two North Miami PD officers were standing away to the left, one young, one old, fingers hooked around their belts, smoking cigarettes, looking bored. The rest of the Park staff had all congregated in the public tunnel and were watching the scene through the wire. Neither forensics nor back-up had arrived.

Meanwhile, behind them, Max and Joe could hear the zoo's inmates getting increasingly restless. Ever since they'd arrived they'd heard loud, fearsome roars coming from the trees. It sounded like a lion, only angrier and edgier, with more to prove. Howler monkeys – the veterinarian had explained with a smile, when she'd seen Max and Joe exchange worried looks – it was what they did in the morning to warn off any competition: nothing to be scared of, they were harmless, all bark, no bite. Then they'd heard more sounds, coming from other kinds of monkey – screeches, hollering, howls and something like the high-speed cackling of a hen on steroids. The noises, uninhibited and completely abandoned, came together in a mad primal cacophony, not unlike a bar filled with drunks speaking in tongues.

There was plenty of accompanying movement in the jungle too, the unmistakable sound of disturbance, crashings in the trees and bushes, branches snapping, things being knocked over and broken, all of it getting louder, clearer and closer.

Max looked over at the jungle – an impressive but completely incongruous legion of tropical trees, too tall and wide for the area of flatland they occupied and way too tall for Miami – and clearly saw monkeys, lots and lots of them, hopping from branch to branch and tree to tree, heading towards the high perimeter fence.

Max stood up and walked over to the corpse's feet. The ends of the toes had turned completely black and sticky. He noticed puncture marks in the legs, teeth and claw marks, all of them leaking clear slimy fluid, some already squirming and yellowy with maggot nests.

He looked along the body and into the trees, then returned his gaze to the area of grass beyond the feet. A stretch of grass behind and beyond the head, approximately the width of the dead man's shoulders, was lying flat. The grass in front of the toes, leading to the main building, was upright. The body had been dragged here.

Max got up and began to walk towards the jungle, looking down the whole time. He traced the trail of flattened grass all the way back to the forty-foot-high wire fence. There was a sign on it, a big stark banner warning of electrocution. It was the same kind of fence they had in maximum security prisons, only theirs hummed with lethal current. This one was quiet. Which meant it wasn't working.

He reached the beginning of the trail. It ended at the gate. He tried it. It was open.

Something on the grass to his right caught his eye. He

turned around and found himself looking at a row of eight monkeys sitting on their haunches, staring right at him. They were beige, apart from their arms, shoulders and heads, which were light grey. Their faces were also grey, except for the area around their eyes and nose, which was a horizontal figure of eight in white, like the Lone Ranger mask, while their eyes and mouths were surrounded in black borders. How long had they been there? Had they dragged the body over? He couldn't exactly ask them.

Suddenly he heard heavy footfalls from behind the fence. Two large, ginger-haired monkeys with long flabby chins were leaning over a log, glaring at him like two badass desperadoes in a saloon bar, waiting to be served. How long before they came through?

Max hurriedly returned to the body. More people had arrived – two more uniforms, medics, the forensics team and a guy who seemed to have come straight off a yacht, if his clothes were anything to go by: white duck pants, espadrilles, a blue blazer and a red cravat. He was talking to Joe.

Max beckoned his partner over.

'Our guy died in there.' He motioned to the jungle. 'Musta stunk the place out so bad the monkeys dragged him out. Forensics'll have to go in.'

'Even if there isn't another crime in the city for a whole month, we still don't have the manpower to cover an area that big.'

'I know, Joe, but it's not our problem once the local dicks get here. Any word on when that'll be?'

Joe was about to answer when the man in the blazer got between them.

'Are you in charge here?' he asked Max.

'Who are you?' Max looked at him like he was a piece of shit who'd grown legs and a mouth. He had round rimless glasses and reddish blond hair, thinning to a threadbare strip in front, like a short length of moth-eaten carpet.

17

'Ethan Moss, director.' He held out his hand. Max ignored it. 'How long will you be?'

'However long it takes,' Max said.

'How about an estimate?'

'Forensics have to do their job.' Max nodded to the team working over the body, while uniforms were planting metal rods in the ground and cordoning off the area with black and yellow tape. 'If this turns out to be a homicide, the whole place could be shut down for weeks.'

'*Weeks?*' Moss went pale, then looked at his watch. 'You've got two hours at the most. We've got VIPs coming.'

'Not today you haven't, sir.' Max kept the officious side of polite. 'This is a crime scene. You can't open for business until we're through.'

'You don't understand, Detective. Time is money.' Moss was panicking. 'We're expecting a Japanese film crew. They're shooting a commercial.'

'Sir, it's outta my hands,' Max said. 'We're just following procedure.'

'But, you don't *understand*, Detective. They've come all the way from Tokyo. It took *months* of negotiation.'

'I'm really sorry about that, sir, but you've got a dead body here. A crime may have been committed. This is a police investigation. That supersedes everything else. OK?' Max spoke slowly, feeling a little sorrier for the guy because he looked like his balls were on the line, his feet stuck in cement and he'd just heard the express train whistle. 'Can't you film someplace else?'

'No. It has to be here. It's in the contract. Bruce in his natural environment.' Moss turned to look towards the jungle.

'Bruce? Who's Bruce?' Max asked.

'You mean you haven't heard of him? Bruce – our gorilla?'

'You got a gorilla . . . called *Bruce*?' Max smiled, looking over at Joe, who'd heard and was mouthing 'fuck you' at him.

'Yes. That's right. What's so funny?' Moss snapped.

'Oh, nothing – private joke,' Max replied. 'So what's Bruce do that's got the Japs interested? He sing?' He looked at Joe again and winked.

'No. He smokes.'

'*Smokes?*'

'Yes – smokes.'

'Like what – cigarettes?' Max was incredulous.

'Yes, Detective, cigarettes, cigars. He smokes,' Moss answered. 'I can tell you don't watch TV. Bruce has been all over the news.'

'For smoking?'

'That's right,' Moss said, 'and the Sendai cigarette company has paid us a lot of money to use Bruce in their ad campaign.'

'Jesus!' Max shook his head, shocked and incredulous at human cruelty. He smoked himself, but it was an informed decision – albeit a stupid one he was starting to regret. The animal didn't have a choice.

'Look – Detective Mingus,' Moss took another tack, dropping his voice a few notches and drawing closer to Max, who knew what was coming, 'couldn't we make some sort of, er, arrangement. I'm in a spot here –'

He didn't get much further because he was interrupted by a loud commotion to their right.

A uniformed cop, who'd been putting up a cordon around the scene had just fallen flat on his face. He was shouting and swearing and yelling for somebody to come and help him. His legs were tied together with the same tape he'd been using to close off the space around the body. What at first looked like a stupid prank on the part of a colleague, became a matter of public hilarity when one of the beige monkeys Max had seen jumped on the cop's back and started bouncing up and down, clapping its paws, grinning and squawking like a manic bird. The officer tried to knock it off, first with his left hand, then his right, but the monkey deftly leapt over the swiping hands, causing the zoo staff watching from the tunnel to cheer. This pissed the cop off. Furiously, he pulled himself to his feet, most likely thinking he'd rid himself of the animal that way. But the monkey wrapped its tail tight around the officer's forehead and clung to him while he hopped around screaming for help.

Moss went over, but the monkey saw him coming and scampered away across the grass. Moss took out a pen-knife and cut through the plastic tape around the cop's ankles. Once free, the cop got back up and ran off after the monkey.

Suddenly there was a gunshot.

The police automatically hit the deck, everyone else panicked; a few screamed. The sounds of the jungle suddenly died.

At first Max thought the officer had shot the monkey, but then he heard agonized sobbing and moaning and saw that the cop was on the ground, clutching his left leg below the knee. A few metres away, the monkey was sitting on its haunches, nearly motionless and completely subdued, staring at them all. The animal was evenly spattered, head to foot, in red. Standing in a row behind it, were the other monkeys. The blood-soaked monkey turned and joined the others.

Max got up and raced over to the officer. As he drew closer, he noticed the monkeys were doing a kind of Mexican wave.

Blood was pouring out of the officer's leg, running over his hands.

'What happened?' Max asked.

'I just got fuckin' *shot*!' the cop gasped.

'You got shot?'

The officer's holster was empty. Max looked for the gun, but couldn't see it anywhere.

Then he realized what the monkeys were really doing.

They had the gun – a black .44 Smith & Wesson Special service revolver – and they were tossing it to each other, underarm, down the line, like a football; passing and catching.

Behind him, everyone was up on their feet. Joe and a paramedic were running over.

Max heard the unmistakable sound of a hammer being cocked. He turned and saw the gun bouncing down the line of fur and grinning teeth, primed to fire. Without looking away, he held up his hand and motioned for Joe and the medic to get down. Joe shouted the command over to the others, who all hit the deck.

Max grabbed the officer by the collar and dragged him back towards the building. Looking over his shoulder he couldn't help but notice what was going on in the background, by the fence. The gate was wide open and dozens of monkeys were spilling out onto the grass and heading towards them, led, it seemed, by the two large ginger primates he'd last seen on the other side. They stopped a few feet behind the beige ones. Max picked up speed – the wounded officer screaming as he bumped along the ground.

The beige primates had up until now been happily playing pass-the-lethal-weapon. Then, one of them turned around and noticed the ginger badasses coming up behind them, droopy chins swinging like irate pendulums.

Suddenly, the badasses roared so ferociously and so deafeningly loud they drowned out the sound of the gun going off. Max saw the flash and the smoke and threw himself to the ground. One of the beige monkeys was down on its back, but it scrambled to its feet and ran straight for Max in its desire to get away from the ginger primates and the horde of other beasts the jungle was disgorging – gorillas, baboons, chimpanzees, macaques, great apes, orangutans – now advancing on the crime scene at a fast clip.

As Max got up, the monkey jumped in his arms. The thing was shaking with terror and very very smelly. Max turned and ran, carrying the animal in one arm and dragging the cop with the other. He ran towards the open door of the building where cops, medics, forensics, Park staff and his own partner were pushing each other to get inside before they were overrun by screeching, excited primates. Max, the monkey and the cop were the last in.

The corpse stayed where it was, soon once again disappearing under the bodies of other species.

3

Gemma Harlan, medical examiner at the Dade County Morgue, liked to play music when she performed autopsies; something soothing, but at a loud enough volume to drown out the procedure's unique noises – the sawing and hammering of bone, the sticky squelch of a face being peeled back from a skull, the occasional farts and belches of released gasses – sounds of life's straggler particles leaving the building seconds before demolition. And then there were other things the music helped her get away from, the little things she hated most about her job, such as the way the spinning sawblades sometimes smoked as the bone dust landed on the hot metal and gave off a sour, ammoniac smell; the toxic aerosol jets the same saws sometimes threw back when they hit soft tissue; the way the exposed brain sometimes reminded her of a big ugly shellfish when she'd pulled the calvarium away from the lower skull. The music also drowned out the feeling that was always with her since she'd turned forty two years ago, a lengthening shadow with an icy cold centre. It was the notion that one day she would end up someplace like this too – an empty shell, her vital organs cut out, weighed, dissected then thrown away, her brain pickled and then examined, cause of death confirmed, noted down, filed away, another stat.

She hit the play button on her portable cassette deck. *Burt Bacharach and His Orchestra Play the Hits of Burt Bacharach and Hal David* – instrumental versions of those beautiful sunny songs she so loved and cherished, no vocals to distract her.

'This Guy's in Love with You' came out of the speakers as she looked down at her first cadaver of the morning –

the John Doe found in Primate Park, whose discovery had sparked a mass breakout by the zoo's entire population of monkeys. Four days later they were still recovering them all over Miami and beyond. Many had died, either hit by cars or shot by people who thought they were burglars, aliens or dangerous. One had been found lynched. A few had escaped out into the Everglades where they'd joined the dozens of exotic pets dumped there by their owners every year. Lions, tigers, wolves, pythons, boas had all been spotted in the swamp.

Gemma worked with three other people. There were two pathologists of opposing levels of competence – Javier, originally from El Salvador, was almost as good as her, whereas Martin, five years into the job, still occasionally threw up when the sawing started – and an autopsy assistant, or diener, as they were known in the trade. The city's medical budget didn't stretch to hiring one full time so they usually had to make do with either a med school student on work experience, or someone from the police academy. These greenhorns usually all either puked, fainted, or both. It was here Martin proved invaluable. He'd played a little football in his youth and was still quick on his feet. He'd catch the falling interns before they hit the ground thus preventing injuries and lawsuits. Of course this was dependent on him being upright at the time of crisis, which he usually was. He still had a jock's pride about fainting in front of an intern.

Death had changed a lot in Miami since the cocaine explosion of the mid-seventies. Prior to that the bodies she'd inspected had been victims of gunshots, stabbings, beatings, drownings, poisonings – crimes of passion, home invasions, street and store robberies, suicides; although she'd occasionally also had to inspect the results of political assassinations and piece together the remnants of a mob hit which had floated to shore in instalments stuffed in oil drums. Cocaine had made her job far more complicated. The drug gangs didn't simply kill their victims, they liked to torture them to within an inch of their lives first, which meant she spent more time on a body because she had to be sure the victim hadn't died from the barbaric suffering he or she had been put through before they were dispatched. Even the weapons were excessive. When they used guns, they didn't use pistols or even shotguns, they used machine guns and automatic rifles, riddling bodies with so many bullets it often took most of a working shift just to dig them all out. There was a hell of a lot of peripheral death too: innocents caught in the crossfire or having the misfortune to be in some way related to an intended target. Gemma had never seen anything like it, not even when she'd worked in New York. Miami had gone from having a below average murder rate, when it was predominantly home to Jewish retirees, Cuban refugees and anti-Fidelistas, to the off-the-chart-and-still-rising homicide epidemic it was experiencing now.

The morgue was full. They'd recently had to lease refrigerator trucks from Burger King to store the overflow.

She needed a break, a long one, or maybe she needed to change jobs. She didn't even like Miami anymore. What had seemed like a great place to live after the dysfunctional urban nightmare of New York, now seemed like more of the same, only with better weather and different accents.

First she examined the outside of the body, noting for the record that it was completely hairless. Shortly before his death, John Doe had had a full body shave. Even his eyelashes has been trimmed off.

'Don't the hair and nails, like, keep growing after you're dead?' a young and unfamiliar voice piped up behind her. It was today's diener, Ralph. They'd only met five minutes ago, so she didn't know what he looked like because she could only see his eyes – blue and intelligent – under his green overalls and face mask.

'That's the movie version,' Gemma said, with a weary

sigh. She was glad she'd never gone into teaching. She didn't believe in fighting losing battles. How could you compete with Hollywood myths? 'After death, the skin around the hair and fingernails loses water and shrinks. And when it shrinks it retracts, making the nails and hair look longer, and therefore giving the impression they've grown. But they haven't really. It's an illusion. Like the movies. OK?'

He nodded. She could see from his eyes that it had gone in, that he'd learned something new today.

She carried on, noting the sixteen puncture marks around the lips – eight above and eight below, as well as a series of deep indentations along the lips themselves, some of which had broken the skin. The mouth had been sewn up.

She looked at the nose and saw a puncture mark on either side, right through the middle, very slightly encrusted with dried blood; on the underside of the nostrils was a small horizontal cut, the same width as the marks on the lips. Nose sewn up too. The object used to make the hole had been thick and long, a needle, she estimated, with an eye wide enough to hold something with the density of a guitar or violin string, which was what she thought had been used to fasten the mouth and nose. She'd seen this before a couple of times, but she couldn't remember the specifics. Once here, once in New York; some kind of black magic ritual. She made a note to cross-reference it on the computer if she had the time and that was a big *if*.

'Are we going to look inside the head?' Javier asked. She usually left that to him.

'Depends what the insides tell us.'

'The Look of Love' began to play as she made the T-incision from shoulders to mid-chest and all the way down to the pubis. It was around about now that the dieners would start dropping.

She opened up the body and inspected its insides. It was a predictable sight, looking a lot like a butcher's shop might two weeks after the owners had suddenly closed it up and abandoned it with all the contents inside. The organs hadn't just changed colour – reds and maroons had turned shades of grey-blue – they'd started losing their shape too, becoming viscous, and some had been disconnected from the main framework and shifted position because hungry insects had eaten through the cabling. Surprisingly Ralph and Martin had hung on in there. Ralph even looked like he was enjoying himself.

Gemma took a large syringe and extracted blood and fluid from the heart, lungs, bladder and pancreas. Then she spiked the stomach and started filling the syringe barrel with a sample of its contents – a green liquid, the colour of spinach water – but then something solid got sucked up by the needle and blocked it.

After they'd removed and weighed the organs one by one, she sliced open the stomach and emptied its contents into a glass container – more green liquid came out, murky at first, then clearing as a gritty white sediment with the consistency of sand floated to the bottom of the receptacle, followed by small shiny dark scraps of something that could have been plastic.

She noticed the stomach wasn't quite empty; there was something that hadn't come out. She opened it up a little more and saw a pale, sticky greyish ball of matter stuck to the lining. It reminded her of a shrunken golf ball. When she held it up to the light she saw it wasn't a single object, but small overlapping squares compacted into a ball.

Using tweezers she tugged and pulled at the ball until she'd managed to prise loose one of the squares. It was about a third of an inch long, made of cardboard, printed on both sides, miraculously intact despite the digestive process. One side was black, the other was multicoloured – reds, yellows, oranges, blues – but she couldn't make out the design.

She unpicked the rest of the bundle, laying out the squares one by one at the end of the slab, until she found herself staring at a jigsaw.

She spent the next hour piecing it together. Fifteen minutes in, she began to recognize the thing she was assembling.

The image she had before her was familiar, but the design differed in many ways. The drawing was more sophisticated, more detailed, the colours richer and more vibrant – what there was of it, because it wasn't complete. At least a quarter was missing. She guessed where she'd find it.

'Javier, open up his throat,' she said.

The victim had choked to death on the remaining cardboard squares.

When Javier had finished and handed her nine missing pieces, she completed the jigsaw.

It was a tarot card depicting a man sitting on a throne with a golden crown on his head. The crown was in the shape of a castle turret and studded with brilliant red rubies. In his left hand he held a blood-flecked gold sword, blade plunged into the ground; in his right fist a thick chain was wrapped tightly around his knuckles. The chain was fitted to a black mastiff who lay at his right side, head raised, teeth half bared, paws out in front. The dog's eyes were bright red and it had a forked tongue, to go with its mean, bad-tempered expression on their faces, an anger caught midway to eruption. Despite where it had been and what it had been through, and the fact that it was in pieces, the card seemed very much alive. She found herself staring at it, enraptured by its terrible beauty, unable to pull herself away. This was like no other card she'd ever seen. The man on the throne had no face. In its stead was the blank, plain white outline of a head. It seemed like it might have been a printing error, given the richness of the detail, but the more she studied it, the more she felt the design was intentional.

'You know tarot?' Javier said behind her.

'What?' She turned around, then laughed. 'No. I don't believe in that kind of stuff.'

'The King of Swords,' Javier explained, looking down at the foot of the mortuary slab. 'The card represents a man of great power and influence, an aggressive man also. It can mean a valuable ally or a fearsome enemy, depending on where and how it turns up in the reading.'

'Is that right?' Gemma said. 'So what does it mean when it turns up in someone's stomach?'

4

'Preval Lacour,' Max read off a photostatted report as Joe drove. 'Forty-four years old. Haitian. Became a US citizen in 1976. Taxpayer, registered Republican, churchgoer, married, four kids. Good credit score, home owner, modest Amex debt. Recently became the proud owner – with his business partner, Guy Martin – of a lot of real estate in Lemon City. He was plannin' to redevelop it. No priors, no record, no nothing. I don't get it.' He looked at Joe over the pages. 'Here's a guy well on his way to getting his piece of the American Dream. No history of mental illness, or violence. No drugs or alcohol in his system. How and why the fuck did it all go so wrong?'

'People go crazy, Max,' Joe said. 'Sometimes somethin' just slips. You know how it is. We see it all the time.'

'I'd say somethin' more than just "slipped" with this guy.' Max continued reading from the report. 'He killed his business partner and secretary. Why? These were childhood friends, godfathers to each other's kids, never known to have had a serious quarrel, business was on the up.' Max turned the page. 'Then he puts the bodies in his trunk and drives over to Fort Lauderdale and kills Alvaro and Frida Cuesta. *Then* he drives over to Primate Park, breaks in and chokes to death on his own vomit – all in seventy-two hours.

'The other people he killed, the Cuestas: they were his main business rivals. They went head to head over the Lemon City project. But the Cuestas lost out. Why kill 'em? And there was a *third* guy in the running too – Sam Ismael, Haitian, Lemon City local, runs a voodoo store. He was the lucky one. He was out of town the day Lacour went on the rampage, otherwise he might've been murdered too. The whole thing's insane. Don't make sense.'

'Sometimes it just never does.' Joe sighed.

They were on US1, driving towards Kendall. It had been two weeks since they'd found Preval Lacour's body in Primate Park. The incident had made the national news, thanks to the hundreds of monkeys which had escaped from the zoo and run riot all over Miami and beyond.

Lacour's fingerprints had been taken at the morgue and run through the computer. Five days later the machine had matched them to the murders of Guy Martin and Theresa Morales in a Hialeah motel and to the Cuestas in Fort Lauderdale. Lacour's car – a black Mercedes saloon – had been spotted speeding away from the scene. A witness had taken down the number plate and phoned it in.

Lacour had dumped the Mercedes in a car park in North Miami Beach, where it had stayed until the weekend before the Primate Park discovery. A caretaker had noticed a horrific smell coming from the car and called the police who had found the decomposing bodies of Lacour's business partner and secretary.

Now Max and Joe were going to Lacour's home address. Max had called the house before heading over to North Miami, but there had been no response. He'd checked with Missing Persons. Nothing on record.

'And what about that shit they found in his stomach?' Max flicked through to the autopsy notes and read out the inventory. 'A tarot card, sand – mixed with bits of ground-up bone, possibly human, as yet unconfirmed – plus vegetable matter, also as yet unidentified.'

'Sounds like some kind of potion,' Joe said.

'His lips had been sewn up, nose too.' Max closed the report and threw it on the back seat. 'What d'you think about that? Some kinda ritual?'

'I ain't thinkin' too hard 'bout this one,' Joe answered,

''cause it ain't gonna be our problem after next week.'

'True.' Max lit a cigarette and wound down the window. As of the following Monday, North Miami PD took back the case, which had been theirs in the first place, as the body had been found in their jurisdiction and the matter wasn't deemed either urgent or sensitive enough to be dealt with by the Miami Task Force – commonly known to cops and the press as the MTF – which Max and Joe worked for. North Miami PD, sinking under the burden of a record number of unsolved homicides, had begged MTF to handle the Primate Park stiff, but they for their part were under exactly the same pressure, if not more so because, as Dade County's supposed elite task force, they were expected to solve crimes at lightning pace. Max and Joe had thirteen unsolved homicides and twenty-two missing persons on the case board in their office. And Eldon Burns, their boss, was breathing down their necks hard, screaming at them to bring him 'Results, results, results – GOOD. SOLID. FUCKEN'. RESULTS!'

Theoretically they shouldn't even have been out here, working the Primate Park case, but Max had wanted to get out of the office and do something simple to accomplish and tick off. He and Joe always did this whenever they hit a wall with their cases – look for something easy to do and solve and then come back to their problems with renewed confidence and a fresh perspective.

They headed down North Kendall Drive, passing the Dadeland Mall. The previous July the mall had been the scene of one of the worst shootings in living memory. A posse of cocaine cowboys had rolled up on a rival and his bodyguard and sprayed them with submachine-gun fire in the middle of the day when the place was crowded with shoppers. The incident had put Kendall on the map. Prior to that it had been one of Miami's best kept secrets, known only to real estate brokers and locals.

If you had money and craved attention you lived in Coral Gables, where guides would point out your house to tourists with Instamatics, otherwise you made your home in Kendall. Part of its appeal lay in its anonymity. Drive through it and you wouldn't know you were there. It could have been anywhere residential, its main streets lined with modest houses sporting flagpoles and the occasional motor boat outside. Beyond the main streets lay larger, more expensive houses, but you'd need to know where you were going to find them. The area appealed to the retired or semi-retired, who liked the fact that it was far enough away from the beach to avoid the hustle and bustle of tourism, but still close enough to central Miami for shopping, socializing and emergencies. Kendall was also especially popular with ex-dictators and their henchmen, fugitive foreign embezzlers, exposed conmen, political exiles, lapsed criminals and disgraced public figures from all walks and stumbles of life.

Before he'd spun out of control, Preval Lacour had been doing OK. He'd lived on Floyd Patterson Avenue, a road lined with arching banana palms where all the houses were situated inside gated compounds with their own private security, closed-circuit cameras and individual hotlines to the emergency services. This way of living – away from the street and under armed guard – was becoming more and more popular with upper-income Miamians scared by the city's escalating crime rate. Home invasions had risen by 150 per cent in the last six months alone, and they'd become far more violent: where once criminals would have tied up the homeowners before making off with their money and belongings, now savage beatings and rapes were commonplace, as were murder and arson.

They stopped outside the entrance to the Melon Fields estate, Lacour's address. Max badged a security guard behind a double gate and told him who they'd come to see.

'Now this is *some* livin',' Joe said as they drove into a wide cobbled courtyard with an ornate water fountain in the centre, depicting four dolphins, back to back, frozen in a mid-air leap, water coming out of their open mouths and landing in a wide round shallow pool filled with pink and yellow flowers.

The three storey houses with their tiled ochre roofs and shuttered windows were partly hidden behind bushes and trees like shy, magnificent beasts. The Lacours lived in the second from last house on the right. Max and Joe headed up a short driveway and parked next to a white Volvo station wagon which was covered in leaves and burst seed pods – debris from the recent rainstorms.

Joe rang the bell. Gentle chimes, but loud enough to hear outside. Max looked through the window to the left. He saw a room set up for a party: gold tinsel hanging across the ceiling, deflated balloons, a fully laid dining table with several bottles in the middle and two jugs but no food and no people. But Max swore he could hear something behind the window, and there were shadows moving about the room.

Max drew his gun and stepped away. Something crunched under his shoe. He looked down and saw he'd just obliterated part of a long procession of green-bodied hister beetles making its way into the house. He followed the line as it disappeared under the door. He was about to go on when he noticed another column of the same beetles on the opposite side of the steps, except this one was exiting the house and moving at a slower pace. When he looked closer he saw the insects were carrying small scraps of pale matter and live maggots in their mandibles.

Joe rattled the letterbox. A dozen blowflies whizzed out, carrying with them a gust of air so foul it made him gag.

Max turned around sharply. He saw his partner backing away from the door with his hand clamped over his mouth and nose.

Then he smelt it too.

'There'll be more'n just one this time,' Joe said over his shoulder, as he hurried down the steps to call it in.

They found six bodies.

Most of them were strewn around the living-room floor, contorted, twisted, bloated, skin stretched out to a greyish near-translucence, big balloon people, bursting out of their clothes – tuxes for the men and glittering designer gowns for the women – threatening to float off up out of the room, over the house and into the Miami sky.

The room was decked out for a party. A gold and red tinsel banner was strung from either wall over the room reading 'Felicitations Prevail!'. Bunches of balloons, wilted and wrinkled by the evil heat and poisoned air, hung from pieces of string fixed to the four corners of the room. A lot of the furniture – armchairs, a sofa, a black granite coffee table – had been moved out into the hallway. They'd been planning to dance after dinner.

They'd been shot dead to a record called *The Joys of Martinique* by the Swingin' Steel Band. It was still playing, after a fashion, because the needle was stuck in the run-off groove and the album had warped a little so the turned-down edge was scraping the side of the turntable, making a sound like a spitball hitting a hotplate – *TAK! – pffssttt . . . TAK! – pffssttt . . . TAK! – pffssttt . . . TAK! – pffssttt* – a warped metronome keeping time over the scene.

Max and Joe walked around the room with plastic covers on their shoes, rubber gloves on their hands, nets over their hair and menthol-scented surgical masks over their noses and mouths. The window hadn't yet been opened because a woman from forensics was dusting it for prints. Plenty had turned up under the black powder.

Max picked up a spent shell casing from its chalked circle, numbered with a marker on the floor and compared it to a blown-up photograph of one of the casings found at the

Martin/Morales murder scene. Same strike marks on the end.

'Six bodies. Twelve shots fired – at least,' Max said, holding up a glassine evidence bag with a fragment of the shell that had been dug out of the windowsill. As with his previous two murders, Preval had used hollow-points on his family – bullets with quartered tips, which fragmented on impact, flying off at four different angles, causing maximum damage. Back in patrol Max had known a cop who'd been shot in the kneecap with a hollow-point. It had blown his lower leg clean off. 'Someone musta heard *something*.'

'These houses are too far apart.'

'He killed his whole family, Joe, with a .38. That's a lotta noise.'

'Then there's the time of day this happened. Late enough and everyone woulda been sleepin'. Dunno 'bout you, but when I sleep, man, I *sleep*. I'm Lazarus. Take Jesus himself to rouse me.' Joe looked out of the window at the activity in the driveway – paramedics with stretchers, uniformed cops keeping back a news crew, curious neighbours.

'What about the guard? What they pay him for?'

'Keep the bad guys *out*,' Joe said.

Lacour had been as systematic as he'd been merciless. He'd killed them anti-clockwise, beginning with the old woman in the black and green dress to his left nearest the door. She'd been sat at the end of the table. He'd shot her twice in the forehead, once from a distance and then the second time from very close up, the muzzle practically touching the skin. Then he'd turned on his two teenage sons, sitting side by side in the middle, their backs to the window. The first – and oldest – had tried to shield his brother and had been shot first in the shoulder, and then executed like the woman he'd been sitting close to. His brother had been grazed in the neck by the bullet fragment Max had found embedded in the windowsill. He'd crawled under the table Max guessed, following the small morse code of bloodstains on the floor. The old man in the wheelchair had then tried to protect him by swinging one of his two thick walking sticks at the gunman. Lacour had shot at the man mid-swing and blown his stick apart. There were splinters and slivers of wood buried in the old man's face, as well as part of a bullet which had entered his head through his eye. He'd then been shot one more time for good measure, before his murderer had dispatched the boy on the floor. Most of the corpses still had the gold cardboard party hats they'd been wearing at the time of their deaths stuck to their ruptured heads.

Apart from the turntable and Max and Joe's whispering, it was utterly quiet in the room. Five forensics staff were working on the scene, scraping, bagging, stoppering glass tubes, lifting prints, lifting hair, lifting lips to look at teeth, lifting hands and legs, lifting bodies to one side, left and right. They measured holes in the wall, distances between bodies, sizes of entry and exit wounds, range of spatter. Everyone worked efficiently and precisely, but also very quickly and without pause, as if they couldn't wait to get away.

The hister beetles were moving freely and unimpeded throughout the room. Once inside the house they'd branched out into two trains, one making for the stairs, the other going into the living room. There, a few feet into the room, they'd forked again, four subdivisions taking a body apiece. They crawled up fingers and feet, shoulders and necks and disappeared under hems and collars, up sleeves, through rips and tears in fabric. Meanwhile, from each corpse, a separate string of beetles exited from another aperture and made its way back across the living room, gradually linking up with other departing bug lines to form a pulsing shiny green caravan out of the house and back to the earth it had come from. From up where Max was standing, the bugs seemed like a network of veins, pumping in and out of the earth, a conduit straight to its deep dark heart. He thought for a moment how he too would one day be reduced to a lump of rotting, seeping meat and this troubled him enough to think of insisting on being cremated. Fuck the headstone.

'I don't get this one, Joe. This – this family, this house, this kinda life – this is something you kill *for*.'

'That's the second thing I hate about this job.' Joe nodded. 'Shit you never get to understand 'cause the perp took all the answers to hell with him.'

'What's the first?'

'The ones that get away, the ones you never catch, the ones that are still out there, lookin' for the next kill, the invisible monsters.'

'Well, it's like you once told me back in patrol, Joe . . .'

'*Way it is, partner. Do your best and learn to live with it, 'cause it'll always be a lot worse tomorrow,*' Joe finished the sentence Max liked to quote back to him, and to every pale-faced rookie who came up to him and asked him for advice after they'd found out what being a cop was really about. Joe hadn't learned those words off anyone. They'd just come to him, the effortless way wisdom does to someone who's had to struggle for everything in his life from the day he was born.

They looked around some more. There was a drinks trolley near the stereo system. On it stood a large punch bowl, part-filled with thick, sticky bright pink syrup. The top was completely covered with a crust of drowned blowflies.

They looked over the eight-foot-long dining table and its white cloth and full dinner service – fine heavy silver cutlery and china crockery, immaculately laid out with small ivory winged rests for the knives, silver rings for the napkins and three different-sized crystal glasses at each place setting. In the middle of the table were uncorked bottles of red wine, a magnum of champagne and, either side of them half-empty jugs of water. A large framed colour photograph stood near the bottles: Lacour to the left, Guy Martin to the right and the mayor of Miami in the middle, beaming. There were thin lines and spots of dried blood all over the table – impact spray from the bullets.

'He killed his own first,' Max said. 'Then he went after the others.'

The two detectives looked at each for a brief moment, one seeing the other's horror and revulsion and the thought that informed the looks: just when you figured you'd seen it all – the very worst thing man could do to his fellow man – something that little bit more horrific came shimmering down the pipe, a big bloody grin on its face. They left the room.

A black, open-toed high-heeled shoe stood upright at the foot of the stairs. It had a diamanté pattern of creeping ivy around the heel and diamanté laurels around the toe opening. It was surrounded by a chalk mark. There were two more bodies on the hallway stairs, one on top of the other, lying in a wide pool of dried blood, which had soaked the boards and dripped off the side of the steps onto the ground below, some catching on the wall. A woman, shot in the back and then behind her ear, was lying face down on top of a little girl, no more than seven or eight, executed in the same way as the others. The mother had been trying to protect her daughter. Her long black hair partly covered her daughter's face. The beetles were busily working their way through them both.

Lacour's study was next to the living room – a large mahogany desk faced the door as they came in, behind it a plush leather reclining chair and lampstand. On one wall hung a crude painting of giraffes in a dense forest, while on another was a large posed family photograph in a gilt frame. All the victims were there. Lacour was in the middle of the second row, his hands on the shoulders of his two teenage sons, beaming proudly. His wife sat in front – a good-looking, if slightly plump dark-skinned woman smiling an unforced, good-natured smile. Next to her was the old man in the wheelchair. Max guessed, from the strong resemblance, that he was Lacour's father. He was holding a baby in his lap. To his left, was his wife. Lacour's young daughter was sitting up on the floor between them.

'No sign of the baby?' Max asked Joe.

'No,' Joe said. 'Maybe someone was lookin' after it while they partied.'

'I don't think so. This was a family party. Just them celebrating the Lemon City deal. The baby would've been there too.'

'So what do you think? He took it with him?'

'Perhaps,' Max said.

Joe walked away to check out the rest of the study. Max continued examining the faces in the portrait. They wouldn't hold the slightest clue as to what had happened and why, but he wanted to imagine them alive, going about their day-to-day business, what their voices sounded like ringing around the house, what their habits were, what united and separated them. He'd always done this, humanized the dead, summoned their ghosts and listened in on them. Thinking about them as people instead of statistics helped keep him focused on the job and what it was really about. A lot of cops working homicide became so jaded and indifferent, so numb inside, that death was a numbers game to them – one they were resigned to losing before they'd even started playing. They forgot they were dealing with people just like them, people whose lives had been cut short before their time. Yet, looking at the Lacours, Max felt for the first time a sadness and something collapsing within himself, a support giving way and an ideal crashing to the ground: if this is what people were doing to each other now, turning in on

40

themselves and those closest to them, there was no hope any more. And if there was no hope, there was no point in being a cop.

'Max,' Joe called out, 'come see this.'

Joe was standing by the windowsill, holding up one of a row of photographs he'd picked up from there. It showed Lacour standing on a stretch of grass with his sons and daughter. They were all holding hands with chimps dressed in shorts and Primate Park T-shirts. When they looked closer they saw the picture had been taken at roughly the same spot on the grass verge where they'd found Lacour's body.

'Looks recent,' Joe said. 'Maybe that's why he went back there.'

'Who knows?' Max sighed. 'Who'll *ever* know?'

Max noticed the evidence bag Joe was holding.

'What've you got?'

'Found it in the parents' bedroom.' He handed Max the envelope. 'Smells of almonds.'

It was a small red and white striped candy wrapper.

'Where d'you find it?'

'Under the cot.'

'Babies don't eat candy.' Max gave him the bag. 'And this house is clean and tidy, orderly. My guess is, when they run prints on that wrapper they ain't gonna find any, 'cause the person who dropped it was wearin' gloves. But if they *do* get something, it won't belong to any of these people.'

'So you're sayin' . . . ?'

'Yeah,' Max nodded grimly, 'Lacour didn't do this on his own. He had help.'

PART TWO
April–May 1981

5

'Man. I dunno why you keep on lettin' freaks like that out, 'cause y'all *know* they gonna do it again – sure as man followed monkey,' Drake murmured, passing Max Mingus a book of matches over his shoulder. They were from a motel called the Alligator Moon in Immokalee, a small town right in the middle of the Everglades.

Max memorized the address as he lit a Marlboro, and then gave the matches back without turning his head. He now had the information he needed: the child-killer Dean Waychek's whereabouts, his hiding place, the rock he'd crawled under as soon as he'd come out of prison.

Drake and Max had been doing business like this for most of the ten years Max had been a cop. Drake was by far and away the best snitch he had. The guy was plugged into the Miami criminal mainframe like no one else. He knew everything there was to know and everyone who was doing it.

Max would tell him what he needed and Drake would call him back with a time and place to meet – always breakfast at a diner, usually one that had just opened up because, Drake reasoned, the food was more likely to be better in a new joint, as they'd be making an extra effort to attract repeat custom. The two would sit back-to-back in adjoining booths and whisper to each other out of the corner of their mouths.

Today they were in a place called Al & Shirley's, off 5th Street in Miami Beach. Max remembered the building well. It had once been a photographer's studio. The owner had taken some shots of Muhammad Ali shortly after he'd won the heavyweight title for the first time. He'd blown up one of the photos to lifesize – Ali in his white shorts, championship belt around his waist, throwing a jab, exuberant expression on his face – and proudly exhibited it in the window, only for someone to smash the glass and steal the picture. Max and Joe had caught the thief a couple of weeks later when they'd seen him standing outside a school Ali had just opened, with the six-foot-plus-sized blow-up at his side, waiting for an autograph. The incident made the front page of the next day's *Miami Herald*. The accompanying photograph was a surreal sight: Joe hauling the thief away in cuffs, Max walking just behind them, carrying the Ali blow-up under his arm; while standing very clearly in the background, unbeknown to all, the real Muhammad Ali and his entourage were watching the spectacle and laughing.

Max looked through the same window and took in the desolate view of the near empty forecourt beyond, its entrance flanked by two tall but frail-looking palm trees, with weak trunks and drooping, dried-out leaves. His brown 1979 Camaro was parked in-between a white Ford pickup and a gleaming dark blue Mercedes coupé he guessed was Drake's. It had been there when he'd arrived. The sky above was thick with ash- and sour-milk-coloured clouds which broke the sunlight down to a feeble glow full of shadows. The air was dead and still. Everything was on pause, waiting on the heavens to make up their mind.

Inside were two rows of booths starting from near the entrance and ending at a glossy mural of Old Glory which filled up the back wall, shot-up and dirt-caked, but billowing defiantly – American pride and endurance at its most fundamental.

The cop and his snitch were in the last two booths at the end, to the left, away from the window, Max facing the door as he always invariably sat, even off-duty. He liked to know

46

what was behind him and what was ahead of him as best he could.

The place was nearly empty, which wasn't surprising, given the time – just shy of 9.30 a.m. – but it felt like this was as busy as it was going to get today.

Max listened to Drake eat, the sounds of his chewing recalling a platoon trampling in time across dry undergrowth. Although Drake had once claimed to eat only breakfast, Max wondered where on his six foot three, raggedy-ass bird-leg frame he put all the calories he was wolfing down – a greasy pile of crispy bacon, sausages, ham, hamburger, beans, hash browns, grilled tomatoes, four eggs fried two different ways and toast; so much food, they'd had to serve it up on two plates, one for the meat alone.

Drake dealt coke, poppers, pills and grass to an upmarket clientele of interstate jetsetters, white-collar lost weekenders, college kids with more bucks than brains and Miami's burgeoning gay community. Max helped him by regularly busting his competition and keeping him off the police radar. He also occasionally kicked some of the coke he seized in the line of duty back to him. He didn't feel too good about the last part, but that was the way it was in Miami right now. The town ran on coke and coke ran the town. For every three kilos seized, one would make the papers and two would make it back on the street.

'Ain't no *cure* for *that* kinda evil thing,' Drake continued. 'Ain't no jail *bad* enough, ain't no religion *good* enough, ain't no shrink *shrunk* enough to undo that. Only a bullet can cure *that*.'

Drake was getting worked up, like he always did whenever Max asked him about child abusers and child killers. He hated their kind with such intensity that Max often wondered if he hadn't himself been molested when he was a boy, but it wasn't the kind of thing you ever asked a street-forged hoodlum like Drake – not that he'd ever tell anyway, because it'd make him look how he couldn't afford to be seen: weak, a victim, a sissy. If he got a rep like that it'd be bad for business. He'd have armies of rivals on his tail, and there'd be nothing Max could do to save him.

'I hear you,' Max said, barely moving his lips, 'but you know how it is. It's the law.'

'Then the law's all fucked up. Shit needs changin'. You get mo' time for peddlin' reefer than you do rapin' some lil' girl.'

'I hear that too.'

'Yeah?' Drake leant back a little so his mouth was closer to Max's ear. 'You *hear* so good, why you still a cop?'

'Same reason I had when I joined: I thought – and still *do* think – I can make a difference. Even if it's a small one no one notices. Somewhere, to someone, what I do counts. For better or worse depends on the someone. And that's why I'm still here, meetin' you for breakfast,' Max answered.

'You believe in Santa Claus too?' Drake chuckled and Max could almost hear him flashing his smile, that same sardonic, knowing, each-day-as-it-comes-and-fuck-tomorrow nonchalant expression that had landed him more pussy than he could handle and a bullet in the leg from a husband he'd cuckolded.

Max shook his head and grunted negatively. The mention of Christmas saddened him. He'd driven to Key West with his girlfriend Renée on Christmas Eve, for a make-up or break-up vacation. They'd broken up before they got there, midway down the Seven Mile Bridge. An argument about the faulty passenger window had escalated into one about the faults in their relationship. They'd both said things they shouldn't have, but meant anyway. She'd got out at Mallory Square with her bags and tears streaming down her face, and boarded the bus back to Miami. Max had returned home, where he'd drunk until he'd passed out. The next day he'd called Joe, who'd come over with a crate of beer, a

48

bottle of bourbon and a bag of reefer. They'd sat on the beach and got palooka'd. Max had spent the rest of his vacation that way, and was still finding his way out of that zone, slowly.

The radio was on low and playing Beatles songs back to back, non-stop, still mourning John Lennon, shot dead in New York the previous December. You couldn't escape the programmed grief on the airwaves right after it had happened. Even black stations had played soul, funk and disco versions of Beatles tunes, and whenever Max had turned to talk radio for relief, all he'd heard were people arguing away about the murder and what it all meant and how it was probably a CIA-organized hit. It had driven him nuts. Some psycho misfit with a gun and a grudge plugged innocent family men on the street all the time in Miami and barely anyone noticed or even cared. Even Reagan getting shot just last month hadn't quelled Beatlemournia.

The waitress came over with the coffee pot. Max hadn't touched his. His stomach was burning again – booze-binge acid – and his medicine cabinet at home was fresh out of Pepto-Bismol.

'You no like café?' she asked him. Her name tag said Corrina and she was cute as hell – bright brown eyes, almond-shaped face, tan skin, flawless complexion, beestung lips. She could have passed for twenty-one, but Max suspected she was much younger.

'I forgot to drink it.' Max smiled.

'You want new cup?'

'Sure,' Max said.

She was about to turn and head back when Drake reached out and stopped her with a quick but gentle hand on her arm.

'Any for me?' Drake asked, holding out his empty coffee cup, bright dental beam right behind it.

She apologized with a giggle, gave him a refill, and then hurried back towards the counter.

'She *waaay* too fine. Kinda waitress you wanna order from juss to watch walk across the room, but,' Drake said, leaning over and watching her go down the aisle, 'thass's a whole heap o' trouble on two legs, right there.'

'How so?' Max asked.

'Don't wanna be goin' mad over no pussy when you makin' moves on the street. Gotta keep yo' mind on yo' game, and keep that game *tight*. Fine bitch like dat? Turnin' every nigga, spic and cracker head in dis town? Fo' you know it that pussy be havin' a *entoorage*, an' you gotta be swattin' 'em away full time, so you got no time to be makin' money, dig? Pussy like *dat* be worse fo' a nigga than dope.'

'So you only date ugly women, is that it?' Max said.

'They ain't *ugly*, 'zactly – they mo' . . . You know them hey-good-lookins always turn up wit plain Jane as a best friend, make deyselves look better? Plain Jane be the one I be flyin'. Most o' tha time she be so got-damn grateful to even *have* herself a man she do *anythang* fo' a nigga – cook, clean, wash yo' back – every damn thang. An' most of 'em fuck real good too. Them good-lookin', straight-offa-cover-of-a-magazine bitches? They ain't *never* gonna do that 'cause they think they too *good*.'

'Whatever floats your boat, Drake,' Max said. He did exactly the same thing in clubs, but he didn't want to start comparing scoring technique with his snitch. You had to keep a professional distance. 'Me, I like to have something nice to look forward to when I wake up in the morning.'

'I work anti-clockwise,' Drake said.

Max chuckled and pulled out a Marlboro. He lit it and took a deep drag, tasting lighter fuel mixed with the tobacco. He thought about Dean Waychek.

Dean Waychek had killed Billy Ray Swan, aged four.

Dean Waychek hadn't gone to trial because his lawyer had managed to convince the grand jury that his confession had been obtained under 'duress'. He'd produced photographs of Waychek's bruised torso and an X-ray of his broken nose. Max had claimed that Waychek had taken a dive out of their car. Joe had backed him up. It wasn't enough. Apparently there should have been more broken or fractured bones. Max wished he'd been able to beat him up a lot more. Joe wished he hadn't pulled him off, saying, 'You don't want to kill him.'

He hadn't then. He did now, but not by his own hand. Not this time. He'd do something else with the information Drake had given him.

After Waychek had walked, Max'd finally come to the conclusion that he didn't want children of his own. They would bring him no pleasure, only dread: he'd seen what people could do to them, and he knew he'd be such an overprotective parent he'd make their lives a misery. So he'd had a vasectomy at the end of January. He hadn't told anyone about it. He'd just booked himself in and had his tubes snipped. The procedure, the surgeon had informed him, was completely reversible. But the things he'd witnessed and the effect they'd had on him were not.

A few moments later Drake said goodbye and stood up. He was dressed head to foot like a tennis player – white shoes, socks, shorts and a polo shirt. He even had two blue-finished metal rackets with him. It was always a different look with him.

Max watched him leave and was surprised he didn't get into the Mercedes, but instead walked out of the forecourt altogether, turned left and continued down the road.

Max finished his cigarette and went over to the counter to pay.

The brown-skinned man in the emerald-green suit and shiny shoes he'd noticed come in half an hour ago was still there, perched on his counter stool like a ravenous crow. He had brilliantined wavy hair and wore a thin gold bracelet on his right wrist. He was holding Corrina's hand close to his mouth, poised to kiss it. She was blushing and looking at him through wide, sparkling eyes. She was smitten. Was he her boyfriend? It didn't seem so. He looked a lot older, early thirties.

Max reached the counter and pulled out his wallet. Corrina didn't notice him until the man nodded Max's way and straightened himself up. She apologized, took the check down from a hook near the register and handed it to him.

But something was nagging at him, stopping him in his tracks. The guy was all wrong.

None of your business, he told himself. Pay and go.

Max had the right change, but he handed Corrina a twenty so he could stick around a little longer, check the guy out some more. Wouldn't hurt.

The guy watched Corrina's back as she turned. Max followed his stare to her ass, watched as he licked his bottom lip and mumbled something to himself.

The guy wasn't her boyfriend.

Max broke him down: the suit and shirt were real expensive, the sort that spoke money to burn. No one dressed like that to go to work, and most people couldn't afford those kind of clothes.

He checked the shoes. Black and green gator loafers, gold band across the middle – $500 a pair.

Drug dealers didn't dress like that in the day time.

But pimps did.

The guy sensed he was being observed because he turned his head and looked straight at Max. They locked eyes. The pimp had sharp green eyes, which matched his suit and probably explained why he'd chosen it. He had a smattering of freckles across his nose. Hispanic with a black bias. Handsome motherfucker, but with a very hard edge to him.

He frowned aggressively at Max and stiffened his posture. A challenge moved to his lips and his eyes narrowed. Then he caught sight of Max's gun on his belt under his jacket, read the situation and turned away in one almost interchangeable motion.

Max told Corrina to keep the change and walked out.

6

Hot bitch, thought Carmine Desamours as he watched Corrina bend over to pick up the spoon she'd just dropped.

'You a dancer, baby? *Es usted bailarín?*' he whispered to her, taking in the shapeliness of her ankles, the smooth, almost mannish musculature of her calves and the width and firmness of her thighs. She was two or three inches over five feet tall – the kind of size most men would want to protect. Protect and fuck: the perfect combination in a woman. He could almost see the money he'd make off her sweet ass.

'No,' she said, turning her head round and smiling at him over her shoulder, a strand of hair falling down past her cheek. He swore right then she was the best little thing he'd seen in at least six months – a straight up Diamond with Heart potential.

'Coulda fooled me.' He smiled, still keeping his voice low so he wouldn't wake the old codger sitting snoozing at the end of the counter by the kitchen door – Al, the manager. He could see Shirley back in the kitchen smoking a cigarette, listening to a Beatles song on the radio, lost in her memories.

They'd had their grand opening on the Monday John Lennon got shot, 8 December, last year. He and his friend Sam had been their first paying customers, coming in after gator hunting out in the Glades. That was when he'd first clapped eyes on Corrina.

The diner was close to deserted as usual. He counted four other people. In the window booth near the entrance, a woman with short grey hair and a bright yellow T-shirt, nibbled on a bagel, while the man opposite her was shovelling scrambled eggs and toast into his face and talking at the same time, spraying his plate with debris. Right at the very back were two other customers – a black man dressed up like Arthur Ashe, and a broad-shouldered white guy in a leather jacket, despite the stifling humidity outdoors.

After she'd served him the first time, Corrina had come back and told Carmine the white guy stank so bad she wanted to heave. He'd sprayed the inside of her wrists with the little bottle of French aftershave he always carried around with him, telling her it would ward off any evil stench. He'd held her hands and blown the perfume dry on her skin, looking her straight in the eyes as the alcohol evaporated. He'd watched her olive skin blush purple as that little bit more of her gave in to him.

'Stinky Man no drink iss café,' Corrina said as she put together a clean cup and saucer, and added the spoon she'd picked up off the floor.

'Maybe he was so loaded he mistook this place for a bar,' Carmine said.

Corrina laughed and walked over to the end of the diner with the coffee pot in one hand, the crockery in the other.

He checked her figure out some more as she walked down the aisle. Unlike most white girls, she had real ass, high, round and firm like a black woman's. Nothing a man liked more than an ass like that: the better the cushion, the better the pushin'.

First he'd change her name to something commonplace, forgettable and untraceable. Next, Sam would break her in and break her down. He'd teach her to do absolutely everything she was asked to do and never say no. And when she was good and ready, he'd put her to work.

The way he saw things was very simple. In his world all women were potential hos. He rated them by looks and earning potential and categorized them by playing card suits. In order of superiority: Hearts, Diamonds, Clubs and

Spades. No royalty, no faces and *strictly* no jokers – just numbers.

Corrina's starter Games would be with rich old white tricks who had boats named after the trophy wives they'd lost their houses to the year before and crushes on their teenage daughter's best friends. They'd treat her real nice and gentle, purr all poetic and gaga through their drool and their dentures. The sex would be undemanding but uncomfortable, what with having to pretend she was getting the monster fuck of her young life under all that soft wheezing blubber. She'd learn to work them like cash registers. She'd call them 'Big Daddy' and nickname their temperamental peckers 'Tonto' or 'Hot Rod' or 'Big Rocket' or sumsuchshit. She'd learn to feign love and attentiveness and interest, and in the process she'd grow a hard heart.

Then she'd move on to her rightful place, the escort circuit – aka the Diamond Trail. Her tricks would be younger high rollers, the ones who rented girls out for the weekend.

Starting price for a Diamond was $850 per day for a basic weekend rate, an extra $250 per day on holidays. The prices were for the girls only and excluded accommodation and transport. Carmine insisted his Cards travel and stay first class all the way, unless the trick was renting a villa or sumsuchshit, but if they could afford to do that then most likely they could afford to upgrade their Card to a Heart as well.

Hearts started at $2,000 a day, and they were worth it. They were perfect in every way, like God had designed them from a wet dream – faces out of *Elle* and *Cosmopolitan*, bodies out of *Playboy* and *Penthouse*. Corrina was almost there, but not quite. Her face had a touch too much wetback about it, mostly around her mouth, which sagged slightly at the bottom when she spoke, showing too much lower gum and betraying the *barrio* paddling in her gene pool. He could see that side of her becoming more prominent in her looks as time went on, because one thing about the life he was about to lead her into was that it always brought out a bitch's true nature, no matter how much make-up and affectation she buried it under.

All things working out as intended, he'd keep her in play until her looks peaked. She'd already told him she'd lied about her age to get this dogshit job. She was really seventeen, not twenty-one. That didn't matter. With the right clothes and make-up, she could easily pass for twenty. And at the age she was now, provided she kept herself in good shape, avoided drink and drugs and didn't eat too much, she could be a cash cow for at least seven or eight years.

When they were done Diamonds either left the Game outright and split back to the shitholes they'd run away from, or else they carried on. He busted the lingerers down to Clubs and made them work the hotels and uptown bars. The money wasn't as good, the risks were higher and they had to turn twice the number of tricks they had before, but it was still way better than being the next suit down – Spades – and working the street, or else – the worst option of all – getting some kind of regular nine to five. He'd known a few who'd tried just that. 'Going straight,' they'd called it. Yeah, right. Within months they'd all gone straight back to him. No point in selling your soul if you don't get the right price.

It wouldn't all be smooth sailing with Corrina. He took that for granted. In his business, there were ten shitstorms to every sunny day. Any number of things could go badly wrong every time a Card went out on the Game – cops, pregnancy, VD and violence. Carmine would have the Diamond and Heart tricks checked out first to make sure they weren't pigs or feebs, and then he'd find out how much they could afford to pay and how much they had to lose. He used a PI called Clyde Beeson to do the background checks. Beeson was expensive, but he was as quick as he was thorough. It usually took him under a week to find out everything and anything about a person.

Of course, there was just no predicting people, especially the rich. Some tricks turned nasty and liked to knock a bitch about, just for the hell of it, 'cause they could. Most of the time the damage was nothing too serious – a split lip or a black eye, but occasionally they'd overstep the mark and fuck their looks up good. His operation didn't skip more than a beat or two because he'd recycle the Card back as a Club or, if they were fucked-up beyond what a reasonably priced surgeon could fix, he'd use them as Spades. In truth, that was a pretty extreme scenario and had happened only twice in the seven years he'd been running his Deck.

A hot Creole Card called Hortensia had gone out to the Caymans with a Wall Street type for the weekend and didn't come back when she was supposed to. The guy rang Carmine up and said the bitch had freaked out on him and gone AWOL that morning. Carmine sent Beeson out to look for her. He found her thirty-seven hours later, back in Miami, holed up in a shitty hotel, a loaded gun in one hand, a bottle of sleeping pills in the other, trying to decide which way out she wanted to go. Looking back and seeing the state of her now, Carmine didn't know why the bitch hadn't just gone ahead and pulled the fucking trigger. He would've done. Mr Wall Street had given her a shot which had put her to sleep while he'd tattooed the whole of the bitch's beautiful face so she looked like someone out of Kiss. Although Carmine had wanted to cut Hortensia loose, she'd begged to be kept in the Deck. Good thing he'd agreed to it too, because now she had a small but loyal clientele of weirdo freaks who went in for her kind of looks. Then there was Valerie, a Diamond who'd been jumped outside a hotel and pack-raped by a bunch of jocks in the back of a van. When they were through, they'd thrown her out at seventy miles an hour on the freeway. She survived but looked like the

Elephant Man's twin sister. Carmine couldn't think of anyone who'd want to fuck that, but men never stopped surprising him. Like Hortensia, Valerie had her paying devotees.

'*Su perfume es bueno,*' Corrina said as she came back from serving Stinkyman, sniffing her wrist and beaming that smile at him. He thought it her worst feature. It made her look simple and stupid. He'd make her drop it.

'*Solamente el major,*' Carmine replied. It often baffled him how dumb a lot of these bitches were, believing any old shit they were told as long as the teller looked the part.

Corrina was a case in point. She thought he was a photographer from New Orleans called Louis De Ville. That's what it said on the business card he'd given her. It was a classy-looking thing – thick textured cream card with his name embossed in metallic emerald-green capitals. His profession, address and number were printed in smaller lettering below. The number and address were for a downtown office block. The office was empty but for three phones and three answering machines, each corresponding to one of his chosen identities. He had a specific profession and business card to match a target Card's dreams. They all wanted to be at least one of the impossible trinity – actress, singer or model – in that order. Accordingly, he'd pose as a talent scout, an agent or a photographer; never too big a cheese, like a director or producer, because that came over as too good to be true and even the dumbass ones'd get suspicious.

He'd already broken the ice with Corrina. He'd taken her out twice, walked her home twice. The last time he'd kissed her goodnight on the doorstep of the shithole house she rented a room in. He knew she wasn't a virgin from the way she kissed. She'd stuck her tongue in his mouth. He could have gone further with her then, but he hadn't fucked a target since the first month of his first year on the job. That had been a mistake. The intimacy had messed with his head, made it harder for him to get nasty with the bitch when she'd got out of line. He'd shared something with her, something fragile and unguarded, something that was all his and she'd tried to turn it on him. She hadn't got far, but since then he'd vowed never to let one of those bitches get close to him again. He left all that to Sam.

Corrina was going to meet Sam tonight, although she didn't know it yet.

Carmine checked his watch. It had gone 10 a.m.

The brother in the tennis-player costume settled his bill and left. He looked like he belonged in the Village People in that get-up. Carmine followed him out the door with his eyes, the slow walk across the forecourt, the way he stopped to check out his fine Mercedes coupé and then looked back at the diner to see if he could spot its owner, probably correctly guessing that it belonged to the fly-looking, green-eyed brother he'd seen as he'd left. Carmine thought the brother might be getting into the dirty-brown Camaro parked nearby, but it wasn't the right kind of ride for him. He figured him as a classier type, a Porsche or Ferrari man – *if* he had the bread.

A few minutes later the white guy in the leather jacket came up to the counter to pay his bill. Close-up he looked a bit of a mess. His face was pale, unshaven, sweaty and bad tempered; there were bags under his bloodshot blue eyes. Carmine could feel him scrutinizing him from the side, taking in his fine suit and shoes. It was an intense looking-over too, the kind a guy wanting to start a fight might give you to get you riled up enough to ask him what was up.

The man gave Corrina a twenty and drew a bit closer to Carmine.

The motherfucker stank like he'd fucked a skunk in a distillery: shitty bad breath, booze, cigarettes and stale sweat.

The guy's stare stayed on him until he started to feel small, like he was being looked at under a microscope.

What's with this guy? thought Carmine. Is he a pissed off redneck?

Carmine put his game face on and turned to Stinkyman and looked him straight in his squinty eyes.

Stinkyman met his glare full-on and threw it back at him.

Scary ass motherfucker! thought Carmine, but he didn't let it show. Bitch! Give this peckerwood his fucken' change so's he can be outta my damn face!

Then he saw something glinting under the guy's jacket. He broke the stare and followed the light to a pair of cuffs and the piece Stinkyman was wearing on his hip.

Shit – a cop!

Carmine felt like a pussy but he turned away, none-of-my-business, look-the-other-way, you-just-carry-on-and-act-like-I-ain't-here style. He thought about having to explain the switchblade and the roll of cash in his pockets. He thought about the cigar tube full of the beans he'd picked up from Sam's for his mother.

He'd never been in trouble with the police his whole life. He ran his business real careful and, besides, the SNBC saw to it that the right palms were greased.

The cop was still staring at him. Corrina barely had any bills in the register so she was counting out his change in quarters. He could almost feel the guy *knew* what he was, like he could look into his skull and read all his thoughts, see all his plans.

Bullshit, he told himself. Cops ain't psychic. They just get lucky.

Corrina was turning to give the cop his change when he told her to keep it and abruptly walked out of the diner.

'*Comemierda!*' she hissed, and dumped the quarters back in the drawer and hit the no sale button.

'He ain't that bad,' Carmine said. 'He gave you money for nothing.'

'Den him *grande comemierda*,' Corrina said, holding out her hands wide apart.

You'll go far, thought Carmine.

Ten minutes later Carmine walked out of the diner and headed for his car.

He was real proud of his dark blue Mercedes coupé convertible with its beige leather interior and gunmetal blue rims. Driving it was pure pleasure, gliding through the streets in his own unassailable, aerodynamic little world, top down, radio on, volume up.

He took his car keys out of his pocket and smiled. The morning had been a success. Now, if the bitch was waiting for him where he'd told her tonight, he'd be made. After he was done with her, he'd take a drive around Coconut Grove and reconnoitre for some more targets. That was his favourite part of the job; the one which only he could do. Any motherfucker could be a pimp – nigger, spic, peckerwood, nip, slope, it didn't matter. But no man had his special talent, his *magic eye* for Card-spotting. God hadn't given him much, but he'd given him that.

His right leg suddenly smacked into something he hadn't noticed, something hard and solid. He fell flat on his face and his car keys shot out of his hand. He started to push himself up when something heavy landed on the middle of his back, and pinned him down on the ground.

'Hands out, palms flat, spread your fingers,' a voice above him said. The man smelled of dead booze and fresh cigarettes.

The cop frisked him and tossed his pockets. Out clattered his gold lighter, switchblade, bankroll, his small bottle of aftershave, his wallet and the grey cigar tube. The cop picked up everything except the aftershave and lighter.

Shit! Not the tube!

'Get up!'

Carmine did as he was told and came face to face with those mean, blue, booze-boiled eyes again. The cop was shorter than him but much broader and way stronger-looking.

'Louis De Ville, photographer . . . Jack Duval, agent . . . Harold Bernini, talent scout . . .' The cop read aloud from the small set of business cards he'd found in Carmine's wallet, flicking each at his face when he was done. 'Who the fuck *are* you? What's your name?'

'Louis De.Ville,' Carmine answered.

'That so?' The cop looked at him angrily. 'Where you from *Lou-wee*?'

'Around here?'

'Not with that accent,' the cop said. 'What is that? Haitian? You Haitian?'

'No,' Carmine lied. 'I'm from New Orleans.'

'I know New Orleans. Which part?'

'French Quarter,' Carmine lied again. 'Left a long time ago though.'

'But your accent never went there.' The cop snorted. 'I say you're Haitian. What d'you want with that girl in there?'

'What would you want with a fine bitch like that?' Carmine smiled, trying to get some man to man empathy going, but deeply regretted it when, out of nowhere, the cop slammed his fist into his solar plexus. Pain exploded all the way to Carmine's spine and up into his chest. He fell to one knee with a sharp cry and clutched his gut hard as the punch reverberated all the way up to the base of his skull. Then he retched hot orange juice all over his $850 suit.

'You're a pimp and you're recruiting her.'

'Fuck you!' Carmine spat. 'I ain't no pimp, you racist redneck pig motherfucker!'

The cop squatted down next to him and shook the grey cigar tube.

'What's in here, Willie Dynamite? Drugs?'

'No – seeds.'

'*Seeds?*' The cop unscrewed the tube.

'Yeah – seeds. Like what you plant in the ground and watch grow motherfucker.'

The cop shook out the smooth beans into his palm. They were dark brown and shiny, like giant kidney beans dipped in thick chocolate.

'What you growin'?'

'They ain't for me, they're for my mother.'

'What? You got one?' the cop said, looking at the seeds once more and putting them back in the tube.

'Very funny,' Carmine replied. 'Look. We can do us a deal here, man. You gimme back the tube and the rest of my shit and let me get on outta here; you can keep the money.'

The cop looked at him and right then Carmine flinched because he swore the thunderous look the cop gave him was a prelude to another punch.

'I could bust you right here and now for attemptin' to bribe a police officer,' the cop said. 'What's your name? Tell me the truth or I'll take you in.'

'I ain't got to tell you *nothin'*, 'cause I ain't done nothin', 'cept in your imagination. Y'all bent out of shape 'cause you see a black man drivin' a nice car, wearin' nice clothes and gettin' hisself some fine-ass pussy,' Carmine said angrily.

'You got me all wrong. I ain't got nothin' against black folk. Quite the contrary,' the cop said. 'I just hate pieces of shit like you. See, *I* only exist because *you* exist. *My* role in life is to make your life constant fuckin' hell, and *your* role in life is to suffer or die – preferably the latter after a lot of the former.' The cop picked up Carmine's car keys. 'On your feet.'

Carmine got up and almost fell over. The pain in his gut was so intense he had to look to make sure he wasn't bleeding. He was sure the bastard had fucked him up inside.

The cop made him get in the car and cuffed his hands to the steering wheel.

He popped the trunk and rummaged inside. He didn't find anything besides cleaning products, cloths, a jack and a spare tyre. He looked in the glove compartment and found his licence and registration.

'Carmine Des-a-moures,' the cop read out. 'Kind of name's that?'

'It's a name. What's yours?'

'None of your business.'

'Suits you.'

The cop studied the licence for a long moment, probably trying to see if it was fake or not. It was the real deal, but the cop didn't look convinced. He tossed it into the car and uncuffed Carmine.

'Remember me and remember this: I am going to be in your shit for the duration. I catch you tryin' to recruit girls again I'll bust you for real, and I'll see to it you share a cell with some redneck ass *bandido* who turns you out so much you'll shit a whole watermelon with a smile on your face,' he said, tossing Carmine his wallet, lighter and aftershave bottle. 'Now *go*.' He stabbed his finger towards the exit.

'What about my seeds, man? You don't need 'em,' Carmine pleaded.

'Which part of "go" did you miss, shitstick?'

'Motherfucker!' Carmine spat as he started up the car.

7

Max found a payphone on 5th Street and called Striker Swan.

Striker was Billy Ray Swan's uncle. He'd done ten years for armed robbery. He'd been a serious badass before he'd gone away. He'd met his match behind bars and the experience had changed him from the inside out. He'd been rehabilitated of his worst excesses but he still wasn't doing straight time, making his living mostly running hot cars in and out of the state, yet the violence he'd been notorious for in his youth never re-entered the frame.

He'd loved his little nephew more than he'd loved anyone in his whole life – except, perhaps, for his sister-in-law Rachel on that one hot night when Billy Ray was conceived, or so people said. The two did look more than a little alike, even though that could just have been the Swan family genes. Whatever the reality, Striker had been the most broken up by the kid's murder.

Swan answered the phone at the fifth ring. Max spoke to him through a handkerchief over the receiver and in the only accent he could make fly – Jimmy Carter *Jiowja*.

'Striker?'

'Yeah,' Striker answered in a yawn. 'Who's this?'

'Never mind that. I got me a message to give you. Dean Waychek, guy that killed lil' Billy Ray? Wanna know where you can find him?'

Max didn't wait to hear the answer. He told him.

Max had met Swan once, very briefly, outside the police station, the day Waychek had been freed. Max had apologized to him. Striker – six feet two of white-trash muscle, tattoos and freckles – had given Max the briefest of nods and the faintest of smiles, as if to say, 'You're a pig, so I hate you, but you're OK.'

Striker didn't say a word on the phone. He didn't even reply when Max asked him if he'd got the name of the motel.

But Max knew he'd got it all right.

Max hung up and got back in his car.

As he drove away he thought of Dean Waychek, remembered his smugness in the interrogation room, the way he'd been so sure he was going to get away with it.

'Adios, motherfucker,' Max said.

8

Carmine would never admit it to anyone, but he was scared of thunder. He didn't have a big quake-in-your-boots phobia, yet whenever the skies rumbled he'd get a sense of real and imminent danger, of something about to go very wrong in his life. He'd have to get out of the way, find a building to shelter in until it was over. He didn't like people seeing him afraid, especially not his Cards, current or prospective, and most of all he didn't like nobody knowing about the twitch he got in his upper left cheek, a spasm so strong and violent it jerked his face halfway up his skull, closing his eye and opening up the side of his mouth to show the world his teeth. He was getting it now, listening to the storm raging outside, through the walls of the bathroom, over the sound of the tap filling up the tub. He slapped himself hard to make it stop. As usual, it didn't.

He looked around the vast bathroom – spotless white tiles covered the floor and walls; the large basin, bidet, toilet, deep bathtub and separate shower area were all gleaming, while all the fixtures, down to the pipes, were gold plated. There were white scales and a mirror by the door. But the highlight was the turquoise aquarium that ran almost the entire breadth and half the height of the wall opposite the tub. It was filled with a multitude of beautiful fish which glided, wriggled, hung or hovered across various tiers in the tank, some close enough to the surface to grab, others occupying the middle and showing off their colours, while a few avoided the limelight altogether and hid out in the rocks and vegetation below. They, Carmine decided, were the schemers and scavengers, the ones with the agendas, the plotters, the ones he related to the most. Sometimes, when the bathroom was dark, and the light, shadow and current in the tank came together in the right way to create a gentle, billowing effect that ran from one end of the glass to the other and back again, the aquarium resembled a magical bejewelled tapestry floating in mid-air.

When he was growing up in Haiti, his father had told him that thunder was the sound of the gates of heaven opening up so the angels could come down and kill the world's sinners. All the flashes and bolts of lightning were their swords, cutting the heads off the evil ones, and the rain that came afterwards was to wash their bodies away into the sea. If he was good, his dad had told him, he'd never have to be afraid of thunder, *ever*.

Back then they'd all lived in a two-bedroom house overlooking the Carrefour slum in Port-au-Prince. They hadn't been rich but they hadn't been as badly off as their near neighbours who never had enough to eat and walked around in rags. Carmine's mother was a *mambo*, a voodoo priestess: she cast spells, read fortunes, talked to the spirits of the dead and practised abortion. She had quite a clientele, ranging from the poor-as-dirt country folk who walked ten days to see her, to senior government ministers and society women who'd come to the house in chauffeur-driven cars. She was rumoured to have briefly cured one of Papa Doc's daughters of lesbianism and another of myopia. Carmine had been her *hounci* – her assistant – as soon as he could walk. He'd helped her pick the herbs and prepare the animals she used for her potions, sat in the same room when she told people their fates with tarot cards, and, when he was old enough to know his way around town, he'd delivered messages from his mother's lips to the ears of her clients.

His mother didn't like talking about his dad. Depending on what kind of mood she was in, she would head off the subject when she sensed it coming up and turn the conversation in another direction, or she'd clam up altogether and shake her head threateningly, or else she'd get out and out aggressive. The closest she ever came to talking about his dad was when she'd tell him that he *looked* just like him, and that he *was* just like him, only even more of a *loser*. And she only ever said that when she got what he had dubbed the ShitFits – terrifyingly intense rages she flew into once in a while.

Carmine's memories of his dad were few but mostly very fond. He remembered him as tall and handsome, always in a black suit and fedora, despite the heat. He was around the house a lot more than his mom: he used to sit outside smoking cigarettes – Comme Il Faut, the Haitian brand – and either reading the Bible or a tattered brochure about holidays to America. He talked about how one day they'd go there together, just the two of them, father and son; maybe they'd even stay for good, not come back *ever*. He made Carmine promise not to tell his mom, just like he made Carmine promise to keep another secret from her too.

His mom would often travel to see her most important clients. She'd be gone for days, even weeks. When that happened all kinds of women would come by the house to see his father, mostly at night, but once in a while in the day too. They always woke Carmine up with the noise they made in the bedroom. He never complained. In fact it made him laugh. He remembered there being many different women at first, then it became just the one, his favourite. She was called Lucita. She was light brown and green eyed like his daddy, with the same soft curly hair too, only hers was longer and fell past her shoulders when she let it down. Her and his daddy spoke in Spanish as opposed to the Kreyol he usually spoke to everyone else. She always brought Carmine candy, stroked his face and asked him how he was doing. She smelled great too, like marshmallows and French soap. She was his first love.

The only memory he had of his mother and dad together was when they fought over him. She'd been the disciplinarian in the house, the one who made the rules and beat him for disobeying. She had a thin stick with flayed ends and dried buds growing out of the side. If he disobeyed her or talked back she'd beat him with it across the knuckles, which hurt like a bitch, or across the ass and the backs of his legs. At least that was the idea, but whenever she got it in her mind to beat him, a ShitFit wasn't far behind and when it overwhelmed her she'd switch from the stick to her fists and feet. One day she'd started beating him because he'd forgotten to run an errand. For the first time ever his dad intervened. He came into the room, wrapped his arms around her, picked her up and carried her, kicking and screaming, into the bedroom. Carmine heard them shouting – well, more his mother – for what seemed like for ever. She'd screamed at his dad that she hated him, that Carmine was just like him, that he could get out of her house and take his son with him. So his dad had done just that. The two of them had walked out of the house and gone into Port-au-Prince. There his dad took him to Lucita's house. He didn't know how long he stayed there – it seemed a long time, maybe a month – but he was happier than he'd ever been at home with his mother. In fact, looking back, it was the happiest time of his life. His father and Lucita took him out to the beach, to the Dominican Republic, to carnival. He started playing with other kids his own age which his mother had forbidden him from doing. He never got beaten. And Lucita used to sing him to sleep some nights, in words he couldn't understand but loved anyway.

It all ended very suddenly one afternoon when a group of armed men came to the house in a long black car. They'd knocked on the door, yelling for his dad to come out or else they'd burn it down. His dad had gone to the door and they'd grabbed him and dragged him into the middle of the street where they'd forced him to lie face down on the ground. One man put his foot on his dad's head, while another patted him back down and then drew an X on his shirt in red pen and shot him in the spot. Carmine had run out of the house screaming. He'd tried to grab his dad's arms to pick him up off the ground, but he was convulsing, arms and legs slapping at the asphalt like an epileptic swimmer's as foamy blood pumped out from under him. Carmine remembered how his dad had tried to say something, but couldn't get any words out because of the blood filling up his mouth. As Carmine became schooled in the ways of the street and learned about guns, he discovered that one of the most painful places to get shot is through the heart because, in its final panicked moments the brain diverts the blood flow to the open wound to close and heal it, causing brief but absolute agony for the dying victim. His father's convulsions stopped, until the only sign he was still alive was a twitch in the left side of his face, a violent tugging which Carmine had thought at the time was an invisible angel, trying one last time to pull his dad up on his feet before it was too late. The men bundled Carmine into their car and drove off.

On the way a storm broke. There was nothing like those Haitian storms. They sounded like all the wars in heaven had broken out on earth; lightning lashed at the landscape and thunder roared and boomed, followed by a deluge of rain. His father's killers had pulled over and stopped until it passed. Carmine had looked out of the window, trying to see if the rain would carry his dad's body into the sea. He saw nothing. He concluded his dad had been a good person.

They drove him to his mother's house. She was waiting for him at the doorway and led him to the bathroom. There was a large round grey metal tub in the middle. It was filled with hot water doused with Dettol. She'd never washed him before, it had always been his dad. Carmine's clothes were covered in blood and when she asked him to take them off

he told her he wanted to keep them on. His mother produced her stick and said, 'Do as I say because there's no
one else here for you now. It's just me and you for as long
as I say so. Now, take off your clothes and get in the bath.'

And so, realizing he had no choice but to surrender for
the time being, he did as he was told without further protest
or hint of complaint. That was the beginning of their
relationship, which had then evolved into one of tyrant and
subject, mistress and slave, one growing ever more powerful
as the other grew slowly weaker and more insignificant. Or
so he let it appear.

They left Haiti for Miami when he was about eight or
nine. Memories of his father moved to the back of his mind,
to a place he retreated to when things with his mother got
real bad. He replayed them there and thought of what might
have been and how different his life could have turned out
if those men hadn't come and killed his dad; men he knew
his mother had sent. He created a fantasy world, a padded
panic room he could run to when the humiliation of the
real one and the reality of his place in it got too much. In
that world he was with his father and Lucita. He himself
was still six years old, with everything in front of him and
everything to live for. He often thought about Lucita and
wondered what had happened to her. He couldn't remember
if she'd been there in the road with his father, or if she'd
stayed in the house. Had the men killed her too?

It had long bothered him, the not knowing – not just
about her, but about his father too. He didn't know where
he was from originally, what he'd done before he'd met his
mother. He didn't even know his name. His mother kept all
that from him.

He sliced his fingers through the water in the metal tub.
It was boiling hot and reeked of Dettol, that safe but sour
plastic stench he associated with his father's murder. Just
like he associated the tub with that day. The tub had come

with them from Haiti – the sides dented, the handles and bolts rusted, a film of lime scale dried into the dull metal, the inside encrusted with greeny-grey grime. It had once been big enough for him to drown in – she'd tried once, when he still talked back – but now it was too small for him to do more than half crouch.

She always made him take his baths too hot, deliberately, so the water would scald him and the metal would heat up and burn his feet. She'd had a special tap and boiler installed, just for him to fill his tub. He was forbidden from using the main tub. That was for her alone. Normally she'd shower, but whenever she was seeing her lover, she'd have a bath and it would be a real occasion. She'd be in there at least two hours. She'd put candles at the end of her tub and sweet-scented oils in the water; she'd turn off the lights and play tapes of the sea washing up on the beach.

He heard the familiar sound of his mother coming down the stairs, the clippety-*clop*, clippety-*clop* trotting pony rhythm of her feet on the boards, followed by the sound of the two gold lockets she wore around her neck bumping together with a *shhhh*-put, *shhhh*-put as she approached the door. Thankfully the thunder had stopped a while ago and with it his twitch, so he had no problem putting on his game face – the game being that of the dutiful, loving and admiring twenty-nine-year-old son, happy to see his mother who was coming to give him his bath.

She entered quickly, all 4 feet 9 inches of her, opening and closing the door so fast he could've sworn she'd walked right through it like a ghost. No smile, no nod, no hello, as usual.

Eva Desamours was more striking than she was beautiful. Her skin was dark and rich, unlined and unmarked, bar a single pockmark beneath her left eye; her forehead was wide, her cheekbones high and prominent, while the lower half of her face tapered down acutely to a pointed, well-defined chin, accentuating her prominent downturned mouth whose full lips – dark brown with a hint of purple – for ever reminded Carmine of a drying grape whenever she pursed them. He never looked her in the eye because he was scared to. Marginally slanted and unblinking, cold, near motionless and very very black, her eyes fixed on the world with a merciless detachment, as if she already knew its fate and didn't care to change it. She was also completely bald – whether naturally or by choice, Carmine had neither plucked up the courage to ask nor been able to work out. She wore an array of wigs styled in a straight black bob that fitted her so well they looked like her real hair.

Eva had a man. They'd been together for as long as he could remember. It was a casual relationship. Either he'd come visit once or twice a month, or she would disappear on long weekends. Carmine had never met him nor seen him nor heard his voice. Nor did he know his name. Eva just called him '*mon type*' – her guy. He'd sometimes heard the two of them going at it – loud, raucous and rapturous, her cries duetting with his bull-like snorts and gasps to the accompaniment of quaking floorboards.

'Take your clothes off and get in your bath. I haven't got long,' she snapped. They spoke English to each other and had done ever since they'd come to Miami, twenty years ago. Carmine had learnt his English from the black kids in his neighbourhood, and he'd picked up Spanish from the Cuban kids he'd hung out with. He was often mistaken for Cuban, something he never corrected because to admit to being Haitian in Miami was tantamount to tattooing 'loser' on your forehead.

He took off his robe and hung it on the hooks by the towel rack. He felt his skin rise in goosebumps even though the bathroom was warm. Sometimes she came straight out and told him what was bugging her but usually she liked to wait, hold on to it, let it brew and ferment and build some more in her head, circling him all the while before getting to the point. It was always worse when she prolonged it because he could always sense her fury, always knew what was coming. He could virtually see the rage massing behind her brow, those dark and very deadly legions of anger she had total command over, which she could unleash or withdraw at the drop of a hat.

'Wait,' she said as he was about to step into the water. 'Turn around.' He did as she asked. He'd never been ashamed of standing naked before her. She'd seen him naked every day of his life since the day of his father's murder. 'What's that?' She was pointing at the cauliflower-shaped bruise in the middle of his abdomen.

'Someone hit me,' Carmine said.

'Who?'

'A cop.'

'Why?'

'I don't know,' Carmine said. He hadn't told her about the waitress. She'd been intended for the other Deck he was building, the one his mother didn't know about.

'Did you provoke him?'

'Of course not.'

'Where did this happen?'

'Out near Coconut Grove.'

'Were you working?'

'Yeah.'

'Did he *see* you working?'

'No. It wasn't like that.'

'And his name? What is his name?'

'He didn't tell me *that*.' Carmine chuckled at the stupidity of the question. She gave him one of her fierce black-eyed looks, the kind that could cut through walls.

'Was he in uniform?'

'Plainclothes.'

She came up close to him and touched the heart of the

bruise. It smarted and he caught his breath as memories of the pain echoed back through his body. Sam had given him an ice pack for it at the shop, but it hadn't helped much.

'Did he take the seeds?'

'No. I've put them in the kitchen.' Luckily for him Sam had ordered plenty of extra calabar beans. Failure to bring them back would have provoked the ShitFit to end all ShitFits, because it would have meant they couldn't go through with tomorrow night's ceremony.

She put her nose close to the bruise and breathed in deep and long through flared nostrils. Eyes closed, she held her breath and tilted back her head and rocked it gently from side to side, moving her mouth like she was tasting what she'd inhaled. Then her face turned sour and she opened her eyes and breathed out.

'This cop drinks,' she said. 'He will be a problem to us. A big problem.'

'How?' he asked.

'I don't know yet,' she said. 'Now get in the bath.'

She'd washed him every evening at 6 p.m. sharp since the day of his father's murder. He knew it was way wrong, that it shouldn't be happening at his age, but who was he to stop her, to protest or even complain? He'd tried to, in his late teens, but she'd said that because she was his mother she had a right to wash him, even when they were both old. For most of his life he'd gone along with whatever she'd said and done, whatever she'd asked of him without question, not because he'd wanted to but because it was the easiest way. The alternative didn't bear contemplating. A long long time ago he'd tried his hand at rebellion and the consequences had been disproportionately severe.

The water was cooking him, as always, but he was used to it now. Just like he was used to the hard scrubbing brush she cleaned him with. Years ago, when she'd first bought the brush, the bristles had been fairly soft, but two decades of calcified soap had turned them into mini stalagmites which tore hairline strips out of his skin, especially around the bonier parts of his body. His back and chest were covered with a latticework of fine interwoven pale scars, which, when they caught the light, made his upper body seem enveloped in a wet gossamer web, like he was a spider's prey.

She soaped the brush with Dettol soap and scrubbed his neck, shoulders, arms and upper back first. Then he stood up and she handed him the soap so he could wash his cock, balls and ass with his hands, the only concession to self-administered hygiene she'd permitted him in the past ten years, after allowing him to wash his face and brush his teeth. They didn't talk at all. The bathroom filled with the sound of the bristles' shallow scrapings on his skin, almost the noise of a saw inching through a plank of wood, accompanied by her two lockets, the *shhhh*-put of the lockets clapping together under her blouse, keeping time with her motions and the swing of her heavy pendulous breasts. The bristles dislodged scabs from still tender healing skin and bit deep into old wounds. He stared hard at the aquarium, disassociating his mind from the sparks of pain flying through his nerves. He concentrated on a group of half a dozen oranda goldfish swimming in the middle of the tank. They were graceful fish, like amphibian roosters with their feathery dorsal fins and bushy tails, and traffic-signal-red heads and the metallic orangey-blue of their bodies. He watched them move in single file, equidistant one from the other, simple and perfect. And then, as he stood up, he noticed a flutter at the end of the line as the last oranda collided with the one in front. That goldfish dropped down an inch allowing the last one to take its place in the chain. It hovered without moving for a moment, seemingly confused, before swimming upwards and rejoining the line. It never recovered its pace. It perpetually lagged behind, only following the group in quick spurts, where it would catch up and briefly regain formation before dropping out. When Carmine looked harder at the oranda he thought he noticed an off-coloured patch on its side, a small dull grey mark close to its dorsal fin. But it was gone before he could see for sure.

She washed his feet and legs last, and then he stepped out of the water and onto the floor. Later he'd have to empty the tub, clean and disinfect it and then dry it before carrying it downstairs to the basement where he lived.

After washing him, his mother dried him vigorously top to toe with a white towel, except for the parts he'd washed himself, which he did once she'd finished with him.

'The ceremony's for tonight,' she said.

'But it's *Friday*.'

'It's happening after midnight.'

'*After* midnight . . .' Carmine knew that meant it would be a sacrifice as opposed to a simple execution – which meant this would be a Saturday Night Barons Club and he'd have to attend in full dress. 'Who is it?' But he knew before she told him.

'Jean Assad. You know how Solomon feels about thieves and drug addicts in the organization.' She fixed him with one of her immobile, cut-through-anything looks. Carmine met her stare but, as usual, found he couldn't hold it and looked away at the gleaming white bidet. He'd known Jean Assad in Haiti and they'd been on good if distant terms in Miami. Jean had been on the run for six months.

'Where'd they find him?'

'In Canada,' she said. '*L'imbécile*. Thought he could escape us.'

9

The cigar tube of calabar beans was waiting for her in the middle of the kitchen table. The tube reeked of Carmine's fear, a thin metallic smell of old coins and vinegar that came from him whenever he'd done something wrong. It was so strong she could smell it from the doorway. Eva wondered if he hadn't momentarily lost the tube on his way over. It would be just like him. Clumsy.

Eva went to the cupboards under the sink and pulled out one of the brand new, white plastic chopping boards she used for her potions. She then took out a scalpel and a mortar and pestle, also all new, and brought them over to the table. She opened the tube and emptied the contents on the board – oval shaped like American footballs with the ends filed down, their shiny maroon-brown skins the colour of eggplant crossed with chocolate, hard on the outside, deadly on the in, eight like she'd asked for. She put seven back in the tube and closed it.

After she was done making the potion she'd incinerate everything to make sure it wouldn't end up getting mixed with food. The beans were poisonous. It took just half a bean to kill a man. She'd once fed one to someone in a fresh salad and watched him croak. It hadn't been pretty. First he'd salivated uncontrollably, spit bubbling out of his mouth like he'd swallowed a stream, then his eyes and sweat glands had opened up, as the poison had gone into his veins and arteries, gradually constricting them as it flowed, closing down his blood flow and slowing down his heart, beat by beat, until all the life in him was throttled from within. It was said, by people who'd seen someone die of calabar poisoning, that once the poison started closing down the inner circuits, they had heard the flapping of wings. The closer to death the louder the flapping became until the final five minutes, when their faces froze completely and the only movement came from their eyes, which were still fully conscious. Many said they looked upwards, high above them, in mid-space, and their eyes were utterly terrified. Her victim had got that look too.

She went over to the refrigerator and took out a black clay bottle of holy water and poured it into a metal stewpot, which she then set on the gas hob and lit. As the water began to heat, she quartered the bean, put it into the pestle and ground it to a sticky paste, which was then put to one side of the table.

She went back to the cupboard under the sink and took out a packet of handmade, specially designed Charles de Villeneuve tarot cards, imported from Switzerland. They were the only ones she ever used. The packet was brand new. The cards came in an elegant dark brown wooden box which contained the cards in a drawer lined with purple baize, which never failed to remind her of a huge matchbox merged with a coffin. The cards were wrapped in a black velvet drawstring bag, closed at the side with a red wax seal bearing the company's insignia, this time reminding her of the Smith & Wesson logo on the grip of her .38. The cards were thick, high-quality cardboard. The backs were mostly black with a deep crimson border and a small, almost cartoonish image of the sun, rendered, in gold leaf, as a round, slightly cross-eyed face set in the middle of sprouting rays. Without turning them over, she fanned the pack out on the table and counted anticlockwise from the beginning. The manufacturer always packed the cards in the same order. Minor Arcana last, in suits – first Cups, then Coins, then Swords, then Wands. Fourteen cards in each suit, face cards first, then the numbers: King to Ace. She found the card, turned it over and smiled.

The King of Swords.

Depending on the reading she was giving, the King of Swords could either be a powerful and influential ally and friend or a fearsome enemy, one who would stop at nothing and use force if he had to.

The thing she loved second about the de Villeneuve cards – apart from their magical powers which, if the person using them had the right amount of faith, could turn them into periscopes into the future – was their rich and vibrant colours. They reminded her of the voodoo paintings she'd grown up with in Haiti.

She put the card on the chopping board, then gathered up the rest and put them in a black refuse bag. She took the scalpel and sliced the card lengthwise into six strips. She then sliced each strip a dozen times, so she had something close to confetti. She added the card to the pestle and mixed it in with the ground calabar beans, before scraping the contents out into the now boiling water.

Once complete, the potion would have to settle and cool for a few hours before being fed to its recipient.

Eva was about to begin to speak her spell when she heard Carmine lumber past the door with the tub on his back, heading for the basement where he lived, out of sight and sound. He made as little noise as possible, like he always had, the little creep; even at his age he was still as terrified of her as he had been when he'd been a little boy – terrified of little old her, fifty-four years old, under five feet tall without her lifts and ninety-eight pounds soaking wet. *Pathetic.*

Carmine went to the basement and put the tub down on the floor. There were no windows in there and it was pitch black without the light, but that was always comforting to him after the harsh, sterile whiteness of the bathroom. He took off his dressing gown and threw it where the leather armchair was ready to receive it. He knew every inch of the room so well he could find the smallest things in the dark. It was a trick Solomon Boukman had taught him, back when they'd been as close as brothers, before the organization had grown into the multi-tentacled monster it was now and he'd evolved with it and in the process grown cold and distant, even with those he'd come up with, those who knew him best and would do anything for him.

Still, standing there naked, back in his world, Carmine couldn't help but smile a little at his cleverness and cunning. He may be pathetic in his mother's eyes, but he was fooling her this time, and fooling her *good*. Every tyrant must fall. She was no exception. And her fall would be mighty, all the way back to hell.

10

Jean Assad opened his eyes and immediately wished he hadn't. He'd woken up in the heart of the abattoir, with mere moments left to live. He prayed – no *begged* – that Solomon would show him mercy and do him quick; that he'd forget all about the bad stuff that had brought him down here and remember the good: their long history together, the way he'd been there with him from the start, always loyal and dependable, always a believer. Yet one look at them all, the diadem of bleak accusatory eyes bearing down on him through the death's head paint, and he knew it wasn't to be. He was going out the bad way.

He'd heard rumours about this place, about the things that went on down here, but he'd never believed any of them, ever. He was as superstitious as any Haitian, but he hadn't bought into those stories people came out with about the circle of twelve giant Baron Samedis and the man sat in the middle and what happened to him.

It was all true. So far.

He couldn't move at all, not a muscle, except for his eyes. The rest of him was frozen, locked down, paused between heartbeats. His body felt unbelievably heavy, bones made of mercury-filled lead, propping up skin weighted down with cannon balls. He couldn't open his mouth. His lips and jaw wouldn't part. So he was breathing through his nose, and that with great difficulty, the air having to scrape its way through tightly blocked nostrils, barely making it into his lungs. And then there was a great painful, immovable mass at the bottom of his stomach, like he'd eaten a huge meal his digestive juices just couldn't break down; it was hanging around in his gut, going nowhere, slowly festering.

He looked up and all around him, as far as he could. He met twelve pairs of eyes looking down with interchangeable hatred and contempt. He couldn't tell old friends from lifelong foes, but he was sure they were both there, side by side – that's what he'd heard happened. Their faces were completely unrecognizable under the make-up – half pancake-white from forehead to upper lip, then black from there to the lower neck, taking in the mouth, ears, nose and around the eyes. They were dressed identically too, in top hats, tailcoats, pinstriped grey trousers, white ruffled shirts, black gloves. He couldn't understand how come they were so tall – at least twelve or fifteen feet high. Or was it just the way he was sat, or the state of mind he was in, or something they'd given him to mess with his head?

How long had he been here? The last thing he remembered was waking up in bed in Montreal, blinding flashlight in his eyes, gun to his temple, man's voice: 'Get up! You gots places to be.'

He knew they'd find him eventually. He'd known that when he'd gone on the run, the realization that it didn't matter how far he got, how deep down he hid, sooner or later he'd be caught, sooner or later he'd be made to pay for what he'd done. Still, he'd been real careful at first, moving around a lot, never staying in one place longer than two days, avoiding the ghettos, avoiding all Haitians and Dominicans, staying out of small towns, but what was it he'd heard said time and time again? 'When Solomon Boukman is after you, the world becomes a small place with glass walls.' He might have stayed on the run longer if it hadn't been for his habit. Smack: needle not foil. That had narrowed down their search. The only way a junkie can stay underground is if he's got a big enough stash, or else if he kicks. He hadn't done either. A junkie's got to go out to cop. They'd just pulled on that chain around his arm and reeled him in.

Who'd sold him out? The dealer he'd copped his last dose from? That shit had been suspiciously good, so good he'd got a rush just holding the loaded syringe. Before he'd gone under his last thoughts had been paranoid ones. Montreal wasn't famed for the quality of its smack. The stuff he'd been shooting up until then had been a modest stone, enough to get him under the surface but nowhere near the quality of the dope he'd boosted in Miami. *That* had sent him all the way down to the warm silk cocoon where time stopped and nothing mattered and he was free of everything. Same as his final hit had done. Right before he'd nodded out, he'd wondered if Solomon hadn't finally found him, if his people weren't going to come through the door the moment he'd slipped away from himself, but then the smack had melted his every worry away like hot coffee dissolves sugar cubes. And then they *had* come for him. Just like he'd thought. And here he was now, waiting to meet the King of Swords, waiting to die.

A bright light was trained on him from behind, illuminating his immediate surroundings: a cold grey cement floor with reddish brown markings painted thickly on it – a cross to the left, a star to the right, a long vertical line dividing them. It was a giant *vévé*, a voodoo symbol used, in part, to invoke gods and spirits in ceremonies. Usually a *vévé* was drawn in flour, sand or cornmeal, but this one had been painted in what looked like blood. Beyond that stood the barons, facing him. His feet were in a metal fire bucket, filled with water. His hands were resting on his thighs, palms down.

He saw that he was completely naked and that his arms, legs and what he could see of his chest were completely hairless and oddly shiny. Then he noticed that there were no bindings of any kind on him. He was technically free to stand up.

He felt ashamed of his nakedness and wanted to cover

up, but he couldn't move his hands that short distance to his crotch. Then he tried to take his feet out of the bucket, but they stayed where they were, without even a suggestion of motion about them. Then he attempted to lift his arms. Nothing happened. He tried again. He heard the command come down from his brain, clearly, urgently and in his own voice, but it had no effect; his authority disappeared into cold meat and bone. His arms and legs stayed exactly where they were. He couldn't feel a single damn thing. He wasn't even getting the cold shakes from smack withdrawal. It was as if his being had become completely disconnected from his body and was now imprisoned in it; only death would release it.

Jean Assad, you poor motherfucker, thought Carmine, looking down at him on the chair, a born again baby; skin greased up and gleaming, frozen out of his body by the potion, his lips sewn tight together, his nose part-stitched so he could still get some air, still alive enough for Solomon to come and snatch his soul. Assad was sat in the middle of the sacrificial *vévé* – the symbol drawn in his own blood.

Jean le Chat, they'd called him in Haiti – the Catman, for short. Back then he'd made his living stealing cats and kittens, black ones in particular, to sell to the *hougans* and *mambos* to use in their fortune telling. The most popular and reliable method was for the priest or priestess to kill the cat and leave its body on a grave for the night. The next morning they would fry and eat the animal's guts with squill and galanga root, and then they'd see into the future.

That was how the Catman had met Carmine's mother. He used to come round to the house in Haiti with a thick, wriggling burlap sack on his back, his hands and face always scratched and bleeding. His mother would choose a cat, usually the wildest and most vicious, the ones who went for her with tooth and claw, the ones with strongest spirits who'd take a good while to kill. Carmine remembered Jean's gap-toothed grin, the way he didn't say much, just smiled, and his unusually soft hair. It was said he was the bastard son of one of the wealthy Syrians his mother had worked for as a maid – hence his family name. Ask him about it and he'd shrug his shoulders and say he really didn't know and he cared even less. He was who he was, he said, and that was the best he could do. Who knew where names came from?

On Eva Desamour's advice, Solomon had brought Jean Assad into his enterprise, a year or so after it got started. He did petty minor-league stuff – shoplifting and housebreaking mostly. He was good at it, but he'd never be better than his limitations. He had neither the ambition nor the balls or brains to progress to new, more complex areas, so he stayed strictly bottom rung, doing exactly as he was told, without question; a dependable soldier – as long as you didn't expect too much. When Solomon expanded into drugs and had to divide his enterprise into sub-sections, he got Jean to be a driver for one of his call-out dealers, the ones who sold to the wealthy, upwardly mobile crowd. Jean loved the job, loved the driving around in the air-conditioned Cadillacs he kept real clean inside and out, loved wearing a nice suit like he was somebody special. He thought he'd been promoted. He used to tell people he was starting to feel American.

Then he'd killed Tamsin Zengeni, the dealer he worked for. He beat her to death with a tyre jack and stole her smack stash.

No one understood it at first. No one had known the Catman used drugs, let alone that he was a junkie. Solomon had started digging. He found out that Assad had been buying heroin from one of Solomon's other dealers, a guy who worked in the Broward County division called Ricky Maussa. There were strict rules about drug use in the organization. Solomon had executed Maussa and his entire crew in the same way he was going to execute Jean. Carmine remembered the ceremonies. Maussa and his crew had been made to watch as one by one Solomon killed them, starting with the most recent recruit and moving upwards. Maussa had pleaded his innocence, that he hadn't known Assad's identity, but that in itself was no excuse. All Solomon's dealers had to be sure their customers weren't narcs, stoolies, rival gang members or one of their own.

Carmine found it impossible to hate Jean Assad. Jean had always been cool with him. He'd intervened more than once when his mother had been beating up on him. He wasn't scared of her like everyone else was. He'd even told her she was taking it too far.

Carmine cast a sweeping gaze about the room. The eleven other barons were stood around the figure they towered above, motionless on their stilts, expressions of sealed-in impassivity. As usual he couldn't recognize anyone he knew under all the make-up, and he was sure it was the same for everyone else. They all looked identical. They were the same height – thirteen feet tall – and, thanks to padding and clever tailoring, the same shape. Even their hands, encased in black gloves, were equal in length and width.

When the ceremony was over, they'd all walk out and go off into individual cubicles. They weren't allowed to talk until they were well outside the building, back to being gangster civilians. Those were the rules. Break them and you ended up here, in the middle of the circle. It had happened once before, a long while ago, never since.

There were people watching from a long balcony off to the left; a small select crowd, mostly new recruits, children as young as ten, and a lot of the newly arrived island immigrants, fresh off the boat; Haitians, obviously, but Cubans, Dominicans, Jamaicans, Bajans, people who'd talk about what they'd seen, evolve the myth. This was mostly for their benefit. Get them young, dumb or impressionable, tell them the myth, show them some magic, get them to spread the word, exaggerated and distorted so no two versions matched, even though they meant precisely the same thing. This was the key to Solomon's power, making people think he was more than just flesh and blood like them, making them believe that he was other, a demon – Baron Samedi, voodoo god of death, reborn as a Miami gang leader.

Here was the popular misconception about Solomon Boukman's organization, that it was actually called the Saturday Night Barons Club or SNBC for short. It wasn't. That was the name of the ceremony.

The organization itself didn't *have* a name. It never had. This was deliberate. A gang with a name is an immediate target, a recognizable entity, just begging to be shut down. If you don't know your enemy's name, how can you find him? Solomon had wanted to differentiate it as much as possible from American gangs, which cops and rivals were used to dealing with and approached in the same way. As for a structure, it didn't really have one. It was Solomon and a few key allies, most of whom didn't know each other. People were never sure who was working for Solomon Boukman and who wasn't.

The drums began – one beat, three seconds apart – a deep echoey sound like that of a heavy load hitting the bottom of a long deep dry well. At the beginning they hadn't had any accompaniment, then they'd used tapes of authentic voodoo drummers recorded in the Haitian mountains, and now Solomon had flown the drummers over and set them up in Miami. When they weren't playing the ceremonies they worked the club circuit from New York to New Orleans.

At the twelfth beat the barons linked hands with a flutter and slap of leather on leather. Then the light behind the Catman went out. For a moment they stood linked together in complete darkness. Carmine could feel the nervous pulse of the guy to his left; he heard him swallow and breathe a little harder through his nose. It was probably his first time here.

When the drum was struck for the thirteenth time a dark but powerful purple light gradually came on, bathing the circle in its rich, almost liquid glow.

At the fifteenth drum beat the barons began to move, slowly, anti-clockwise, one step at a time, one step per drum beat.

Christ! Jean thought. He's coming.

The giant figures were moving around him, turning slowly but deliberately like the mechanism of some ghastly machine; a complex lock gradually opening, unlocking horror.

He was scared now, real scared; scareder than he'd ever been – absolutely and utterly terrified.

He knew what was about to happen, those things he hadn't believed before – slicing your neck, drinking your blood while you were still alive, draining your life out of you before your very eyes. Then they'd take his soul.

The drum was beating faster. He could feel it in his stomach, stirring the contents, making them jump, making them come to life. He suddenly felt like he'd swallowed a sack of live toads, and they were hopping around inside him, jumping at his stomach, trying to get out. It was hurting him real bad, not nausea, but pain like he'd been punched by a cast-iron fist.

The drum got faster. Another joined in, slipped in behind it, a snare, building up a rhythm. The barons were moving in time, picking up speed. They were starting to blur, the whites into blacks, losing their shape. He tried to focus on one and follow him, but he couldn't move his head. He tried closing his eyes but he couldn't do that either. He tried looking away, but even that wasn't an option.

Jean knew he couldn't win. He knew it was over, that he was finished.

They were now spinning so fast they'd become an indistinct grey mass, but the purple light they were bathed in was hitting their waistcoat chains and belt buckles, and these were spitting out weird bright red, blue, green, yellow and orange reflections in the shape of deadly bats.

He was getting dozy. He felt part of himself fading away, slipping under, not even bothering to put up a struggle.

His stomach was killing him. He felt like he'd swallowed a live hungry rodent, scratching and clawing and biting him for all it was worth.

As they turned they began to chant:

> *Vin Baron*
> *Baron l'ap vini icit,*
> *Vin Baron*
> *Baron l'ap vini icit,*
> *Vin Baron*
> *Baron vini icit,*
> *Vin Baron*
> *Baron l'ap vini icit*

The lights were dazzling him now, burning his eyes like pepper spray. He felt tears running out of them.

The chanting went on as they spun around him:

> SSSSO-LO-*MON*
> SSSSO-LO-*MON*
> SSSSO-LO-*MON*
> SSSSO-LO-*MON*

There were more drums now, a whole battery of them, pounding, hurting his head, killing his stomach.

The chant had been picked up by others he couldn't see, getting louder.

SSSSO-LO-*MON*
SSSSO-LO-*MON*

Worked every time, thought Carmine, the chant. It had nothing whatsoever to do with Solomon, didn't even mention his name, but as they turned, the words ran one into the other and produced a new word people thought they recognized and chimed in with. The onlookers got swept up in the moment and began to repeat it.

The barons were now spinning so fast the colours had leached out into a thick dirty white cloud, while the reflections had blended into one another forming a thick crimson band around the middle of the circle.

The chant was growing ever louder and the pain in his stomach was intensifying, like he had a boxer in there, flailing away. He wanted to cry out, but he couldn't move his mouth.

And then Solomon appeared. He rose up slowly from out of the ground, a swirling red and orange light shining beneath him, like flames. He was dressed as the barons were, except all in white, right down to the make-up on his face.

Solomon crossed his arms over his abdomen and drew two long swords from under his coat. The blades caught the light and threw it into Jean's eyes, sharp and white and hot.

Solomon began whirling and twirling the blades through the air, slicing through the purple darkness.

Jean followed their deadly progress, feeling like someone getting sucked towards a spinning fan, dragged towards his death, their pull obliterating his resistance.

His terror had flatlined into panicked resignation. He hoped for the best he could. That he'd go out quick and clean. No pain.

But something else was happening to him too. Inside. The pains in his stomach were gone. He couldn't feel a thing.

And then he was drawn back to the man who'd come to kill him. He'd crossed the blades into an X and was drawing nearer. The light from the cross filled his eyes, warming them with its heat, blotting out his vision, until finally it was all he could see – pure white light.

His hearing faded. He could hear absolutely nothing.

He couldn't speak. He couldn't taste. He couldn't smell. He couldn't touch. He couldn't see.

He wasn't sure he was still breathing.

Was this it? Was *this* death?

Although it was difficult for him to move, chant and pay attention to what was going on, Carmine caught a glimpse of Solomon rising out of the ground and heard the excited gasps and screams of the simple-minded idiots watching from the balcony. They didn't realize this was an act, exactly like the circus or a pantomime.

He saw flashes of Solomon doing his dance, twirling his two lethal razor-sharp blades through the air like propellers, slicing, coming closer and closer to Jean Assad, as he sat there facing death without being able to so much as blink or scream.

The drums rose and rose to a booming crescendo of roaring cannon strapped to the back of a herd of stampeding bulls, before suddenly and quite abruptly dying back down to the same single, solitary heavy beat that had started the ceremony. The barons slowed their movements down one beat at a time, until, by the tenth, they were walking in step with the drummer.

At the twelfth beat Solomon swiftly raised and back-handed his swords across the middle of Assad's exposed throat, leaving a thin, dark, almost black line. By the fourteenth beat blood had geysered out of the veins and arteries, heavy jets and fine fountains, coating Solomon's painted face and white clothes.

Solomon then covered himself and the body with his cloak. Both were lowered down into the ground, prompting more screaming and shouting from the balcony.

Then the lights went out and the abattoir was plunged into darkness.

Carmine drove out to Miami Shores. There was a potential Heart working a bar off Park Drive which was popular with the rich old men who were members of the nearby country club. They'd go there after playing a few holes of golf. Carmine didn't understand golf. It wasn't a sport to him but a status thing white folks did once they hit a certain age or income bracket or both. Hitting a ball around and taking a leisurely stroll to where it had landed so you could hit it again – what was the whole damn point of that?

He drove down a pitch-black street where the lights were busted and all the houses were derelict and boarded up. Some had been demolished and were just piles of rubble surrounded by wire fencing. Desolate palm trees tilted over the road like drunks, their trunks hacked, drilled and graffitied, their leaves droopy and dirt-coated. He turned into another street where all the buildings had been levelled. The road was coated with thick dust. It reminded him of a picture he'd seen of Hiroshima after the bomb had hit it, nothing standing. All over Miami construction companies were blowing up or knocking down old buildings and then just leaving the mess right there instead of clearing it up and reconstructing.

Suddenly a car pulled out in front of him and he hit the brakes. He wasn't wearing his belt so the jolt threw him hard against the steering wheel and he smacked his forehead on the windshield.

'Motherfucker!' he yelled and punched the horn. The offending car drove off regardless.

'You still drive like an idiot,' a familiar voice said behind him. He turned around and saw the faint outline of someone in the back seat.

'Solomon!' Carmine hadn't noticed anyone when he'd got in the car after the ceremony, nor the whole time he'd been driving. 'How did you – how long you bin in here?'

'I get around,' he said. 'Keep driving.'

Carmine set off down the road.

'Put on your seatbelt,' Solomon said, his voice still the same, a clear, forced whisper, his words hollowed out and filled with silence.

Carmine plugged in the belt. He felt his boss's stare bouncing back at him from the rearview mirror, even though he couldn't see his eyes, let alone his face.

'Keep your eyes on the road. Concentrate,' Solomon said.

'Where we goin'?'

'Wherever you are.'

'I'm workin'. Got a possible Heart lined up.'

'A Heart? That's good. We need more of the high-class ones, less of the low,' Solomon replied.

'I hear that,' Carmine said. 'I'm doin' my best out here, you know?'

'Your best at what?' Solomon asked.

'My best at what I do, Solomon,' Carmine answered, mouth drying, a little tremor in his voice. He hoped Solomon hadn't found out about his and Sam's side project. They'd been so damned careful.

'How's your mother?'

'She's good.' Carmine searched the mirror quickly, but all he saw was a silhouette. He hadn't been face to face with Solomon in five or six years at least. They always met like this, in dark or shadowy places when Carmine least expected it and not often. Carmine had heard that Solomon had had extensive facial reconstruction, that he'd bleached his skin close to white and wore his hair straight and long, that he was so unrecognizable you could pass him on the street without knowing who he was, and that he used doubles and soundalikes to fool his enemies. Carmine wasn't really sure he wasn't talking to an impersonator right now.

'Send her my regards.'

'I will.'

'Take a left here.'

He turned onto North East 101st Street and drove on for a short while.

'Pull over after the Cordoba there.'

Carmine parked in front of a black Chrysler. The road was empty.

'I heard about that cop who assaulted you. We're looking into it.'

'It's no big deal,' Carmine spoke to the mirror. A sliver of stray light coming from the street had fallen across Solomon's mouth. It was bullshit what they'd said about him bleaching his skin; he'd probably started the rumour himself. He was into that – 'misinformation' he called it.

'It *is* a big deal.' Solomon smiled.

And then Solomon licked his lower lip and Carmine saw what had always freaked people out. It wasn't something Solomon let everyone and anyone see, but it was the one thing about him that left the deepest impression, usually to the detriment of his other features. People who'd seen him went on and on about his eyes, their luminous quality, the way they looked through you, the way they saw your secrets, but none of them had ever seen Solomon Boukman's *tongue*. It was forked, split in two from the middle out, with its tips splayed and pointed and curved slightly downward, like two small pink talons. Carmine remembered when his mother had done that to him, sliced the thing down the middle on a butcher board with a knife. Solomon hadn't even flinched.

'You take care now, Carmine.'

'You too, Solomon.'

Solomon opened the door quietly and slid out of the car

and made his way towards the Cordoba. As he walked he was slowly absorbed by the darkness, before disappearing into it completely.

'Hey, no smokin' in the car. New ride, new rules,' Joe said as Max put his fourth Marlboro of the morning to his mouth. It was just after 8 a.m. They were driving to work in Joe's new car, a chocolate-brown '79 Lincoln Continental with a V8 engine, chrome wheels, fine beige leather seats, wood appliqués in the cabin and two pine-tree air fresheners hanging from the rearview mirror. He'd won it a week ago in the SAW – Slain and Wounded – auction, where money was raised for the families of dead or disabled cops by selling the seized and confiscated property of criminals who'd been sent away for more than twenty years. And, as had been the custom since the auctions had started, a symbolic $100 donation was also made to the family of the first Miami Beach cop to be killed in the line of duty – David Cecil Bearden – shot dead by car thieves on 20 March 1928, at the age of twenty-four. The Continental only had 160 miles on the clock. It had briefly been used by a mid-level dope courier who was starting a seventy-eight-year stretch at Union Correctional.

'Smell gets in the upholstery, it don't come out. It'll bring the price down, time comes to sell,' Joe explained. They were on North East 2nd Avenue, stalled in a tailback caused by an earlier collision between a cement truck and a Winnebago. The truck had come off worst.

'I'll open the window,' Max said.

'The hell you will, Mingus. You're in *my* ride, you respect *my* rules. *No fumar en auto*,' Joe practised the Spanish he'd been learning off tapes for the best part of six months. Word was Miami PD brass were talking about setting up a fast-track promotion scheme where preference would be given to Spanish speakers, so Joe thought it best to get a head start. Besides, Spanish was most of what you heard on the streets nowadays. People could plot any old shit they wanted to if you couldn't understand what they were saying. Max had followed his partner's lead and bought a set of Berlitz tapes and books, but he hadn't as yet taken them out of the packaging. Why the hell should he learn a foreign language to talk to people in his own country? He'd pick up the basics as he went along, same as he did with street slang.

'There's worse outside, Joe. Pollution, exhaust, bird shit. That'll depreciate your car faster than any damn cigarettes.' Max grumpily put his smoke back in the pack. He'd showered, shaved and ironed his clothes but he still looked and felt like a wreck. Before he'd left his home he'd swallowed a mouthful of Pepto-Bismol to douse the burn in his stomach, but it was still smouldering. The doctor told him he didn't have an ulcer, just an acid build up caused by a cocktail of job pressures, booze, coffee and not eating a balanced diet at the right times of day. And he badly needed a damn drink. *And* a cigarette. 'Next thing, you're gonna tell me is they're bad for me.'

'They *are* bad for you.'

'You smoke cigars.'

'Not any more.'

'You quit?'

'Uh-huh,' Joe said smugly.

'No wonder you're actin' like such an asshole.'

Joe laughed.

'You should think 'bout quittin', Max. For real.'

'Think about it all the time. *For real*,' Max said gloomily. And he had. After the first cigarette of the day, he didn't like smoking. The next nineteen to thirty were all reflex and habit, things to do with his hands, things to relieve stress, things to help him think, things to do for the sake of something to do – the necessity of addiction. But that initial cigarette – the curtain raiser – was still one of the best three or four experiences he'd had outside of sex, his job and the boxing ring.

It had all the makings of turning into another nice spring day in Miami. The sky was a limpid clean blue, the sun was bright without being intrusive and there was a good but not forceful breeze cutting through the column of palm trees at the side of the road. January through to May were the best times to be in town, climatewise – warm but never hot, humidity low, rainstorms likely to last hours rather than days like they did in the summer.

The traffic was moving at a slow, loud, angry, crawl. Midtown to downtown, the cars were bumper to bumper, horns were being tooted, people were leaning out of their windows or standing up shouting and cursing, yelling, screaming. At least they hadn't started shooting each other, like they did in LA, but that couldn't be far off.

'You hear from Renée?' Joe asked.

'No.'

'You called her?'

'No.'

'You gonna?'

'No.'

'Best way. Clean break.'

'That's right: clean break.' Max nodded. 'What about you? How's your love life?'

'Not as bad as yours.' Joe laughed. He was a big man – six and a half feet tall and 245 pounds of mostly muscle and bone. He looked like a monument when he was standing still and a boulder when he was coming at you. His car seat was pushed way back to accommodate his long thick legs, and the wheel looked like ribbon in his wide hands; hands that were so solid and dense they looked like padded heavy bag mitts, barely a hint of bone showing anywhere, except for the obelisks he had for knuckles.

Unlike Max, Joe rarely used force on people. He didn't often have to. The sight of him alone made people think twice about messing with him, although the few times Max had witnessed him hit someone their bones had been as tough as matchsticks. Outside work and when he was with people he knew, Joe had a friendly cartoon bear's face which complemented his genial, disarming manner. On the street or in interrogations, however, it was a different matter: he had his game face on – that of a very big and very mean dog whose tail you'd just trodden on.

'So you met someone?' Max asked.

'Uh-huh,' Joe said smugly.

'That why you stopped smoking?' Max asked.

'New love, new leaf.'

'Sounds like she ain't wasted her time gettin' you by the balls, Joseph. She got a name?'

'Lina,' Joe replied. In the decade they'd known each other, Joe had had two serious relationships, both lasting close to three years. When they'd been on patrol he'd dated La-Shawna Harris, a radio dispatcher who'd sounded a lot better than she looked. That had finished when he and Max made Detective in 1973. Then Joe had met and moved in with a Dominican nurse called Marisol. They'd gotten engaged and set a wedding date, but then Joe found out that she already had a husband and two kids she was sending money to back home. He hadn't talked about the break-up all that much. The little he had said was straight off the nearest shelf – shit happens, life goes on and then we die, etc. – the kind of catchphrases people resort to when they want to keep their pain to themselves. Max could tell his friend had been hurt real deep. It was in his eyes and manner – the dull, wounded look in his stare, a general lack of enthusiasm for life and a quickness to cynicism. Before Marisolgate, Joe had believed that most people were basically good and if you helped them out they'd be grateful. Now he was closer to Max's outlook, which was that if you offered someone a helping hand you'd best take a rabies shot first because they'd probably bite you. He'd also become a better cop. When he'd been with Marisol, he'd never been the first through a locked door, always the second to go up to the window of a suspect vehicle. After the relationship was over, he threw himself into the job – first one through, last one out. Any hesitation, any half step was a thing of the past. But now Max guessed he'd revert to his old happy self once his new flame turned into a home fire and this worried him a little. For the last three years they'd been a kick-ass team, regular superheroes. They'd broken big cases, made solid collars and secured a 97 per cent conviction rate – the highest in Florida. They'd won commendations for the last four years. They were both on their way to big promotions. Before they'd done well, better than most, but once you'd done great, doing well was a poor substitute.

'What does she do?'

'She's a teacher. First grade.'

'When d'you meet?' Max asked.

'Two months ago.'

'Two *months* . . .' Max said, surprised Joe hadn't told him anything about her earlier. 'What? Was this like a you-start-off-friends then realize you got a hard-on kind of scenario?'

'I just wanted to be sure of her first.' Joe smiled. 'And I am now.'

'I'm happy for you, Joe. You deserve it. Where d'you meet?'

'You ain't gonna believe this, Max . . .'

'Try me.'

'Church.'

'*Church?* Since when do you – Joseph George Liston – go to church?'

'As of two months ago.'

'Yeah – *right.*'

Neither cop was a churchgoer, but whenever Max needed to think things through, be it a case, or a personal problem, he sought out the nearest and emptiest church. It was a habit he'd developed on the back of a whim during his first year as a detective. One hot afternoon, he'd decided he needed to find somewhere cool and dark to mull over the case of a serial rapist who was posing as a repairman to get into women's homes. He'd gone into the first nearest appropriate place he'd found – Plymouth Congregational Church on Coconut Grove. He'd cracked the case within five minutes of sitting there on a hard varnished pew, in the semi-darkness, the smell of candle smoke in his nostrils. He'd simply remembered something an eyewitness had said about the design of one of the victim's bedroom curtains, something he couldn't have known about unless he'd been inside the house. It had come to him within moments of homing in on all the information he'd absorbed, sifting it out, breaking it down and then breaking it down again. Ever since then, whenever he couldn't see straight, either professionally or personally, he'd go and sit in the nearest church and mull things over.

Meanwhile Joe would wait outside. Joe didn't believe in God and avoided going into churches. His father had been a preacher who drank and regularly beat his mother and all Joe's siblings, before leaving them for good one Christmas Eve. He was both impressed and worried by Max's church sessions. He was glad they helped him break cases, but he hoped to high hell his partner wouldn't get the Jesus bug along the way too and see the hand of God instead of his own fingering the perp.

'Told you you wouldn't believe it.'

'And, you're right, I *don't.* So, c'mon, where d'you meet her?'

'I just told you.'

'Stop pullin' my dick, Joe.'

'I ain't pullin' your dick.'

'You been goin' to church for *two months* and you ain't told me? You're pretty quiet for a born again Christian. Shouldn't you be standin' on your car roof shoutin' hosannah and hallelujah?'

'I ain't been born again, Mingus. Once was enough.' Joe chuckled, stepping on the gas. The traffic had begun to move faster now, although the cars were still jammed nose to tail. 'Remember when my moms broke her leg? She asked me to drive her to church. So I took her to this service she goes to on a Wednesday night and I went in with her and sat through the thing. The place was crowded, every seat taken. And after a while it hit me.'

'What?'

'Never in my life had I seen such a collection of fine, free and *available* women under the same one roof. So, the next day, I went back there by myself to get a closer look.'

'Get the fuck outta here, Joe!'

'I'm bein' serious. There are some *fine* chicks in them churches, Mingus, some fine chicks.'

'Did you say "church-*ezz*"? As in, you been to more than one?'

'Yeah, sure. The Baptist ones are the best for eye contact, chit-chat and hand-holding. They're informal, the preachers play guitars like they just sittin' around a campfire with a few brews. The worst ones are the Catholics. Uptight as hell. All the fine women are with their mammas.'

'You're a sick man, Joe,' Max said with genuine distaste. He may not have used churches for their actual purpose either, but the last thing he'd use them for was as a meat market. He had bars and clubs for that. 'You go to church to get right with God, not to get *laid*.'

'Ah, He don't mind. He ain't lobbed a thunderbolt at me.'

'*Yet . . .*' Max cautioned, half seriously.

'You should try it.'

'Fuck off.'

'See, you bein' white – *and* a cop – I know it's harder for you to get with the sisters nowadays, 'cause of McDuffie and the riots. *But*, you meet a sister in church – if she Christian enough to be in there then she gonna be Christian enough to look past your colour too.'

'I do all right as I am,' Max said, but Joe had a point. Post-McDuffie, people were sticking close to their own kind and hunkering down like they were under siege. It was harder for Max to get to talk to black women he fancied. Instead of the looks he used to get – interest mingled with suspicion and light unease – now he saw fear, resentment and sometimes outright hostility – and that was *before* he told them he was a cop. It didn't happen all the time, but it happened more often than not, and a lot more than it had a year ago.

McDuffie had even split the cops into unofficial racial factions, blacks in one corner, whites, Hispanics and Asians in another. Although, it being Miami, with its disparate, cross-pollinating racial mix, things hadn't been quite that clear cut. Black Hispanics had tried unsuccessfully to occupy a middle ground, before throwing their lot in where they had the most friends. Max and Joe were unaffected. Their friendship had long surpassed the point where they thought of each other in terms of race. In fact, Max had earned the respect of the black cops when he'd refused to give money to the McDuffie murder officers' defence fund, just like he'd refused to shake their hands when he'd accidentally run into them all in a bar one night. Instead he'd called them cowardly killer motherfuckers and told them he hoped they went to jail for life. Joe had had to get him out before things had turned seriously ugly.

'You do all right, huh?' Joe countered sarcastically.

'I do just fine,' Max insisted.

'You doin' just fine now?'

'Fuck you.'

Joe laughed, Max joined in a few beats later.

'My relationships don't last, Joe, because I am, a.) an asshole and, b.) a bastard. I start goin' steady with someone and end up fucking their best friends or their sisters or their first, second or third cousins. I don't commit, I'm thinkin' about work when I should be thinkin' about them, and the last thing I want to do right now is settle down. Race and religion ain't got a damn thing to do with it.'

'You ever even been *out* with a white girl?' Joe asked.

'Nope, never. First girl I ever kissed was black. She was called Jasmine. She was my first girlfriend, I guess. And you know what they say, "Once you go black, you never go back." Well, it's true – as I found out at the age of six.'

'You never been with a white girl, how would you know the difference?'

'I don't *want* to know the difference, Joe. I love black women and brown women. Ain't nothin' finer in my eyes. That's what I like, same as guys who only go for blondes or brunettes. Where's this all coming from anyhow?'

'Just thinkin' ahead that's all. If you wanna get beyond Captain by the time you're forty, you gonna need to get with the programme a little. Conform. See, the police is one racist minefield, the further up you climb. Everywhere you step there's a redneck with two heads. You're Miami PD's rising star, the cop every rookie with a brain wants to be. And there you are, bringing black girls to the ball every damn year. Some of the black cops don't like it 'cause they say you stealin' their women, and the white folks don't like it 'cause they racist assholes. Say, sooner or later, against your better judgement, you meet the right girl, and that girl happens to be black, you're gonna have to choose between her and this.'

'So what are you sayin'? I should get myself an Aryan cheerleader or somethin' to improve my career prospects? That's reverse racism.'

'Don't *have* to be a white girl. How about a Latina?'

'I *have* been out with Latinas.'

'Mingus, they was *black* Latinas.'

'I'm a *cop*, Joe, a policeman not a politician. I ain't *never* gonna be a politician. That's for them pansies over at IA. I'll go out with who I damn well please. And anyhow it's no one's damn business. You seen the Chief's wife? She looks like a fossil. No wonder the old guy looks so miserable, that's what he wakes up to every morning. If she's what you're tellin' me I've gotta marry to get ahead in this job I'll quit and become a lifeguard.'

'Plenty of hot white girls out there, Mingus,' Joe said.

Max looked out of the window. The traffic was flowing without pause into the heart of downtown, its buildings catching and reflecting the sunlight and sky like scraps of broken mirror.

'Tell you what, Joe. *You* run for office and leave the women and the police work to me, OK? Then, when they make you God or Mayor, you can make me Chief. How's that sound?'

'Sounds great.' Joe sighed, shaking his head.

'This girl of yours, Lina? She know you ain't really a Jesus freak?' Max asked.

'We don't talk about religion, Mingus.'

'You mean you avoid the subject?'

'Fuck you,' said Joe. They both laughed.

They stopped at the lights near the Freedom Tower, one of the oldest and grandest buildings in Miami, 225 feet of Mediterranean revival architecture bearing more than a close resemblance to the Giralda Bell Tower in Seville, Spain. There was graffiti on the walls and most of the windows were broken. The giant red on white 'For Sale' sign draped around the middle of the building seemed more like a plea than an offer.

'This town's goin' to shit,' Max commented, 'and it just keeps gettin' worse and worse. Don't know how bad things have gotta get before they get better.'

Max just didn't know what he could be throwing away, thought Joe. Pissed him off sometimes, the way he just scoffed at the opportunities being presented to him on a plate, his for the taking. Fuckin' white people just didn't know how easy they had it. Or maybe they were just *too* used to it. Walk right through doors that opened without them even knowing they were closed to almost everyone else.

Max had everything going for him. He was widely recognized as being the most talented cop on the force. No one came close to him. He also had the right connections. Eldon Burns wasn't just his boss, he was also his mentor. Burns was the most powerful cop in Florida, some said even the whole of the South. He had everyone's ear. Rumour had it he even knew Reagan. It was Burns who'd persuaded Max to join the police. And it was Burns who watched over him like a guardian angel with six guns – not that he'd ever needed to intervene, because once Max was on the streets he took to the job like he'd been doing it for a hundred years, and doing it well. As long as Burns was there, Max would rise up the ranks, probably make Major by the time his boss stepped down. Then the rest would be up to him, and that would be a tough climb – politics not police work got you those top jobs, as Max well knew, and thought he was having none of it.

If Joe had been in Max's shoes, he would've played the game, made the necessary sacrifices and given the powers that be what they wanted. You couldn't get anywhere in life without losing a little of yourself, without giving some part of yourself away that you would have liked to have held on to. But that was just the way it went. The trick was to make sure you got what you wanted for what you lost. Max didn't know anything about that kind of deal yet: the circumstances that would force someone to the point where they had to cut part of themselves off to move on up. Maybe he never would. Joe had burnt virtually every bridge he'd ever crossed to get to where he was today. He didn't talk to his four brothers because he was a cop, and most of his childhood friends had disowned him when he'd told them he was signing up with the PD; they'd called him a house nigger and an Uncle Tom. Not that they'd exactly turned out too right since. Two of his brothers were dead, one in 'Nam, the other of an OD. One was in prison for dealing, the other was on welfare. Those of his friends who weren't behind bars were either dealing drugs or hooked on them, or else were pimping, or walking around in the middle of the day, drunk. Liberty City was a hard rut to climb out of. Ghetto gravity pulled at you the hardest. You had to be tough and determined to get loose of it. Most weren't. They were either genuinely happy where they were or too scared or weak or stupid to see it for the deadly shithole it was.

Joe had barely touched on this with Max. He'd mentioned that he was estranged from most of his family, but hadn't gone into it too much. It was best to have some secrets.

Max was his closest friend. Unlike a lot of white and even a good few Latin cops on the force, he wasn't a racist. He never talked down to black people, never discriminated against or for them. This was probably because when he'd been growing up most of his friends had been black, on account of his being around the kids of his dad's jazz band colleagues. Joe had never said it out loud, but he reckoned Max's attraction to black women was in part due to the fact that his moms had always hated them after his dad left her for a sister he'd met on the road. Changing his habits would be hard, but Joe was determined to make him see sense. He wanted Max to fulfil his potential as a cop, and he himself wanted to get as far up the ladder as he could. He wasn't part of Burns' inner circle the way Max and certain others were. All those guys were hotshots, current or future, kings and their heirs. Joe was therefore relying on Max to do well so he could follow in his wake and move up with him. It was thanks to Max refusing to work with another partner, that he'd made Detective, and again thanks to Max that he'd been brought into MTF. He knew he was succeeding on Max's terms, rather than his own, and that his progress wouldn't have been as quick otherwise, but for now that suited him just fine; it was up instead of down, right where he wanted to be and where he wanted to stay. Besides, he'd met the woman he was going to marry and settle down with. They were already talking about moving in together.

Despite the traffic, Max and Joe still had twenty minutes to spare before their shift started. Usually they timed it so they had around twice that so they could stop off at Sandino's Grill – a café run by a seventy-year-old Cuban called Cristobal who sat outside from opening time to closing time on a foldaway chair in a beige or olive-green cotton suit, panama hat, sparkling shiny black leather shoes and a gold-topped mahogany cane, smoking cigars, watching and chatting to passers-by. Max had thought it an eccentricity of his, a way he'd chosen to spend his retirement, but it was how he drummed up business. He'd greet people he saw every day and, sooner or later they'd start talking and before long they were his regulars. He knew them all by name. The café was run by his identical twin sons, who did the cooking and waiting. They were called Benny and Tommy. You never knew who was serving and who was cooking.

Max and Joe had breakfast at Sandino's most mornings, before or after their shifts ended, but today they only had time for black coffee and Cuban sandwiches to go.

The café was cool and sombre inside, with polished wooden tables and a varnished floor. The walls were draped with the Cuban flag and map, as well as framed black and white photographs of the island, pre-Fidel. Cristobal had played drums in his youth. There were pictures of him in a white tux and black bow tie, playing with an assortment of bands – trios, quintets, sextets, big bands. There were pictures of a smiling Cristobal surrounded by beautiful young women, shaking hands with priests, soldiers and – on two different occasions – with a young Frank Sinatra. He told a great story about how early one morning in 1947, Sinatra had walked into a club in Havana where he and his two brothers were playing. He'd got up on stage with them and sung a few songs – 'Close To You', 'One For My Baby' and 'These Foolish Things'. Cristobal – the only one of the three who could speak any English – had kept in touch with the singer ever since. Sinatra had made a habit of coming by Sandino's whenever he was in town, usually right after closing time, when there was no one around.

Max and Joe sat down at a window table as they waited for their sandwiches to be made by Benny or Tommy. Max gratefully lit a Marlboro, took the first drag and held it in his lungs for a few seconds before slowly expelling the smoke through his nostrils and then his mouth. He took a sip of his Cuban coffee and looked at Joe, expecting to see disapproval. Joe's eyes were glued to the TV behind him. Max hadn't paid it any mind. Breakfast news, same as what was in the paper.

'Well, look at that.' Joe tapped him. 'Dean Waychek.'

Max turned around and saw Dean Waychek's face – thin, pockmarked, goateed, bespectacled. The picture cut to a reporter standing outside the entrance of the Alligator

Moon. Behind him were two police cruisers and an ambulance. The reporter said Waychek had been shot seven times.

'Ain't that a shame,' Max murmured.

'Couldn't have happened to a nicer person,' Joe said. 'No one's gonna be in a hurry to catch his killer either.'

He looked at Max searchingly for a second.

'What?' Max asked.

'You kinda quiet.'

Suddenly they heard police sirens outside. Lots of them. Joe got up and looked out of the door.

'Something's happening at CC,' Joe said, meaning the Miami-Dade County Courthouse, two blocks away and right opposite their headquarters.

'The Moyez trial. That started up again today, right?' Max said as the two went back to the car to get their bulletproof vests out of the trunk. 'Isn't today Pedro de Carvalho's big moment on the stand?'

'Yeah.' Joe nodded.

'Shit.'

13

8 a.m. and a nice day in Miami, Bonbon smiled as he looked out of the window of the Mercedes, which was stuck in traffic, right close to the Freedom Tower. When he'd first arrived in Miami off the boat, they'd sent him there to get himself checked out and naturalized. When he told the immigration officials he was Haitian they didn't believe him, because all the Haitians they dealt with were skinny-ass famine victims.

He reached into the brown paper bag between his legs and took out a piece of candy wrapped in red and white striped plastic. This was his favourite kind of confectionary, imported straight from Haiti, where he'd first tasted it as a kid – a white, almond-flavoured oval filled with liqueur. But, in truth, he loved all kinds of candy. He ate it all the time, morning, noon and night, which was how and why he'd got his name. He liked it. His habit defined him. He was 255 pounds of fat packed onto a big-boned six-foot frame. He was still quick on his feet and didn't get out of breath as long as he didn't have to run up too many stairs, not that people expected him to do too much of that. The parts he played were more particular.

Candy had taken all Bonbon's teeth, so he wore dentures. He'd got real creative here, letting his imagination and wallet run wild. He had eight sets for different occasions. For partying he favoured his gold or diamond-studded ones. He loved to dance. His moves may have been limited to a side-to-side shuffle and a few hand claps and finger clicks, but he had a great sense of rhythm and his timing was perfect. When he was working he wore either standard dentures, like the ones he was wearing now, or, if he had to regulate someone for Solomon he wore the sharp pointy ones he'd had modelled on piranha teeth. Usually the sight of those things in his mouth would be enough to freak any motherfucker out enough for them to do any damn thing that was required, but once in a while he met resistance; the brave types who thought he was all bluff and no blow. He'd shown them right. One time he'd bitten a guy under his left ear and ripped an inch-wide strip of skin clean off his skull all the way past his nose. Then he'd taken some pictures of the fucker's face and had 'em made up as postcards to send to people ahead of his visits. Sometimes it paid to get a little savage and bloody.

He chuckled to himself and looked over at Marcus, the driver, then shifted his bulk around.

Sitting in the back were his deputies Danielle and Jane. Jane was the darker and prettier of the two. She had long slender legs and liked to show them off every chance she got. She had on a short leather skirt and a black bolero jacket with a white blouse done up to the collar. She was originally from the town of Bánica on the border with the Dominican Republic, where her pops came from. She spoke four languages – Spanish, Kreyol, French and English. Bonbon had known Danielle since they were kids. She'd been a skinny little thing back then, arms and legs you could pick your teeth with, always half dead from hunger. Like a lot of kids who'd come up in the slums and then had money, she'd gone from bone to blubber in no time. He didn't blame her. Before coming to America the only meat she'd eaten had been rats and mice. She wore her clothes loose and long to hide the bumps. She and Jane were lovers and had been ever since they'd met, twelve years ago. The Kreyol word for their kind was *madivine*, but he didn't ever use it to their faces. He had too much respect for them and he liked their style. They had his back. They could get as mean and nasty as the best guys he knew but, when he asked them to, they put on the sweetest, most sensual shows for him. Nothing he liked better than watching two or three girls together, especially if one of them was getting turned out. He liked to see the new-to-its fight it – and when girls fought each other, *man* did they *fight*. They didn't quit either, kept on coming back at you, again and again. Sometimes watching them fight was better than the sex that followed.

In-between Jane and Danielle, wearing a nice new grey suit, white shirt and tie was Jean Assad, the Catman. He didn't look too bad, considering what had been done to him. There he was, bolt upright, legs pressed tightly together like he didn't have no nuts, hands palm down on his thighs, just like he'd been in the last SNBC. His face was stone – expressionless, no motion – and his eyes were gone, relating to nothing they were seeing, the life in them locked away. Back in Haiti he'd heard *houngans* say that zombies got that look they had because all they could see was the gap between this world and the next.

When the lights changed they drove on towards the courthouse.

They stopped the Mercedes and waited near a phone booth on North West 2nd Street, right behind the courthouse.

At a few minutes before 10 a.m., Bonbon got out of the car and walked over to the booth. He was dressed in a black pinstriped suit, white shirt, red tie and dark grey waistcoat. He might have gone unnoticed on a street predominated by business types running to meetings and lawyers and their clients going to and from court, most dressed elegantly, some expensively so, but his hat and the way he wore it made people do a double-take. It was a black stovepipe top hat with a red and white candy-striped band around it. It added a good half foot to his height and an air of undertaker-cum-ringmaster to his appearance.

The phone call came dead on ten. Everyone in the organization wore the same Swiss-made Compuchron digital watch with the red LED screen, all synchronized to the exact same time.

Bonbon picked up the receiver.

'*Palé map kouté,*' Bonbon said. Talk I'm listening.

'*Yo tout là,*' a man's voice answered at the other end. They're all there.

'*Sèten?*'

'*M'sèten.*' The reply. He was sure.

Bonbon got back in the car and nodded to Marcus.

They drove over to the courthouse and stopped opposite the entrance. Danielle opened the door and got out. Bonbon turned around to look at Jean Assad.

'*Allay netwaye fatra andedan,*' Bonbon said, slowly and clearly as he'd been instructed.

Without his face changing from its impassive frozen mask, Jean Assad slid off his seat and out of the car and walked away towards the courthouse, Danielle following him a few paces behind.

When she returned they drove a little further down West Flagler Street and found a parking space which gave them a clear view of the courthouse's impressive white granite steps.

Bonbon unwrapped another almond oval and slipped it in his mouth.

The murders of officers Patti Rhinehart and Leo Crews on the evening of Tuesday 6 March 1979 were considered among the most brutal in the history of the Miami Police Department. They shocked everyone, from hardened cops who thought they'd seen it all, right down to the raw recruits who heard about it in the academy and quit there and then.

Victor Moyez, a drug dealer from Venezuela, had just concluded the biggest deal in his fifteen years of shipping first cannabis then cocaine from his country to Florida.

Instead of dealing with the Cubans or the Jamaicans or the Overtown and Liberty City crews, he'd gone and cut himself a deal with the new player on the scene, a Haitian who had plenty of money and an awesome distribution network, but who was notoriously difficult to get close to. It had taken Moyez and his people over a year of negotiations just to set up an initial meeting, and then another year to work out terms. It was a double victory for Moyez, firstly, because under his previous deals he'd had to guarantee his drug shipments from Venezuela right up to Miami and regularly lost a good third or more to US customs. Under the new deal, his cocaine was getting flown to a private airfield in Haiti and unloaded there. His new contact would oversee its passage to Miami. The Haitian had also agreed to launch two new projects Moyez was developing on the streets – *cocaína de mendigo* – beggar's cocaine – a very cheap variety of freebase coke aimed at the breadline masses instead of the trustfunders. The other project was *Erythroxylon Moyez*, a cross between two rare coca plants with a 2–2.5 per cent content of the ether-soluble alkaloids forming the basis for cocaine. It was hoped that the cross – if successful – would result in a doubling of the alkaloid content, meaning he could manufacture either stronger cocaine or more cocaine from less plants. If either or even both took off they'd completely revolutionize the industry and he – Moyez – would be in pole position to make another fortune before the imitators began fighting back.

The only thing that had troubled Moyez about the deal was the Haitian himself. He'd never seen him. Or, rather, he didn't know which – if any – of the three people who'd called themselves Solomon Boukman was actually the real deal. It certainly wasn't the blond-haired surfer dude he'd initially made contact with in the Biltmore suite. And it might not have been the middle-aged black lady he'd met in Fort Lauderdale, also calling herself Boukman. And it quite possibly wasn't the old man who'd concluded the deal that day in a house in Coral Gables speaking only in Spanish. He'd heard that was how the Haitian did his business, never personally, only through spokespeople – or, sometimes he'd deal with you direct but you'd never know it was him for sure because of all the other people you'd spoken to. The dumber folk said Boukman must be the Devil himself to be able to do that, but he didn't believe that for a minute. The Devil wouldn't need to do business deals with people like him. Still, he'd felt that bit uneasy throughout the whole deal, for the first time in his life an inferior part of a greater whole, not in control of his destiny, at the mercy of overpowering forces. Whatever it was with this guy, it was a freaky situation.

That had been furthermost from his mind once the deal was done, because Moyez had thrown a party in his stretch limo with a few hookers, champagne, half a kilo of cocaine and music. They'd driven around Miami in the small hours of the morning. Moyez, bored that the speed of the vehicle wasn't matching that of his heartbeat, ordered his driver to go faster and faster until the limo was doing a steady hundred.

It was then that Patti Rhinehart and Leo Crews had pulled the limo over and met their respective fates. Moyez, blitzed on coke and champagne and pissed off that his party had been interrupted, ordered his men to bundle the two police officers into the limo and steal their car. The officers had been driven out to a warehouse and tortured with ice picks, razor blades, cigarettes and – as was Moyez's speciality – scorpions. The autopsy revealed traces of both scorpion venom and an anti-serum; in other words the cops had been stung repeatedly by the scorpions, experienced all the symptoms brought on by their venom – from severe stomach cramps, vomiting and diarrhoea to difficulties in breathing – before being cured so they could be stung again.

The officers were tortured for ten days before finally being killed with their own revolvers. Their bodies were then dressed in their uniforms and put in the trunk of their patrol car, which was driven to police headquarters and parked outside.

Moyez had gone back to Venezuela but left one of his trusted lieutenants, Pedro de Carvalho, in Miami to act as a liaison with Boukman.

One night de Carvalho got into an argument with a man in the bathroom of a nightclub. The argument had escalated into a fight which de Carvalho had been losing until he'd pulled a gun on his assailant. Unbeknown to him the man was an off-duty cop. When de Carvalho walked out of the club he'd found the police waiting for him, guns drawn. They searched him on the spot and found his most prized possession on a chain around his neck – Patti Rhinehart's badge. De Carvalho was arrested for the officers' murders.

Facing the electric chair, de Carvalho had cut a deal with the DA. He would lure Moyez back to Miami and testify against him in open court. His sentence would be commuted to twenty years, served in a soft prison in New England.

It was cold in the courtroom because the air conditioning had been turned all the way up to regulate the heat generated by the hundred or more members of the public crammed close together into the uncomfortable seats – among them dozens of antsy TV, newspaper and radio reporters – as well as the extra lights for the two film crews from rival networks who were covering the trial.

Today was the big day, the trial's decisive episode, Pedro de Carvalho's star turn on the stand.

The TV cameras were trained on Victor Moyez, a squat and compact man with swarthy weatherbeaten skin, dark eyes, whose intensity was undiminished by the pebble specs he'd worn throughout the trial, and a black beard, with a streak of white running from his chin to his left jaw, so heavy it obscured his mouth. Were it not for the crisp, tailor-made double-breasted navy-blue suit with a white handkerchief in the breast pocket, he could have passed for a political prisoner gone slightly insane during confinement.

Some of the more perceptive journalists who'd been following the trial since it had started the previous month, noted how Moyez wasn't simply calm and composed, but actually appeared to be enjoying himself, chuckling as he listened to the translation of the charges against him through headphones, sometimes laughing out loud and clapping his hands as the more daring or violent episodes of his life were described. Flanked by his two lawyers, Harvey Winesap and Coleman Crabbe of Winesap, Mcintosh, Crabbe & Milton of Park Avenue, New York, the country's most in demand narco lawyers, rumoured to cost upwards of $2,000 a day, he seemed inordinately relaxed for someone facing either the death penalty or life in an American penitentiary, most probably Marion, Illinois.

Moyez had every reason to be relaxed. In the next few hours, he'd be a free man. When Pedro de Carvalho took the stand to sing his traitor's hymn, he'd get the shock of a lifetime. His beloved mother, sisters and young daughter would be brought in by two of Moyez's lieutenants and sat in the front row, right in his sightline. Moyez had had them kidnapped and brought to Miami. De Carvalho knew what it would mean for them if he opened his *mamagüebo* mouth. He'd have to retract everything and the case would collapse. He was all the *gringos estúpidos de mierda* had.

At least everyone agreed about what happened in the first five minutes of the trial – and even if they hadn't, the two cameras captured it all very clearly. The state called Pedro de Carvalho and out of a door to the left of Judge Leo

Davidtz emerged a short and pale-looking man who bore only the slightest resemblance to the puffy-faced, mustachioed *bandido* of his widely circulated mugshot. De Carvalho's round, double-chinned mien had shrunk back to skin and bone, and he'd lost the facial hair too, revealing a prodigious overbite which made his head look like that of a shrunken Inca. He stopped when he came face to face with his old boss, and for a good few moments stood stock still, like he'd grown out of the ground, staring at him, while his expression began to crumble into tremors and tics. Had he been allowed to stand there any longer he probably would have screamed or burst into tears or both, but courtroom guards moved him along to the witness stand.

Meanwhile the cameras had swung to Moyez, sitting back in his seat, hands folded across his chest, smiling so hard at his former charge that his beard had assumed a boat-like shape.

De Carvalho took his oath, sat down and reached for the glass of water on the edge of the stand, but knocked it over. Moyez laughed out loud. The judge scowled at him.

The guard nearest de Carvalho picked up the glass and went to refill it. The DA stood up and began to go through the preliminaries, asking the witness his name, age, place of birth and relation to Moyez.

De Carvalho had begun to answer when he heard the main courtroom door open and glanced to see who had walked in.

No one paid much attention to the bald black man who came into Court 15. He was dressed in a grey suit, white shirt and black and white striped tie. He didn't stand out too much unless you looked at his face and noticed that his eyebrows and eyelashes were missing. But then people in the courthouse didn't stare too hard at each other because they never knew who they might be looking at and what the person might do. The black man was virtually invisible here, just another guy in a suit in a place where almost everyone wore one.

The man proceeded up the aisle between the pews.

Although the first five rows nearest the defendants were full, the man was able to find a seat in the middle of the third row because two people – a man and a woman, both blond – parted to give him a seat. The man took his place as the DA was asking de Carvalho about his association with Victor Moyez.

When he saw the black man walking in instead of de Carvalho's family, Moyez scowled at Coleman Crabbe. Crabbe made a small placating gesture and gave his client his most reassuring smile. They'd be here shortly. Everything was going to plan. Not to worry.

Moyez turned his furious look on de Carvalho who was telling the DA how he'd first met Moyez in the town of Cabimas when he'd been looking for work in the oil refineries. De Carvalho caught his boss's eye and the words, up until then coming in a fluent flow, suddenly curdled in his throat and stopped.

Then Moyez saw his deputy's eyes leave him and move to his left, towards the courtroom door. His face suddenly turned ashen.

Moyez smiled and the edges of his beard stretched outwards with glee.

The man in the grey suit stood up slowly, as if he was trying to leave while causing the least disturbance. Then he raised his right hand and shot Victor Moyez through the back of the head with a .357 Smith & Wesson Magnum. Moyez's face exploded all over the legal papers piled up on his table and his body fell forward.

In the next five seconds the gunman felled Winesap with a shot through the cheek as he turned his head in instinctive curiosity to look at where the first bullet had come from, without properly realizing what had just happened to his client. Coleman Crabbe was quicker. He managed to crawl under the table and curl himself into a foetal ball, with his arms covering his head, but the gunman killed him with a shot that smashed through his overlapped hands and punctured his brain.

There was pandemonium in the courtroom as everyone hit the ground. Then the guard nearest the judge – who'd also thrown himself to the floor – shot the assassin four times, the bullets all hitting him in the heart in close formation. He dropped his revolver, tilted backwards on his heels and then collapsed forward, going head first over the pew onto the people cowering below.

Bonbon let the phone in the booth opposite the courthouse ring twice before answering. He heard what he needed to hear and walked back to the car as the air around him began to swarm with the sound of approaching police sirens.

PART THREE
May 1981

14

'So, gennellmen. Where we at?' Deputy Chief Eldon Burns asked, looking sternly from Max to Joe and then back to Max, where he let his gaze settle and stay.

Eldon was harassed and pissed off, Max could tell, not just from the strained sound of his voice and the colour of his eyes – usually a clear grey-blue, now dark and murky like a low-lying cloud – but also from the purplish tinge of the small wart on the right side of his forehead. Normally the blemish blended in with his swarthy skin to the point where it was unnoticeable, but when he got angry it took on the hue of an overripe grape. Eldon was also wearing his wedding band. Although he'd been married for thirty-one years, he never wore his ring to work, something he'd learned in patrol: criminals were more inclined to mess with you if they thought you had something to lose and someone to live for. When he had to meet his superiors and paymasters, however, he made sure his ring was on, to better project the image of dependability and security that went hand in hand with being a high-level, high-profile cop.

He cut a fearsome figure. His face was broad and damaged. His nose, twice busted in the boxing ring and both times badly set, was out of alignment with the natural order of his features. It listed to the right and threw his physiognomy out of whack, to the point where the opposite halves of his face differed quite distinctly one from the other: the left side sagged a little and puddled about the bottom lip, while the right was firmer and tauter, and belonged to a man ten years younger. Boxing also accounted for his disjointed eyebrows, split in two with a thin vertical band of scar tissue replacing hair. Whenever he frowned his eyebrows steepled and looked like a drawbridge stuck in mid-opening, letting nothing through either way.

There were other scars on his face too, cruel gouges and corrugations which bore testament to a time when policing Miami hadn't been the desk-bound bureaucratic endeavour of modern times, but a daily hand-to-hand war with the criminals who'd followed the new money into the city during its major boomtime in the 1950s.

And then, of course, there was Eldon's reputation – the myths, rumours, stories and quasi-legends which preceeded him like pilot fish announcing a great white shark; none of which Eldon refuted, all of which he encouraged. He liked to tell people how he'd got his scars and leave it to others to describe how he'd avenged them. Max wasn't sure how much bullshit the stories had leaked in the hold from being passed around from teller to teller, but he believed their core and, most of all, he understood their point – you fucked with Eldon Burns at your deepest peril.

'No ID as yet on the shooter, so he wasn't the crazed, lone-gunman type, 'cause they always have ID on 'em – wanna be remembered. This was a well-planned hit,' Max said, looking through the four sheets of notes he'd bashed out on his electric typewriter ahead of the meeting.

It had been a week since the Moyez murder. The case hadn't just gone nationwide but worldwide: the shocking footage of a gunman striking at will right in the heart of Miami's judicial system had been beamed out into billions of homes, prompting two hour-long TV documentaries, marathon radio debates and countless newspaper and magazine articles about the city's decline from comfortable retirement home to lawless war zone. The more sensationalist types were labelling Miami one of the five most dangerous cities in the world after Moscow, Tehran, Kabul and San Salvador. The shootings made the covers of *Time* and *News-*

week. It was bad for business. A third of all hotel bookings and holidays had been cancelled, inbound flights to Miami were half empty and outbound ones oversubscribed, the same for trains and buses. Max and Joe had caught the case because they'd been the first homicide dicks on the scene. They both wished they hadn't. High-profile cases were the worst, everyone from politicians and top brass to the media and public breathing down your neck, demanding a speedy resolution, everything done in TV time, like you were *Starsky & Hutch.*

There was no point in snowing Eldon with the positive side of things because he was the sort who looked for the bad in the good, the down before the up, the price tag on every favour rendered. You gave him the worst-case scenario first and then slowly walked back to find something to smile about. And Max *did* have some good news to tell him.

But first the bad.

'No match on the prints,' Max continued, 'no serial number on the gun – that was filed off. The only prints on the gun and casings were the shooter's. The clothes were all from JCPenney, right down to the socks. Nothing whatsoever in the pockets. Now, the soles of the shoes were near spotless, barely used outdoors, which means that the shooter only wore them a very short time outdoors – I'd say enough to walk a short distance to the courthouse.' Max glanced briefly at Joe in case he wanted to say something, even though they'd agreed Max would do the main presentation and they'd answer Eldon's questions between them. He turned to the last page of his notes, the abbreviated autopsy report.

'Whoever put this guy up to the hit knows basic forensics. The shooter's fingernails and toenails were cut and scrubbed clean. Every hair on his body wasn't just shaved, it was *waxed.*'

'So, so far absolutely nothin', huh?' Eldon said, lacing the fingers of his shovel-sized hands together and leaning forward over the thick slab of highly polished mahogany that was his desk. To an outsider, the desk would have appeared a size too small for someone of Eldon's stature, but Max knew this was deliberate and completely in keeping with Eldon's thinking: the smaller desk made his boss look bigger, more imposing. Eldon was already slightly over six feet tall, but he wore his greying mousey blond hair in a modest pompadour which added a couple of extra inches to his height.

'Not quite,' Max said. 'Remember the Primate Park stiff?'

'How could I forget the *fine* job you two did there? You know they scraped two dead gorillas off US1 just this morning?' Eldon retorted, his sarcasm made worse by his Mississippi drawl, which added a mocking dimension to his tone. He'd been born and raised in Hattiesburg and hadn't lost a hint of his accent, despite moving to Florida when he was seventeen.

'There's a connection with the Moyez shooter.' Max ignored him and spoke a little louder to stake out his ground. Eldon had already torn into them over Primate Park, but that fiasco had made a laughing stock of both MTF and, by association, him, so he made a point of bringing it up every time another escaped monkey turned up. Max knew better than to complain because it only made things worse. Eldon didn't like getting talked back to, especially when he was right. 'Got the toxicology report this morning. The Moyez shooter had the exact same contents in his stomach as the Primate Park stiff: sand; crushed sea shells; three sorts of vegetable matter, as yet unidentified; seeds or beans, also still unidentified; plus Kool-Aid and semi-digested scraps of cardboard. Put them together and it made up part of a card – a tarot card – sort you can tell the future with: the King of Swords.'

'The King of Swords?' Eldon frowned and his split eyebrows turned into thick circumflex accents.

'I did a basic read-up. All tarot cards have two meanings, positive and negative, depending on which way up they are,' Max explained. 'If a tarot card is the right way up its meaning is positive. If it's upside down it's negative. The positive meaning of the King of Swords is an authority figure, like a judge or a general or a company director. It can also represent the outcome of a legal situation. On the flipside, the card represents cruelty, evil, a very powerful and destructive person.'

'Like a hit man?'

'Yeah, could be. Now, we're still lookin' into this but I'm guessing it's some kind of black magic thing, and that other shit they found in the shooter's stomach? That'll turn out to be some kind of potion. Either he drank it a few hours before he went out, or else he was force-fed it. Maybe it was something to pump him up, 'cause this guy *must* have known he was walking into certain death. We'll know the exact composition when the lab comes back to us in a week or so. And there's another thing. As far as I know, all tarot cards have faces. These don't. The faces are blank. Means they would be exotic. Easy to trace.'

'OK,' Eldon nodded. 'What about the stuff they found in the Primate Park stiff?'

'North Miami PD didn't analyse it.'

'Why not?'

'They figured it was a done deal. The guy flipped out, killed everyone close to him and then dropped dead himself.'

'They keep any samples?'

'No, just a few Polaroids of the tarot card.' Max took them out of the file and handed them to Eldon, along with the dozen autopsy snapshots of the card taken out of the Moyez shooter's stomach. The latter had been more corroded by stomach acid, the colours faded to mere outlines in many places, but the overall design was still recognizable. 'Same card.'

Eldon sat back in his chair and studied the Polaroids for a moment then handed them back.

'What about the shooter's helpers?'

'We're still looking,' Max replied, shifting in the uncomfortable, thinly padded pine chairs Eldon had his subordinates sit in when conducting official business. The chairs creaked and were too narrow to settle in without being pinched and squeezed at from the sides. Whenever a case was successfully concluded, they'd sit at the opposite end of his spacious office, where there was a black leather couch and two thick armchairs around a large glass coffee table. Eldon would pour the drinks – high-grade malt whisky or bourbon – and hand out Cuban cigars and compliments to celebrate jobs well done. Then the jokes, laughter, gossip and backslapping would go on for a good few hours. But they were pretty far from that now, still at the foot of a steep and slippery mountain. Professional hits were next to impossible to solve, even if it was obvious exactly who was behind them. A good hit man would leave no traces, collecting his victim's life like a ghost. Yet this was different, something they'd never seen before – a suicide-assassin.

Max and Joe had gone through the available TV camera footage from the courtroom: of the blond man and woman who'd made room for the killer to sit down and then retrieved his gun after the shooting. There wasn't too much to see, only a few seconds of them standing up and leaving their seats, their faces impossible to make out because they'd kept their heads averted from the camera. They were almost indistinguishable one from the other, the only way to tell them apart was the cut of the beige suits they wore. They were of the same height and build, had similar hairstyles and, according to seven eyewitnesses who remembered them and gave details to police artists, looked almost identical, with high cheekbones, blue eyes and sharp dimpled chins. Some sketches had them both wearing earrings too.

They'd also checked out the courthouse security camera footage. There were cameras at the entrance and on every floor. The couple had arrived at the building at 8.30 a.m., and passed through the metal detectors. They were then seen waiting together on a bench outside the courtroom, no doubt so they could be first in line to get their places.

'We're pretty sure they didn't bring the gun in. A Smith & Wesson .357 would not have made it through the metal detector. The gun must have been taped under the seat before the courtroom opened. Those two were there to occupy the seat until the killer came in,' Joe said.

'Insiders. Thought so,' Eldon said. 'Whole city's wriggling with worms.'

'We're currently interviewing everyone – cleaners, security, court staff and as many of the journalists and spectators as we can track down. So far everyone checks out – except for the blonds. Two press passes were issued to a Ryan Connor and Clare Johnson from the *LA Times*. Only, when we checked with the *Times* you know who Ryan Connor and Clare Johnson are? Their horoscope writer and cookery correspondent. One's fifty-five and bald, the other's a brunette. Airtight alibis for the day of the shooting too: they were at an editorial meeting with thirteen other people.

'Now, we've talked to an eyewitness who says the blonds got into a dark green two-door Cutlass Supreme with a white hardtop. Didn't get the plates. The witness is a guy called Hector Manso who sells ice-cream cones opposite the courthouse. He gave the clearest description because he stopped right by the car to sell a cone to a kid a few minutes before the blonds came out. Says he thinks the car was either a '74 or '75.'

Eldon nodded grimly and then stood up and walked over to the window on the right. His office was on the top floor of MTF headquarters, facing the courthouse and overlooking the street. He stood there for a while, arms behind his back in a loose V, his posture straight yet reluctantly so, as if he was fighting the urge to slump under the burden of responsibilities which had physically manifested themselves on his shoulders.

He came back and sat down. He glanced from Joe to Max and then settled for the odd way he had of looking at neither and both at the same time, subtly moving his gaze in and out of their orbits.

'Earlier this morning I got a call from NYPD Homicide. The offices of Moyez's lawyers were broken into and all the files, taped depositions, everything they had on Moyez was lifted. Guys walked in dressed as security and took the files. They had keys and passes.'

'When did this happen?' Joe asked.

'The night of the shooting. Didn't get noticed for three days.'

'How come?'

'No one thought to check, I suppose,' Eldon said. 'But things get way worse: Winesap and Crabbe always gave copies of all the files of cases that were going to trial to their office manager, Nora Wong, for safekeeping. She stashed them in her country house in the Catskills, and then, when the trial was over she put them back in the office.

'The morning of the trial she phoned in sick. Stomach cramps, food poisoning. Said she was going to see her doctor. Her office didn't think this was unusual because she'd been complaining of dizzy spells the week before. She'd also recently given birth to a little girl. Her third child.

'NYPD found Nora Wong, her husband and two of her children in the basement of the Catskills place late yesterday night. All shot. They'd all been tortured first. The file's on its way down here. It won't be pretty.'

'What about the baby?' Max asked.

'They didn't find it. Probably sold on the black market.'

Just like the Primate Park stiff, Max thought.

'Now, these are bad times we're living in, gennellmen. The worst I've ever known,' Eldon spoke quietly but very firmly. 'We're getting hit from all sides and we're sinking. We've got the Colombian drug gangs, we've got the Cuban crimewave, we've got the blacks, we've got the Aryan Defence League. These fuckers are walking right over us.

'So we need a result on this one. And I mean one big loud result. Something that yells from every rooftop, something everyone will remember, something that lets these scumbags know that *no one* fucks with our justice system. I want you to bring me not just the guys who did this, but every piece of shit who helped them. *Everyone*.

'Every week we're gonna feed the press a success story. Every week there'll be people in custody, every week there'll be a breakthrough. Starting next Tuesday.'

'*Tuesday?*' Max began, but Eldon silenced him with a raised hand and a shake of the head.

'*You* don't have until Tuesday. You have until Monday. A week.'

Max and Joe exchanged perplexed glances. They were doing all they could: every cop in Miami was working on this and every single one of them was getting nowhere.

'We'll do our best, Eldon.' Max sighed. He would have protested more – a *lot* more – but he sensed there was something else behind Eldon's mood, something he hadn't yet got to, so he held back.

'Gennellmen, you're MTF *not* MPD. We don't "do our best" here, we *are* the best. That's what's expected of us, that's what we deliver. Now this is the biggest case we've had. They've hit us. We're on the ropes. We need to hit back. And *hard*. So get to it.'

Max and Joe stood up to leave.

'Not you, Max. You stay a moment. Liston, please wait outside.'

'Yes, Mr Burns,' Joe said and left the office.

15

Yes-*suh*, Masser Burns, no-*suh*, Masser Burns – go *fuck yo'
self Masser* Burns, Joe thought as he sat fuming outside the
office, angry and humiliated, and real close to getting up and
walking out. It was always this way at these face-to-face
meetings, had been ever since he'd joined MTF. Sixdeep –
that's what he called his boss, short for Sixth Degree Burns
– treated him like he wasn't there, never looked at him,
never asked his opinion, never asked him a single question
about anything, only ever addressed him when he was with
Max, and then just hello, goodbye and wait outside. He was
letting him know he didn't count for shit around here.

Sixdeep's secretary sat behind her desk right opposite
him, tapping away at her computer keyboard. She hadn't
even looked at him when he'd come out, treated him the
same way her boss did. Helga Martinez – aka Miss Irontits,
although no one said that too loudly in case the wrong ears
heard it – real fearsome, no nonsense and every bit as scary
as Sixdeep in her own way. Stout, dark-skinned Cuban
mother of five, with an extra roll in her neck and the
beginnings of a second chin. She'd worked for Sixdeep ever
since he'd been important enough to have someone do his
paperwork.

The phone was ringing but she ignored it. She was locked
deep into the mechanical groove of pecking out words on
the keyboard, her green nails and the piping of the jacket
over her chair matching the phosphorescent letters marching
left to right across the black monitor screen. She'd been the
first member of staff in the Miami PD to learn how to use
a word processor, and was probably one of only five or six

who were on first-name terms with the things in MTF. Joe had signed up for a night course at Miami University, starting in a month. Computers were the future and he wanted to be five steps ahead of police policy, just like he was with his Spanish lessons.

Max and Sixdeep were up on the roof, discussing whatever clandestine shit that got plotted when he wasn't around, quite possibly even discussing him. Max never told and he knew better than to ask. Max was loyal to Sixdeep; they went back years and years, to when Max was a teenager and Sixdeep had taught him to box at the 7th Avenue gym in Liberty City. If it ever came down to it Joe was sure Max would throw him over if his boss asked him to. He wouldn't like doing it, but he'd do it just the same. Max was a great detective, true, but he was a soldier in Eldon Burns' private army, following orders and executing commands.

Joe thought about his lot, second fiddle to Max Mingus, star cop. He thought of Lina and how they'd talked about moving in together, getting a place, an apartment or maybe a house, but in a good neighbourhood. That would cost money. He'd need a promotion and a bigger salary. That would only come if he carried on riding Max's coat tails and keeping up the dutiful house/nigger act. It hurt his pride and it pissed him off. He knew it wasn't like that for Horace Calderon, the only other black man in MTF, or for Sara Valdeon, one of the few women on the squad, also black. They were in Sixdeep's inner circle, part of the gang within the gang, part of the Cutmen.

And the shit he'd heard about *them* was enough to fill a city sewer ten times over. People talked plenty about the Cutmen and plenty more about Sixdeep – mostly black cops, a few of the younger Latinos, no whites – and none of it was pretty, let alone legal. He'd once mentioned the rumours to Max and his partner had told him it was all bullshit, stories envious losers made up to feel better about having been stepped over and left behind. Joe thought otherwise, but he hadn't said anything so as to keep the boat he was in on a straight and even keel.

Play the game, brother, he told himself. One day you'll be the man up in this beast.

Max liked it up on the roof. There was always a cool salty breeze blowing in from the sea, even in the hottest days of summer when the atmosphere was at its heaviest and the air tense and thick with building storms. You could lose the sense of the sea in the streets, where man-made fumes stunk out nature. Down there it was predominantly the dead heady smell of fuel being belched up into the sky but recently, with all the demolition work that had been going on around the city, Max had sometimes picked up a strong accent of fried cordite in the wind, especially where the contractors had used cheap illegal dynamite from South America. Then he'd feel on edge, like he was walking through the middle of a shoot-out, expecting to run into an ambush at any moment.

He could see much of the city from the roof: on one side the yellowy-grey spread of the streets and low-lying buildings broken up with dashes of intense tropical green, which went on to dominate the landscape the further out you looked; and then, when he turned around, he saw the port, marinas, hotels, beaches, the ocean and the bridges reaching out across it like fossilized tendrils.

The roof was where everything really happened at MTF; everything that counted and made a difference. It was where Eldon communed directly with his inner circle – no bullshit, no filtering out his words, no playing by the rules for appearance's sake; it was a place where no records were kept and every word spoken was carried away and dispersed in the wind once it had been heard.

'The Turd Fairy came by this morning,' Eldon said.

'Right,' Max replied as he lit a cigarette. That explains your mood, he thought.

The Turd Fairy was Victor Marko, but people only called him by his real name to his face. He was the mayor's fixer and all-round performer of unpleasant tasks, many of ambiguous legality. For the last twelve years he'd worked for whichever politician was running Miami. He had no party affiliations and no identifiable ideological convictions. In fact he was only loyal to whoever would pay him the substantial sums of money he commanded for his services. He'd earned his nickname because he either got shit done or fucked shit up. Today, Max guessed it was the latter.

Max had only seen him once: tall, bald, unsmiling and with udder-like jowls. His face and the way he carried his large head at a slightly upward angle from the rest of his body made Max think he might have modelled himself on the bust of a particularly nasty Roman emperor. His skin had all the radiant pallor of someone who spends most of his days indoors with the air conditioning on at full blast, and his upper body had a cushioned set to it that hadn't quite declared itself fat. Max imagined the Turd Fairy rarely exercised and had a balanced diet of wrong and right foods.

'He's all over the Moyez case,' Eldon said.

'Figures.'

'This isn't for the mayor though. Not this time. *Oh no.* As of now the Turd Fairy flies a higher path.' Eldon paused for effect and looked at Max with a wry smirk. 'None other than our beloved President Reagan.'

'Who'd he fuck over to swing that?' Max was incredulous and suddenly worried about the dimension the Moyez case was going to take. He hated it when it got political, because it became about more than just solving a crime and punishing the perps; when there were elections to be won, minorities would be charmed and pandered to, only to be ignored and bypassed once they'd delivered victory.

'There's only two places to go in politics – somewhere or nowhere. And these days the Turd Fairy is going somewhere.'

'What's *Reagan* want with Moyez?'

'Didn't you follow his campaign?' Eldon feigned indignation with a smile.

'No, I just voted for him,' Max said.

'Like the good registered Republican you are!' Eldon laughed and clapped Max on the back, which made him choke on the smoke he'd just drawn into his lungs, and provoked a coughing fit. Eldon watched with distaste as Max first struggled to clear a thick blob of phlegm from his throat and then spat it out with a retching noise.

'Reagan's planning a new offensive in the war on drugs. He wants to stop our kids getting high – bring the fight into the home,' Eldon explained. 'As you know there are two main drug cartels in Colombia, the Cali and the Medellín. The CIA's decided to go after the Medellín cartel. They're the bigger of the two, and they're exporting most of the coke that's coming into Florida. The cartels are headed up by the Ochoas, José Gacha, Pablo Escobar and Carlos Lehder. Moyez worked for Lehder.'

'But I thought Moyez was an independent. In the case file it says he got his stuff straight from the Bolivians. De Carvalho backed that up and was going to testify to it,' Max said, puzzled, but then saw the expression on Eldon's face – anger mixed with resignation and impatience – and knew what was coming next.

'Evidence from the investigation you're conducting will prove Moyez was *really* working for Carlos Lehder all along. And that it was Lehder who had him killed so he wouldn't name him.

'Lehder's the one they're going after first. He's the easiest one to get 'cause he's operating out of Norman's Cay in the Bahamas. Him and his crew have taken over the whole island. They're importing something like three hundred kees of coke *an hour* from Colombia and shipping that shit back here. We build a case against him and our government will send Special Forces out there to get him and his whole crew.

'So, first up, I need you to haul me in a low-level chain of command – bottom- to mid-level street guys, all spics – South Americans, *not* Cubans, and Colombians best of all. Usual drill: bring me the people, bring me a story, make 'em fit and make it stick. Can you do it, Max?'

'Yes, Eldon.' Max nodded. 'I can do it.'

'Good.'

'What about the Wong murders?'

'Put it this way,' Eldon smiled, 'by the time we're through with him, Lehder will have killed the Kennedys.'

And this was the way it sometimes went at MTF, and how it had sometimes gone from the moment Max had started working for Eldon Burns. Crimes got solved, but the guilty didn't always pay and politics and politicians sometimes rigged the scales of justice.

'That's the first thing,' Eldon said, and then looked Max directly in the eye. His pupils were back to their usual light steely grey. 'After this case is done, I'm assigning you a new partner. I'm replacing Joe Liston.'

'*What?*' Max reeled. '*Why?* What do you mean "replacing" him?'

'He's off the unit.'

'Why?'

'He's not one of us, Max.'

'What's that supposed to mean?'

'He doesn't fit in here. Never has. No matter how hard you've tried to make it so.'

'No matter how hard *I've* tried? I wasn't the one started calling the two of us "Bruce and Clarence" and *Born to Run*. That was you. *You* made us the Dynamic Duo, Eldon – *you!*' Max was angry now and starting to yell. It was hardly a surprise. Eldon didn't like Joe and never had. He made it quite obvious: no eye contact, no warmth in his exchanges. Joe had only spoken about it once when Max had brought it up, and all he'd said then was that he was sure Burns was one of those hard to get to know types and that they'd get on in time. Max hadn't wanted to put him straight, tell him that Eldon cold-shouldered people he didn't like – kept contact to a minimum and civility at a functional level because that would have made him feel he wasn't part of the unit.

'I made an effort with him, sure, more than usual. I cut him some slack on account of how tight the two of you are and what you represent.'

'What we *represent*?'

'It's a great look for the press and TV, a salt and pepper crime-fighting duo for a salt and pepper crime-choked city.'

'Then why are you changin' it?'

''Cause I don't like him and I don't trust him, so he's got to go.'

'Joe's a good guy, Eldon. And a great cop.'

'*Bullshit!*' Eldon snapped. 'A great cop he ain't. He's a mediocrity at best. At heart he's a by-the-book, process-driven lunk with a badge and a gun. He wouldn't cross the fucken' street if it wasn't in the manual. He's one of those guys who thinks about going home as soon as he clocks on, the kind of guy who treats this work like a job, not a vocation, not a *duty*. In short, he ain't *you*. Or Harris, Brennan, Ford, Whitlock, Valdeon, Guzman, Valentín, Calderon, Teixeira. He ain't no Abe Watson and he sure as shit ain't me. Break down any door, go through any window, any skylight, that's what I was like back in the day, and that's what my guys are like now – all of you. Same methods, same dedication. And don't give me that what "a good guy" he is crap either. Good guys don't belong in the trenches. Good guys are what we protect not what we are.'

'Joe's cut plenty of corners, Eldon,' Max said quietly, chastened by his boss's outburst.

'What? Beating up on suspects? Call that cutting corners? Tell me something, Max: you ever told him about what you really use the Comic Book for? He know what Seeds are? You told him how we *really* do things around here?' Eldon looked at him, got up close. Max picked up a hint of coffee in his breath.

'No.'

'Why not?'

Because I wanted to keep him out of all this, Max thought and almost said, but held back. Why bother speaking his mind? Did he tell Eldon the truth? Eldon was going to get rid of Joe and there was nothing Max could do about it. He should have seen it coming. For the last six months, Eldon had pruned MTF of all the underachievers and people he plain didn't like or trust.

'Thank you!' Eldon interpreted Max's silence as point taken. 'I've carried Joe Liston because of you. And hell, yes, because I had no homegrown nigras in the division too.'

Nigras – the word always made Max wince whenever Eldon used it, which he always did in private. The way he said it sounded real close to 'niggers'.

Eldon read the look on Max's face.

'Hell, Max! This ain't a race thing! You know there ain't a bigger nigra lover than me on the force. You know what the good ol' boys in command call me? "The EFO Man" – the Equal Fucking Opportunities Man! My record speaks for itself: I'm the only white face on the Rebuild Liberty City Committee, the NAACP has just shortlisted me for their Cop of the Year Award, and me and the Reverend Jesse Jackson are praying together at St Agnes next month – in front of the TV cameras.' Eldon smiled and showed his teeth – large and white like bathroom tiles. He'd never been much of a smiler until he'd started appearing on television. After the first few times someone must have said something to him about the state of his mouth because he'd had his teeth bleached and straightened.

'Don't worry about Joe. I'll look after him. He'll do real well for himself for as long as he wants. He'll make Detective First Grade at the end of the Moyez case. Then, in six to nine months he'll do and pass the Sergeant's exam – all that and a nice desk in Public Relations.'

'Public Relations! Public Fucken' Relations! Jesus, Eldon! Joe's a *street cop*. He's a Miamian born and bred! You can't stick him behind some fucken' *desk*!' Max was ranting, but he might as well have been doing it to the walls for all the reaction he was getting. Eldon stood where he was, his expression rigid but his eyes bright and smiling.

'Miami's changing, Max, and the Miami PD is gonna change with it. And I'm gonna make Joe its poster boy. Literally. From September we're gonna be running a recruitment drive, aimed at attracting us some ethnics and women. I've designed the billboard myself.' Eldon looked at the sky and extended his hands outward in a straight line. 'The poster will show a line-up – two women, a spic, a nigra in the middle, a white guy, and some kikey-lookin' college type with glasses. The nigra'll be Joe Liston, wearin' his biggest, proudest, happiest, ear-to-ear shit-eatin' grin. The new improved Miami PD, our rainbow force. And the headline? "All races, *One* Police Force". Whaddayathink?'

'You should work in advertising. You're wasted here,' Max retorted sourly. He wondered how long Eldon had been planning this, how long he'd been digging away at the ground under his feet. And did it matter?

'Aw, come on, Max!' Eldon said. 'You don't stay partners if you got ambition. Do you see me with a partner? Hell, no! You can't carry *and* climb, Max. There's room on that ladder for you and you only. Get to where you're going first, *then* – if you feel so inclined – dispense a little favouritism.

It's no different to when you was boxing, remember? Champs only come in ones.'

The thought of what was going to happen to Joe and his complicity in it, sent a nauseous spasm all through Max's guts. The spit in his mouth turned warm and his throat tightened. He was already in poor shape. He'd averaged two hours sleep a day since the Moyez shooting, most of it snatched in twenty-minute instalments in his car. He hadn't even been back home in three days. He'd eaten, washed, shaved and changed in HQ. He'd also been drinking too, a nip of bourbon here and a slug there, most of it in the near-continuous stream of coffee and Cokes he'd been floating on. And then there were the 30 mgs of dexedrine he'd been popping every six hours to fight off the worst of the fatigue.

'I've got big plans for you too, Max,' Eldon went on. 'You'll make Lieutenant next year, have your own division by 1985. And by 1995 you'll be Deputy Chief or more.'

'With you always one step ahead of me, right, Eldon?' Max said wearily. Clearing the path and then blocking the way, he thought. 'And what about you? The Turd Fairy gonna wave his wand and make you Chief when this is over?'

Eldon smiled and put an arm around his shoulders.

'I was like you once, you know, Max. I believed it was all about merit and hard work and that should be enough to get you through. But life ain't like that. It's not about how good or how clever you are – that counts, sure, but it's other stuff that sees you right: who you know and how far you're prepared to go to get what you want. You've gotta break eggs and hearts to get what you want. That's just the way it is.

'You do Moyez right and it'll be a beautiful thing. You boys'll be heroes. Don't worry about Liston. It'll be for the best and he'll come to see it that way.'

Max heard the sounds of traffic and voices carrying faintly up to the roof. He thought about having to face Joe when he came out of the office, then of working this last case with him, and then, more than anything, he realized he wanted a drink – and it wasn't even midday.

16

Max sat in a booth at the Well and slung back his second shot of Wild Turkey, chasing it with a gulp of Schlitz and a long pull on his Marlboro.

He felt seriously bad about Joe, the worst. He hadn't been able to look him in the face when he'd come out of Eldon's office. They'd ridden the elevator down to their floor in a tense silence. Joe normally asked him how it had gone, but this time he hadn't said a word; like he knew – which he probably did. He'd once told Max that black people had a sixth sense when it came to trouble, for knowing when something was wrong even when everything seemed right. He called it NSP – Nigger Sensory Perception, a genetic survival tool.

Once back at their desks, Max had taken the Comic Book out of his bottom drawer and said he'd be gone for an hour. Joe hadn't replied. He'd know where to find him if he needed to.

'Fuck you, Eldon,' Max mumbled into dead space. He couldn't resist his boss's decision any more than he already had. It was final, no argument, no compromise. Typical. What Eldon said went.

And it had *always* been that way, ever since Eldon had trained Max as a boxer.

They'd first met on 8 March 1964 when Max, then aged fourteen, had walked into the 7th Avenue boxing gym in Liberty City late in the afternoon. It wasn't his idea to go there. He was tagging along with his friend Manny Gomez, who'd wanted to learn how to fight.

Eldon and Abe Watson owned the place. Abe had retired from the force and was running the gym on a day-to-day basis, while Eldon trained amateur fighters four nights a week. Eldon had been Golden Gloves champion in both Mississippi and Florida and had briefly fought as a pro before becoming a cop.

Abe was Eldon's old partner. In 1957 Eldon had been the first white detective in the South to work with a black partner – a good three years before the Miami PD was officially desegregated. He'd personally gone to Chief Walter E. Headley with the request, arguing that it would help build trust with the black community and improve community relations if they saw at least one white cop working alongside their own kind. The Chief partnered Eldon up with Abe, the best detective in the police department's black division. It was a deeply unpopular move. The white detectives refused to let Abe sit in the same office as them, so he was given a cramped, stinking cubicle in the basement of police headquarters, very close to the holding cells. Eldon moved down there with him, and between them they got some serious results, closing close to 98 per cent of their cases; solid collars resulting in solid convictions.

Eldon had greeted Max and Manny like he did every wannabe who walked through the gym's saloon-style swing doors: no hello, who and how are you, just, 'OK. Hit me in the face.' It was his way of sorting the shit from the serious at the starting gate, and those who'd follow orders from those who'd question and hesitate.

Manny threw an awkward version of a jab he'd learnt from the street and watching fights on TV. Eldon casually moved his head out of the way and it missed him by a mile. Max hit Eldon flush on the chin with a short right hook which sent him to the ground with a thud like a sandbag landing on a pyramid of barrels. Everyone in the gym stopped what they were doing. No one had so much as landed a glove on Eldon since the gym had opened, let alone put him down.

'*Nothin' to see here, ladies. Back to work,*' he'd called out to his gawping charges as he got up off the floor. Then he'd looked at Max and Manny and said, 'I'll see you two tomorrow, 6 p.m. sharp. Bring shorts, a T-shirt and gym shoes. And don't be late.'

Max had been that rare thing – a fighter with the sort of natural, God-given ability that only needs pointing in the right direction and then keeping focused and on track. He was state and national middleweight Golden Gloves champion. Everyone thought he was going to do really great things – win gold at the Mexico Olympics and then go on to be an undisputed World Champion.

Although in public Eldon hadn't treated him any differently to the other fighters in the gym – infrequent and highly begrudging compliments breaking otherwise uniform criticism and barracking – in private they forged a close bond. They were a perfect fit: Eldon didn't have any sons, and Max's jazz musician father had bailed on him when he was nine, leaving him in the care of a mother who was largely absent from his life because of the two jobs she worked to keep the roof over their heads and the food on their table. Eldon took Max under his wing and looked out for him, encouraging him to work hard at school because boxing wouldn't last long and he'd need something to fall back on when the ring didn't want him any more. Max opened up to him, talked to him like an older, wiser buddy, asked him for advice – mostly about girls, which Eldon was an expert on. It was thanks to boxing that Max lost his virginity. When he'd taken his first trophy, a mere three months after walking into 7th Avenue, Eldon had bought him an hour with a hooker – something he did for all his fighters whenever they won championships. Eldon also introduced Max to his friends, a close-knit group of cops nicknamed the Cutmen who hung out at the gym. They adopted Max as their mascot and came out to support him at all his fights.

But Max never made it to the Olympics.

In November 1967 Max and Manny Gomez travelled to Atlantic City for a Golden Gloves bout. Max fought first and won easily, but Manny ran into problems with Kid Fernando, a local fighter also known as the Hands of Stone. He was knocked out close to the end of the last round and slipped into a coma. He came out of it a week later, but he was blind and paralysed on his left side.

Max hit a losing streak after that. He lost his nerve in the ring, played it cautious and safe where he'd once taken risks and gone out on a limb. He was suddenly scared of getting hurt. He lost nine bouts in a row, the last three to fighters so mediocre Eldon wouldn't have let them into 7th Avenue.

In the gym during training everyone could see the fight going out of Max, the way it sometimes did with naturally gifted boxers. One minute they had it, the next they didn't. Boxing was a sport of gradual peaks and sharp troughs. There was no gradual decline, just the sky, and then the ground rushing up to your face as you crashed towards it.

'So, do you know what you wanna do with the rest of your life?' Eldon asked him after he'd lost his tenth fight.

'Yeah,' Max answered. He'd always known.

The Well was small, cramped and always sombre, the main sources of light came from TVs fixed to brackets in each of the four corners, bulbs above the booths and bar counter, and the gaudy neon signs and tube lights advertising liquor, beer and cigarettes on the walls around the bar, all of which combined to suffuse the place in a dull and sticky blue-pink twilight.

Max turned his attention to the business at hand, the

thick and heavy blue file he'd bought with him: the Comic Book.

It was called the Comic Book because you used the pictures and words to make up stories. It was the MTF's Gideon's Bible. There was one in every detective's drawer.

The Comic Book was a 550- to 600-page directory containing details on every serious criminal and suspect known to be at large in Florida. It was arranged into four sections – Murder, Drugs, Sex, Other – with the people they covered, known informally as Characters, arranged in alphabetical order. An individual page contained a Character's mugshot or most recent photograph, zip code, basic particulars, family details, known associates, main crimes, MO. The pages were updated as many as five times a day. Gretchen Varadera, the MTF database manager, brought them round to each detective and then took away the out of date information. The data was collated by a surveillance team whose job it was to monitor the Characters and keep the information up to date and accurate.

The book had two uses. It was primarily a reference tool. If a particular crime fit one or more of the Character's MOs, or was similar, then the Comic Book provided a list of possible suspects. To access more information on one or more Characters, a detective would get Gretchen to print out the full file on the database and, if necessary, get a larger print of the photograph. But the directory also had another purpose, the one Max was using it for.

Eldon never referred to what he ordered his inner circle to do as 'framing'. He called it 'getting results' and 'making a difference'. As far as he and everyone who worked for him at MTF were concerned, anyone who made it into the Comic Book was a scumbag who needed taking out of circulation one way or another. Whether they'd actually committed any crimes that were being actively investigated really didn't matter. They would be preyed on just like they preyed on innocent Miamians.

The surest way to set up a Character for a fall was by sowing Seeds – planting evidence for forensics to find. Even the best defence lawyer found it next to impossible to argue away fingerprints found on a murder weapon, hairs, fibres, teeth and traces of fluid found at a suspect's home. MTF collected plenty of samples from all the cases it was working and carefully stored them in climate-controlled conditions in various safehouses around the city. When it was a Character's time to go down, the Seeds would turn up in his or her home – never too much to alert suspicion, but enough to put guilt beyond any reasonable doubt.

In addition to the evidence, some of the houses were used to store sizeable amounts of coke and cash, the former to plant on Characters, the latter mostly to pay certain sympathetic judges to sign search warrants. The going rate for this public service was around $20,000.

Octavio Bolivar Grossfeld, twenty-nine, Colombian.
Ideal.

Grossfeld had entered the US on a student visa in 1974 and studied land economy at Miami University for a year, before getting kicked out for drug offences. He'd not only been caught smoking grass, but he'd been dealing it on campus too. His three brothers and their girlfriends had been bringing brick-packed kilos over from Colombia. He was arrested and locked up for a month before his arraignment and was repeatedly assaulted and raped in prison. He was bailed and then disappeared. A bondsman who caught up with him in Boca Raton ended up dead with multiple stab wounds. Grossfeld was believed to have slipped back into Colombia.

But, in July 1979, he re-emerged as the leader of a small-time gang who'd been importing heroin into Florida. He'd been using Colombian women as mules, bringing them over by the plane load, guts filled with skag balloons. Some of the women had turned up dead with their stomachs hacked open and half their intestines missing. In September 1980 one of the mules was found alive and, against all odds, survived to give an accurate description of Grossfeld as the man who'd attacked her.

MTF officers had tracked him down to an address in South Miami Heights.

Max called Gretchen from a payphone and got more details on him from the database. He cross-referenced them with the factsheet he had on Carlos Lehder. They were a perfect fit. Both had shared German ancestry through their fathers who'd emigrated to Colombia from Germany, and both had mothers who were avowed Nazi sympathizers.

Next Max called Pete Obregón, a senior supervisor at airport customs. Pete was also a friend of Eldon's.

'*Como estas*, Max?'

'*Bueno*, Pete. You got any fresh mules in the tank?' Max asked.

'Been a real busy day. We got seven. Three Colombians, two Nicaraguans, a Panamanian and some girl from Georgia swears she's Jamaican.'

'The Colombians? Can they speak English?'

'No.'

'They been processed?'

'Two have. We can't X-ray the other one 'cause she's pregnant. We're lettin' her sit and shit.'

'OK. Can you get her in an interview room? I'm coming over.'

'This on or off the books?' Pete asked, in case he needed to get an interpreter to sit in with them. Otherwise he'd translate himself.

'Off,' Max replied.

'I'm on it,' Pete said.

Joe sipped the cup of coffee he'd poured himself ten minutes ago and had only just remembered. It was now tepid and tasted like caffeinated dishwater. He was waiting for Max to come back from the Well, his mind doing bitter laps as it churned over the events of the morning.

He knew for sure now Sixdeep was going to get rid of him. And knowing the way Sixdeep's mind worked, it wouldn't look like he'd been fired at all. He'd get a desk job in a departmental backwater like Archives, Complaints, Traffic, or maybe even Public Relations, which would mean no recognition and slow death by stalled career. The only people he knew who worked desk jobs were women, former cops who didn't want to retire, the disabled and people who didn't want to be cops at all but liked the uniform. Once you were behind a desk it was next to impossible to get back on the street. You were deemed soft and out of step. It had happened to three MTF detectives before, the ones who'd fallen foul of Sixdeep, who hadn't toed the line and gone along with his way of doing things – Meredith, Allen and Gonzalez. Meredith had been made deputy head of police kennels. He had a well-known allergy to dogs. He quit the force on medical grounds a month later.

It would play out something like this: they – that was him and Max, but mostly Max – would 'crack' Moyez. Which meant they'd patsy-out the case on some evil scumbags every jury in the world would just *want* to find guilty and that would be it – case closed, radioactive headlines, another positive notch on the stats board and Sixdeep looking better than ever, the Saviour of Miami or some crap like that. And while the real perps got away clean, they – Max and Joe, but mostly Max again, because he was more photogenic and, let's face it, *white* – would get fêted as heroes; medals would be pinned on their chests and they'd appear on a few local talkshows. They'd be flavour of the week, All-American Heroes, the Good Guys. Then, when it had all died down, Sixdeep would call Joe into his office. His next boss would be sat in one of the two chairs facing his desk. Sixdeep would say congratulations he'd got a promotion. New boss-man would then stand up and clap him on the back and shake his hand and say, 'Welcome to the team! Good to have you on board!' If he refused to go Sixdeep would tell him it was his way or the highway, and nothing in-between.

Christ, he hated him!

But there was absolutely nothing he could do about it. OK, there was. He didn't have to stay and take it. He *could* quit and go into another line of work. But what would he do? Drive a truck? Security? Run a bar? *Bullshit!* He didn't want to do that. He wanted to stay a cop – and a Detective too. He was good at what he did. Damn good. A lot better than *any* of these motherfuckers gave him credit for – except Max. Max was his biggest fan, his staunchest supporter. He'd never taken solo credit for anything. It had always been the two of them.

Joe remembered the day he'd first met Sixdeep. He was in the locker room, getting dressed and waiting to meet his new partner when he heard all conversation stop and saw everyone around him suddenly get busy doing something. Sixdeep had walked in. He was head of Robbery and Homicide at the time, but already a long-established legend. Joe had never met him, just seen his picture in newspaper reports. It was two weeks to the day after Joe had buried his partner Rudi Saunders, shot dead while they were making a routine stop.

'Joe Liston? Eldon Burns. Sorry for your loss.' He held

his hand out. 'I lost my partner too. Four guys turned him into a teabag for kicks. It's a tough break, but life has to go on and we've got a job to do. Here's someone I want you to meet. Came top in his class in the academy. Joe Liston meet Max Mingus, your new partner.'

Max had been so green that day, a scared and embarrassed look on his face, standing next to Sixdeep in his new, fresh-out-of-the-plastic uniform, his shiny shoes and his left-parted regulation-cut hair. Still made Joe laugh when he recalled the image and juxtaposed it with the way Max was now, a decade older and wearing every second of it.

He'd known what it had all meant: Sixdeep was making him *responsible* for Max. At the time, Joe had a great record on Patrol. He'd made an over the average number of arrests and every one of them had resulted in a conviction because he was thorough and meticulous about detail and procedure. He didn't cut corners. He interviewed every witness and wrote down everything they said (he'd aced the departmental shorthand course). Sixdeep wanted Max to learn everything he could from him and then move on to bigger and better things. Max was the chosen one, the heir.

Sometimes Joe wished he and Max hadn't become friends, that Max had simply moved on after his time was up. That way Joe would've stayed in Patrol and eventually made sergeant. Oh, it was a tough job, the hardest. You were a soldier, right there on the front line, street level with the criminals, the one most likely to take a bullet. But there were no politics inside your car. It was you and the guy you rode with. You made it work.

Joe looked around his office – one huge, strip-lit, open-plan space of pale green carpet tiles and off-white walls, soundproofed to keep the noise of forty overworked, over-caffeinated, stressed-out detectives from leaking upstairs into the meeting rooms or downstairs into Files and Records. Today it was a third full, but its unmistakable polyrhythm was present and correct, like several very familiar tunes being played at the same time, over and over at low volume – shouting, swearing, singing, conversations, phones ringing, phones being talked into, phones being slammed down, all underpinned and locked in by the stop-start metallic babble of various proficiencies of typing. The office was windowless and the lights were always on, 24/7, 365 days a year, so the only way you could tell whether it was day or night in there was by checking who was in the office against the shift roster. It was air conditioned to the point of making you shiver, and completely smoke free. If you wanted a cigarette you took the elevator two flights down and went and stood out on the balcony.

They were nominally managed by Captain Gabriel Ortiz and his two Lieutenants, Jed Powers and Lou Barlia. Ortiz was in his late fifties, celebrating his thirtieth wedding anniversary and looking forward to becoming a grandfather for the second time. He was short and stocky, with meaty hands, a barrel chest, gold-rimmed specs and jet-black hair that was badly dyed because he missed the greys at his nape. He always had his head buried in and behind a huge pile of papers. His main responsibility was triple checking all the reports and then signing them off. Powers and Barlia ran the Detectives through their oral witness statements and rehearsed them for shooting boards, IA hearings and court appearances. Every angle was covered, scenarios were improvised, scripted and learnt so the stories, when they came to be delivered for the record, were without contradiction. They even worked on the tone. It was like being forced to take a lead role in a play. Once, when there was a majority black jury that needed to be swayed, Joe had been told to mangle his syntax to make his speech more 'ethnic'. He found it offensive as hell, but they got the conviction they wanted so it was deemed to have worked.

Joe and Max sat at the back, in the furthest right-hand

corner. Their territory was marked out by a giant blow-up of Bruce Springsteen's *Born To Run* album sleeve which took up half the wall behind their desks. It had been MTF's gift to Joe on his birthday last year.

Joe loved Bruce. He'd first heard him in October 1973: his second album, *The Wild, the Innocent & the E Street Shuffle*, was playing in a bar he'd gone drinking in after breaking up with his then girlfriend, a waitress called Bernadette. They hadn't been together long, three weeks and a couple of days, so the split wasn't too hard to take, and, truth be told, he was quietly relieved to be rid of her because he didn't think she was right in the head. That night she'd told him she was becoming a Buddhist and that his being a cop was all wrong for her karma. He'd nodded, wished her all the best and gone for a beer. As he was getting through his first bottle a documentary on world religions had come on the TV – focus: Buddhism. Ten minutes were devoted to the famous case of the Saigon monk who, in 1963, had soaked himself in gasoline and set himself on fire in protest at the government's anti-Buddhist policies. The image of the burning monk had come on at the very moment Joe heard the words to the song that was playing on the jukebox – *4th of July, Asbury Park (Sandy)* – Bruce singing about how a waitress he'd been seeing wouldn't set herself on fire for him. Joe had laughed out loud. He'd been a Bruce fan from that moment on and never looked back.

Theresa came over with a FedEx package addressed to him and Max.

It was a copy of the Nora Wong file, from the NYPD.

Joe opened it. A stack of photographs slipped out and splashed across his desk with a wet plop. Glossies. The photographer was the conscientious kind: he or she had taken two of everything.

Torture was commonplace in Miami these days, but Joe had never seen anything like this. It looked like a pack of ravenous killer dogs had been let loose on the victims. They'd suffered all the way to death's door, their expressions frozen in extremes of agony. Blood everywhere. A twisted carnage of rape and then disfigurement; flesh ripped from faces clean through to muscle and bone, exposing the head's inner workings, reminding him of vandalized billboards with strips of one poster torn off and showing part of the one underneath and the one underneath that. The woman had been scalped. And they hadn't spared the children – if anything they'd got it worse.

Sickness gripped and squeezed and twisted his stomach. He gasped as the breath went out of him and the vomit reflex constricted his throat. Sweat prickled his brow. He stood up, his legs weak, hollow, trembling. He went to the bathroom. He tried, but couldn't puke. Nothing came out. He splashed water on his face and breathed deeply. His hands were trembling.

Back in the office he took Max's pint of Wild Turkey out of his bottom drawer and had a long swig.

Then he grouped the pictures together and turned them over.

He read the reports. The bitemarks were human. The assailant had worn dentures modelled on piranha jaws. There were also high concentrations of sugar in the wounds, indicating the assailant had eaten large amounts of candy directly before each of his attacks.

Then he looked through the list of recovered evidence and something caught his eye. Something familiar. He cross-referenced it with a photograph.

'Jesus!'

He picked up the phone.

18

'Is this your first child?' Max asked Marisela Cruz. They were sitting at a wooden table in one of the interview rooms in the two-floor detention building, behind the hangars. There was a small square window through which they could see the stars and stripes fluttering on a nearby flagpole and beyond it planes taking off against a clear blue sky.

'*Es este su primer bebé?*' Pete translated. He was sat beside her, speaking low and tenderly, father to young daughter, a safe haven between her and the blue-eyed, mean-faced *gringo* cop opposite.

'*Sí.*' She nodded. Marisela was very pale and very, very scared. She had long, lank black hair that went with the shadows under her dark brown eyes, bloodshot from crying and sleeplessness. She was dressed in faded blue jeans, a thin grey sweatshirt and flip flops. She had the acrid pine stench of prison soap on her. With make-up on she'd looked like a perfume model in her mugshots, dressed as she had been in a pinstriped business suit and blouse, a little too perfect according to the customs officer who'd pulled her over.

In the middle of the table was a small pyramid of twenty-one latex balloons filled with cocaine recovered from her guts. It amounted to over half a kilo, pure and uncut. They'd fed her laxatives in her dinner and water, just like those who'd paid her to transport the drugs would have done. Only low-level players used mules. The big timers were bringing it in by the boat and plane load.

'You're in a lot of trouble, Marisela.'

'*Usted está en muchos de apuro.*'

She met Max's eye and quickly looked at Pete.

'*Sé.*'

'How old are you?'

'*¿Cuántos años tiene?*'

'*Tengo veinte años.*'

'Says she's twenny.'

That's what it said on her forged Argentinian passport. Max gave her his full-beam I-don't-believe-you stare.

'*No mienta. Hará cosas peores,*' urged Pete. Don't lie. It'll make things worse.

'*Diecisiete.*'

'Seventeen.'

'How old is your mother?'

'*¿Cuántos años tiene su madre.*'

'*¿Mi madre?*'

'*Sí*, your *madre*. How old is she?'

'*Treinta dos.*'

'Thirty-two.'

'Look at me, Marisela,' Max said, taking the girl by the chin and holding her head until they locked eyes. 'You'll go to prison for thirty years. You'll be older than your mother is now when you get out. Your baby will be born in prison and taken away from you. You won't see your child again. By the time you get out it'll be an adult. And who wants to know a mother who's been to prison for smuggling drugs?'

She talked to Pete. She grabbed his hands and held them tight. She told him she'd been put up to this by her boyfriend, Miguel. He lived in Miami. He'd given her money and some nice clothes. He'd told her she'd get a lot more on delivery. She said she was sorry. Over and over again, that she didn't know what she was doing, that if she knew what was in the balloons she would've said no. Max could almost have believed her if he was hearing this for the first time instead of the millionth. Her words dissolved into pleas and sobs. He waited until she'd finished, giving her a hard impassive look that let her know none of what she said or did would make any difference.

'Marisela, there's a simple solution to your problems,' he said. She wiped her eyes and nose with her hands. 'If you do exactly as I say, you can have your baby here, and then afterwards you can go home, back to Colombia. Would you like that?'

'*Sí.*'

Then she grabbed Max's right hand with both of hers and squeezed them tight and went into a quickfire monologue, crying the whole while she spoke.

'Same shit,' Pete said when Max looked to him for a translation.

'OK. OK. I know you're sorry and I believe you.' Max quieted her and turned on his soothing voice, 'You are going to help us catch the man who brought you and others like you into our country with drugs.'

'Miguel?' she asked.

'Not, Miguel, no. The man he works for. The man who paid him to recruit you.'

'*No le conozco.*' She looked lost. I don't know him.

'You will,' Max said. 'Don't worry. It'll all make sense.'

After Max had explained to her that she would be moved to a safehouse the next morning, a guard came and escorted her out of the room and back to the cramped hot cell she was sharing with six other girls, mules like her.

Max and Pete lit cigarettes.

'You know, they'll probably kill her family in Colombia if she testifies.' Pete blew out a stream of smoke.

'We'll keep her anonymous.'

'Not for long. Money talks. And those *narcotrafficantes* have got a lot of it. Plus they got long arms. Reach anyone anywhere.'

'This is an MTF operation, Pete.'

'You guys . . .' Pete smiled and shook his head.

'There'll be a place in heaven for you for this, for sure.'

'Or hell. Right next to you and Eldon.'

'Have some faith in the system, will ya?'

'That's just it, Max. I do.'

Max drove out to the 7th Avenue gym to see Eldon, who'd gone there for a workout.

Post-McDuffie, the area was fast turning into a ghost town. The money was fleeing and with it the life and soul of the neighbourhood: half the stores had either been burnt down or were boarded up with 'CLOSED – FUCK YOU & THANKS A LOT' painted across their fronts in white. The ones that were open weren't doing much business because there was next to no one around on the wide streets. The few people he passed were either drunks and junkies weaving across the sidewalk in slow stumbles, teetering on the verge of collapse, or else locals moving at jogging speed, heads down, shoulders tensed, as if trying to get home before a coming storm. Traffic was sparse.

Max parked his brown Camaro next to the only cars on the lot – Eldon's Oldsmobile and Abe Watson's brand new Chevy Monte Carlo.

He walked into the gym, and, as usual, the feel of the place in mid-training session electrifed his senses and took him right back to his teens, when he used to push hurriedly through the same door, duffel bag in hand, heart full of ambition and a head full of dreams.

Unlike most boxing gyms, which tended to be cramped and close to decrepit, 7th Avenue was cavernous, with a high, vaulted ceiling fitted with powerful fans to keep a chill breeze wafting through the building at all times. It made no difference whatsoever to the smell that greeted everyone when they came in – a heady blast of fresh and stale sweat, dry blood, liniment, rubbing alcohol, rubber, antiseptic and new and old leather, bound together by an atmosphere of intense concentration and calibrated violence.

Max crossed the floor and headed towards the match-sized ring in the middle of the gym where Abe was putting Eldon through his paces. Eldon was in a faded yellow T-shirt, sweatpants and boxing boots. He was working on the pads, firing jabs, hooks, uppercuts and crosses into Abe's hands. He was slow, compared to everyone else in the room, but he could still move and his punches were powerful and accurate, the force of each making Abe shudder all the way down to his toes. Abe never lost his balance or composure, just calmly switched the gloves around, called out a punch or a combination. Eldon was red-faced, soaked in sweat, his hair plastered across his forehead, breathing hard. When caught out he'd mumble or curse under his breath and fire a harder shot than was necessary into the mitt, prompting Abe to congratulate him on hitting like a man.

When the buzzer went Eldon walked to his corner, where one of the assistant trainers handed him a towel and bottle of water. Abe saw Max standing ringside and came over.

'Hey, Max!' He smiled. 'Long time.'

It was true. It had been nine months since they'd last seen each other. Max and Abe had never been close the way he was with Eldon, but he'd been around Abe just as long and felt a strong bond with him. Abe wasn't the most demonstrative guy in the world. He rarely showed his emotions, positive or negative, but once, when Max had won his very first Golden Gloves championship against Alonzo Wilson, an opponent everyone had expected to defeat him, Abe had put his arm around him, congratulated him and told him how proud of him he was. That had meant the world to Max, more than the two whores Eldon had bought him as a reward.

'How's it goin', Abe?'

'Ah, you know. Same-O, same-O.'

He was a tall slender man with greying hair and a shining bald spot in the middle. He kept his moustache neatly trimmed. There was an air of sadness about him, his face dragged heavily and reluctantly behind each expression and his eyes seemed to be either on the verge of tears or recovering from them. He hadn't really been the same since his eldest son, Jacob, had died from a heroin overdose in 1977. Jacob, once a promising basketball player, had come back from Vietnam in a wheelchair after he'd taken a bullet in his lower spine. He'd been in near constant pain, which he'd used increasingly large doses of street heroin to quell.

'Any pugs I should be watching out for?' Max asked.

'Some.' Abe cast his eyes around the gym, where about twenty fighters from their teens to their early twenties were going through their paces. 'These kids comin' up now, they ain't hungry like they used to be. That do-or-die drive just ain't there no more. They want the victory and the rewards that go with it, but they just don't wanna run to the finish line. They wanna drive there instead – preferably in the back.'

Eldon came round the side of the ring, wiping his face with a towel.

'Don't be a stranger.' Abe took his cue with a nod to Max, and then slipped under the ropes and walked over to observe a fighter putting combinations together on the heavybag.

'What've you got?' Eldon asked. They never talked business on the phone, unless it was above board.

Max told him about Octavio Grossfeld, stressing the German parentage and Lehder's Nazi sympathies.

'Good. Very good. That's my boy. We'll just have to amp the Nazi angle and the kikes'll have a field day. Reagan'll *love* us for this. I can see those headlines now: "Drugs – the new Holocaust".' Eldon smiled broadly and gave Max a one-armed hug. Great drops of sweat broke out on his forehead and cascaded down his face, lingering off the edges of his chin and jaw and nose like big transparent warts before falling and splattering to the ground. His T-shirt was soaked through and he was giving off the acrid and slightly sulphurous smell of people who eat too much protein.

'Bring Grossfeld in the day after tomorrow. Early morning. Plant if you have to,' he said.

'OK.' Max made to go but caught a glimpse of something out of the corner of his eye that made him stop and turn to his right where the speedbags were. A young black boy in grey sweats, around eight or nine, was standing on a chair, hitting methodically, left fist to right. 'Who's that?' Max said.

'I was just about to introduce the two of you.' Eldon beamed, then turned the boy's way. 'Frankie!'

The boy stopped what he was doing, jumped off his chair and came running over. He was a cute-looking little kid, Max thought, with a skinny face and large eyes that were both innocent and very sharp, as if he was already living on his wits.

'This here is Frankie Lafayette,' Eldon said, putting his wet hand over the boy's shoulder and shaking it playfully. 'Found him here a month ago.'

'You hit him in the face?' Max asked the kid. Frankie didn't reply, just looked up at Eldon.

'His English ain't so good yet. Abe found him here one Monday morning, sleeping in the ring. He walked in one day and hid out until everyone'd gone.'

'Where are his parents?'

'Who knows? He says they're back home in Haiti. He came over here on a boat. Illegals. They're comin' here all the time, just like the Cubans. He's a natural. God knows what he'll do; how far he'll go.' Eldon looked down at Frankie, smiling. Frankie smiled back. 'I'm seriously thinking of adopting the little bastard.'

'*What?*'

'Becoming his legal guardian. He ain't got anyone else,' Eldon said.

'How does Lexi feel?' Lexi was Eldon's wife.

'She's thrilled. You know, we never had boys, so it'll be a change. Plus the girls are all growing up fast, so it'll be good for her.'

Max wanted to ask Eldon what would happen if it turned out that Frankie didn't want to box. What would he do then? Dump him in the sea and tell him to swim back home? But he didn't want to jinx the kid's future, or say anything bad around him, even if he wouldn't be able to understand. The kid was entitled to keep however much of his innocence a place like Haiti had left him with. And he seemed happy enough with Eldon.

'You know what, Max? Frankie here reminds me of you, the way you were. All that natural aggression, all that raw talent just waiting to get shaped and directed,' Eldon said, his big flushed face slippery and shiny with sweat, his smile dazzling in its cosmetic whiteness.

Max remembered his past life, here in the gym, all that optimism for the future, the great things he was going to do, the titles he was going to fight for and unify and he felt a little sick for everything he'd lost and missed out on, and for where those failed dreams had led him. And suddenly he feared for Frankie and what would become of him if he didn't live up to his brightest hopes. Would he too become a cop who drank too much, slept too little and really couldn't remember when exactly he'd crossed the line?

'You know how to pick 'em, Eldon,' he said wearily, a little sarcasm trickling into his tone.

'Of course I do,' Eldon replied with a laugh, 'look at you.'

19

Max got back to MTF an hour later, tired as hell. The benzedrine had worn off. His tongue felt like galvanized rubber, there was a coppery taste in his mouth, dull aches in his arms and legs, and a hangover waiting to drop on his head from an almighty height. He looked forward to going home and crashing.

He started heading towards his desk and saw Joe sitting there, thick arms folded across his big broad chest, looking right at him with an almightily pissed-off expression.

'You said an hour. It's been four.' Joe glared at him when he sat down. There were plenty of people in the office. Alex Teixeira, who sat nearest to them, was eating lunch off a yellow styrofoam plate – black beans in thick sauce, white rice, fried sweet plantain and avocado. He never touched meat but always denied being a vegetarian.

'Got a break on the Moyez case. Had to run with it.' Max sat down, opened his top drawer and pretended to rummage for something so he wouldn't have to meet Joe's eye.

'Oh yeah? You find the perp at the Well? What's his name? Jack Daniels?' Joe sneered.

'I ran a check on this guy, Octavio Grossfeld . . .' Max began, then stopped when he realized the absurdity of what was about to come out of his mouth: that he'd been looking through the Comic Book and somehow found the perp right there, between the pages; that he'd then, on a hunch, rung Pete Obregón up and, lo and behold, he happened to have a mule in custody who said she was working for the suspect; and then he'd have to try and get Joe to believe him. Here they schooled you to lie to everyone but each other. That you chose to do on your own. 'Can we get a drink?' he said instead.

'No. No more drinks for you. You've had enough.' Joe shook his head. 'What you need is Cuban coffee, food and aspirin to get yourself right. *Then* we'll talk.'

'You know, the first time we got one of these cases, ones that *seemed* to just solve themselves – the Jerome Perabo case? I wondered about that one for the longest time. I mean that lead come out of nowhere, right? As good as if it fell right out of a tree – knowhumsayin'?' Joe wiped his mouth after he'd finished eating. They were in Calle Ocho, Little Havana's main drag, in a small restaurant right opposite Maximo Gomez Park, where the old men played dominoes, smoked cigars, reminisced about the good old days and bitched about that *singao* Castro. Joe had ordered everything in Spanish. He'd gone for shrimp tortillas and fresh orange juice, while Max had opted for a deluxe Cuban sandwich – half a pressed and toasted baguette with spicy roasted pork, ham, melted Swiss cheese, dill pickles and mustard – delicious, but he'd only managed to eat one bite of it before he'd felt full. The dexedrine had killed his appetite for anything other than liquid and cigarettes. He downed his sweet, thick Cuban coffee and ordered another.

And there was another reason he couldn't eat: Joe was talking about the very first Turd Fairy mission they'd done – the first time Eldon had asked Max to find a patsy to fit up for a headline-grabbing case and make it stick. They'd never discussed the case before.

Thursday 26 May 1977, St Alban's primary school, Coral Gables. As the children were going home someone started shooting at them. Two fifth-grade girls were killed immediately and seven others, including two teachers, badly wounded. Three died from their injuries within days, among them Anthony Tabrizi, the nephew of a New York mobster Aniello Pastore, a high-ranking member of the Gambino family. The two girls, Norma Hughes and Charlotte Mazursky, were best friends who always sat together in every class. The gunman got away. Witnesses reported seeing a blue Eldorado speeding from the scene. A burnt-out blue Eldorado was later found in a stretch of wasteland near Overtown. The car was traced and found to have been bought from a second-hand dealership in Atlanta. Not that any of this ever came out because that wasn't the direction the investigation went in. Eldon had had other ideas.

'Jerome Perabo, out of town mob trigger man.' Joe shook his head with a smile. 'Man, I never told you this at the time, but I really *wondered* about that one. Kept me up nights. How could someone like him get so careless? Remember what we found when we tossed his house?'

'Yeah.' Max lit a cigarette for something to do to distract his mounting nervousness. Where was Joe going with this?

'A pistol with his prints on it. The pistol had been used in a hit on Ángel Quisqueya, who owned all that beach-front land in Miami Beach. Perabo's prints matched a shell casing from an M1 carbine we found in some bushes opposite the school.'

'What's wrong with that whole picture?' Joe asked.

Max shrugged. The waitress set down his coffee.

'Trichloroacetic acid,' Joe said. 'As in the shit they use in face peels. We found three big bottles of that in Perabo's pad. Perabo was a real *meticulous* motherfucker. He'd been doing hits since he could crawl. He used the acid to peel the skin off his hands, get rid of gun residue.'

'How do you know?'

'I asked him.'

'*When?*'

'Last year. I went to see him in prison. A little off the record chit-chat.'

'Why?'

'I needed answers,' Joe said. 'Like how it was that some-one who went to the trouble of burning off his skin would leave a shell casing with his prints on it at a murder scene. And don't even get me started on the pistol. A nickel-plated Colt. Mingus, that's a born-to-lose stickup kid's gun! All shiny and flash. Perabo would *never* have used shit like that in a hit. Too visible. And no way in hell would he have held on to it. Professional hitmen *always* lose their pieces.'

'So what d'he tell you in prison? That he was innocent?' Max laughed and took a sip of coffee.

'Of killing those school kids? Yeah.'

'And you believed him?' Max did his best to appear casually amused, but he couldn't pull it off. His stomach was tightening.

'What Perabo told me was the day he was meant to have killed them kids, he was really out smokin' some mob rat in Fort Lauderdale. Guy called Vinnie Ferrara.'

'So?' Max finished his cigarette and crushed it out on the ashtray, which had Castro's face on it. 'Doesn't prove he didn't do the Coral Gables shooting. He could've killed Ferrara too,' Max said.

Joe shook his head.

'I believed him. He didn't do it.'

'Why?'

''Cause I never believed *you*. You found an asthma inhaler in the bushes, remember? You had a cast made of the footprint too.

'I didn't say nothin' at the time. I thought maybe someone else found the bullet. But you told me to leave out the inhaler and the blue Eldorado. Said they were "irrelevant". You already had Perabo in the frame for this. It all had something to do with them South Beach hotel develop-ments. Gave the city an excuse to investigate them, and we all know what got found.'

Max put another cigarette in his mouth but fumbled trying to light it with his brass Zippo.

'It wasn't Perabo I was interested in. One way or another he gets the chair. But I want you to tell me what happened to the real perp.' Joe took the Zippo off him, lit Max's cigarette and snapped the lighter shut.

Right then Max felt like one of those cartoon characters who unknowingly sprint off the edge of a cliff, spend a few seconds treading thin air before realizing where they are, and then plummet to their own destruction surprised and suddenly very stupid.

'Why do you wanna know *now*, Joe?'

'You think I'm Stevie Wonder, Max? Think I need Braille to read what's going on, huh?' Joe leant over the table, just like he did with suspects, when he got in their faces to intimidate them. He had sweat in the creases of his brow. 'Which part of Alaska's Eldon transferring me to?'

'*Shit!* How did you know?'

'NSP – Nigger Sensory Perception. Works every time.' Joe eyeballed Max. 'You weren't planning on tellin' me, were you?'

'No, I'm sorry, I . . .'

Joe cut him off with a wave of the hand and sat back. 'I understand. It ain't your call. Eldon's never liked me. Way it is everywhere. Doesn't matter how good you are at your job, if your face don't fit no way are you going anywhere. Where's he puttin' me?'

'Public Relations.'

'I s'pose it beats Traffic.'

'I tried to talk him out of it.'

'I'm sure you did, Max. You shoulda gone and talked to the wall instead. He tell you when?'

'Once we wrap up this Moyez thing.'

'As I thought.' Joe nodded. 'Go out in a blaze of good publicity.'

'Eldon says there's gonna be big changes in the force. Give it a year or two and you'll be back on Homicide.'

'Bullshit and you know it, Max. I ain't goin' anywhere he doesn't want me to go. I predict that within two years they'll have brought all the different Miami police departments under one big roof, with Eldon sitting on top running things. That's going to be his trade-off for doing the Turd Fairy's bidding.'

Max didn't know what to say. Joe was right. Eldon had often talked about how he'd reform the police force, turn it into the Southern equivalent of the LAPD, with specific units tackling the city's biggest problems – cocaine and money laundering. And MTF was his pilot, the trailer for the big picture.

'Now. Back to Perabo,' Joe said. '*You* killed the real perp didn't you?'

Tanner Bradley. White male, forty-six years of age, five feet ten inches, 217 pounds. Taught English and gymnastics at St Alban's Primary. Taught Norma Hughes and Charlotte Mazursky. He'd been there for two years. His pupils all loved him. Felt he was their big brother, their best buddy. They had a nickname for him, 'Tan Your Hide Bradley', but it was meant affectionately. He was well-respected by his colleagues – always on time, always willing to help out in after-school activities, but, they all said after he disappeared, something of a loner. None of them really felt they knew him.

And they were right about that. If the school had bothered to cross-check his references it would have found them to be bogus. Tanner Bradley hadn't spent the last ten years as a teacher in Hawaii and LA, like it said on his resumé. He'd worked as a caretaker in an orphanage. He'd molested five girls in his care. He liked them blonde.

Norma and Charlotte were blonde.

That's what Max got back when he ran the prints they'd found on the asthma inhaler. Ray 'Tanner' Bradley. Got his teaching qualifications in San Quentin – that was when he wasn't getting assaulted and raped by the inmates. Prison was hell for everyone who didn't want to be there, but it was double that if you were a kiddie rapist. It was open season on you and everyone was taking their best shot. The guards wouldn't help – as far as they were concerned, you had it coming.

The footprint was from a size 12 US Army issue paratrooper boot. You could see the markings quite clearly on the sole. He'd also found a small scrap of olive-coloured fibre in the bushes, which could have come off fatigues. He'd killed the girls because they'd presumably threatened to tell their parents he was molesting them.

Max had never had time to discuss any of this with Joe because Eldon had called him up to the roof and told him they were going to pin the killings on Perabo and make them stick. When Max tried to complain, Eldon told him the Turd Fairy had visited. He had no choice but to follow orders.

The Perabo bust went like a dream. They gave him the option of voluntarily putting his prints on the carbine shell and pistol they planted in his apartment, therefore voluntarily fucking himself. When he refused, two MTF officers broke his right wrist and got their evidence anyway. Max and Joe took the credit and got the glory, but all they'd had to do was listen to Perabo calling them criminals for twelve hours straight.

After Perabo's arraignment, Max broke into Bradley's apartment in Opa Locka. He found pictures of Bradley in full Second World War US Marine uniform. In all of them he was holding the carbine. Max didn't find the gun or the uniform, but he did discover a pile of Disney lunchboxes filled with Polaroids of naked blonde girls. Among them were pictures of Norma and Charlotte. And he found the boots. He scraped some dirt off the sole and had it analysed; it matched the dirt from the bushes.

He tracked down the car dealer who'd sold the blue Eldorado spotted leaving the scene. He identified Bradley as the buyer from a mugshot.

Max told Eldon. Eldon told him to do what he felt had to be done, only he couldn't bring Bradley in because of Perabo. Max was confused. So Eldon told him about all the people he'd taken down 'off the books' because it was the right thing to do and the world was better off without them, but there hadn't been enough physical or corroborative evidence to get a conviction. Then he told Max that if he chose that course he was on his own as far as MTF was concerned. This was an extra-curricular kill and all on him.

Max bought a second-hand Browning BDA 380 and filed off the serial number. Wearing thick surgical gloves, he loaded the magazine with thirteen hollow-point shells and slipped one in the chamber.

Two nights later he broke into Bradley's home, gagged and blindfolded him and put him in the trunk of his car and drove him out to a clearing near Lake Surprise. It was part fresh, part saltwater and home to crocs and gators alike.

Bradley had got on his knees, looked Max in the eye and started crying. He'd said he was sorry, over and over again. He said he wasn't a bad guy, he just needed help. He said he was no different to faggots and people who fucked animals. He said he had a medical condition.

And when it came down to it, Max found he couldn't do it. Not like that, not in cold blood. He lowered his gun. It could all end peacefully. He'd tell Bradley to get out of Florida immediately and stay gone.

But before he could speak, Bradley began to cough and splutter. Then suddenly he'd stood up. Max told him to get the fuck back down on his knees. Bradley wasn't listening.

Bradley was coming at him fast. Max raised his gun. Bradley reached for his waistband. Instinct overruled sense. Max shot him twice in the head and Bradley fell backwards.

When he checked Bradley's pants he found what he'd been reaching for – his asthma inhaler. He'd been having an attack.

He wiped the Browning down and tossed it off the Rickenbacker Causeway into the ocean. A while later he pulled over to puke.

Then he'd gone to a club on Washington Avenue for a drink. A fat woman in a silver sequinned blouse and gold satin pants called Harriett asked him if she could join him. He realized she was his alibi if there was any comeback; he was thinking like a murderer and wanted to be sick again. He said sure, sit yourself down, my name's Max Mingus, and I'm a cop. Evenin' officer, she'd giggled. They'd danced a while and then he'd taken her home and tried to get her so drunk she'd pass out. But she could handle her liquor, so he'd had to fuck her. He'd kept his eyes closed through most of it and thought of Pam Grier. He'd asked her what his name was. She'd called him Daddy or Danny or something in-between.

The next morning she couldn't remember his name at all, no matter how many times he told her. She didn't believe he was a cop either. In fact, she really didn't want to know him. She insisted she'd never done anything of the sort before. She was happily married, she said, with a son called Max.

No one missed Tanner Bradley, at least not after they found the pictures in his house and discovered his past. The headteacher at St Alban's resigned, as did the head of personnel who should have checked his references.

Max never forgot him. Not his face, not the way he'd looked, not the way his body had shaken when he cried, not the way he'd pissed his pants as he begged for his life, for forgiveness, for understanding, for a *cure* for the way he was. The memory had diminished a little over the years, but the colours were still fresh. It didn't matter that what he'd done might have been right to a lot of people; to him it had felt wrong. He'd crossed a line then for sure. Again. Another one.

Up on the roof, the morning after he'd done it, Eldon had given him a simple piece of advice: 'Never kill someone who's looking you in the eye, 'cause you're the last thing they see and the first thing they take away with 'em. Always turn 'em around. Shoot 'em in the back. You'll sleep sweet that way.'

Which is exactly what he did when he shot the next two child killers he'd discovered but hadn't been able to move on officially because the Turd Fairy had spotted another opportunity to make capital out of atrocity.

'So, how did you know?' Max asked, when he'd finished talking.

'I'm a detective. It's what I do,' said Joe. 'But you gotta be careful now, 'cause there's a real clear pattern forming. Child killers and rapists ending up dead in the middle of nowhere, close-formation double-tap entry wounds to the head, nine millimetre hollow-point shells fired at point-blank range from an automatic – speed shootin' – your speciality. Guns different both times, but the victims and MO are identical. Points to a cop on a spree.'

'There's nothin' tyin' me into any of this.'

'I know,' Joe said. 'But sooner or later, someone somewhere will be asking questions.'

'So what are you sayin?' Max lit another Marlboro. He'd smoked so many today they were burning his throat.

'Stop before you get caught. Stop *now*.' Joe looked Max in the eye and held his gaze. 'Think about it. Is killing those scumbags worth destroying your life for? They catch you they'll give you life. And you know what happens to ex-cops in prison, Max. Eldon's filled your head up with his good ole boy, Wild West vigilante bullshit. I've heard all his campfire stories, how he used to bring people in tied to the back of his Crown Victoria. Times are way different now, man. You can't be takin' people out to the Glades and cappin' 'em. Doesn't matter what they've done. We're the *police*, Max. We *uphold* the law. We don't break it.'

Max knew Joe was right, that what he'd done was indefensible, but then what about the people he'd killed? Thanks to Eldon and the Turd Fairy, he'd had to let proven child abusers go free, unpunished, and – inevitably – emboldened by their success at evading the law, primed to strike again. And they *always* struck again. And again, until they got caught or killed. Knowingly letting one of them off the hook to walk the streets wasn't something he was sure he could live with. Killing them was a different matter. He was protecting the public. Doing his job.

'Now I want you to see this.' Joe placed the NYPD file he'd brought with him on the table.

Max looked. He was glad he hadn't eaten much because his stomach contracted hard, like he'd taken a right hook to the gut. Then he couldn't look any more, so he read. He came to the list of recovered evidence. He saw something familiar.

Joe was holding it up – the red and white striped candy wrapper they'd found at the Lacour family home – sealed in a glassine evidence bag.

'You were right: Preval Lacour *did* have help,' Joe said. 'Drugs plus property equals money laundering equals a highly organized gang. And don't start running Eldon's case past me neither. We both know it's bullshit.'

'So what d'you wanna do?'

'This is gonna be my last case as a real cop. After that I'm window dressing. I don't want it to be some bullshit frame-up. I want to be able to look at myself in the mirror and know I did my best at all times, that I did what I swore to do.'

'You wanna take these guys down?'

'No.' Joe shook his head. 'I want to bring them in, through the front door, cuffs on their wrists. I want to see them get booked, tried and executed. I want to see them punished, not by us, but by the *law*. Will you help me?'

'If we do this –'

'There's no 'if' about it. You're either with me on this or I'll take my chances alone.'

'What about Eldon? The Moyez case?'

'We'll work his phoney shit too,' Joe said, '*and* we'll go after the real perps.'

'Say we bring 'em in, it'll throw out the Moyez case.'

'We'll cross that bridge when we come to it. For now, all I need to know is whether you're with me.'

'I'm with you,' Max said without hesitation, but inside he was worried as hell. He was backing Joe over Eldon. In other words, he was going up against Eldon. And no one did that – *especially* not one of his own. They'd have to work the case in secret, make sure no one found out. And they'd have to work it quick too, crack it and bring it in before Moyez was wrapped up. It was impossible. Maybe that's what he was counting on.

'Are you sure about this?' Joe looked him in the eye, reading him. 'I'll understand if you don't want to do it.'

'I am sure,' Max said, holding out his hand. 'We're partners, remember?'

'Then it's done.' Joe smiled and they shook hands across the table.

God help us, Max thought, for we know not what the fuck we're getting into.

20

Eva Desamours laced together her long, bony fingers and bent them back until she heard them crack twice and then pop in all three joints. She smiled slightly as she felt the warm effervescent current of released tension bubbling and fizzing back and forth under her skin, enervating her nerves and priming her senses.

Opposite her at the round table she sensed Solomon Boukman wince in the darkness. She knew he hated her doing it, but he should have learnt long ago to live with it; it was the last of the rituals she performed before she read anyone's cards – and she'd been reading his for over twenty years, since he was her apprentice in Haiti.

First she'd shower, soap herself clean and then she'd bathe. She'd scatter a mixture of herbs, flowers and shaved roots at the bottom of the bath tub – mint leaves to clear all paths, belladonna flowers to free the self from the body, mandrake root for the courage to step through any door, vervain for protection against corruption, High John the Conqueror root for the strength of thirty, goldenseal to open the eyes and a mixture of lavender oil and holy water to bind all these powers together. She'd run the bath hot to better free the mixture's essence. Then she'd step into the tub, lie back, close her eyes and let the powers seep into her as she watched the beautiful fish in the aquarium.

After an hour she'd towel herself dry and, naked, walk upstairs and go into the room where she kept her cards.

The room was small and sparse, with dull brown unpainted plastered walls and smooth bare unvarnished floorboards. A wide circle of stolen church altar candles studded with fragments of vulture bones, standing on black-painted iron saucers, and the small crude wooden cupboard where she stored her two decks of cards in specially designed black velvet envelopes were the only furniture. There was no light in the room whatsoever. She'd had the window bricked up when she'd bought the place.

Although she couldn't see anything once she'd entered the room, she'd placed the cupboard sixteen paces to the left of the door. She'd retrieve her tarot cards, make a half turn on her heels and then walk thirteen steps until she was at the edge of the candle circle. She'd step inside and grope around the floor until she found the matches. She'd light the candles anti-clockwise and squat down on her haunches, watching while the room assumed the dull purplish tone of a healing bruise as the oily orange glow coming from the floor combined with the wall's hidden pigmentation.

Then she took the cards out of their envelope, cut them, shuffled them thoroughly, cut them again, and then dealt them anti-clockwise in a circle, face down.

She squatted in the middle of the circle, took a deep breath and began to speak, in reverse, the names of the clients she would read for that day.

Sometimes it took minutes, sometimes an hour. There are no clocks in the afterlife, only time and the dead aren't bound by appointments.

The cards changed. They came alive. The designs transformed from crude etchings to beautiful visions, as their dull colours grew brighter and fuller and far more vivid than they were in the cold light of day or to the untrained, uninitiated eye. The crimson borders of the de Villeneuve cards thickened and liquefied, as the golden suns they enclosed glowed with a deep rich light, becoming skull-faced ingots mounted on a hellish necklace.

It was then they came, those who watched over her

clients: their guides, their counselling voices, the sources of all their instincts and feelings, those who forewarned them in dreams and premonitions, those who pointed to uncanny parallels in events commonly known as fate and sometimes dismissed as coincidence.

To Eva – as to all clairvoyants and mediums – the spirits were human in appearance, assuming a shape she could recognize and relate to. They looked not as they had in death, but as her clients would remember them best, right down to the clothes they wore and the things they brought with them to jog their charges' memories. They came singly mostly, but pairs were fairly common, and once in a while she had to cater for groups of up to seven if a person was particularly loved. The spirits had two things in common – they all looked happy, verging on euphoric, and they told her their names and who they'd come to talk to. They stood in front of her, outside the circle of candles and waited to be summoned in.

The bad spirits came too. They always did, right behind the good, shadowing them, just to mess with the natural order of things, to wreak havoc on an innocent life, destroy it if they could. They always tried to fool her into letting them in too, but she'd long ago learnt to spot the things they couldn't quite fake – the glint in their eyes, the vulpine hint in their smiles, sometimes the things they carried or didn't. She would firmly but politely refuse them entry and tell them to go back to where they belonged.

Yet occasionally the bad spirits got in. It was inevitable. They had genuine business with her clients, debts that needed collecting, earthly transgressions avenging. These ones she *had* to let in. That was the deal. Some people just *had* to be stopped before they went on destroying the natural order of things. Balance had to be restored, wrongs done to reach right.

And some bad spirits tricked her. That was inevitable

too. They'd been great liars in life, who'd just gone on getting better and better now that time was no obstacle and the prospects were limitless. They were good at acting good.

Solomon Boukman always had his guardian come visit, the one he took his name from, the great one, who'd started it all.

Boukman was the slave turned voodoo priest turned rebel leader who in 1791 started the slave uprising that set Haiti free. The French colonial ladies knew about his extraordinary powers of foresight and used to ask him to read their fortunes in their palms. He didn't need to look. He knew they would die savage and bloody deaths. At night, in the slave quarters, he'd prophesy the overthrow of the French colonial masters and the imprisonment of the 'dwarf who led them'. They said he saw his own death, his head paraded around on a spike for all to see. They said this was what led him to start the uprising that would become a revolution. They said this was what drove him to savagery. He spared no white man, woman or child. He killed them all. He'd rape wives in front of their husbands and then kill their children before he killed them. He was without mercy or compassion.

When he came to talk to Solomon, he came naked, but for a shackle around his ankle, a bloody machete in his hand and white face paint in the shape of a skull. Even though he could do nothing to Eva, she was always a little scared of him.

Nearly all fortunes tellers are fakes and most of the real ones lie. If something bad's coming your way, they'll be the first to know and you the last. They'll snow you under with platitudes and upbeat clichés, tell you everything's going to be all right – *anything* but the truth.

Eva Desamours was an exception to the rule. She prided

herself on *always* telling the truth, no matter how much it hurt.

She had two kinds of clients – winners and losers, or, the way she saw it, those with futures and those without. She couldn't do anything for the latter, except take their money and look at them pityingly. Their lives weren't just in the toilet but spiralling away down the pipes – the chronically ill, the unemployable, the heartbroken, the all-round desperate. What she told them was rarely pretty. She knew she could have made things easier by sugaring the pill, but what was the use in that? You always got to the poison. She considered people natural optimists, and therefore congenitally dumb: they only ever believed what they wanted to believe, even if the contrary was staring them in the face and shaking them by the hand.

The people with futures she treated differently. After all, there was more to play with and more she could use. They were as vulnerable as their negative counterparts, sharing almost identical needs, desires and aspirations, yet they had more going for them. They had important careers, money, influence and contacts. For them the answer was never, 'No, it isn't going to happen', but, 'Yes, anything's possible – depending on how much you really want it.'

Their replies were invariably the same: 'More than anything.' As was hers: 'I'll see what I can do.'

Eva Desamours was more than just a fortune teller; she was a fixer. If she saw that what they desired wasn't coming for them, she could arrange it so it did. She couldn't change the future – that was completely beyond her powers – but she could delay it for a short spell, distract it so it missed its stop. And while it was finding its way back, she moved things around, so destinies became misplaced: the lonely career woman suddenly started dating the work colleague she'd secretly loved for a year; the married father of three got it on with a waitress he'd lusted after; a business man got a career-making deal; an ambitious employee an unexpected promotion; a couple drowning in debt got a windfall. What she never told them was that in order to do good for them, she dealt with powerful bad spirits – conmen, thieves, fraudsters, murderers; the clever, gifted ones who'd evaded capture in mortal life – and that their moment of bliss came with a hefty price tag. The work colleague turned out to be a hitter, the waitress a herpes carrier, that glorious business deal would lead to its maker's downfall, the glamorous job would be utter hell, and the windfall would come from an insurance payout when one of the couple died in a horrific accident and the other was crippled for life. It was wrong for the uninitiated to mess with the future: the punishment for undeserved happiness was roughly three times its equal in misery. Yet payback didn't happen immediately, and it was in that honeymoon period that Eva capitalized on the goodwill to sort out some business for the SNBC. As she never charged for fixing futures, she accepted favours from her business contacts in kind – setting up offshore accounts, shell companies, helping to broker real-estate deals and buying up businesses to launder the organization's huge amounts of drug money.

Eva had been born with the gift of precognition. She came from a long line of seers and sorcerers, stretching back to Haiti's colonial days. Her great-grandmother Charlotte had been one of the country's most famous *mambos*. She'd been President Jean-Pierre Boyer's most trusted and – some said – most influential adviser, using spells and sacrifices to keep him in power for twenty-one years.

Eva could read tarot cards at the age of three, and at four she saw her first spirit. By the time she reached her tenth birthday she was telling wealthy Haitian society ladies their fortunes, reeling off details of adulteries, abortions, names and ages of bastard offspring, complex financial and property swindles, and births and deaths with pinpoint accuracy. When she was twelve she was talking to the dead. At fifteen she was enlisting their help in fixing the futures of the living.

In 1963 she was chased out of Haiti by Papa Doc, her former friend and sometime client, after she'd foreseen the end of the Duvalier dynasty.

She took the well-trodden Haitian exiles' path to Miami with her nine-year-old son Carmine and her helper Solomon Boukman then aged eleven. She'd taken Solomon as payment from the family of a barren woman she'd helped get pregnant, but who'd died while giving birth to him.

For the first year, they lived in a house in the Liberty Square Housing Project, a collection of shacks known to the locals as 'Pork 'n' Beans', because of their pinkish-orange colour. There were a handful of other Haitian families there, but it was mostly home to poor black Americans. The two groups didn't get along. The Americans resented the Haitians for moving in on the little turf they had: Liberty Square had, after all, been set up for them alone. The Haitians regularly got robbed, beaten up and sometimes killed. The cops did nothing. To them it was just niggers offing niggers, so who cared as long as it didn't cross racial lines.

A month after they'd arrived, Carmine got attacked by a gang of kids on his way back from the local 7-Eleven. They robbed him of his ten dollars grocery money and kicked him unconscious. Solomon went out, found the gang and attacked them with a razor-sharp machete. He left each of them missing a hand, finger, or an arm, an eye and – in the case of the leader – a nose. He took back the money they'd stolen.

Soon after, Liberty City's Haitian kids formed their own gang, with Solomon as their leader. It was the start of the SNBC. They fought all the local gangs with fists, feet, bats, switchblades, machetes and zipguns. Solomon was always in the thick of it, his combat skills the stuff of street legend. They robbed people, houses and stores. They fenced the goods. They stole cars to order. They ran protection rackets, first for Haitians, then for anybody who'd pay. They worked too for Vernell Deacon – aka the Charmer – Liberty City's most successful pimp. He paid them to watch his whores and guard his brothels. But he didn't think to pay them to watch his back, and he wound up getting shot in a club toilet. Solomon added pimping and prostitution to his gang's portfolio. The more Haitians came to Miami, the bigger the organization became. Solomon then divided it into subsections, giving the most trusted members control of key areas, which freed him up to get into the narcotics business.

Meanwhile Eva Desamours told fortunes to tourists in South Beach. She rented a fold-up table, two chairs and a parasol and joined a line of half a dozen Jewish and Cuban women who read cards, tea leaves, palms and gazed into crystal balls for anyone who gave them five bucks. The first week she read for twelve people, the second she doubled her clientele, and by the fourth, she had to turn people away. She had Carmine with her at all times, holding the money, because he wasn't much use for anything else – especially not Solomon's gang. In the beginning she seriously contemplated sending him back to Haiti, because he was seemingly useless, but then she began to note what a hit he was with women, how they cooed over his caramel skin and doe-like green eyes – just like those bitches had over his scumbag father. And she also noticed how he revelled in their attention and flattery, how sweetly he smiled at them when they told him how pretty he was, which only made them coo and cluck even more. Her cowardly little boy had a way with girls. He sought out their company. He knew how to put them at ease and make them laugh and gain their trust. She understood then his role in her new life.

Eva cut the deck of tarot cards and slid them across the table to Solomon.

He shuffled them twice, riffle and strip. She watched his short thick fingers handle the cards with a dexterity belying their shape. His nails were opaque, twisted and yellow, completely overlapping the fingertips and crowning hands rendered grotesquely large and heavy by his thin arms.

When he'd finished, he cut the deck and gave it back to her.

She laid the cards out face up in a descending pyramid, twenty-eight in all, beginning with a single card at the top, then two below, three after that, then four, and so on until she completed the spread with a final row of seven. The last cards on the right-hand side of the pyramid told the future, the ones before them represented significant past events and the undercurrents influencing it.

To an outsider the cards would have appeared flawed, because none of the court cards had faces, their heads represented by outlines around a white inside. Yet they had been specially designed that way, intended only for the most powerful fortune tellers. Once she'd started her reading, Eva would meditate on the court cards, staring deep into the blank space: the features of whoever they were meant to represent would begin to form in her mind's eye, sometimes as clear as a photograph, at other times only faint traces of a face would come through.

'What d'you see?' Solomon asked.

It wasn't good, not at all, but she wasn't going to say anything just yet.

At the top of the pyramid was the King of Swords, which represented Solomon – a powerful, bellicose man who was in a position of high authority in an organization. The second and sixth cards were the Knight of Swords and the Knight of Wands. In-between were three sixes – Wands, signifying plans and ideas; Pentacles, representing money, business and security; and Swords indicating conflict, trouble and strife. But it was the final card in the spread that was the most damaging – the Tower, the great destroyer; harbinger of ruin.

She couldn't understand it. The future had been so bright the last time. What had gone wrong?

'Two men are working against you,' she said, pointing to the Knights.

'Who?'

She stared at the blank space that was the Knight of Swords' face. She saw bloodshot blue eyes staring back at her and almost immediately smelled gunsmoke. She picked up the card, held it to her nose and breathed in deeply. A horrid taste formed at the back of her mouth. She broke it down: alcohol, earth, blood, chemicals, cigarettes.

'This man has killed in cold blood. More than once.' She put her finger on the Knight of Swords. 'He's not an assassin. He's killed for other reasons. Principles. And a sense of failure. But he's weak: he smokes, drinks and has taken drugs.'

Of the other man, she could only see his dark brown eyes, yet she sensed his massive, intimidating build. When she smelled and then tasted his essence it was at first a honeyed sweetness, indicating an even, good-natured temperament and a basic honesty – he was the sort of man who'd always help a friend and never cheat on his wife. Then, almost as soon as she was ready to conclude the man posed no real threat to them, she tasted a hint of vinegary sourness buried in the nectar. As she isolated it and drew it out, the taste became so unbearable she had to spit it out.

'The other man,' she wiped her mouth with a handkerchief and moved her finger to the Knight of Wands, 'is ambitious, but he hides it well. He's the initiator.'

'*Who* are they?' Solomon asked impatiently.

Before she could answer, Eva saw Carmine down on

the ground clutching his gut like he'd been punched. She remembered the Knight of Swords' taste now.

'They're police,' she said and looked at the spread again. 'They're acting alone.'

'Are they from here?'

'Yes.'

'They won't be a problem,' Solomon said.

And then the spirit of Boukman appeared at Solomon's right side. He was holding up a glittering tapestry of the original Haitian flag – blue and red, with the crest in the middle – and pointing to a single thread hanging off the edge. He had his eyes closed as he pointed. Then he opened them, looked at the thread as if seeing it for the first time and pulled it. The tapestry fell apart on the table in an ungainly heap of material and very quickly turned to a spread of dust which Boukman blew away.

She understood what it meant: there was something the cops hadn't seen yet, the tiniest detail, but if they found it, it would spell the end.

She asked the spirit what the detail was, but he didn't answer. It either meant he didn't know or she wasn't meant to know. Which it was, she wasn't allowed to ask.

And for the first time ever she felt afraid.

'We need to find out who these men are,' she said to Solomon, 'and then they must be killed.'

21

1 p.m., Coconut Grove. Miami's village they called it. Lots of palm trees keeping everything shaded and cool, cute boutiques and restaurants everywhere. The people all relaxed and unsuspecting and rich, taking their time and talking real low. You didn't come around here unless you had money or wanted to see what it was like to have money.

Now *this* was living, *this* was where it was at, the place he wanted to be – Can't-Afford-Me-Anyway-So-Don't-Even-Bother-Asking Central, thought Carmine, as he squeezed the lemon slice into his Perrier water and looked around him at the rich ladies lunching outdoors at Dubois' Fresh & Natural, a healthfood place on Grand Avenue. It had round tables, parasols made from recycled wood; they served you on plates made by indigenous South American Indians, and you spent a lot of money on their specialties – nutroast, seed loaf, soya sausage, dried-berry pudding and tofu fuckin' *everything*. Every time he ate there he spent a week shitting his guts out.

Still, there was nothing he liked better than sitting here in the lap of luxury, dressed to the nines and studying all those haughty trophy bitches through his dark-blue-lensed Ray-Ban Aviators with the gold Bausch & Lomb frames. They all sat around in their expensive clothes and discreet jewellery, branded paper shopping bags at their sides and those ugly manicured poodles standing to attention at their feet. Them damn dogs all looked like they got their fur sculpted by the same hairdresser who did their mistresses' hair. The women all looked the same, give or take – starved down to bone, nervous tics, with so much plastic surgery added in they were like shopfront mannequins who'd been brought to life by Frankenstein when he'd run out of cadavers.

This was his playground. Here he liked to amuse himself and play God in his head, load the dice and turn the tables. He'd take away the rich husbands, the bank accounts, the property portfolios, address books and wardrobes, disconnect the phone and send the staff packing. Then he'd imagine them coming to him with their sob stories, and him acting all boo-hoo-hoo sensitive *mucho simpatico*, before telling them that there was a way out of their dilemmas, that they had to use what they'd got – or what the plastic surgeons had left them with. Oldest trade known to man, shit that's been going on since man was a monkey and lived in a tree. Hell, even Mary Magdalene started out that way. They wouldn't like it at first. They'd slap his face and call him scum, but sooner or later they'd realize it was his way or no way. How low could they go? All the way down that social ladder. After Sam had turned them out good, he'd pimp out these stuck-up cunts to cab drivers, shoeshiners, waiters, bellhops, store managers, gardeners, pool men, cooks – anyone they'd been rude to or turned their noses up at. They'd all get a piece. Once in a while he'd bring them back here and rub their old lives in their faces; only they wouldn't want to eat salads and fruits, they'd be begging him to go to Wendy's or BK, get themselves some *real* food. He chuckled quietly to himself: *man*, he was a *nasty* motherfucker when he wanted to be, scared himself sometimes. But life and his evil-ass mother had made him that way, so tough shit and too bad and boo-fuckin'-hoo-hoo-hoo.

Today he was here on busy-ness. Waitress called Dominique. Potential Heart. Only this one wasn't going to his mother. Oh no, he was keeping this piece for his own Deck. White, long blonde hair (real), big round baby blues that had this way of going wide like she was hearing or seeing something new and wonderful for the first time, slender body, tall, long-legged, narrow waist, good hips and a great pair of tits; real healthy glow to her skin, classic all-American apple-pie blonde straight out of the Christie Brinkley/Chris Evert gene pool. Yessir. Looking just like her workplace, Fresh & Natural.

He'd been working her since before Christmas, taking it real slow, reluctant at first, truth be told, because he wasn't too sure about recruiting on his own turf, but in the end he'd recognized she had way too much potential to pass up. In fact, she was the one who had initiated contact, not the other way round. He'd noticed her OK. Damn near couldn't miss this fine piece of cornfed ass. He'd just come back from posing as a photographer around Biscayne Bay, and she'd asked him if he was 'a professional'. He'd laughed at the unintentional irony of what she'd said and she'd thought he was laughing at her. She'd blushed and looked hurt, which was a perfect entry point for him. He'd made up some shit about how he'd just got called an amateur that morning, blah blah blah, and they'd hit it off. She'd told him she came from Vegas. She'd tried making it as a model in LA, but hadn't got anywhere, and now here she was. He did the usual – got to know her, made sure she had no one around – husband, long-term boyfriend, family. When she said it was just her and her ambition he mentioned an assign-ment he had coming up in the next few weeks. He shot a few Polaroids of her and gave her his card. Sam had almost come when he'd seen the photographs, so he'd decided to move in today, final phase – date her a couple of times, gain her trust, then introduce her to Sam, the turn-out man.

'Hey, Louis!' Dominique called out to him and smiled in that high-voltage white flash-bulb way she had. *Louis De Ville, photographer.* That's what it said on the card he'd given her.

'Whassappenin', princess?' Carmine smiled at her and

pushed his glasses up. He made his fingers into a rectangle and framed her. She posed, pouting, holding up her hair. The mannequins looked their way. Carmine got up and kissed her on the cheek. Had to tiptoe up a little. Bitch was taller than him by an inch or two *and* she was wearing flat shoes; some fat old dwarf would *love* her.

She'd just started her shift. She'd work late today, right through to midnight closing. After sundown the place was popular with young couples who sipped fruit-juice cocktails while looking into each other's eyes. She said she hated that time of day the most because seeing those happy couples only reminded her of her loneliness. It never ceased to amaze him the kinds of intimate shit bitches told you when they trusted you – kinds of shit he could turn to gold.

'I've got some real great news,' he said to her, slipping into pro photospeak. 'That job I told you about? It's a new Calvin Klein shoot.'

'Calvin *Klein*!'

'Thassright.'

'With Brooke Shields?'

'No.' He laughed. 'I ain't all *that*. This is like a local campaign, aimed at Florida. And they want some local models, so I thought of you.'

'Oh, mi God! Oh, mi God!' She jumped up and squealed loud enough to turn every starved head in the place their way. She hugged him tight, pressing herself right against him.

'Now hold on, hold on.' He disentangled himself. 'Lots we got to talk about first. Like what the process is gonna involve, and how you gotta be gettin' yourself a good agent.'

'Sure, OK.'

'How's 'bout I pick you up after you get done, an' we can go get ourselves a bite to eat, an' I'll talk you through what is what?'

'I get out of here about 12.30,' she said.

'Kahmyne?'

Right behind him, he heard it, but it didn't fully register.

'I'll be here,' he said, then he heard it again, clearer and closer.

'Kahmyne?'

Dominique was now looking over his shoulder, knots of puzzlement in her happy expression.

'Kahmyne Dezzamoo!'

Oh *shit*! It was Risquée!

'Kahmyne Dezzamoo – nigga, turn yo' ass arown when I address yo' redbone ass!'

There was a hand on his shoulder and a real pissed-off voice bellowing in his ear.

He turned around. Risquée, one of his own Cards. What the fuck was she doin' here? Bitch looked like all kinds of shit. She was squeezed into a short 'n' sheer pink pvc dress, so tight it made her flabby thighs spill out over the hem. She stood unsteadily in leopard-skin heels, and had a handbag to match. Big gold Africa earrings and a short black wig that looked like she'd scraped a dead crow off her porch and glued it to her scalp. She was sweaty faced and wild-eyed, anger over all what was left of her looks.

'Sorry . . .' he started. 'Do I . . .'

'Do you *what*, nigga?' she snapped, hands on hips, getting up real close to him. He could smell reefer and malt liquor on her breath. 'Do you know me? Thass what you was gonna say to me, right? – *Bitch*!'

He hadn't seen her in five months, not since she'd got herself busted and slung in jail. He was supposed to bail her out like pimps usually did, but she'd been so much trouble he'd decided to cut her loose and let her rot. Drinking too much. Doing way too much blow 'n' reefer. Robbing johns. Stealing from him. She'd piled on the pounds too now, gone for that skidrow skeezer look. Time was when she was a sexy little piece. Dangerous and sexy. She'd even got him a little hard come to think of it – and that hadn't happened to him with a ho since a good while.

Now her bloodshot eyes were dancing all over him, taking him in and spitting back contempt. Her voice was hoarse, like she'd been screaming all night and basing all day. He remembered how Sam had had to stuff her panties in her mouth when he'd turned her out, on account of her yelling so loud while he was doing her. Johns had loved that about her though, made them feel like ten Tarzans, even though she was faking it.

'Listen . . .' he began, but his mouth was all dry and the words wouldn't come. He had a cold, churning feeling in his gut. He wanted out of this picture quick. Every eye in the place was on them now. The waiters and waitresses had stopped what they were doing to look at the commotion.

'Who dis white bitch, Kahmyne? Huh? You playin' her like you played me? What you tell her it is you *do*? Huh?' She pushed past him and changed her tone to something as close to polite and civil as she could get, 'Wassyo'name, suga?'

'Hey, leave her out of this,' Carmine managed to say.

'I *AIN'T* TALKIN' TO YOU, YOU PUNK-MADE *BITCH*!' she yelled in his face, spraying him with spit. She turned back to Dominique. Carmine tried to catch her eye, but she was focused on Risquée. Dominique looked scared and confused. Carmine doubted she'd seen anything like Risquée outside of television.

'What you say yo' name was, baby?' Risquée was back to sweetness and light, kind of voice she used on johns to talk their dicks up and their wallets open.

'Dominique.'

'Thass a *nice* name, baby. Yo' momma give you that?'

'Yes.'

'What this –' she curled her lip up in disgust – 'this "man" tell you his name was?'

Dominique looked at Carmine. Carmine shook his head at her, and twirled his index finger around his temple to tell her Risquée was crazy, but Dominique looked away.

'Louis. Louis De Ville.'

'*Looooweeeee*!' Risquée scream-laughed like a hyena on fire. 'An' what did *Looooweeee* tell you he *does*?'

'He says he's a photographer,' Dominique said, looking at Carmine with sudden anger now, seeing him as he really was for the first time. He wanted to run off, get away, but he couldn't fuckin' move. His feet felt like they were part of the ground which had just given way beneath him.

'He tole *me* he was a talent spotter fo' a record company. That was some long time ago. Said he was gonna make me Tina Turner. He give you a card, right?'

Dominique nodded.

'Well, lemme tell ya, suga – this motherfucker here – he's a *pimp*. Ya hear me? He's a motherfuckin' PIMP. He was fixin' to *ruin* yo' sweet lil' self. An' this is juss about the luckiest fuckin' day in yo' life, baby.'

'That's – that's – that's not true!' Carmine found his voice. 'Dom, listen to me – this woman –'

'Shut yo' fuckin' mouth, *bitch*!' Risquée span on her heel and slapped him so damn hard across his face it shook the fillings in his back teeth and made him cry out in pain.

'Don't *ever* come near me again, you lowlife,' Dominique said to him, ice cold. 'If you do, I'll call the cops. You *disgust* me.'

'What?' Carmine started. 'You *believe* her!'

But Dominique had turned her back on him and was walking quickly away, probably to get the manager.

Carmine felt like he wanted to faint. Risquée's palm print was burning his cheek.

She grabbed him by the arm and started dragging him out of the café, away from the mannequins, away from the place he had, until very recently, most loved to be. She dragged him down the street like he was a big rag doll, her heels clickety-clacking loudly on the sidewalk, her plastic dress squeaking as she moved, pushing her way past people. He tried to pull away from her, but her grip was fast, her hand welded to his arm.

They got to where he'd parked his car. She slammed him up against the wall.

'You *owe* me, nigga!' she screamed at him.

'Listen, I – I'm sorry I didn't bail you out of the joint. I was havin' problems makin' my paper, you know?' he said, realizing he was whining. She back-handed him. He felt her bones connect with his cheekbone and yelped.

'Fuck dat! Fuck everythin'! Gimme my money, *bitch*! Where it at?'

She didn't wait for an answer. She grabbed his nuts and squeezed them with her left hand; her free hand quickly patted his trouser pockets until she found his $4,000 roll, various denominations held together by a solid-gold clip. He was proud of that clip, the dull green really brought out the gold.

She quickly counted it and then dropped the roll in her handbag.

'What you doin'?' he whinged. 'Thass all the bread I got!'

'No, nigga. Thass all the bread you *had*. Iss *my* bread now!'

'Damn, bitch! After everything I done for you!'

'What you *did*, Kahmyne Dezzamoo, was leave me in the motherfuckin' joint. Ain't a damn pimp in the *world* leaves his girls in no joint. Thass part o' the deal. Only you done violated that deal. You got no pimp *ethics*. You done broke the golden rule o' pimpin'. You can treat yo' girl like shit, you can beat her black and fuckin' blue, take her last dicksuckin' dime, leave her ass broke 'n' hungry, but you *always* bail yo' bitch out.'

'I'm sorry,' he repeated.

'Well, I *ain't*.' Risquée smirked. 'I learned some things

'bout yo' ass in there. See, all that while I was out there peddlin' *my* ass, I thought I was one o' yo' mamma's girls. Only I wasn't. I ain't got that playin' card shit tattooed on my thigh, an' I ain't got me no *retirement plan* neither. Yo' mamma's girls get to keep ten dollars outta every hunnert they make, an' she puts aside another ten dollars on that for when they can't ho no mo'. You bin rippin' me off, nigga! An' you straight up *lied* to me 'bout how I was workin' fo' yo' mamma too. I bin workin' fo' *yo' ass* the whole time. An' I *know* you playin' yo' po' mamma, runnin' hos on the side without her knowin'.'

Carmine didn't reply. She had him. She was completely right.

'I *was* gonna go see yo' mamma, tell her *everythang*, only ain't no money in that.'

'How much you want?'

'Fiddy thousand bucks.'

'I ain't got that kind of money.'

'*Get it*,' she snapped coldly. 'Today's Tooseday. You got till next Tooseday, or I'll go see yo' mamma. And maybe I won't gonna go alone neither, 'cause I'm *sure* you runnin' plenty other bitches out here. Meet me at yo' boyfriend Sam's store at eight.'

'He *ain't* my boyfriend,' Carmine said bitterly.

'Way that nigga passed up my pussy fo' my ass that night? He straight fag-fucked me, nigga.' Risquée sneered. 'You the only pimp in the world don't fuck his bitches, you know that? Hell! You ain't even a *pimp* – you a motherfuckin' *pimple*!' She laughed her hyena screech. 'An' I'ma gonna *squeeze* you like the pimple you is, nigga! Next Tooseday. You better be there – an' you better have my money.'

With that she turned and walked off, squeaking and clicking down the street, head up, swinging her bag.

Carmine got in his car and drove off.

Humiliated and panicked, he went through Coral Gables,

barely giving it a glance, even though it was one of his favourite drives. Normally he loved cruising past all those beautiful big homes, along the smooth, ficus-tree-lined roads, his top down, the warm wind on his face, the smell of big money and fresh grass in his nose. Now he just sped over the Blue Road Bridge, not even glancing at the boats parked in the seawater canals behind their owners' houses. And he didn't even bother marvelling at the Venetian Pool. He didn't give a fuck about all this man-made beauty. He wanted to get the hell away from what had just happened.

He went down Miracle Mile, faintly aware he'd planned to scope out two potential Cards – Diamonds, one for him, one for his mother – but he felt like such a failure he didn't even want to think about doing what he did best.

Christ! That bitch *knew*!

He'd been running his own Game for three years now without a hitch, being real careful about *everything*. And now that cunt Risquée was threatening to blow it all. Solomon would kill him for sure. Didn't matter what history they had. Didn't matter that they'd been virtually like brothers from Haiti up. None of that shit mattered to Solomon. He'd torture him too. He'd do him at an SNBC. And what about Sam? What would happen to him? Sam was his best friend, his *only* friend. Sam was in this shit as deep as him.

When he got to Little Havana he felt better. The whole place was so run down and poor and derelict it suited his state of mind. Shitty little spic stores. Shitty little spic bars. Shitty little spic diners. Even the *sky* was shitty little spic something here.

He should *never* have brought her in. Bitch hadn't even worked nowhere *nice*. She'd worked at fuckin' *Wendy's*! A burger chain!

And she'd hit him. Twice. Just like his mother did.

It just wasn't *right*! It was too much. He had to stop.

He pulled over and parked on Calle Ocho. Opposite

him a man was standing near a flatbed truck loaded with coconuts. He was cutting the ends off and selling them as drinks to passers-by. Carmine watched him work. Simple job. Simple life. Simple guy. Right then he would've traded places with him in a heartbeat if he could. Let that fuck deal with Risquée.

Bitch had taken his money. Bitch wanted to take more. Bitch was gonna tell his mother. Bitch was gonna tell all his other Cards too. He'd lose them all. And he was so damn *close* to getting away. *So damn close.*

A solitary tear ran down his face, still throbbing on both sides from the slaps. He hated himself for crying. He hated himself for being such a fuckin' pussy. Bitch was right. He wasn't no *real* pimp. A real pimp would've broken both her arms and then gone to work on her face. He wasn't no *real* pimp.

Maybe it was time he started behaving like one. Maybe it was time he grew some balls.

He wiped his face. He was going to see Sam.

He started his car, pulled out and drove on.

Risquée wasn't going to get his money. No way.

No fuckin' way.

Every morning Sam Ismael – a tall, very slim and straight bald man, with a long bulbous nose and yellowy-brown eyes – washed the sidewalk outside his store with an infusion of jasmine, mint and rosewater. It was a Syrian shopkeeper's custom passed down to him from his parents who'd run a supermarket in Port-au-Prince. The smell was meant to attract prosperity and peace.

Sam was certainly prosperous, and, partly because of that, he was mostly at peace with himself. His store, or botanica, Haiti Mystique, on North East 54th Street in Lemon City, was doing great. It sold all kinds of voodoo paraphernalia from drums, spirit-calling sticks, candles, dolls, plaster saints, to all manner of herbs, roots, leaves and seeds, and also sacrificial animals – roosters, chickens, doves, goats and snakes. He also did a highly lucrative trade in under-the-counter goods used in black magic, much of it stolen from churches and graveyards – the skulls and bones of nuns, priests and murderers proving exceptionally popular. Everyone came to him from Haitian *houngans* and *mambos*, Cuban and Brazilian Macumba priests, African witchdoctors, home-grown witches and fortune tellers, satanists to kinky-sex freaks, musicians and tourists.

The store stood out a mile in the drab and derelict street. It was an antidote to an otherwise depressing grey vision of row after row of boarded-up buildings, empty warehouses and low-lying tenement blocks that were home to squatters, junkies and ever increasing groups of Haitian migrants.

Sam didn't believe in *vodou* any more than he believed in any religion, but he understood the hold it had on people and he appreciated and respected what the belief could do.

He thought little of most of his customers – charlatans, quacks, hacks or simply deluded crackpots; people who'd made a living out of being born with weird faces and staring eyes and a perfect aloofness – yet he was still undecided about Eva Desamours. She sometimes scared him enough into believing in the supernatural. Once, on a rare visit to the shop, she'd seen a German couple who were looking at coin chains, and she'd said to the woman, a brunette in her early thirties: 'It's a boy and you'll name him after your father, because he won't live to see him born. He's ill and hasn't got long.' The couple had left in a hurry, much to Sam's fury, because tourists were easy spenders. But last year they'd come back with their young boy, looking for Eva, to ask her how she'd known.

Sam was also a money launderer, specifically for Solomon Boukman, but also for a growing number of senior officers in the Haitian army, who were making serious cash from cocaine smuggling. They'd built private airfields in the north of Haiti and were landing Colombian cartel airplanes stuffed with coke, refuelling them and flying them off to Miami. US Customs never suspected a thing because of where the planes were coming from: Haiti wasn't cocaine country. The Haitian connection was the source of all Solomon's narcotics, and the cornerstone of his massive wealth. Sure, he had a hand in almost everything illegal, but nothing paid like drugs. And he owed it all to Sam who'd got him started in the big game, simply by telling him about the airfields in his homeland and arranging a few meetings with the main players. Prior to that Solomon had been strictly a small-bills and dime-bag operator.

Sam's services varied from straightforward routing of money through offshore banks to accounts in Switzerland, Monaco and Luxemburg, or, in Solomon's case investing the money in businesses and property. Sam was the frontman for the Lemon City project, and in some ways the brains behind it. He'd had a vision of sorts. He'd been driving back through Coral Gables with Carmine one day after the two of them had been gator hunting out in the Everglades. Carmine had been talking about how the area had once been orange groves until George Merrick had come along and decided to build a city there in the 1920s. Twenty minutes later they'd found themselves stuck in traffic in Little Havana. He'd seen a sign on the kerb reading 'Parking For Cubans Only. All Others Will Be Towed'. He'd been shocked at first by the audacity of it, immigrants doing this to their host nation, but then it had occurred to him they could get away with it because it was *their* area – built, owned and run by the 'Freedom Flighters', the Cubans who'd fled Fidel. And that's when he'd had his vision of a similar area for Haitians: a 'Little Haiti'.

Sam had seen that whole chunks of Lemon City were being sold off and he'd suggested to Solomon that he buy it all up as a long-term investment. Sam had even told Solomon there was a bizarre symmetry between Lemon City and Coral Gables, because back in the early 1900s Lemon City had earned its name because of its abundant lemon groves. Between them, they'd be building a modern version of the Gables. It took some convincing, but Solomon had gone along with the idea. To him the place would just be one huge money laundrette.

Not so for Sam. Although Syrian by birth, he considered himself Haitian. He spoke French and Kreyol fluently – as well as English, Spanish, Arabic and Circassian. He loved Haitians and wanted to do something for them. He'd come to the island as a baby and lived there until his early twenties, when he'd gone to the University of Miami to study economics. The country had been good to him and to his parents, Rafik and Zada, who'd made a considerable fortune with their supermarkets, thrift shops and garment factories.

Sam had met Solomon nine years ago, shortly after he'd

first opened the store. Solomon had sent Bonbon round to collect protection money. Sam had pulled a shotgun on him. Bonbon had waddled off, warning him that he'd made a big mistake.

Sam had heard about Solomon Boukman and his gang. Solomon was a neighbourhood legend, and impressionable minds were already ascribing mystical powers to him. The Liberty City Haitians considered him their guardian. The rest of Liberty City feared him. This hadn't fazed Sam, who'd thought it was all bullshit, but had still taken precautions and always kept the gun to hand in the store.

Solomon had never come to him in person. He'd sent Eva. She'd apologized for Bonbon, said it wouldn't happen again. Then she'd looked around the store, bought a John the Conqueror root and left. She'd returned the following week and bought two chickens and a toad. Both times he sensed her scoping him, looking into him, even though their conversation was limited. On her third visit she told him Solomon needed someone to help manage his money.

How had she known he was good with numbers? Sam guessed she'd done a little research into his background, possibly found out he was managing his parents' investments here in the US. It wasn't exactly a secret. They liked to boast that their son was a whizz with money, a regular Richie Rich.

He didn't want to do it. He wanted to make his money honestly, like his parents had, but Eva mentioned his sister Malika, studying in Gainesville, and he understood he had no choice.

Sam met Solomon face to face a month later – after a fashion. They'd sat across from each other in an empty room with closed curtains. It was late afternoon and the sun was going down. Solomon was an ambiguous silhouette in the feeble light, appearing to change shape as night encroached on the room and merged more and more with his outline. They'd talked business. Solomon's voice was soft, American-accented with the mildest hint of Haitian. His words, although few, were well chosen and precise; he wanted to make sure he wasn't misunderstood. He'd struck Sam as highly intelligent, as clever if not cleverer than the brightest people he'd known at university. He had a quick mind and remembered every detail of what was said to him. He'd asked Sam to set up six savings accounts – four for him, two for Eva, but not in their names. He'd then asked about numbered accounts in Switzerland. Sam had told him he needed serious capital to get one of those. 'It will come,' Solomon had said. And it did.

Whenever they'd met, it had always been in places with poor light or no light at all. For all Sam knew, Solomon might not even have been there in person on every occasion; he could have been meeting one of the doubles Carmine said he regularly used. Not that it really mattered one way or another, because, apart from his voice, Sam didn't have the slightest idea what his employer looked like. Solomon could have come into the shop and Sam wouldn't have known it was him.

Things ran very smoothly, or had done until the murders of Preval Lacour and Mr and Mrs Cuesta over the Lemon City project. Sam hadn't approved, but he hadn't disapproved of their being out of the picture either. He was, above all, a businessman, and business was about taking advantage of whatever opportunity came your way.

On Wednesday afternoons, the slowest time, his assistant Lulu gave him a manicure. Sam was fastidious about his appearance. Hands and teeth were exceptionally important in his kind of business, he had found, along with his brains and book of contacts, the key tools of the trade. A good smile with healthy teeth drew someone in and gained their trust, and a firm handshake bound them to you.

He was inspecting Lulu's fine work when the bell above the door rang and Carmine walked in, looking sweaty and pissed off.

'Salaam, Carmine!' Sam called out happily. He walked over and kissed his friend on each cheek and then stood back to look at him. Carmine was lightly bruised about the face. 'What happened?'

'Not here,' he said, looking at Lulu, who was packing away her manicure set.

'Why don't you go downstairs and clean up?' Sam said in English, which Lulu was still trying to master.

By downstairs Sam meant the lower basement, two floors beneath. The floor directly below where he kept his animals. Until very recently he'd had a chimpanzee there. It was a runaway from Primate Park he'd found sitting outside his shop, seemingly half dead with exhaustion. He'd taken it in and let it stay in the empty goat cage, before selling it to a Congolese witchdoctor.

The lower basement had white tiled floors and walls, and a whitewashed ceiling with a long rail across it hung with stainless-steel hooks. It was spotless and reeked heavily of industrial disinfectant. There was a marble mortuary slab in the middle with a sluice drain next to it. There were four white rectangular freezers around the slab, humming a quiet but deep note.

This was where Sam stored the carcasses of the gators he and Carmine went out and hunted in the Everglades once a month. Sam drove the airboat and Carmine shot them through the eye with a hunting rifle. He was a great shot, hitting the beasts dead on target every time.

When they were done they'd bring the gators back to the shop, hang them up, gut them, clean them and pack them in ice. Later Sam would ship them out to his parents' factory in Haiti where they got turned into shoes, belts, luggage and souvenirs – the heads and feet being big sellers to tourists and religious freaks.

Carmine washed his face and then scooped out some ice into two trash bags and put them against his bruises.

When Sam came down a few minutes later, Carmine told him what had happened. Sam remembered Risquée well; trouble from the moment she'd stepped into their lives. She was a Diamond, albeit one still clinging to the coal. When Sam had put the $2,000 on the table, she'd asked him for more, saying she wasn't going to suck on his Ayrabb dick for less than $3,000. Sam had paid up. Then she'd asked for another Quaalude so she could imagine that he was hung like John Holmes and fucked like Mandingo. Sam had liked her, but she'd scared him limp. She was a ready-made hustler who didn't give a shit.

'What are you going to do, Carmine?'

'I can't give in to no blackmail, man,' Carmine said. 'I do that, she'll take it all.'

'And who knows what else she'll do,' Sam said.

'What do you mean "what *else*"? She already said she'll tell my *mother*. She finds out, we're both fuckin' *dead*. Don't matter what you do for Solomon, how useful you are an' shit. You cross him, you're gator food. The guy is straight up ruthless. Shit don't mean shit to him.'

'Then there's only one thing to do.'

Carmine nodded but didn't meet Sam's eye.

'You want me to take care of it?' Sam offered.

'No, man,' Carmine said, 'I gots to handle my own shit.'

'You're not a killer, Carmine.'

'Yet.'

'You're *not* a killer,' Sam repeated firmly. 'And you don't want to walk down that road. Let me sort it out. Put some-one on it.'

'Who?'

'Someone. There's so many killers in Miami they'll have a union soon.'

'No man. It's my thang, you know. This bidniss is mines, so this problem is mines. How you expect me to survive out in the desert if I can't deal with one greedy bitch? I'll handle this.'

Carmine looked at his reflection in the mirror above the sink. 'My face, man. Look at me. I gots to be collecting the rent off these hos about now. That Lulu? She got some – er – make-up or somethin'? All girls always got make-up on 'em, right? See if she got some foundation I can put on my face.'

'Foundation? OK.' Sam turned around and started heading for the stairs, clenching his jaws so he wouldn't laugh.

'Hey, don't tell her it's for me, right?' Carmine called after him.

What Sam hadn't told Carmine was that Solomon and Eva knew all about his sideline. Sam had kept them informed from the very beginning. He'd had to. They would have found out easily, and he and Carmine would've wound up as human sacrifices.

They hadn't taken it badly. In fact Eva had been amused that her useless, stupid son had even *thought* of making it on his own.

23

They busted Octavio Grossfeld at 4.30 a.m. on Thursday. Recon had told them that he was alone in the house. One way in. No way out.

Max, Joe, Mark Brennan and Jimmy Valentín went through the door.

They found Grossfeld in the bedroom, naked, face down on his bed, passed out from hitting a large blue springing-dolphin-shaped glass bong; so deep under the stone he didn't hear them.

Brennan and Valentín tossed the house, while Max and Joe tried to wake Grossfeld. They stood him up, slapped him around, shone a light in his face.

'*Buenos dias*, motherfucker!'

Grossfeld's eyes peeked out from under heavy lids and went back in, as he smiled a sloppy grin, mouth half open, drool dribbling out the sides.

They took him into the bathroom, dumped him in the shower and turned the cold water on full. Grossfeld came to screaming.

They frog-marched him into the living room and stood him up against the wall, dripping wet.

The room was a tip and smelled like God's own outhouse. The floor was carpeted with used pizza boxes, flattened and taped together.

Valentín came back from the kitchen holding a plastic bowl filled with coke balloons.

'Hey, they ain't mine!' Grossfeld yelled.

'No? What they doin' here then?' Joe asked.

'He planted them there!'

'Right,' Max said sarcastically.

Brennan meanwhile, had found a surgeon's bag in a cupboard. He took out three scalpels, duct tape and a saw, all covered in dry blood.

'Don't tell me,' Max said to Grossfeld. 'He planted them there too right? And the prints we're gonna lift off 'em ain't gonna be yours either?'

Grossfeld didn't say anything, just looked at his feet, dripping water, covering his balls. He was short, pale and skinny with a tattoo of the Virgin Mary covering his chest.

'What you like doin' better, Octavio? Dealin' dope or cuttin' girls open?' Max asked.

'Fuck you, *puta*!' He spat at Max's face and missed hitting Joe's jacket. Joe wiped it off with his handkerchief.

'I look *estupido*, man? That dope ain't *mine*. I ain't gonna keep my shit in here!'

'Where you stash it?' Joe asked.

'Eh?' Octavio grimaced. 'You *plant* this fake shit here, and now you ask me where I keep my *real* shit. You're dumb in three dimensions, *chardo*.'

'You know a man called Carlos Lehder?' Joe asked.

'*Si*. He fucked your mamma in the jungle and made you, *mono negro*.'

'You tryna get a *rise* outta me, Octavio?' Joe said, looking down at him, bringing all his build to bear, dwarfing him. 'Let's get some panties on this bitch before we read him his rights.'

Max went back to the bedroom and found a pair of jeans and a dirty pink T-shirt lying next to a half-eaten pizza.

'Put these on, fuckhead!' He tossed them at Grossfeld.

As he was getting dressed Jed Powers walked through the door. He took a look at Grossfeld and called Brennan and Valentín outside. Max heard them murmuring and then Powers and Valentín came back in.

'What are you doin' here, Lieutenant?' Max asked.

'Been a change of plans. We ain't takin' him in.'

'What? Says who?'

'You know who,' Powers said. 'You two get over here.' He beckoned.

'Hey! I want some compensation for that door, *puta*!' Grossfeld shouted out and started coming forward.

'Shut up you! And back up where you were!' Powers barked, stopping Grossfeld in his tracks. He retreated to the wet patch he'd previously occupied.

As Max and Joe were approaching Powers, Valentín stepped past them and shot Grossfeld twice in the chest. His back blasted out and splashed thick crimson treacle on the wall. Grossfeld fell face down on the floor.

'WHAT THE FUCK?!' Max yelled.

Valentín walked over to the body, holstering his piece. He took a silver .38 out of his waistband.

Powers motioned for Max and Joe to step outside.

'OK, you two saw it. You came in and took fire. Valentín popped him. Simple.'

They heard a single shot go off in the house.

'When was this decided?' Max asked. He was shaking with shock and anger. Joe was ashen and silent.

Valentín came out.

'All clear,' he said.

Lights were going on in the neighbouring houses, doors were opening, people were starting to come out on the street. The monotonous chirping of crickets was giving way to the wail of sirens.

'Eldon'll explain everything once we get through the debrief,' Powers said, then looked at Joe. 'You OK, Liston?'

'What do you think?' Joe growled low.

Powers gave him a long hard look, then stared at Max.

'You two best go help control the spectators.'

'Did you know that before he got busted the first time, Octavio Grossfeld was top of his class at Miami University? His parents were dirt poor farmers. He was a scholarship kid. Got through on his own brains and merit,' Eldon said to Max.

They were up on the roof. It had gone 2 p.m. The sky was thickening to thunderstorm black, sunlight only breaking through in patches. There was no breeze at all. The heat hugged them close, tight and humid. Below there'd been an accident on Flagler, and traffic was backed up halfway down the road.

Max had just been through his witness report – taped and written. He'd repeated what he'd been told to say: he and Joe had gone in first, with Brennan and Valentín behind them. Grossfeld had come out and shot once in their direction. Valentín had returned fire twice, hitting Grossfeld in the chest at point-blank range. It was self-defence; a good call which had saved their lives; exemplary police work.

Then he'd had to type up two reports because Joe was too messed up to concentrate. It had taken him five attempts before he'd got it right.

'And that's why he had to go,' Eldon continued. ''Cause there ain't nothin' worse for a cop than an intelligent criminal. He'd've caused us all kindsa problems when he came down offa his bong cloud. Happened before with his kind. This way's better. We can pin what we want on him and make it stick. Dead men tell no tales and all that.

'Look, I'm sorry I didn't warn you about it, but I wanted you goin' in there with a clear head. Mind on the job,' Eldon said.

Max didn't know what was pissing him off more – what he'd just witnessed, or the fact that Eldon was so fucking matter of fact and even jovial about it.

'How's Liston?'

'What do you think, Eldon? He's never seen this kind of shit first hand before,' Max said, 'so he's kinda confused.'

'Confused?' Eldon frowned.

'Yeah, you know. His right and wrong compass is all fucked up.'

'He gonna be a problem?'

'No.' Max shook his head. 'Joe's a hundred per cent solid. With you all the way. I mean, he ain't got a death wish, right?'

Eldon smirked at that. 'You're upset, ain't you?' he said.

'You could say that, yeah,' Max said, drawing hard on his Marlboro. 'What went down today was wrong.'

'*Wrong?* No, it wasn't wrong, Max. It was right. *Wrong* was that guy. He was a piece of shit. Brought young Colombian girls over here and gutted 'em like they was kingfish. Hell, why am I even tellin' you this? You *know*. It was you who picked him outta the book.'

'It's still murder.'

'Huh?' Eldon stepped closer to him and craned his head down a little, looking Max right in the eye. 'I can't believe I'm hearin' this. From *you*, of all people. You a little shell shocked, Max? You got amnesia? Macon PD have three unsolved murders on their books – three kiddie rapers with double tap entry wounds in their heads.'

'That was different.'

'Oh? How so?'

'They were guilty but you made me let 'em go because their faces didn't fit whatever political agenda you and the Turd Fairy were workin' to that month.'

'But you still popped 'em.'

'I was doin' the job you wouldn't let me do the right way. Those guys? They preyed on defenceless children. I gave the kids and their heartbroken families justice. Justice *you* denied 'em!'

'*I* denied them justice? Bullshit! Those families *got* fucken' justice, Max! You see them complainin' in court? They didn't give a flying fuck it was the wrong guy.'

''Cause they didn't *know*!'

'But *you* got the real perps, Max. And the creeps we put away? They hurt kids too. So what's the fucken' problem? Two for the price of one. And you're talkin' to me about *justice*? I say what we're doin' here is justice — justice at its *purest*. Those fuckers all deserved to go down. Octavio Grossfeld sliced girls up, Max. Young girls, with families too. He was a scumbag. He got what was comin' and good fucken' riddance!'

'We weren't even gonna arrest him for *that*,' Max said bitterly but weakly, feeling the protest drain out of him. Eldon was right: he wasn't in any kind of position to protest, and there was even a warped truth in what he was saying.

'Look, Max,' Eldon put his hand on his shoulder, all fatherly and concerned, 'you're upset 'cause I didn't keep you in the loop. Is that it? It was a last-minute call. You and Liston'll get the credit, don't worry. It's still your baby.'

Fuck that, Max thought, looking away, over to the sea.

'What about Marisela Cruz?'

'Who?'

'The mule who was gonna testify against Grossfeld?'

'What about her? Things have changed, so the deal's off. She'll be charged and go to prison.'

'But I promised her . . .'

'Not in writing you didn't. Verbal promises ain't worth shit. Who was with you when you talked to her? Pete?'

Max nodded yes.

'He'll deny the whole thing.'

'What about her baby?' Max almost whispered. He felt sick and dizzy. He dropped his cigarette on the ground and stamped it out.

'Her kid'll be born here and fostered or adopted. Best

thing for it. Would you wanna grow up in Colombia? I wouldn't.'

'That's fucked up,' Max said, disgusted. 'Can't you at least deport her?'

'Not my call.'

'*Bullshit!*'

Eldon was taken aback by Max's fury, but only for a second.

'We send that girl home, know what'll happen? She'll be back on the next plane over, and the one after that too. And then maybe she'll bring her baby along for the ride. You know they use babies to get coke in here, right?' Eldon said.

'Forget it then,' Max said. 'I want off this case.'

'*What* did you just say?' Eldon's face tightened.

'You heard me.' Max looked him straight in the eye.

'Ain't gonna happen.' Eldon shook his head.

'No? Then I'll quit.'

'The fuck you will!' Eldon snarled.

'Watch me,' Max said coldly and turned to go.

Eldon grabbed him by both shoulders and spun him around so fast he lost his balance and stumbled, and his cigarettes and Zippo fell out of his breast pocket.

'Now you *listen*,' Eldon seethed, face flushed, eyes small and fierce, wart turquoise going on purple, index finger jabbing at Max's face. '*I* run this division. *You* work for *me*. I decide who stays and who goes. Not you. The only place you go is where I tell you.

'You wanna walk outta here, Max? Fine, fuck off. But you'll be taking Liston with you. And I'll make *sure* he knows that his arrogant little prick of a partner was willing to wreck his life over some spic mule.

'That girl? She's surplus to our requirements. She broke our laws. She goes to our prisons. End of fucken' story. You *got* that?'

Max didn't reply. The thick veins in Eldon's muscular neck had sprung up like a nest of snakes and his face was beet-red. Max hadn't seen him so mad at him since his boxing days.

'I didn't fucken' hear you,' Eldon said, getting right up in his face, so close their heads were practically touching.

'I got it, Eldon.' Max backed off a step, feeling pathetic and whipped and all kinds of small. Back when he was training him, Eldon had used one of two approaches to get results. Patient, friendly encouragement when he'd lost confidence in his abilities, or full-scale public verbal bombardments when he'd lost sight of his ambition. Eldon had known him so long he knew exactly which buttons to press and how hard.

'You *what*?'

'I said I got it. I understand,' Max said more loudly, keeping a firm hand on his wounded pride so it wouldn't turn to anger.

'Good.' He stood glowering at Max, soaking up his protégé's capitulation. And when he'd had his fill, he packed the anger away, smiled, and put a firm but friendly arm around Max's shoulder and walked him over towards the edge of the roof.

'A little disagreement's always healthy, huh?' he said. 'Clears the bad air.'

Max replied with a noncommittal, 'Hmmm.'

'Me and Abe, God, we used to fucken' disagree all the time. You know why? Abe was extra efficient when it come to dealin' with his own people. He was rougher and nastier and more intolerant than any o' those Klan-affiliated Patrol cops ever were. Whenever we was interrogatin' nigras, he had this bat he used to take out, intimidate 'em with. Thing was filled with lead shot. One tap'd turn bone to powder. Know what he used to call it? His "nigger knocker". Can you imagine that? Abe was a great cop, one of the best ever had a badge, and the finest I ever worked with. But, you know, sometimes he went *way* too far trying to prove he was bluer than black, one of us. Boy did we argue! Things he used to say. Close your eyes and you woulda sworn that was some redneck talkin' to you.'

Max had heard all the stories about Abe, although never directly from him. Abe didn't talk about the past much. Joe despised Abe, called him a self-loathing sellout – and that was when he was being polite.

Eldon took a deep breath of the dense dead air and sighed.

'I love this fucken' city, don't you?' Eldon swept his free hand across the view of the flat landscape, his tone now warm and friendly.

'It's all right, I guess.' Max shrugged his shoulders. He wanted to get Eldon's paw off him.

'It's "all right, you *guess*"?' Eldon laughed. 'You're Miami born and bred, Max. You don't know no better. Me? I love this city more'n I love most people. That's the honest truth. Always been that way, always be that way.

'First time I came here, I was ten years old. Came here with my daddy, Eldon Burns the First. He was a sheriff in Mississippi. Caught himself a fugitive wanted by Miami PD. So we drove him down. Guy was in the back seat. I was up front with Daddy. We handed him over and went down to Miami Beach. The first sight o' that was so fucken' beautiful. The beach, the sea, them rows of art deco hotels. Those places were really somethin' back then, you know? Not like the dumps they are now. To me they were little palaces and everyone stayin' in 'em was royalty. I made myself a promise that when I grew up I'd be sheriff of Miami. Look at me now, huh?'

Yeah, look at you now, Max thought bitterly. Your daddy woulda been real proud of you, Eldon Burns the Second.

'There ain't no place like Miami,' Eldon continued. 'We got it *all* here. Back in my days in uniform it was whites, tourists, Cubans, kikes and nigras who knew their place and were happy to stay there. Now we got World War Three going on out here with these Colombians and the street gangs. They're bringing this shit into our city, right under our noses and fucken' it up for everyone. They're walkin' into our courtrooms killin' people on national fucken' television! Tourism's down, money's dryin' up. Breaks my heart to see what this place is comin' to.

'Only, you know what? Miami ain't gonna get no lower than this. Things are gonna stop and things are gonna change. Like it or not, Max, we're at war. They're winning right now, but we're fightin' back. We're like a guerrilla unit. We're the Miami Resistance. We're outnumbered, outgunned, outfinanced. And we're fighting not one but fifty invading armies, and they're all at war with each other, and they're all at war with us. The Cubans are fighting the Colombians. And the Colombians are fighting each other. But we're gonna win. 'Cause this is *our* city and *our* country. We're gonna reclaim Miami, bullet by bullet. We're gonna help turn it around, give it back its looks, its glamour and its money. We're gonna make it beautiful again.

'And you, Max, are gonna help me do it.' Eldon looked him hard in the eye and squeezed his shoulder. 'You're the next best cop it was ever my honour to know. And I mean that. Together, you, me and this division – we're gonna make a *real* difference. And when the smoke clears and the dust settles, Miami won't be Murder Capital USA no more. It'll be the greatest city in America, the place everybody wants to come to and be part of. Just like it used to be.

'And do you know what the best part about it is? After I'm gone, one day, this'll all be yours. Everything you can see. What do you think of that, Max?'

I think you're full of shit, Eldon, Max thought. Bullet by bullet? Are you totally fucken' *insane*?

'I think that sounds real great, Eldon,' Max said flatly. '*Real* great.'

24

'"One day this will all be yours". Kind of fucked up shit is *that*?' Joe laughed sourly and then took a pull on his Miller. He was sitting on Max's balcony looking out over Ocean Drive. The balcony was wide enough for Max to stretch out in, but Joe was so tall the only way he could sit anywhere near comfortably was by resting the backs of his ankles on the iron railing.

It was late afternoon, but the sky was so dark and thick with cloud it felt like night had come early. The beach was the colour of graphite, while the sea had the tone and stillness of mercury. There was going to be one hell of a storm.

'What he said,' Max replied. He'd related the whole conversation to him as soon as they'd sat down.

'Crazy muhfucker,' Joe grumbled.

'What I thought.'

'But you didn't tell him, right?'

'What difference would it've made?'

'Were you serious about quittin'?'

'Still here ain't I?'

''Preciate the loyalty man.' Joe clicked his bottle against Max's.

'It was an empty gesture,' Max said.

'Not to me, man,' Joe countered. 'Not to me.'

It had taken Joe most of the day to recover his public composure. After they'd taken him through his statement, he'd gone back to his desk and sat there for an hour with his chair turned away, facing the wall. He hadn't said a word. The phone had rung and he hadn't answered it. People had talked to him and he hadn't acknowledged them. Then he'd got up and left the office. When he came back two hours later Max had smelled the booze on him, but he'd been more communicative and had managed to laugh at the way Max got his finger caught in the typewriter keys when he was writing up the report.

They hadn't discussed what had happened and wouldn't for a while. It was too close to Joe. He never talked about traumatic events until he'd got a good distance away from them.

'Emperor Burns was right 'bout one thing though,' Joe said, looking down the street with its still pretty pink side-walks. 'This used to be one helluva beauty spot. Sure ain't like it now.'

'I hear that,' Max said.

'Why d'you live here, man?'

'So I can tell chicks I gotta view of the sea,' Max quipped and lit a Marlboro. 'Besides, it's cheap.'

The press called Ocean Drive 'the ghetto by the sea'. They had a point. On either side of Max's building were some of the old exclusive art deco hotels Eldon had talked about – the Shore Park, the Pelican, the Colony, the Carlyle – now exclusively home to Cuban refugees and infirm Jewish retirees living out their last days in the sun. Fifty dollars or less got you a room for a week. The buildings were cracked and crumbling, pastel paint flaking off the walls in chunks, and the neon signs barely came on any more, either because the tubes were burnt out or because the owners were saving on electricity. Washing hung on lines from almost every balcony, and Spanish-language radio playing Spanish-language tunes to drown out Spanish-language arguments was all you ever heard. In the daytime, in Lummus Park, on the other side of the road, the old women would sometimes sit out in groups on folding metal chairs. They'd knit and talk in Yiddish about the past, hair covered in headscarves, drab-coloured dresses down to their knees, flip-flops on their feet. Between the 1940s and 60s the park had been a lush stretch of nature, densely planted with palm trees, but many had been uprooted in storms and never replaced; now it was mostly grass, ratty and clogged with trash. It was a magnet for bums, drifters, runaways, junkies and dealers. Every day one or two bodies would be found in the park.

Max was playing the album he'd been listening to all week because he hadn't bothered to take it off the turntable – Donna Summer's *Bad Girls*. The album had hit its dull ballad quarter. He usually skipped these tracks when he was on his own and dropped the needle on the synth-heavy anthems at the end, starting with 'Our Love'.

'I reckon you only like this shit 'cause o' the covers,' Joe said, picking up the sleeve of *Bad Girls*. 'You're too embarrassed to go get yourself a copy of *Black T 'n' A*, so you go to the record store instead.' Joe looked at Donna's half-open mouth, and come-hither stare. 'She sure is fine though.'

'Gimme that.' Max snatched the cover back. 'Fucken' hypocrite. Get your own copy.'

'Yeah, take it.' Joe laughed. 'Fuckin' *disco*, man! Shit's *over*. Thank goodness and good riddance. White man annexed that music soon as he saw how much money it could make. Same with rock 'n' roll. Elvis was *that* poster child, same way John Travolta was disco's blue-eyed boy. Hell, they even dressed him up in a *white* suit to make sure we got the message. Might as well've put a white hood on him too.'

'That was a *film*, Joe, c'mon!' Max laughed. 'You been smokin' reefer again?'

Whenever they'd smoked weed together, Joe would start talking conspiracy theories about everything from Christianity to the Iranian hostages, and every conspiracy had racism as its prime motive. Some of them had a kernel of debatable truth, but most were utterly ludicrous.

'Nah, man, I'm off that shit for good. I'm just makin' an observation. Hollywood's the best propaganda machine the USA has. See, we do as much if not worse stuff around the world than the commies, but Hollywood always has Uncle Sam as the good guy, always doin' the right thing, savin' the planet; so simple-minded people see it and believe it. You know *Birth of a Nation* was the biggest recruitment ad the Klan ever had, right? Same with *Saturday Night Fever*. People see that, they believe the white man can dance!'

'And *you* can?' Max laughed loudly, remembering Joe's dancing. 'You move like George Foreman on valium.'

'Fuck you, Mingus!' Joe cackled.

'You wanna another brew?'

'Let's talk about our thing first.'

They hadn't had time to discuss how they would go about tackling the real Moyez case, but Max had jotted down a few ideas on a notepad, as had Joe.

Max started.

'Here's what we gotta go on – similarities with the Lacour case. Both Lacour and the Moyez John Doe were completely hairless and they'd had their lips sewn up. Contents of stomach: squares of tarot card – the King of Swords – plus a mixture of bone, sand and vegetable matter. The tarot cards were already part digested, which means they were in their stomachs before they did their hits. I'm thinking this was part of a potion, and I'm also thinking these guys didn't know what they were doing. Lacour killing his family was like a dry run, a test to make sure whatever it was he had inside him was working – that he'd kill on command and without hesitation.

'And there was someone else there with him when he killed his folks. And whoever this person was was the same one who did the Wong family.'

'The Candyman,' Joe said. 'I'm gonna contact NYPD, see if they got a print off that wrapper they found. And I'll see if North Miami PD came up with anything on their side.'

'Good.' Max nodded. 'Then we'll have to look into gangs who use black magic.'

'That's five phone directories' worth – just for Miami alone,' Joe said. 'Seein' that shit more times than not now. The Mariel crims all got Santería altars in their homes. Most of 'em offer up prayers and sacrifices to their gods before they go out and commit felonies.'

'I could be wrong, but I don't think this is a Cuban thing,' Max said. 'I'm thinkin' Haitian.'

'*Haitian?* If they ain't drivin' cabs or cleanin' floors here, the most they do is muggings and stick-ups in 7-Elevens – strictly small-time shit.'

'You gotta keep an open mind, Joe.' Max riffled through a couple of pages. 'Preval Lacour was Haitian. As was his business partner, and so's the only guy he didn't kill – Sam Ismael. And Sam Ismael runs a voodoo store in Lemon City called Haiti Mystique. He was one of the bidders for the redevelopment project Lacour won. Ismael's on my list to interview.'

'He clean?'

'Totally.'

'Moyez wasn't Haitian.'

'Wasn't Cuban either.'

'Best you keep an open mind too.' Joe winked, jotting down some notes.

'Sure will.' Max smiled and lit another cigarette before going on. 'We don't know who the Moyez shooter was yet. No fingerprints on file. But he may have killed before – possibly a person or persons close to him.'

'So we gotta check on families or such reported missing or murdered in city and state,' Joe said.

'If he was from around here. If not, we'll have to do a nationwide search. Shouldn't take long if it's multiple murder. He used a .357 Magnum with semi-wadcutters. If it's the same MO as Lacour, he woulda used the same piece on his family or friends, so that'll narrow it down some. Then we'll search for similar-type killings.'

'I got that down too,' Joe said. 'Hairless hitmen with stitch marks on their lips and tarot cards in their guts.'

'Next,' Max flipped over a page, 'the tarot cards. Normally used in fortune telling, but here they were part of a potion. We'll do a search on the cards themselves. There are literally hundreds of different makes and manufacturers. But these *have* to be exotic. They've got no faces. Plus we need to talk to card readers too, find out what they know.'

'Check,' Joe said. 'What about de Carvalho?'

'He's on my interview list, along with *everybody* who was in that courtroom – everybody we can trace.'

'De Carvalho's in a Fed safehouse right now.'

'Know who's in charge?'

'Bill Forsey. He's real tight with Burns.'

'Shit, I know,' Max said.

'We could pretend we're talking to him as part of our official investigation.'

'Won't fly. Forsey's a Cutman. Probably knows as much – if not more – about what Eldon's up to than me.'

'What are we gonna do if Eldon finds out?'

'Say we're tyin' up loose ends.'

'You mean cuttin' tripwires.'

'Yeah.' Max nodded. 'We'll just have to make sure we lie convincingly. He gets so much as a *hint* of the truth and you're done. We can't have that.'

'Let's focus on the positive.' Joe frowned. 'This is gonna involve a lotta paper – reports, lists, photographs. We can't keep it in the office.'

'I've thought of that.' Max grinned. '*Mi casa.*'

'You got the space?' Joe looked back through the window at the untidiness that was Max's living room.

'I got plenty of room,' Max said. 'We'll use here as a base.'

'Dunno,' Joe said. 'Wouldn't put it past Burns to break in here, bug the place, knowwhumsayin'? Why don't we rent us somewhere? My cousin knows a couple of places we can use.'

'You gotta point. Let's do that. Other thing is, we're gonna have to fund this all ourselves. I wanna put my informant, Drake, on this, find out what he knows. He don't come cheap. I got some cash put away. You?'

'Some,' Joe said.

'Then there's time. We do this right, it'll mean doin' double shifts.'

'I know that.'

'Your old lady gonna be all right with that?'

'If she ain't, I ain't . . . with the right girl. She'll be cool. She already knows how it is.'

'We'll start on this next Tuesday, after the news conference,' Max said. 'Which end you wanna bite on?'

'I'll look into missing person reports and multiple murders of families.'

'OK. I'll do the tarot cards and deal with the lab. How soon can you get our base camp set up?'

'I'll call my cousin tonight, soon as he gets home. He should be able to hook us up with somewhere in the next twenty-four.'

'OK. We're on.'

They shook hands.

'How's about that brew now?' Joe asked.

After Joe had gone, Max poured himself a shotglass of Jim Beam and sunk it in one. He took *Bad Girls* off the turntable and put it back in its sleeve. He went to the room where he kept his records. It was supposed to be an extra bedroom, but three of the walls had floor-to-ceiling shelves with over two thousand albums lined up in alphabetical order on them.

There were more on the floor too – wooden crates of LPs, and 12- and 7-inch singles. He'd won half his collection at a SAW auction. It had originally belonged to a drug dealer called Lovell the Lodger, who'd doubled as a DJ. The rest he'd bought himself, or confiscated during busts and kept, if they were rare.

He took out Miles Davis' *Sketches of Spain* and put it on. He flopped down on his brown leather couch. The deep-rooted melancholia of Miles' trumpet pierced him to the edge of his soul and made him feel suddenly very alone and empty, as close to vulnerable as he could be.

He closed his eyes. Quickly he fell asleep.

He awoke four hours later feeling a little refreshed. It was dark and hot and the room smelled of rain. The storm had broken in his absence, but there was still more to come.

He stepped back out onto the balcony. The Drive's pink sidewalks were wet but quickly drying. It was full of people, babe-in-the-woods tourists looking to get skinned, lowlifes looking to give or get cheap thrills. On either side of him he heard the usual barrage of Spanish songs and shouting.

Max took a shower, shaved and brushed his teeth. He dressed in a pale blue shirt, black chinos and leather slip-ons and went out.

25

La Miel was and always had been Max's favourite spot in Miami clubland. It was located in the Airport Hilton on Blue Lagoon Drive. There was no better place for meeting women you'd never see again, because half the club's clientele were travellers on overnight transit, specifically foreign-airline stewardesses. He didn't have to bullshit them about what he did. In fact it was an asset in the pick-up game: once they heard he was a cop, they channelled their *Starsky & Hutch* fantasies and got all starstruck and tongue-tied, and from there it'd be a shortcut from club to hotel room.

Though Max had been going to clubs since 1968, he couldn't really dance for shit – his main moves being either a cracked mirror to what he saw men around him doing, or a sole to sole shuffle that had more in common with defensive boxing footwork than groovy gesticulation. He'd presided over the rise of disco, the 'Theme from Shaft' giving way to quarter-hour long epics with four/four beats, easy to follow bass patterns and empty, innuendo-laden lyrics. He'd loved it and he'd loved discos. They'd been a great racial melting pot – whites, blacks and Latinos coming together for the single purpose of having a good time, everyone getting along, Dr King's dream in platforms, satin, sequins and on lots and lots of cocaine; and it had never been easier to meet black chicks, which was his main reason for going to so many, so often. Then *Saturday Night Fever* had come out and killed it. After that all you ever saw were random assholes in white suits and black shirts aping Travolta, while the women unfailingly wore red dresses and talked in phoney New York accents. He'd been glad when the backlash had kicked in, with the 'Disco Sucks' campaign and the blowing up of a small mountain of records on Disco Demolition Night: it had cleared the air and the wannabe Tony Maneros had fucked off to Kiss and REO Speedwagon concerts, denying their past dalliance like Peter before the cock crew.

When he arrived, just after eleven, the club seemed strangely empty. The DJ was spinning the kind of salsified disco tune that was becoming all the rage in the city, but there were wide-open spaces on the dance floor and most of the people were standing on the fringes, looking on, barely moving.

Max got himself a beer from the bar. The music was too loud and the song was making him uncomfortable, nauseous almost. The bassy beat made the fluid in his guts slosh around, the squealing brass grated against his eardrums, and an adenoidal girl singer was belting out a two-word lyric – *Vamos! Danza!* – over and over and over in a shriek both pained and painful. Suddenly this wasn't music any more, but an endurance test in patience and tolerance, and he crashed at the first hurdle.

He lit a cigarette and checked out the women, but it was too dark to tell the shapes apart. Torture-by-saldisco segued into son-of-torture-by-saldisco. The crowd was still thicker at the edges of the dance floor, the vibe in the place curiously dead, frowns instead of smiles, stillness instead of motion. He began thinking that coming here hadn't been such a good idea and wondered whether it was worth driving to his second favourite spot, O Miami in Miami Springs. He dismissed it as a trek too far and walked over to the dance floor, to see what was keeping the people at bay.

At first he thought it was some kind of competition, or maybe a 'couples only' segment of the night. There were maybe two dozen people getting down to the God-awful shit coming out of the speakers. Nothing special about them at an initial glance, except for the fact they could all dance quite superbly, their movements at one with the musical squall, not a dip or turn out of time. You always got this at discos, the Cinderella effect transforming the drab into deities, deities to dust. But the longer he watched them, the more he realized what was happening: they were all dancing in the same way, and the dances were an incredibly complex mix of dazzling footwork patterns and unpredictable turn sequences. It all seemed pre-arranged, pre-planned and exclusive. To participate you not only had to know the moves, but know the dancers too. The couples were in a loose, tight circle, but were all interacting with each other, the merest look or hand signal announcing a switch in the pattern: perfect physical telepathy. And nearly everyone around them watched in defeated awe, as if suffering from a collective loss of confidence in their own hipster abilities. A few men and a few more women were trying to copy the steps, but they couldn't keep time with the music, or were too uncoordinated to fuse feet and upper body, or simply glanced at the new masters of the dance floor and realized they'd never ever get it right.

Max moved around, beer in one hand, cigarette in the other, trying to find women as bored and pissed off as he was, but their attention was undivided, to the point that the two times he tried to strike up conversations, he was completely ignored, frozen out at the first monosyllable.

He finished his beer and went back to the bar. He didn't want another, but he bought one anyway, hoping the music would change and normality would resume.

Unfortunately torture-by-saldisco had come with her whole fucking family, and after forty more minutes the scene had become so unbearable he began to long for some locked-in-a-timewarp dickheads to stride in in cheap white polyester suits and force the DJ to play the Bee Gees at gunpoint.

At around midnight he left. He'd had three beers and a shot of bourbon and didn't feel remotely drunk. Things had moved on and he was living out his yesterdays. He wished he'd stayed at home.

Driving back he realized he was hungry and didn't have any food at home. He drove to Cordova's on South West 7th Street, in Little Havana. It was a fast-ish food place with wooden tables outside.

He got himself a plate of picadillo – spicy minced beef with raisins, olives, onions and garlic – on white rice, with a side of fried plantain and a can of Colt 45.

While he was eating, an orange Honda Civic parked next to his Mustang and a woman got out and came towards the restaurant. Latina, about his height, slim but with broad shoulders. She had long curly black hair down past her shoulders, copper-coloured skin, gold hoop earrings, black jeans and a denim blouse tied over an inch of bare waist. He noticed they were wearing the same colours, only she wore hers better.

She sat down a few tables away from him. When the waiter came over she waved away the menu and ordered in Spanish. He hadn't touched his food since he'd seen her, not even chewed what he had in his mouth. She sensed him looking at her and turned around to meet his stare. She had big round brown eyes, long dark eyebrows, high cheekbones, a wide mouth with large lips protruding in a natural pout. Then she looked away. She was just about the most beautiful woman he'd seen since he could remember, and that was saying something because Miami was filled with them.

Max weighed up his options. He could try and talk to her, but he was in such a shitty mood she'd probably pick up on it, and he didn't think rejection the best way to round off a lousy evening. So he carried on eating, looking straight ahead of him. Her face stayed in his mind's eye like a retinal imprint of the sun, taking its long sweet time to fade. He read her license plate and unconsciously memorized it. She was local. The car was a '75 or '76 Civic, reliable not flash.

When the waiter came back with her order, he stole a quick glance at her to see what she was having – a Cuban sandwich with a Diet Coke.

He thought about talking to her again. They were the only people outside. But before he could make his mind up the rain suddenly came down. A handful of huge drops scattered across the table and on his plate and then the sky opened up and spilled a tidal wave.

Max grabbed his beer and ran for the restaurant entrance. The girl was already there, standing under the awning, eating her sandwich.

'Hi,' Max said.

'Hello,' she returned. Formal and distanced. Close up and in the light she was even more of a knockout. He told himself not to gawp and looked back ahead of him, where the rain was pounding the tables. He saw his paper plate floating away fast.

'There goes my dinner,' Max said. She didn't reply, biting into the sandwich.

He waited until she'd finished chewing and swallowing before speaking again.

'Heavy rain, huh?'

'Sure is,' she said.

'Did you have a good night?' he asked

'It was short. A friend of mine's getting married this Saturday, but I couldn't stay out too long 'cause I got work tomorrow,' she replied. She was holding his stare. There was a seriousness about her under all the beauty. He detected a slight hint of Spanish in her accent which was otherwise pure Dixie.

'What is it you do?' he asked.

'I'm an accountant.'

'Downtown?'

'That's right.'

'What firm you with?'

'Why?' she asked, frowning, but there was a curiosity in her tone, tinged with amusement.

'I work around downtown too.' Max shrugged. 'I might know it.' He took a pull on his beer.

'Should you be drinking and driving, Detective?' she asked, surprising him.

'That obvious, huh?'

'Clear as if you'd switched a sign over your head saying "poh-lice".' She smiled and wiped her mouth with a napkin.

'This is my first and only,' he lied. 'I'm under the limit, I'm off-duty and it's Detective *Sergeant* to you.' He smiled and winked at her. 'We're kinda touchy 'bout rank.'

'Sorry, Detective *Sergeant*,' she said with jokey sarcasm.

'I'll let you off with a warning.'

She finished eating her sandwich.

The rain hadn't let up at all, still pounding down. The water levels around the tables were rising.

'You local?' he asked.

'Yeah, I live real close to here,' she said. 'Kinda wish I hadn't stopped now.'

'I'm kinda glad you did,' Max said, without thinking, regretting it as he realized how sleazy it sounded. He saw the smile start to leave her face and did his best to mop up the slime. 'I mean I wouldn'a had no one to talk to out here.'

'Right,' she said and looked out towards her car. The rain was coming down so fast and thick it was hard to see more than a few feet ahead. A nearby drain was overflowing, bubbling up at the opening like an overactive tarpool.

'So, your folks, they what? Cuban?'

'My mom's Cuban-Dominican, my dad's black.'

'Nice mix,' Max said. 'You speak Spanish at home?'

'I don't live with my parents any more. But yeah, when I was growing up it was Spanish in the house and English everywhere else. My dad learned to speak Spanish so he could talk my mom into dating him.'

'He musta been real serious about her,' Max said.

'He still is.' She smiled.

'So they still together?'

'Yeah.' She nodded.

'That's nice. How long they been married?'

'You ask a lot of questions.'

'What do you expect? I'm a cop.'

'You're off-duty.'

'I'll be a cop again in a few hours.'

She laughed. She had a small gap between her front teeth.

'My parents have been married thirty-four years,' she said.

'Wow.' He'd placed her at her mid to late twenties. She was probably slightly older. 'You got any brothers and sisters?'

'Three brothers, one sister.'

'Five of you? You the eldest?'

'No, third down. I've got two big brothers. My sister's the youngest.'

'Guess you're a tight family?'

'Yeah, we're real close,' she said.

Max took his cigarettes out of his breast pocket and offered her one. She shook her head with a disapproving look. He lit up, but was careful not to breathe the smoke anywhere in her direction.

They were quiet for a while, both looking out ahead of them. She crossed her arms. He noticed her black alligator-skin handbag and the fact that she was wearing heels, which would make her a few inches shorter than him.

'You still haven't told me where you work,' Max said.

'Bellotte-Peters,' she answered.

'You're right, I don't know it.'

'We're corporate accountants. As far as I know we don't break the law.'

'We're not just there for that, you know,' Max said.

'You don't look like the sort that gets cats outta trees.'

Max laughed aloud. 'I don't look that bad.'

'I dunno ... They say you're not supposed to judge a book by its cover, but you look like you'd use that book on someone.'

'If I had your attitude I'd be lockin' up everybody whose face I didn't like.'

She laughed, looked at him very directly and smiled. His heart beat faster.

'I'm Max, by the way.' He held out his hand.

'Sandra.' She shook his hand quite firmly. She was right handed and wore a ring on her middle and fourth fingers, and another on her left thumb. Her wedding finger was bare.

'Pleased to meet you, Sandra. You got another name goes with Sandra?'

'Your folks stop at Max?'

He laughed again. He was starting to really like her, but to despair a little too. She was as smart as she was beautiful. Everything going all the way right for her. She wouldn't want him. Anyway, she was probably living with some nice guy, with a nice job, who she was hoping to marry someday and live in a nice house in a nice part of town with some nice beautiful kids – everything he couldn't give her.

'It's Mingus', he said.

'*Mingus?* Like Charlie Mingus, the jazz guy?'

'Yup.' He nodded. 'We ain't related though.'

'I can see *that*,' she said.

'My dad changed his name just after I was born. He was a musician, played double bass in a few local bands. He loved Charlie Mingus so much he took his name.'

'What was it originally?'

'MacCassey,' Max said. 'It's Scots-Irish.'

'Max MacCassey. It's gotta nice ring to it.'

'I prefer Mingus.'

'Your parents still together?'

'No. Not since for ever,' Max said. 'My dad split when I was young. He was on the road a lot anyway, so I didn't really see that much of him. Haven't seen him in twenty years. Dunno where he is.'

'That's sad . . .'

'I guess, but, you know, happened way too long ago to get upset about it.'

'What about your mom?'

'We ain't too close,' Max said. 'She moved outta Miami. Went back to Louisiana. Talk once in a blue moon.'

'You married?' she asked.

'Wouldn't be here if I was,' he answered. She smiled at that.

The rain had stopped a good few minutes ago. There was a huge puddle about an inch deep in front of them. She'd be going soon. It was now or never. He opened his wallet and took out one of his cards with his direct line on it.

'Say, seein' as we both work downtown, you wanna meet up for lunch sometime? Or maybe just stand someplace and watch the rain again?' He held out his card.

She took it and looked at it. 'Miami Task Force,' she read out. 'I've heard of that. Aren't you guys supposed to be supercops?'

'Supposed to be.' Max chuckled. 'You got a card? Or a number?'

'They don't like us getting personal calls in the office.'

'OK.' Max couldn't keep the disappointment from showing. She'd probably liked his company enough to let him down easy.

'But they don't mind us making them, as long as we're quick. So why don't I call you next week?'

'Sure!' Max said, a little too keenly for his own comfort. But what the hell? She hadn't said, 'No, my nice boyfriend with a nice job and nice prospects wouldn't like it,' had she?

She took off her shoes and rolled up the cuffs of her trousers. She wore sky-blue nail varnish on her toes.

'So long, Detective – sorry, Detective *Sergeant* Mingus.' She held out her hand.

'Call me Max,' he said, shaking it. 'And call me. Please.'

She smiled and tiptoed out into the puddle. He watched her go. He tried not to disrespect her by checking out her ass, but he couldn't help himself.

'*Qué culo magnifico!*' The waiter sighed quietly next to him, under his breath, translating Max's uppermost thoughts into the little Spanish he knew.

'*Hey!* Watch your manners, fuckhead!' Max snapped at him. He doused his cigarette in the beer can and tossed it to the waiter before wading out through the puddle in his shoes.

Sandra waved at him just before pulling out into the road. He waved back and then stayed where he was until her tail lights had disappeared. He had a huge smile on his face.

26

Carmine didn't immediately recognize Risquée when he saw her waiting for him outside the shop. She wasn't wearing her street clothes. She was dressed in blue denim dungarees, white sneakers and a white T-shirt; her hair was tied back and she was carrying a rucksack. Maybe she was splitting town as soon as he gave her the 50 Gs he had in his trunk. He hoped so.

He wasn't going to kill her. Sure, he'd considered it as a cheaper option, but, when it came down to it, he couldn't see himself doing it. Murder wasn't him.

He parked three blocks down from the store. He wasn't gonna give her the money here. He was gonna walk up to her, take her for a drive, sweet talk her like he'd done the first time he'd seen her; he'd apologize from the bottom of his heart for leavin' her in jail and betrayin' her and then try and get a guarantee from her that she wouldn't say nothin' to his mother. He'd make her see sense, see his way. He knew he could. Plus he even had another 25 Gs in the glove compartment as a token of his appreciation. No way could that bitch resist the combination of green and his smooth charms. They never could. Everyone had their price.

It was dark in the road, with the only light coming from the few passing cars that were around and the one street lamp that hadn't got shot out by kids.

Carmine started walking up slowly, getting his words straight.

'Hey, baby,' he'd say. 'Sorry I kept you waitin'. Traffic was a bit—' No, not 'bitch'; couldn't use no pimpspeak.

'Traffic was hell.' That's what he'd say. 'Traffic was hell.'

'Hey, baby,' a man's voice behind her made Risquée turn around. It wasn't Carmine.

She couldn't quite make him out. He was close by, walking up to her from the right side of the street.

'You waitin' on someone, suga?' the man asked, voice all deep, comin' from inside his stomach like he was imitating Barry White.

'You talkin' to me, mistah?'

'Sure am. Ain't no one else out here on this night.' The man got closer. He had a kind of bounce in his voice, like he was finding shit funny.

'Zzamatta-o-fak I *am* waitin' on someone – *suga*,' she said, putting plenty of boot in her tone, so he knew she wasn't interested. 'An' I *don't* need no company while I'm doin' it.'

He was close enough to see now. Tall and slim, short-sleeved black shirt and loose slacks, a hint of gold in his mouth, gold chain, shiny gators, aftershave – damn, if it wasn't Ole fuckin' Spice! Her pops used to put that shit on his dick after he'd been fuckin' around, so's her moms wouldn't smell another pussy on him. Another no-good dumbass.

'*Whooooh!* Ain't you the feisty one, huh?' The man laughed.

There was something off about him, the way he was standing real close to her.

'Yeah, I'm feisty as fuck, you mess wit' me,' she snarled. 'An' you a *inch* from catchin' that shit! Now, I'm a waitin' on someone and it ain't yo' ass, so why don't you take a long walk outta mah face, OK?'

'Oh, I'm sorry, *mam* – I do apologize,' he said with exaggerated politeness, but then turned pure nasty, 'but I thought you was some cheap ho' lookin' to make a quick five.'

'Oh, I'm sorry, *sah*,' Risquée snapped back sarcastically. 'I remine you o' yo' momma? Or is it yo' daddy like to dress up in women panties?'

He hit her in the mouth. She felt metal in the punch. Brass knuckles.

She staggered back into the shop door. She was dazed, head spinning, blood pouring down her throat and out of her mouth.

She felt the man reach through the fog and grab her arm. He started dragging her up the street, in the direction he'd come.

Her rucksack was gone.

Carmine saw it all. At first he'd thought the brother was a john or some guy out tryin' his luck, but then it occurred to him that only trouble or an idiot walked these streets at night, and, right at the instant he hit her, Carmine realized the man was someone Sam had sent.

Fuck that bitch, had been his first and only thought as he'd quickly turned around and started walking back to his car, more relieved that Risquée was *really* being dealt with for good, than he was mad at Sam for disobeying him. Hell, Sam had only wanted to look after his best interests anyway, so –

Behind him, he heard a scream – a man's scream.

He turned around to see what had happened, but couldn't see shit 'cause it was too far away.

The man was yellin', '*You bitch! You bitch! You fuckin' daid!*'

Then, behind him, an engine started and, as he turned back around, headlights came on full beam and blinded him.

Only her mouth hurt. Her head cleared in seconds.

Ole Spice was dragging her up the road to where his car was parked and the passenger door was open.

243

That fuckin' piece-of-shit-pussy-cocksucker-lowlife Kahmyne had set her the fuck up! She shoulda known. She juss didn't think he had the nutsacks to get her smoked.

She could smell those cheap shit aftershave fumes comin' offa Ole Spice, and stale sweat too. Lazy nigga probably didn't shower regularly.

He had her by her left arm.

She was right handed.

She reached into her pocket and took out the switchblade she kept there, in case of bad tricks. It had a six-inch razor-sharp stainless-steel blade.

Ole Spice stopped when he heard it pop open.

Dumbass ... Dinn think to frisk me, didja? But who's complainin', fukka?

She swung quick and hard and stuck him in the gut. The blade pierced his flesh and ruptured soft tissue. He screamed. She dragged the blade down her like she was pulling on a lever.

He screeched in an unmanly way, reminded her of a little girl getting spooked on a ghost train.

His warm blood pissed out all over her hand and splashed on the ground.

She pulled out the knife; he fell heavily to his knees.

'You fuckin' bitch!' he said, quietly, in astonishment, 'you fuckin' *stabbed* me!'

'No shit, fukka!' she yelled and kicked him in the face. He fell back with a grunt.

Risquée ran up the street, fast as her legs could carry her. She had a great pair of pins on her, sprinter's legs, or so she'd been told. Amount of runnin' away she'd had to do all her life had developed 'em juss right.

She heard Ole Spice yellin' his ass off. Then he shot at her. *Pop-pop-pop.* She ran faster.

Two cars were coming up the road.

Pop-pop-pop again.

She heard glass breaking and the first car suddenly swerved sharply and skidded, crashing into Ole Spice's ride.

She ran even faster, just kept on going, faster and faster, oblivious to her busted-up mouth, and the sounds of more gunfire.

Carmine's ride was stolen right from under his nose. He'd left the top down and the keys in. Didn't think he was going to be gone for more than a few seconds. Little fuckers had probaby been watchin' him from the minute he stopped in the street. They'd jumped in when his back was turned and reversed so fast the tyres had squealed. Then they'd spun around and torn off down the street, as hell had broken loose behind them.

First some shots, then a car had swerved off the road and smashed slap-bang-boom into the hitman's ride. Then there'd been more shots – automatic fire, coming from another car – rat-tat-tat-tat-tattatat – loud – sounded like an assault rifle. Bullets had smashed into the vehicles and started ricocheting everywhere.

Who was shooting at who and why, Carmine didn't know or care because he'd started running the opposite way, running for what was left of his dear, precious, sad-ass life.

27

9.30 p.m. Eldon Burns had a home to go to. His day was done. He was going to go to his gated house in Hialeah, kiss Lexi hello, kiss Vanessa and Leanne, if they were still in, have himself a good hot bath and then kick back with some beers and watch some old fight films in his basement den. Friday nights were his alone, Saturdays he met up with the Cutmen, and Sundays he spent with his family, especially Leanne, the youngest, brightest and sweetest of his daughters. He hated to admit it and did his best not to show it, but she was his favourite. He had high hopes for her – an Ivy League college, then an internship with a congressman in DC, possibly Strom Thurmond, who the Turd Fairy knew very well.

He got in his dark blue Buick Skylark sedan. Leather seats, dark wood panelling, 2.8 litre engine, gold wire wheels, smooth transmission, plenty of room inside, like being in your own private club; an all over class ride. He also drove a Cadillac Eldorado, but that wasn't as practical for me day to day as this baby.

He got onto Flagler. Traffic was fluid.

He popped a cassette tape into the car stereo. It was an advance copy of Sinatra's new album, *She Shot Me Down*, which wasn't due out in the stores for another few months. He'd got it straight from Frank's management, where he had good contacts. He loved Frank, always listened to him on a Friday. It was great end-of-week music.

As Eldon took US1, he decided the album was pretty good for late-period stuff, possibly even the best thing he'd done since *September of My Years*. He wasn't trying to be

246

relevant or appeal to hippies and moptops, and he wasn't doing none of that *Star Wars* bullshit he'd tried on *Trilogy*. No, this was Frank at his best, back in some bar on his lonesome, loaded on Jack Daniels and thinking about how Ava Gardner had dumped him for a bullfighter. The years were showing in Frank's voice, but the material he was singing suited him perfectly. It was a nice album you could kick back to. Lexi might even like it, if he could stop her from playing Kenny Rogers for just a second.

He noticed the black Mercedes which had been behind him since he'd left the car park wasn't exactly shy about the fact that it was tailing him. He wondered if he should do something now or later. He smiled to himself. He had a .357 Magnum in the glove compartment and a .38 under the seat. He preferred revolvers over automatics. They never jammed.

When he reached Hialeah, Eldon pulled over and parked in a well-lit residential street close to his house.

The Mercedes stopped behind him and killed its lights.

'Whaddaya want?' Eldon said, finally looking in the rear-view mirror at the passenger who'd been riding with him the whole way. He could only see the side of his forehead.

'The most powerful man in town shouldn't be leaving his car door open.'

'I didn't,' Eldon said. 'Whaddaya want?'

'Two of your finest are investigating me.'

'Who?'

'I don't have the names. One's black, one's white.'

'How d'you know this?'

'I just do.'

'This more of your voodoo shit, Boukman? The spirit of King Kong materialize in your living room or somethin'?' Eldon laughed.

'You'll never understand,' Solomon said. The leather squeaked as he moved slightly in the seat.

'I'd "understand" if you gave me a name or two.'

'Look into it.'

'You heard of "please", or don't that word exist in Haiti?'

'Look into it – *please*,' Solomon said. No sarcasm in his tone. No emotion. No nothing. Usual flat, dull, personality-free voice. 'We don't want any problems, not with the construction about to start.'

'There's no problems I don't see comin' a month before they show up,' Eldon said. '*I'm* your future, remember? So you got nothin' to worry about, s'long as you remember who's in charge.'

'Long as I remember my place, you mean?'

'Don't gimme that civil rights shit!' Eldon laughed. 'You ain't a nigra, Boukman. You're *Haitian*. Martin Luther King did *not* die for you.'

Solomon didn't answer. He shifted closer to the door on the passenger side.

'Why are you sweatin' this anyway? No one knows what you look like, right? You probably forgotten yourself, way I bin hearin' things. How many operations you had to your face?'

'You remember what I look like, Eldon. You never forget a face, right?' Solomon opened the door and got out of the car.

Eldon watched him walk off to the Mercedes, which had pulled back away from the street light and into the dark. The car then reversed up the road, did a three-point turn and headed back to Miami.

Weirdly, Eldon had the feeling someone was still in the car with him. He switched on the light and looked behind him. There was no one there, but Boukman had left something on the seat, his signature, his calling card: the King of Swords.

Their troubles weren't over. There'd be more killing.

PART FOUR
June 1981

28

'Tarot cards are used in the art of divination, commonly known as fortune telling. They've been around since the fifteenth century, and are thought to have originated in Italy, although fortune telling itself is older than the Bible. The books of Leviticus and Deuteronomy rail against fortune tellers. And in Chronicles, one of the reasons King Saul dies is because he asked a medium for help. You could even say it's the oldest faith,' Phyllis Cole explained to Max in a room at the Tuttle Motel on Collins Avenue, where she taught card-reading and palmistry classes on Thursday nights. She was a professional psychic who also helped cops with their investigations. Max had never used psychics himself, but it was a common, if not publicized practice, especially in missing persons cases. Phyllis had a good reputation: she'd found several people, although they'd all turned up dead.

'There are seventy-eight cards in a tarot deck. They're divided into two groups – Major Arcana and Minor Arcana,' she continued, laying out four on the table. 'There are twenty-two Major Arcana cards; they signify life's prime forces, things over which we have no control – twists of fate, acts of God, the intangibles, the imponderables. They're results too. You're probably familiar with some of them, on account of seeing them on TV or movies – Death, the Devil and the Lovers. None of these are meant to be taken literally. Take a look at the design. What do you see?'

She passed the Death card over to Max, who was sitting opposite her at a table at the end of the room. He saw a giant grinning skeleton in black armour riding a white horse. The horse was trampling over a body. In front of it stood a cardinal in his mitre and robes, hands clasped together in prayer and supplication, while two children knelt beside him, one looking up at the skeleton, the other looking away in fear.

'Oh, I know, I know,' she said before he stated the obvious. 'Looks like a scene of devastation, doesn't it? But look to the right of the picture, behind the horse's head.'

'A rising sun,' Max said.

'Exactly.' She nodded. 'A rising sun. A new day. After the end, a new beginning, a fresh start; change, regeneration. That's what the card symbolizes – one door closing, another opening. And if you look at the rest of the background, you'll see a waterfall, symbolizing the constant flow of life.'

'And tears too, right?' Max said.

'See? You're learning.' Phyllis smiled warmly. She was a short, large, but not unattractive, woman who wore her hair in an almost militaristic afro, cropped close around the back and sides, but higher and pointed on top. It shouldn't have suited her, but it did.

She put the cards away and picked out eight new ones from the deck, laying them face up so Max could see them.

'This is the Minor Arcana, which closely resemble traditional poker cards. There are four suits – Swords, Cups, Pentacles or Coins and Wands or Batons. Playing cards are also used in fortune telling, and when they are, Spades are taken to mean Swords, Hearts are Cups, Clubs are Pentacles and Diamonds are Wands.

'Like playing cards, the number suits run from an Ace to a Ten. Swords represent aggression and drive, as well as pain and suffering; Cups are the emotions; Pentacles symbolize money and all that goes with or without it; Wands mean ideas and creativity, as well as communication.

'Now, the main difference is in the court cards, of which there are four in tarot – King, Queen, Knight and Page – as opposed to just three. The court cards represent people, seniority usually reflecting their age. Except for the Queen. She can be any age.'

One of the cards Phyllis had put out was the King of Swords – a scowling man in robes, sitting on an ornate stone throne, holding a huge sword in his left hand. His right hand was clenched into a fist. Around him, in the background, much smaller than him, were three trees and low-lying clouds. Max understood the card represented someone who dominated with aggression, but – peering closer at the King's wary sideways glance – also someone who was always looking over his shoulder to make sure nothing was sneaking up on him from behind.

'So Swords are bad cards to get?' Max asked.

'Yes and no. It depends where they turn up in a reading. The Ace of Swords, for example, turning up in the middle of good positive cards can mean a heroic triumph over adversity. But the Three of Swords means heartbreak, and the Eight, Nine, and Ten are all bad news.'

Max considered the King of Swords a lot more closely. What was it doing in two people's stomach? Was it a sign, a message, a calling card or part of a potion?

'Now, do you want to know how these work?'

'Please,' Max said.

'Would you like me to read for you?'

'No thanks, mam.'

'You don't believe in it?'

'Not really, no. No disrespect meant or anything.'

'None taken.' She shuffled the cards overhand, but considered him curiously, like she'd noticed something new about him. Max sensed a gentle pleasant warmth behind his neck, close to the nape, as if he was being massaged.

'Tarot readings can be like confessionals. Do you go to church?'

'Sometimes,' Max admitted, 'but not for the religion.'

She frowned.

'I go there to think things through occasionally, when I need peace and quiet.'

'To reflect but not to pray?'

'Yeah.' Max nodded. 'Something like that.'

'To help solve your cases?'

'The difficult ones, sometimes, yeah.'

'And do you solve them?'

'As a matter of fact, when I'm there I find I'll remember things I missed.'

'But do you think it's God shining his light in those dark corners of your mind, wiping away the dust?'

'I really couldn't tell you.'

'You didn't say "no", Detective, which is interesting. It's a short step between the church and what I do, you know.' Phyllis smiled. 'It's all part of the same path ... But anyway, I respect your wishes. We'll do a hypothetical reading.'

She put on her glasses and picked out ten cards. She arranged two in the middle of the table, one crossing the other, then she quickly placed one above and one below the cross, then one card on either side of it. The last four tarots she laid down to her right, vertically, one over the other.

She circled her hand above the group of tarots on the left. 'This first set of cards represents the present, and these' – she moved her finger up and down over the upright line on the right – 'going up, represent the future. Now, let's break it down.

'The two crossed cards in the middle represent the petitioner – that's the person you're reading for.'

The Knight of Swords, riding a white horse, charging into battle, sword aloft, face frozen in aggression, was crossed by the Two of Cups, a young man and woman, each holding a golden chalice, reaching out to touch one another's fingers.

'Typical boy meets girl scenario, from a male's perspective,' Phyllis said. 'The card behind them, the Six of Wands, represents the recent past, what's brought them to this point: news, communication, a letter, a phone call. The one above them, the Queen of Cups, represents what the petitioner hopes for the most. In this case, the Queen of Cups is the woman of his dreams. The card below, the Three of Swords, is what the petitioner's worried about – a broken heart. And the last card in this section, the one in front, is the Three of Cups and shows the present moving into the future. It may be a celebration. A happy time.

'When you read them, you read them in the order you placed them. Tell me what you see, Detective.'

Max studied the cards, which she'd laid out so that they faced him.

'The Knight of Swords is an aggressive young guy. Like a younger version of the King of Swords, always going to war. He meets this girl he thinks is everything he isn't, and that maybe she's better than him, so he's afraid of getting his heart broken if he goes after her. They've been in touch with each other though' – he pointed to the Six of Wands and then moved to the Three of Cups – 'and they've made a date to go to – a party?'

'Very good.' Phyllis clapped. 'You're a natural.'

Max thought it wasn't exactly brain surgery, but he smiled at Phyllis instead of speaking his mind. Then he thought of Sandra, who he'd met twice for lunch close to her workplace in the past two weeks and studied the cards more closely. The Six of Wands – half a dozen branches seemingly falling through the sky – reminded him of rain.

He looked at Phyllis again and got a knowing smile from her.

'You understood that the cards tell a story. Most people, when they start out as readers, take it one card at a time. Not you. You got a girl in your life?'

'Not really, no. Why? D'you see one for me?' he asked

her. The times he'd met Sandra had been brief, but he'd sworn she'd been a bit warmer to him when they'd first met than these last two times. Their lunches – sandwiches and coffee in Avi's Diner on Flagler – had almost been formal, the talk small and polite, her attitude aloof and distant. Yet it was she who'd made all the moves. She'd called him up both times and fixed the where and when. He'd gone there all excited, like the teenage geek who's bagged the best-looking cheerleader in his school, yet he'd come away uncertain as to whether she felt anything for him beyond curiosity. It was an odd position he found himself in, vulnerable and open to hurt in a way he hadn't been since his youth.

'I thought you didn't want a reading,' Phyllis replied, putting away the cards.

'Guess not,' Max said. 'So, how many different kinds of tarot cards are there?'

'All kinds. The one we used here is the Rider-Waite deck, probably the most common and popular, on account of its simplicity, but there are literally hundreds of designs. You can get the ones with Native American Indians, crows, cats, dogs, vampires, comic-book superheroes, old movie stars, baseball players – you name it. They're all based on the Rider-Waite system. There are some exceptions though. Have you heard of Aleister Crowley?'

'Yeah. The devil worshipper, right?'

'That's him. He designed a deck called the Thoth Tarot. It incorporates a lot of Egyptian symbolism in the designs. Then there's also the Golden Dawn Tarot, the Tree of Life Tarot and the Cosmic Tarot, each with a variation in the way they're interpreted.'

Max pulled out three black and white morgue photographs of the card taken from Preval Lacour's stomach, the scraps fitted together to make a whole.

'Seen this one?' Max handed her the photographs.

Phyllis studied them for just a second.

'My God! That's from a de Villeneuve deck!' She was almost breathless. 'Where did you find this? And why's it been cut up like that?'

'It was found in someone's stomach.'

'Someone *ate* this?'

'Ate, swallowed, force fed. We're not sure yet.'

'These are very rare cards. Very exclusive. *Very* expensive.'

'How much do they go for?'

'Five grand a deck, the last I heard, and that was a few years ago. They're not easily available. They're only printed once a year in Switzerland. And they're made to order. Cash upfront.'

'What's so special about them – apart from the price? Why's the face missing'

'All the faces are missing. That's one of their unique qualities. Not just anyone can use them. Only certain people.'

'Like who?'

'People with . . . a very special gift.'

'Can you use them?'

'I wouldn't go near them,' Phyllis said.

'Why not?'

'Did you ever hear of someone called Kathleen Reveaux?'

'No.'

'She was a well-known card reader, quite famous even. She'd been on TV a few times, accurately predicted Nixon's downfall, defeat in Vietnam, the attempt on Ford's life. I knew her very well. She bought a de Villeneuve deck at an auction in New York. She tried using the cards and the images on them *turned hostile.*'

'What do you mean?'

'She said she saw monsters, great beasts with blood-red eyes and white fangs. I told her to burn the cards immediately. But she had a wilful, stubborn side and she persisted with them.'

257

Phyllis stopped talking and tears began to gather in her eyes. She took off her glasses and dabbed at her eyes with a handkerchief.

'What happened to her? If you want to tell me,' Max said.

'She took her life. She threw herself off the Freedom Tower. You must have heard about it?'

'Was that in '78?'

Phyllis whispered, 'Yes.'

'Yeah, I heard about her,' Max said. He remembered the incident, but not well. It was deemed a spectacular suicide, given the location, but a suicide nonetheless. A deranged woman who'd died alone. It made a change from the two most common kinds of death in Miami at the time – cocaine cowboys killing each other and everyone in-between, and South Beach retirees checking out of God's waiting room – but those were the only things about Kathleen Reveaux's death that had registered. He hadn't even known her name until now.

'I spoke to her a few days before,' Phyllis said. 'Kathleen told me the cards were speaking to her, compelling her to . . . to kill herself.'

'She heard voices?' Max asked.

'Just like psychotics do, I know.'

'What kind of voices?'

'Actually it was just the one voice. A man's voice. She said he had a French accent. And every day the voice got louder and louder, until I presume it was all she could hear and all she could listen to.'

She broke off and stared out of the window into the darkness outside.

'Who was this de Villeneuve?' Max asked, bringing her gaze and attention back to the photographs on the table.

'A lot of rumour and conjecture surrounds him,' Phyllis began. 'What is known for sure is that he was a painter in the court of the eighteenth-century French king, Louis XVI. He made a good living painting flattering portraits of the nobility. He was a favourite of Marie-Antoinette, Louis' wife. Some claimed he was also her lover. But there was another side to him. He was a reputed devil worshipper, and – unlike Crowley – he was said to be the real deal, capable of summoning Lucifer himself from the depths.

'The story went that Lucifer granted him the power to change his appearance. He could become whoever he wanted, male or female. He had the power to walk through any wall and open any door. He made a lot of use of this to further his position and influence in court, taking on the appearance of husbands, wives and mistresses, hearing every dirty little secret in the realm, which he passed on to Marie-Antoinette.

'But, as with all pacts, there was a downside, a price to pay. Every month de Villeneuve had to make a human sacrifice to retain his powers. Young women – young girls, actually, because the Devil would only accept virgins. He killed several society women, some say up to ten or twelve before he was caught. The bodies would be found with their throats cut ear to ear, and there'd be a brand over their hearts – a long upright, medieval sword, very similar to the one in the card. The hearts would be missing, although no one knew how because the only injuries the victims had were to their necks.'

'How d'he get caught?' Max asked.

'Well, one day, the king decided to honour de Villeneuve by exhibiting his favourite paintings of himself and his cronies. The portraits were hung in the Grand Trianon – an outbuilding in the Palace of Versailles. Hundreds of guests were invited. They wined, dined and danced in the main palace ballroom and then Louis led them over to see the portraits. There they got the shock of their lives. Instead of seeing portraits of the monarch and themselves, they saw what looked to be a hundred variations of the same painting: a naked young girl, sitting in a chair with her feet in a bucket and her hands tied behind her back. A man in black robes was standing behind her with a raised sword. And all around them, in a circle stood these very tall men with dead-white faces.

'No one knew how the paintings got in there, or what had happened to the original portraits. Then one of the nobles recognized the girl in one of the paintings as his murdered daughter. And then another nobleman saw *his* child in another of the paintings.

'They arrested de Villeneuve and put him in the Bastille, but he escaped. That was in 1785. In 1789 the French monarchy was overthrown and de Villeneuve resurfaced, this time in Haiti.

'Haiti was then a French slave colony. No one knows how, but de Villeneuve had become a wealthy plantation owner; coffee and cane were his main trade. He owned over a hundred African slaves, although, for the times, he was enlightened. He treated them well and gave them a kind of freedom. He paid them and even built a village for them away from his estate. Of course, there was a reason for this. At night, the slaves practised their religion.'

'Voodoo?' Max suggested, mentioning one of the four things he knew about Haiti, outside of Papa and Baby Doc, and the fact that the island was a hundred miles away from Miami.

'No. De Villeneuve's slaves practised black magic, a series of rituals revolving around human sacrifice and the conjuring up of evil spirits. The high priest of the slave village was a man called Boukman. He was said to have all kinds of supernatural powers, including the ability to see far into the future. He used playing cards in his divination.

'De Villeneuve used to attend the ceremonies, both as participant and painter. He and Boukman were good friends, as well as followers of the same master. De Villeneuve designed a set of cards for Boukman to use.'

'And that's the origin of the famous five-grand deck?' Max asked.

'Yes. But it's said that it wasn't really de Villeneuve who was the cards' creator, but Lucifer himself. All the cards are said to bear his signature in the lower left-hand corner: a falling star, symbolizing his fall from grace. And the cards are only really meant to be used by those who follow him, or who are at least familiar with his ways. I can't verify this because I've only seen the cards in photographs, and those weren't close-ups.'

They both studied the card in the morgue pictures, but all four corners were eroded.

'What happened to de Villeneuve?'

'He lived in Haiti until 1805, when once again he disappeared. This time for good. No one knows what happened to him.

'As for Boukman, in 1791 he led the first slave uprising against the colonial masters – a very bloody and violent campaign. De Villeneuve and his property were of course untouched. Although Boukman was eventually captured and executed by the French, the rebellion continued and became a sophisticated military campaign led by Toussaint L'Ouverture. Haiti declared its independence in 1804.

'De Villeneuve is known to have fathered many many children by slave women, including several with Boukman's sister, by whom he had six – all twins. Many of his descendants are still in Haiti and Switzerland, of course, where they produce the cards every October, which was the month they were originally created.'

'So this King of Swords card. What do you think it was doing in someone's stomach?'

'What did the person do?' Phyllis asked.

Max told her about Lacour.

'It sounds like he was possessed and under a spell, to do something like that,' Phyllis said. 'Just like Kathleen was, God rest her soul.'

Max checked his watch. It was past 9 p.m.

He asked Phyllis for the names of shops where they sold tarot cards. She told him she had a list of suppliers and distributors in her files and went out to make him a copy.

She came back with three sheets of paper. He thanked her for her time and help. She walked him outside.

When they were shaking hands and saying goodbye, Max saw her expression change from pleasant to fearful.

'I know you don't yet believe, Detective, but I have to tell you to be very careful,' she said gravely. 'You're heading out on a dark road. It's going to be *very* dangerous – not just for you, but those close to you, people you care about the most.'

'Where does it end, the road?' Max asked.

'It's not where, it's *how*,' she said, looking at him with concern one final time.

'Could you be any more specific?'

She shook her head and walked quickly away, back into the motel.

29

Early the next morning, Max drove to Miami-Dade PD headquarters and went to the library. He looked up microfiche articles on Kathleen Reveaux's suicide. It had made the front page of the *Herald* on Thursday 11 May 1978. She'd jumped from the top of the Freedom Tower in the early hours of Wednesday morning. There were no witnesses. The body had been discovered by construction workers.

The following day the story had been bumped down to a third-page column: Reveaux was identified, and her family and friends were quoted as saying she'd become increasingly disturbed since her return from a trip to New York the previous month.

By Friday 26 May, another column, again on the third page, said the police had ruled out foul play and were marking her death as a suicide. The report mentioned that 'numerous occult objects' had been found in her house on South Miami Avenue, before going on to describe her career as a celebrity fortune teller.

Max then went down to Records.

Kathleen Reveaux's file was thin: incident report, coroner's report, witness statements (two) and twenty photographs.

A Detective Billue had caught the case. His report stated that, based on the damage to the victim's body – head, legs and arms all fractured in multiple places – the victim had fallen from a considerable height, estimated to be the upper floors of the Freedom Tower.

The victim was wearing blue Levi's, a white blouse, white socks and one Adidas tennis shoe on her left foot. Recovered near the scene was the right tennis shoe. Screwed up in her hand was a tarot card: the King of Swords.

Max made a photocopy of the file and took the elevator down to evidence to see if they'd kept anything from the case. All personal effects in suicides were usually destroyed if the next of kin didn't claim them.

There was nothing, but Kathleen's sister had signed for her belongings – her bloodstained clothes and shoes, and the tarot card.

Her address was in Gainesville.

Max called her up and made an appointment to go by her house that evening.

30

Joe sat back on the busted up couch and stretched out his long legs as he finished up reading through the NYPD witness reports on the Wong family murders. He was in the disused garage behind North West 9th Street in Overtown, which he and Max were using as their base. His cousin Deshaun had hooked them up with it for fifty bucks a month. Apart from the couch, a wall of empty metal shelves, a refrigerator, their three boxes of paperwork, a blackboard and a corkboard, the place was empty. Max and Joe went there once a day, sometimes together, but more often individually, before the beginning or at the end of their shifts. They never talked about the case at MTF. Any calls they made were on outside payphones.

The place could have been much better – light came from a single bulb hanging off a flex, and the power supply was temperamental, going off for minutes at a time; plus there was no ventilation, so it was always stifling hot, and the stench of old oil made Joe's head hurt and his clothes stink like a mechanic's overalls. But it was on a deserted side road, and was one of a dozen identical-looking, brown metal-shuttered garages with rusted padlocks, completely anonymous.

Joe liked it here, doing *real* police work instead of framing patsies. He and Max had spent all of the past week putting together an imaginary case against Philip Frino, an Australian dope runner who brought Colombian cartel coke in on a small fleet of cigarette boats. Frino had a place in the Bahamas. The idea was to link Grossfeld to him and then him to Carlos Lehder's middle management. It was something they could've done in ten minutes, but Sixdeep wanted the whole thing carefully documented, a paper trail that would stand up in court, so he'd pulled them both off their eight ongoing investigations and made them go at Moyez full time; so far they'd put Frino under surveillance and photographed him meeting numerous people. Joe was glad he was in on the joke.

This was his third time going through the Wong file, making sure he hadn't missed anything. The NYPD officers had been diligent and conscientious, interviewing damn near everyone who lived on the street. Several witnesses had reported a dark blue Ford transit van with New Jersey plates parked across the road from the Wong house, and three people had described the same man hanging around on the kerb by the Ford – tall, fat and wearing a black bowler hat. The van hadn't been recovered. They'd run the plates, but they'd turned out to be fake.

The candy wrapper had been dusted for prints, but nothing had come up. It was the same with the one found at the Lacour house.

Joe put the file away and got himself a Coke from the fridge. He turned his attentions to the twelve-page computer printout of missing persons reported in Miami between June 1980 and May 1981. Forty-six names per page, 552 in total.

He scanned the printout for families living at the same address. *Nada*.

He scanned it again for matching family names. It was laborious, because the list wasn't in alphabetical order. Twice the light went out and he lost his place and had to start again.

He persevered. He sweated through his shirt.

He got to the twelfth page and swore he'd missed something.

He went back to the beginning.

Spanish names dominated, then English. The French and Jewish ones stood out.

Nothing matched.

He did it by address.

Nine pages in, he hit the jackpot.

Madeleine Cajuste, 3121 North East 56th Street, Lemon City; reported missing: 30 April.

Sauveur Kenscoff, 3121 North East 56th Street, Lemon City; reported missing: 30 April.

That was it. Two people living in the same house had disappeared just before the Moyez shooting. It was too late to check it out now; he'd go the next morning.

Joe wrote it down on the blackboard, which they'd divided in two, Joe on the right, Max on the left. That way they kept track of their current and upcoming tasks, as well as any leads they'd generated.

Max had written that he was currently talking to tarot card sellers and distributors. So far nothing. The de Villeneuve family in Switzerland had refused to divulge their list of buyers, saying they prided themselves on their secrecy and considered their clients an extension of the family. Some family, thought Joe, who'd heard all about their history from Max.

At the bottom of the board, in capitals, Max had written: 'DEVIL WORSHIPPERS/BLACK MAGIC?'

Max had been to Bridget Reveaux's house in Gainesville and photographed her late sister's tarot card. He'd blown up his picture to A3 size and tacked it to the corkboard. Every detail was visible, including the supposed mark of the Devil in the bottom left-hand corner – an inverted five-pointed star with an elongated tip, which, to Joe, looked more like a badly drawn plummeting eagle.

Joe didn't buy into any of that hocus-pocus bullshit, but the card sure freaked him out. The King of Sword's may have had a blank face, but it didn't feel that way. The thing had some kind of presence – and a human presence at that. It was like having someone in there with him. Even with the lights off. He wanted to turn the fucking thing around, but that was a pussy thing to do. It wasn't even a card, but a *picture* of a card.

Fuck it! He turned the damn thing around.

After he was done, Joe locked up the garage and went to his car, parked close to the Dorsey house.

When he was a kid his granddaddy used to take him by there and point it out to him. It was a fine two-storey wooden gingerbread house, with tall trees in the back yard and red rose bushes in the front. D. A. Dorsey was Miami's first black millionaire. He'd made his fortune in real estate and done a lot of good for Overtown, including, among other things, helping build the Mount Zion Baptists church. Joe's granddaddy told him that every black man should aspire to being a little like D. A. Dorsey – help yourself first and then, when your pockets are full, give some of it back to the people around you.

The house had long since fallen into disrepair and neglect. The front entrance and all the windows were boarded up, the white paint was greying, bubbling, cracked and peeling. In some places it had been replaced with gang graffiti.

A bunch of kids were hanging around on the sidewalk outside it, smoking and drinking liquor out of bottles in brown bags. They eyed Joe up, immediately made him for a cop and one by one started to disperse, shuffling off slowly, a dip in their walks, left arms swinging lower than the right.

'Yeah, go on, walk off,' Joe muttered under his breath. They didn't know shit about where they'd been standing.

He looked up at the sad old house, dirt under the slats, smashed roof tiles in the grass. There should've been a statue of Dorsey in Overtown, but the city wouldn't spring for that and who'd come see it anyway? Nobody came to Overtown any more unless they lived here, had a score to settle or a crime to commit. It hadn't always been that way, but it sure was now.

Overtown was one of the oldest neighbourhoods in Miami. In the 1930s it had been called Colouredtown, and its entertainment district, known as the Strip or the Great Black Way on North West 2nd Avenue had almost rivalled Harlem's, right down to the Lyric Theatre, Miami's very own version of the Apollo, where all the greats had played. His granddaddy had talked about seeing Nat King Cole, Cab Colloway, Lady Day, Josephine Baker and many others at the Lyric. The area had been home to the Cola Nip Bottling Company, as well as dozens of hotels, grocery stores, barbershops, markets and nightclubs. It had been a happening place, and a happy, prosperous one too – or as happy and prosperous as black people were allowed to get in the Jim Crow era.

Ironically, Overtown had started dying when segregation laws were repealed. There was a slow exodus of businesses and talent as people relocated to other parts of town. Then the powers that be had driven a stake right into its heart by building the I-95 Expressway right through it, which devastated the already struggling community. Now the place was barely there and easy to miss; somewhere people literally drove over on their way downtown or to get their kicks at the beach.

Joe felt angry as he pulled out and got on the road. Angry at the city, angry at the world he lived in, and mostly angry at himself for burying his emotions behind his badge and uniform. He'd looked the other way and stayed quiet when he should have been pointing his finger and screaming his head off. He'd played the white man's game for the sake of his bullshit career and lost. Stevie Wonder could've seen *that* coming. He couldn't help but feel that he was being punished for the way he'd done things – and for the million things he hadn't done. He'd let his people down. He'd watched them take beatings and humiliations they didn't deserve, and he hadn't lifted a finger or raised his voice in protest. He'd lied for racist cops who would've done exactly the same thing to him, if he hadn't been a uniform. He could've taken a stand and done the right thing, but he hadn't because he'd thought he needed his job more than his soul and his pension more than his peace of mind. He thought of his granddaddy again, trying to instil those good values in him as he'd held his hand in front of the Dorsey house. He'd failed him.

And even now, with what he was doing in that garage – who was he fooling? Max, that was who he was fooling. His best friend – shit, his only damn friend. The guy had always been a straight arrow as far as he was concerned, always looked out for him, no matter how unpopular it made him. Max just didn't care. Joe was his friend and you didn't bail out on a friend, no matter what.

Max was helping him because he thought this was about getting some proper justice and to see Joe go out in a blaze of glory. But it wasn't really. It was about Sixdeep, about bringing him down.

With Max's help, Joe was going to build the *real* Moyez case, uncover the people behind it and hand every detail over to Grace Strasburg at the *Herald*. She was a good reporter, one of the few who didn't think Sixdeep walked on water. He'd do it the day he officially left MTF. It would be his parting shot, his farewell and by the way fuck you to Sixdeep.

It would mean the end of his and Max's careers. Max would come out of it worse – both betrayed and betrayer – and Joe felt genuinely bad about that, but Sixdeep had to be stopped, and that made the ends justify the means.

31

Madeleine Cajuste lived on a stretch of North East 56th Street cops called 'Shantytown Central', because all the houses there looked like they'd been sucked up by a Third World hurricane and dumped on the nearest available strip of Miami wasteland.

The houses stood on bricks or breezeblocks, just like gutted cars, and were made up of five pieces of wood so thin that if you stamped your foot in anger it went through the floor. The roofs were slim sheets of corrugated iron, which split in heavy rain, buckled and ripped open in the heat, or blew off in the wind. Many had clear-plastic sheeting instead of glass for windows. They were hard to tell apart because their colours, although not the same or even similar, all seemed to blend together into a universal shade of pallid grey, like the tone of an overcast day.

The Cajuste house stood out. It was painted pale yellow. There was glass in the windows, which were protected – as was the door – by thick steel bars, painted pea green. It told Joe that Madeleine was doing better than her neighbours.

The illusion was somewhat shattered when he reached through the bars and knocked on the window and made the whole structure shake.

No one answered. He knocked again. Rivulets of dry dirt poured off the ridges in the roof and ran down onto the ground, building up in little mounds. The curtains were drawn. He saw coloured lights glowing on and off in the room to the left of the door.

Outside the house next door, a Rottweiler started barking furiously at him from where it was tethered by a studded collar and chain to a hunk of cement, lunging at him impotently from its spot, half choking itself every time. From behind the flimsy steel fence separating them, Joe flipped the beast the finger and went round the back of the house.

He was surprised to find freshly laid grass there instead of dirt. A child's swing and a paddling pool with a rubber Donald Duck were there too. The water was filthy and smelled rank. Mosquitoes were hovering over it. Madeleine Cajuste wasn't home and hadn't been for a while: someone this house proud – even if that house was a cereal box turned on its side – wouldn't have left that pool out in that state.

There were bars on the back door and windows too. Just to be sure, he knocked again on the windows.

He went to the house next door. The dog snarled and drooled as he approached.

A woman's voice asked him who he was when he knocked on her door. This house was sturdier, but the windows were made out of greaseproof paper.

'Police, mam. It's about your neighbour,' Joe said, holding up his badge.

The door opened a crack. A tiny, very dark-skinned woman with a wild shock of unkempt snow-white hair and white bushy eyebrows peered out and looked him up and down.

'You comin' by *now*? I made that call a month ago. Why ain't nobody come see me?' Her voice was a croak buried so deep in her throat it barely made it into her mouth.

'I don't know, mam, but I'm here now. Is Madeleine Cajuste your neighbour?'

'Thass right. An' I ain' sin her since Easter, juss like I tole the lady police on the tele-fone.'

The Rottweiler was still barking, and there was more barking and growling coming from inside the house – a whole chorus-load. There must have been over half a dozen dogs in there with her. Joe briefly thought about their welfare and the old lady's, but he wasn't here for that and let the thought blow off his conscience.

The old woman stepped out the door and pulled it to behind her as she stood on one of the tiered breezeblocks that made up the makeshift steps to the entrance of her home. She was barefoot and wearing a lavender nightdress down to her ankles. The fabric was so thin and faded it was almost transparent. Joe could see she was naked underneath and wanted to wrap his suit jacket around her to give her back some dignity, but she didn't seem to mind the state she was in, so he let that one go too.

'You made the call on 30 April, right?' Joe said, speaking louder to make himself heard over the dog. The woman looked at it fiercely and clicked her fingers. The dog quieted immediately.

'Thass right. I use ta see her ev'ry day out there, playin' wit' dat baby.'

'She had a child?'

'Not hers. She tole me it belonged to that man she had livin' with her.'

'What was the man's name?'

'Sauveur. She said his name was Sauveur. Means "Saviour" in Hayshun. They's from Haydee, you know, them people.'

'So they weren't married?'

'She callt him her man. Dinn say nuttin' 'bout no marriage.'

'When d'you last see them all together?'

'On a Sunday. In the mo'nin'. I think they was goin' to church.'

'Why?'

'They was dresst up all fine an' dandy. Like what you do when you goin' to church. You go to church?'

'Me? Yeah, sure I do. Every Sunday, mam.' Joe smiled. 'What church did they go to?'

'I dunno. Fact, I ain't sure they went to church, zactly. You know, they's from Haydee. They still eatin' folks out there, what I heard.'

'Did she have the baby with her, when they went out that day you told me about?' Joe asked, trying not to laugh at what the old woman had just said.

'I think so. I didn't look too good though, you know. She wood'na left home without him.'

'Was the baby a boy or a girl?'

'Lil' boy. Sweet thang. Smiled a lot at me – *and* my dogs.'

'Was there anyone else with them when they left?'

'Juss the man drivin' the car.'

'What car?'

'A shiny black one. Fancy and long, kinda like you see at a funeral.'

'What did the driver look like?'

'I dinn' see no dryva. See, I guess't there were a man there cause they's all get in the back. Ain't no car can drive itself – yet.'

'Did you notice anyone coming to the house afterwards?'

'Except you, no. Why it take you so long to come anyway? A whole month done gone by from since I callt.'

'We're pretty busy, mam,' Joe said. 'I apologize.'

'You think somethin' bad happened to her, right? Else you wouldn't be here.'

'I hope not, mam. This is a routine visit. Miss Cajuste might've moved. Did they have any visitors? People who came by regularly?'

'No. But Madlayne's brother used to live wit her for a lil' time.'

'Her brother? What was his name?'

'John or Gene, somethin' like that.'

'What did he look like?'

'I never sin him. Just heard he was there, what she tole me.'

'When did he leave?'

'A long time back. I ain't sure when. One year. Longer. I dunno. He was good to her though. She tole me he sent her money regular. How she get them bars on the house, and that green grass there.'

'You ever see a man with a hat hanging around the house?'

'Near *every* man arown here wear a hat, 'cept you.'

'Tall guy, maybe my height. Fat.'

She shook her head and the thick white explosion she had for hair swayed like ghost wheat in a field.

'Did Madeleine mention any other relatives she had here in Miami?'

'Said somethin' 'bout a cousin over in Liberty. Went by the name o' Neptune,' she said.

'Neptune? Was that it? Anyone else?'

'Not that I can think of.'

'Well, thanks, mam, you've been mighty helpful.' Joe closed the notebook he'd been scribbling in. 'You did the right thing calling us.'

'You coulda got here sooner.'

'I wish we had,' Joe said. 'You have a nice day now.'

Back in his car he went through the missing person's list, running his finger down first names, looking for Neptune.

He found it.

Neptune Perrault, 29 Baldwin Gardens, North West 75th Street, Liberty City; reported missing: 27 April.

Baldwin Gardens was a project building. In Miami they built them way lower than in other cities, on account of the weather, but the principle was exactly the same: officially, affordable housing for the poor with great views thrown in; unofficially, concrete pens to crowd the minorities in like sardines. Meant for four to five people, the tiny apartments

275

housed anywhere up to twice or often three times that number.

Joe took the stairs to the fourth floor, breaking into a sweat as he went up. The building reeked of piss, garbage, alcohol and too much humanity crammed into too small a space.

Neptune Perrault's corridor was dark, hot and wet. Joe heard TVs and radios bleeding through the thin doors, as well as conversations and arguments, most of them in a foreign tongue he recognized as Haitian Kreyol, a hybrid of French and West African.

There was no answer when he knocked at No. 29. He tried the apartment next door. Same thing.

Someone stuck his head out of a door at the end of the corridor.

'Police, do you know . . . ?'

The head went back in.

He tried the next apartment along.

A young girl opened the door wide and stared up at him. She had wet cereal on her face and her hair in braids. She couldn't have been older than eight.

'Hello, sweetie. Are your mummy and daddy home? It's the police.'

A man shuffled up behind her, red-eyed, half awake, a pair of orange Bermuda shorts barely clinging to his skinny pelvis, golfball for a navel. He had an old man's face, craggy, lined and droopy, but an anorexic teenager's body, bone breaking through skin, zero fat.

'Morning, sir. Police.' Joe held up his badge. 'You speak English?'

The man nodded silently.

'Do you know a Neptune Perrault? Apartment twenty-nine?'

The man nodded again.

'Have you seen him today?'

276

The man shook his head,

'What about yesterday? Or recently?'

Another negative shake of the head.

'When was the last time you saw him?'

'April,' the man said with a cough.

'Beginning, middle, end?'

'End.'

'End?'

'That's what I said,' the man replied. He had an island accent – one of the smaller ones, Trinidad or Barbados.

'How can you be sure?'

'I just am.' He shrugged, like Joe was stupid.

'Where d'you see him?'

'Outside Emmanuel's – barbershop across the road. He was getting in a car. He worked at Emmanuel's.'

'What kinda car?'

'Black limousine.'

'Was he well dressed?'

'Better than normal, sure. He was in a suit.'

'Did you talk to him?'

'No.'

'Were you friends?'

'He was a friendly person.'

'But were you *friends*? Did you like him?'

'He was OK. I didn't really know him too well, you know.'

Joe looked at him hard and then looked past him into what he could see of his home. Curtains drawn, several kids in the background crowding around a doorway to see what was happening.

'Did Neptune live with anyone?'

'Sure. Crystal. His girl.' He smiled lazily. Island Man liked her – probably why he hadn't been friends with Neptune, Joe reasoned: jealousy. Joe even went as far as to guess that Neptune might have warned Island Man off his woman.

'Tell me about this Crystal – she got a last name?'

'Never asked her that.'

'What she look like?'

He smiled again. Yellow, tobacco-stained teeth. 'Pretty lady,' he said. 'Built, you know.'

'Pretty lady, built. Very descriptive.' Joe stepped up to him. 'Height?'

'About mine. She was *big* down below. I *like* that.'

'Was she Haitian?' Joe asked, realizing that if he asked the man to describe her face he'd get a cell by cell fotofit of ebony booty. Exactly the way Max described three-quarters of his conquests and crushes.

'No. I think she said she was Dominican. Spoke Spanish only.'

'They have any kids?'

'Just them.'

'Visitors?'

'A few all-night parties.'

'You go?'

'No.'

'Ever see a tall fat guy with a hat around here?'

'No.' He shook his head.

'What's your name?'

'Why?'

'Just asking.'

'Arthur Jones.'

'How long you lived here, Arthur?'

'Two years this May past.'

'What about Neptune?'

'The same. We move in about the same time.'

'Was he friendly with anyone else around here?'

'Whole project knew him, mon. He cut everyone hair.'

'He cut yours?'

'No.'

'Why not?'

Arthur Jones smiled again.

'You fuck her?' Joe asked.

'Every night. In my dreams,' Jones said.

Emmanuel Polk was wiping down one of the three chairs in his barbershop when Joe walked in and introduced himself.

'Yeah, Neptune worked here,' he said. 'I was the guy made the call when he didn't show up for work on the Monday. In the eighteen months he worked for me, he was *always* early and *always* stayed late to help me clean 'n' close. Like they say, "a model employee".'

'Any police come by?'

'Sure.' He read from a card wedged into the mirror frame opposite the chair he was cleaning. 'Detective Matt Brinkley.'

'Right.' Joe nodded, not surprised they'd sent the worst guy in Missing Persons into Liberty City. Brinkley couldn't find snow in Alaska if it was pointed out to him. His specialty was helping old ladies cross the street.

The barbershop was small and cramped, two work stations on the right, one on the left, with a bench right next to it for waiting customers. On the wall were pictures of Kareem Abdul-Jabbar, O. J. Simpson, Jim Brown, Bernie Casey, Leon Isaac Kennedy and Carl Weathers in his Apollo Creed costume.

'When d'you last see Neptune?'

'Sunday, 26 April. Around midday. Came by to get his hair cut. Said he was goin' to some party his cousin was throwin'. I was cool with that, you know. I live just above this place and I was happy to do him a favour.'

'Was he well dressed?'

'Yeah, in a suit. Looked fly.'

'Anyone with him?'

'His girl, Crystal. Dominican. Didn't speak much English, but I know a little *español*, so we got along good. Nice girl.'

'What was her last name?'

279

'Taíno. She said it's the same name as the tribe of Indians that lived on the island when Columbus discovered it. She had that look too. Like Pochahontas, only darker.'

'What else do you remember about that day?'

'They got picked up outside-a here in a black car. A black Mercedes. Tinted windows.'

'Did anyone get out?'

'No. The passenger door opened. Neptune knew the people in there. Said hello and was laughin', all happy, like he ain't seen them people in a while.'

'He say where this party was at?'

'Somethin' 'bout Overtown. I think it was 2nd in Overtown.'

'You tell the detective this?'

'Sure. He wasn't writin' nothin' down though. He ain't called me back neither. I left six, seven messages fo' him.' Polk looked disgusted. He was a bald man of medium height, with grey chest hairs curling over the open collar of his yellow polo-necked shirt and white sparkles in his stubble.

'I'm sorry to hear that, sir,' Joe said, meaning it.

'You one of the good ones, I know, I can tell. Got your book out.' Emmanuel looked at him, paused, then frowned. 'I been cuttin' folks' hair here since '65. Seen boys grow up into men, those same men grow old. I was cuttin' hair of all the construction guys built Baldwin. You know Neptune's the best employee I ever had? He's better than *that*. I ain't hired no one else to take his place, 'cause you know, he might be back. That's where he works right there.' He pointed to the single chair on the left. 'Used to be mine, but I let him have it on account of how popular he is with everyone.'

Emmanuel stopped and looked at the space behind the chair for a long moment, as if he was seeing Neptune there. Then he caught sight of his sad face in the mirror and saw Joe studying him and snapped out of it.

'You didn't see a tall fat guy with a hat around here, did you?' Joe asked.

'No.'

Joe went over to look at Neptune's work station. There was a colour photograph propped up under the mirror. It showed five people – four women and a man in the middle – standing together, arms around each other's shoulders.

'This Neptune?' Joe asked, pointing to the man.

'That's him. See the way he smilin' there? Way he always is. I never seen him unhappy. Girl next to him?' Emmanuel pointed to a stunning, dark-skinned woman with long straight black hair. 'That's Crystal. Prolly the reason he's so happy. The woman at the end? That's his cousin Madeleine.' Madeleine Cajuste was tall and stout with glasses and a shoulder-length perm. Emmanuel pointed to the other two women – an older one in a green blouse, and, beside her, a younger girl in a dark blue Port of Miami T-shirt. 'That's Neptune's aunt – Madeleine's mamma – with Neptune's cousin. I think the aunt goes by the name of Ruth. Way he said it sounded like "root".'

'I'm gonna have to take this, if you don't mind,' Joe said. 'I'll make sure it comes back.'

'You already doin' more than the last guy was here,' Emmanuel replied.

Joe smirked.

Then Emmanuel took a couple of steps back and tilted his head a little.

'Say? You that cop been on TV? 'Bout the County Court murder?'

'Yeah, that's me.'

'You used to live round here too, right?'

'I came up here, yeah.'

'In Pork 'n' Beans?'

'I look that young?'

Emmanuel laughed. Joe slipped the photograph into his notebook.

'Neptune got somethin' to do with that courthouse thang, right?'

'I doubt it,' Joe said. 'Different case.'

'That so?' Emmanuel frowned, disbelief in his voice. 'How come you ain't IDed the shooter then?'

'I can't comment –'

'On an ongoin' investigation. Spare me the man's line, brother. I *knew* the shooter –'

'*What?*'

'OK, I didn't *know* know him, but he came by here maybe two, three times, right when Neptune started.'

'They were friends?'

'They was *cousins*. That shooter is Madeleine's older brother, Jean. Jean Assad. They had different daddies. His daddy was some kinda Ay-rab.'

'How d'you recognize him?'

'Face was clear as day on TV. I'm good with faces. Part of the trade, you know. Faces, first names, names of the kids. Everyone needs a haircut some time.'

'Did you tell the police this?'

'Sure I did. Called them right away.'

'And?'

'They said thank you very much for your information, took my name and number. When I see you comin' in I figured it was 'bout that.'

'Did you talk to Jean Assad?'

'Didn't get beyond "Hello" and "See you again". He talked to Neptune mostly. It was Neptune cut his hair.'

'Neptune talk about him much?'

'Not much. He mentioned one time that the guy was mixed up with some bad people.'

'Did he say who?'

'Haitians.'

'Any names?'

'Yeah, just the one.' Emmanuel smiled. 'Solomon some-one. I can't remember his last name. Guy had a real bad rep. Neptune was scared just talkin' 'bout him.'

'What kind of things did he say?'

'You know what a shapeshifter is?'

'Sure,' Joe said, 'that's like a person that can take on all different kinds of forms – human, animal, whatever. I've seen the movies.'

'That's what Neptune said this Solomon guy is. But you know how in Haydee they got all that voodoo they do?'

'So this guy Solomon is some kind of voodoo gangster?' Joe smiled. 'I seen that movie too. It's called *Live and Let Die*.'

'What I thought too.' Emmanuel laughed. 'I didn't say nothin' though, you know. Respect for the man's beliefs 'n' all.'

'And Jean Assad was working for this guy?'

'Yeah. I don't know what he was into zactly, but one day Neptune said Jean had just upped and left town.'

'Right,' Joe said. And then he suddenly came back and killed Moyez in the courtroom, probably after he'd killed his family.

'Anything else you remember?'

'Not offhand.'

'You think of anything, call me here.' Joe wrote down his home number in his notebook and tore out the page. 'If you get the machine, leave a message. I'll get right back to you.'

'You think Neptune's dead, don'tcha?'

'It doesn't look good,' Joe said.

32

Raquel Fajima – day-shift manager at the forensics lab – smiled broadly when she saw Max standing at her office door, miming a knock. They'd known each other for ten years and still laughed about the night they'd first met, when she was still working call-outs and Max was in uniform. A group of frat boys had blown themselves up in their car with a grenade, and Raquel and Max had had to look for ID in all the gore. Raquel had made a bunch of tasteless wisecracks while Max – still new to gruesome kinds of death – had been trying to hold on to the contents of his stomach because he didn't want to appear weak. Raquel had found a useable index finger stuck to an eight-track tape. She'd bagged the finger and, after she'd seen the tape was Deep Purple's *In Rock*, looked all around at the mess in the car and said, 'Serves you right,' which had made Max laugh so hard he'd puked anyway. She could have slipped into fairly cosy gear as lab manager, spending her time delegating, juggling and going to meetings; instead she played an active role in cases, working on samples that came in, writing them up and testifying in court.

Max and Raquel had remained friends over the years, occasionally meeting up for all-night drinking and bitching sessions, but these were few and far between now she was married and had a two-year-old son.

It was 8.15 in the morning. Raquel was drinking a cup of jasmine tea at her desk. Max could tell she hadn't been in the lab long because she wasn't wearing her white coat, her dark brown curly hair was still down to her shoulders, and she was seated. Every time he saw her he usually had to compete for her attention with the microscope she was hunched over.

They kissed each other on either cheek and Max sat on the chair opposite her desk, which was completely clear of everything bar a phone and lamp. All the shelves were full of files and thick leather-bound medical books, and there were more files on the windowsill. She had no photographs or personal items of any kind anywhere in the office. Here she was all about work. Her personal life stayed at home.

They exchanged pleasantries. Her boy was well, as was her husband. She understood he was in a hurry and cut to the chase.

'What can I do for you?'

'You know the samples you took out of the courtroom shooter's stomach? What've you isolated and IDed so far?'

'The tarot card everyone remembers.' Raquel stood up and went over to a filing cabinet and opened a drawer marked 'Ongoing'. She ran her finger along a series of hanging files, then pulled out an orange wallet folder, which she riffled through to find a list. She then stooped down to the 'Links' drawer and pulled out a grey folder.

'Some meal he had!' she quipped, sitting down and looking through it. 'Shooter's first course was a soup of Kool Aid, sand, crushed sea shell and bone – we're fairly sure it's human, that's still tbt – to be tested. Next, diced sirloin of tarot card. The card was high-quality cardboard and coated with a plastic seal, making it harder to digest. He had that with a tasty side salad of cashew leaves, bressilet – poison ivy – two kinds of stinging nettle, mandrake and a bean, also tbt. Not common. His third course consisted of a side order of choice creepy crawlies: a tbt snake, a few millipedes, tarantula legs, bouga toad and –'

'A *what* toad?'

'Bouga toad. B-O-U-G-A. Their gland secretions are toxic. Cause catatonia in large doses. Shooter's liver and kidneys contained traces of tetrodoxin. Tetrodoxin's another toxic substance commonly found in puffer fish. A large enough dose can put you in a coma or plain kill you.

'This was all in some kind of potion designed to render the person who took it incapable of controlling his own actions,' Raquel said, tapping at the grey files. 'I've seen this kinda stuff before. Look at this.' She slid over the grey file.

It was an autopsy report on a black man, aged thirty-five, who had wandered into incoming traffic on US1 on 13 February 1979. He'd been hit and killed by a Buick, which had turned over, killing the driver and his passenger. The contents of the collision victim's stomach were almost identical to those in Moyez's killer – except for the bean and the tarot card.

And then he noticed something else – the man had been registered deceased on 8 July 1977. He was called Louis-Juste Gregoire, a Haitian resident, who'd lived in Overtown. His grave was in the City of Miami Cemetery. His first death certificate stated he'd died of natural causes.

'I'm sure you've heard of zombies,' Raquel said.

'Sure.'

'Forget what you think you know – *Night of the Living Dead* and all that. In Haiti, Louisiana, certain parts of West Africa and South America they practise two kinds of voodoo. There's the traditional kind called *rada*, which is peaceful and harmless, and there's the Hollywood-movie kind – the dark variant called *petro* or *hoodoo*. This is all about worshipping evil spirits, putting death spells on people, human sacrifice, orgies. Zombies stem from *hoodoo*.

'What basically happens is a witchdoctor will administer a potion on a person either orally or topically. This paralyses them and shuts down key parts of the brain. They look clinically dead. No breathing, really weak pulse, slow heartbeat. They get buried.

'A few days later, the witchdoctor digs them up and brings

them back to life with an antidote. Except they don't fully return to the land of the living. They're very much alive, but their minds are gone. They don't recognize anyone they know: friends, family, whoever.

'You see, the potions they've been given also contain powerful hallucinogens which make the person *believe* they're dead. The zombie then becomes the witchdoctor's personal slave, doing everything their master orders.'

'Like killing someone in a courtroom?' Max asked.

'Sure. It's highly possible. A mixture of hallucinogens and hypnosis alone could turn a person into a killer. In fact, the levels of scopolamine found in the brain and blood of the shooter indicate that he was tripping when he killed Moyez.

'Scopolamine is found in mandrake, which was in his stomach. Mandrake belongs to a class of plants called "deliriants" – very powerful hallucinogens. Under their influence people have been known to talk to themselves, believing they're addressing someone else. Except that there'll be dialogue instead of monologue, because people under the influence take on the characteristics of the person they're talking to – accent, patterns of speech, you name it.'

'Like schizos?'

'Deliriants induce a kind of schizophrenia, yes, but one which comes with a propensity for violence too. I've seen people beat the shit out of themselves, thinking they're attacking an enemy. Most of the time, once the deliriant wears off, a person will have absolutely no recollection of what happened.'

'Like sleepwalkers?'

'*Exactly* like a sleepwalker,' Raquel agreed.

'How common's the stuff you found in the stomach?'

'Garden variety. Except the bean.'

'How soon can you get a result?'

'That's a piece of string question, Max. It's a full house

in the morgue today. And one of them's a cop. A DEA sting got stung on the east side. You hear about that?'

'On the way in, yeah.'

'We think he got shot by one of his own.'

'On purpose?'

'We won't know until the results are in. Cocaine's turned this city inside out and upside down.'

'Tell me about it,' Max said. 'We're in a blizzard, walking blind.' He paused, lowered his voice and leant across the desk a little, 'Raquel, I don't wanna put any pressure on you, but I really *do* need to know what that bean is.'

Raquel looked at him hard for a moment, then leant over the desk towards him and winked. 'This another of your off-the-books crusades, Max?'

'I'd appreciate your discretion, yeah.'

'I should've known when you showed up right at the start of my shift. You normally come in when I'm, you know, right in the middle of something important.'

'I know you're real busy . . .' Max began.

'Eldon know about this one?'

Max shook his head. Raquel drew breath mock-dramatically and mimicked his headshake.

'Let's keep this between us, huh?'

'Sure. What do I get out of it?'

'What can I do for you?'

'Well, what *can* you do for me, Max . . . ?'

'You still drink mojitos?'

'When I get the time.'

'Then the next time's on me. *If* you can stand my company.'

'You know attempting to bribe an officer of the law is a federal crime?'

'You started it.' Max grinned.

'Deal,' she said.

'Can you call me at home, when you get the result?'

'OK.'

'Thanks, Raquel. I appreciate it. Can I get a copy of this Haitian's file?'

Back in his apartment Max sat down at the phone and started going through his list of tarot-card stores, distributors and individual suppliers, asking if they stocked Charles de Villeneuve cards. Many of the stores and distributors hadn't heard of them, but the few that had explained they could only be obtained directly from the family. The solo operators were more helpful, offering to get him a deck and quoting him prices varying from $5,000 to $10,000. Had they ordered any for anyone recently? No, they answered.

After fifteen calls he took a break, made coffee and smoked a couple of cigarettes on his balcony. It was a sunny day with a good cool breeze undercutting the heat; he could smell the sea in the air. Unfortunately the illusion of paradise was shattered when his gaze ranged over Lummus Park below. They should have renamed it Fuckups Park.

He sat back down on his couch and looked at his call list. The next place was a shop – Haiti Mystique, the owner's name one he recognized – Sam Ismael, who'd been one of the prospective developers in the Lemon City reconstruction programme that had been awarded to Preval Lacour and Guy Martin.

Before he could pick up the receiver the phone rang.

It was Joe, calling from a payphone, sounding out of breath and harassed.

'I know who the Moyez shooter was,' he said, 'and I've just found his family. Bring the tools and lose your breakfast.'

33

It was dark and hot inside Ruth Cajuste's house. All the curtains had been pulled shut, the windows closed. The stench was intense, close to unbearable; even behind their masks and the Vicks ointment they'd rubbed under and in their noses, hints of its extremity wriggled through.

Max closed the door and Joe flicked on the light. They were wearing gloves and plastic covers on their shoes. The scene would be examined by forensics and they didn't want to leave even a hint of their presence.

They saw the first three bodies immediately: still, dark bundles lying very close together, to the right of the door. There were two more bodies about twenty feet away.

They checked the rooms: kitchen on the right, empty; two bedrooms on the left, both empty. Last there was the bathroom. The door had been kicked or bashed clean off its hinges. Another body was in a seated position on the end wall, right under a small rectangular frosted-glass window.

There was no back door. They'd checked before going in the front.

Six bodies.

They went back to the beginning and examined the house.

They were in a wide open-plan space which served as both front room and dining area, tiled pale yellow. The area around the bodies was moving, armies of black beetles scurrying and swarming to get a piece of what palatable flesh was left. This wasn't the orderly disciplined stripping and carting off they'd witnessed at the Lacour house, but a frenzied free-for-all. The beetles sensed that time was running out. The temperature in the house had accelerated the process of decomposition.

'What's the date today?' Max asked.

'Third of June.'

'These look *well* over a month old. I'd say they were killed on the twenty-sixth of April.'

The five-week-old bodies had passed the bloated stage and were liquefying from the inside. Puddles of shiny translucent slime had formed about the torsos, mingling with the halos, commas and wings of dried and now black blood that had poured out of the wounds; skin was slipping off bone and turning into grey-green mush. Each body had its own cloud of blowflies hovering right above it.

Joe named the ashen-haired woman as Ruth Cajuste, the man two feet away from her as Sauveur Kenscoff, and the girl lying face down in the red and white gingham dress, he initially mistook for Crystal Taíno, except that her hair and body type were wrong. She looked more like a teenager. He corrected her identity to Jane Doe.

Ruth Cajuste had been shot in the forehead. A writhing nest of yellowy blowfly maggots filled the hole. She was lying on her back, in the corner, hands folded across her chest. Max and Joe agreed she'd most likely been killed first, way before she could realize that her son Jean Assad had just put a bullet in her brain.

Sauveur *had* realized what was happening and had tried to fight back. There was a silver .38 Special next to his right hand, but the safety was still on. He'd had just enough time to pull his weapon before being hit in the shoulder, chest and through the left eye. That last shot had voided his cranium and splattered the contents over the wall behind him. He too was lying on his back.

The blood-wipe pattern between the edge of the door and the teenager's head told them her body had been moved post-mortem. There was an upward arc of high-velocity spatter covering the inside of the door; stray spots of blood had hit the wall above and touched the ceiling, indicating that the girl had been close to the door handle when the bullet struck the back of her head. There were shell fragments studding the wood and wall, along with pieces of bone and two teeth. She'd been shot at close range, the circle of singed hair around the entry wound suggesting the barrel had been mere inches away.

'No one heard it,' Joe said.

'Silencer – must've been,' Max suggested. It was the only explanation he could come up with. The house was in the middle of a row of one-floor homes, each about fifteen metres apart. The walls were on the thin side of functional.

Max looked around the scene. He thought he'd seen something unusual about the bodies, but he couldn't find it again.

The two other corpses in the middle of the room were those of Neptune Perrault and Crystal Taíno. Neptune's right leg was slung across both of Crystal's, his puffed-up, rotting right-hand fingers were interlocked with those of Crystal's left, and his ruptured head – shot clean through the temple – was leaning into Crystal's neck, as if he'd been nuzzling her when he'd died. Crystal was lying face down, shot through the crown.

Max stared at them a good long while, unable to take his eyes away from the sight, as touching and tender to him as it was grotesque.

'He didn't even try to get away, or resist,' he said to Joe. 'He just lay down and grabbed her hand. He couldn't live without her, but he could die with her. They deserve justice.'

'That's why it's just the two of us here, right?' Joe said, looking at Max quizzically, seeing an altogether new side to him. They'd seen far worse than this – a comparatively clean straight kill and relatively painless for the victims, no signs of torture, no dismemberment – and Max hadn't blinked out of turn. He'd studied the bodies, read the scene, come to initial conclusions. The only thing that upset him was when they found children, but that got nearly all cops. They usually got angry, some cried, some couldn't do their jobs. Max was in the first category. But how he was now was new to Joe. Max looked sad, as if he had known the victims. Joe wondered if this new girl Max had started meeting for lunch hadn't opened up his emotional side, if he wasn't a little bit in love with her. He'd been awful quiet about her, which was really unusual for him. He hadn't even told Joe her name.

There were half a dozen spent shells on the ground near the bodies. The shooter had reloaded. Joe bagged two of them and left the rest for forensics.

Up ahead of them was the bathroom, a mess of smashed tiles and blood stains everywhere. Madeleine Cajuste had been shot at least five times in the torso and once through her right hand. The bathroom door had been dead-bolted from the inside.

The window was unlocked and opened out from the side onto a view of the garden – a small strip of lawn, rose bushes and a palm tree at the end.

Max noticed small scraps of white fabric stuck to splinters at the edge of the sill. He plucked one and showed it to Joe.

'You said she had a baby? I think she dropped it out of the window. When the shooting started she ran in here, bolted the door and put the kid out of the way of the bullets. Maybe she screamed for help too. Either way, they took the baby. Let's take a look at the other rooms.'

Joe went to the kitchen. Dry dishes and cutlery on a rack by the sink, rotting and withered fruit in a large bowl on the counter. Everything in the refrigerator had gone off.

Max looked through the bedrooms. Ruth Cajuste's was nearest the bathroom. She'd slept in a double bed, with a Bible and a wind-up alarm clock at her side. The curtains were drawn. There were bars on the windows. Next door was where the teenage girl had slept. Her name was Farrah Carroll. She was fifteen. He found her Haitian passport and return-flight ticket for 5 June. In two days' time her parents would be expecting her home. By her bedside was a photograph of her, Ruth and Mickey Mouse taken at Disneyland. She had kept her room neat and tidy.

Max made for the front door.

He went and stood where he'd been when they'd first come in and scanned the scene of slaughter one more time, first casually, then body by body, trying to find what he'd missed.

The bugs were crawling up Farrah's right leg but not her left.

He looked at her feet. There was a small pile of dead beetles by her shoe. He bent down and studied the sole. There were white stains on it, absent from the other shoe.

She'd trodden in something, maybe slipped. He turned around and looked behind him.

There, that was it: a small circle a few feet away, clearly defined by the crust of dead black beetles all around it. It was a white splash with scraps of dark green matter in it, shredded leaves or herbs, and something small, shiny and dark brown, but unmistakeably part of a bean.

'I think the shooter puked here,' Max told Joe.

Joe went back to the kitchen, got a knife and spoon which Max used to scrape the dried mess into an evidence bag. Then they left the house, turning off the light as they went.

'I'll call it in from a payphone,' Max said.

'Say you heard gunshots,' Joe suggested. 'Otherwise it'll be another year before they send someone round.'

34

'You're a piece a dogshit on wheels.' Carmine sighed as he drove his new ride – a white Crown Victoria – down North West 2nd Avenue. It was a cop car, an *honest* cop's car; only kind of ride pigs could afford on the minimum wage they made outta bein' pigs. The pigs on the cocaine payola drove flashier autos: fresh-off-the-ramp sports cars and rides they'd seen in James Bond movies.

There was method to his downshifting in the style stakes, because today, and every day until he got a location on Risquée, he, Carmine Desamours, was playing at being a cop. He wasn't just driving this shitty ride, he'd changed his look too. He was wearing ugly straight-off-the-rack clothes from JCPenney – a grey sports coat, shitty black slacks that itched the inside of his thighs, a white shirt and scuffed black wing tips. He had himself an authentic-looking fake ID and a pearl-handled .38 snubnose on his hip. He was a regular Richard Rowntree motherfucker. OK, that wasn't *strictly* accurate – RR was a private dick not a cop, but he couldn't think of no black cops he wanted to be in the image of, so Shaft did him just fine.

He wasn't the only one out looking for Risquée. He'd put Clyde Beeson on her trail. Beeson said he'd tried every dentist and hospital in Florida and none of them had any record of her. Beeson said he'd asked around on the streets too. He was sure she'd disappeared; most likely left the state. It would've been the sensible thing to do, what he would've done himself if he'd almost been killed, but Carmine didn't buy it. He *knew* Risquée: when she was pissed any common sense she possessed went out her ears. And she'd be *real* pissed at him. She'd think *he'd* sent that creep who'd tried to kidnap her outside the store. If Risquée had read any of the papers, she'd know her attacker's name was Leroy Eckols, out of Atlanta, said he had 'criminal connections'. Eckols had been killed by the driver of the car he'd shot at. She'd want payback. And he didn't blame her, the way things looked.

So, he was out here, searching for her himself too.

He passed a stretch of dismal row houses and had to slow down for an ambulance that was pulling up outside one of them. Looked like a lot of death had happened there. Another ambulance was already in place, doors open, plus three prowlers and a blue version of his own ride with a red light on the hood. The front door was open and medics with masks on were stretchering out a stiff in a bodybag. There was a whole lot of commotion, as a heavy crowd of onlookers jostled for a view. Uniforms told them to stay back.

This kinda shit always happened around O Town. When he made proper money in Nevada, *no way* would he be living in the nigger towns of this world. No, he was gonna get himself a condo in a fancy high-rise block with white folks for neighbours and security at the door, kind that said 'Good morning' and 'Good evening, *sir*' and told you who your visitors were.

Today, he might've been a pretend cop, but he still had pimp business to attend to for Solomon. Apart from recruiting and breaking in new Cards, today was when he collected from the two street Suits – the Spades and the Clubs.

He turned onto North East 6th Street and saw a Spade called Frenchie getting out of a tan Olds. He waited until the car had disappeared and let her get a good stride in her step. She had on a red vest, red heels and a pair of Daisy Dukes so small and tight they squeezed her big fat wobbly ass cheeks half down her big fat wobbly thighs. She was forty or fifty, something around that – he didn't properly know because she was full of shit, always lying about the time of day – dark skin, hard face, shitty teeth, shitty reddish brown wig she either wore up or all the way down to her elephantine behind. When she was far enough into her walk, he drove up and hit the brakes hard, squealing to a stop right next to her. She scoped out the car in an instant, turned around and started heading in the opposite direction.

The look was good. She'd made him for a vice cop.

He reversed, winding down the window.

'Hey, Frenchie! Git yo' ass back here!' he called out to her.

She let out breath and smiled at him.

'Shit, Carmine, baby, I thought you was a cop,' she said, hurrying over to him. She had a jamambo pair of titties that were the only reason she ever made money.

'Just testin' yo' reflexes, baby.' Carmine gave her his nicest smile. Bitch smiled back at him. She'd always told him she liked his smile the most, said it reminded her of one of her little boys – or was she the one that had girls? – he couldn't remember and didn't give a fuck either way. 'Get yo' cute lil' ass in here.'

She got in the passenger seat and closed the door.

Lil' ass? *My* ass! thought Carmine as she took up the whole seat.

'Watcha got for me, baby girl?'

'Bidniss been slow, baby.'

Even if he hadn't seen her getting out of the Olds, he could smell cum and sweat on her.

'That right?' Carmine smiled. 'Whose car was that I saw you gettin' out of? You got a *chauffeur* now?'

She looked down at her knees, the skin on them all scarred and tough from the amount of time she spent on 'em.

'Like I said, and like I keep on sayin', I got eyes everywhere, kind see round corners, so don't try 'n' play me, baby girl, else I'll send my man Bonbon over to see you.' Carmine enjoyed the fearful look she got in her eyes at the mention of Bonbon's name. He could've used a Bonbon on his payroll to keep his private Cards in line – the likes of Risquée wouldn't've *dared* go up against him. Sam had suggested it and he'd said, nah, I'll be man enough for them bitches. He was regretting it now.

Frenchie reached down in-between her titties and handed him a thin sweaty roll of green. Thirty bucks. One fuck.

'And whatchu' got up there in yo' pussy bag?' he whispered to her.

She opened her mouth to protest, but he shut her up.

'Don't be makin' me go explorin' up in there, bitch!'

She snapped open her cut-off jeans and unclipped the small cloth bag she kept pinned on the inside, under the waistband, and gave it to him.

He took out the money. Eighty bucks. Two fucks 'n' a suck.

'Take off,' he told her, tossing the empty bag in her lap.

She didn't move. Her lower lip trembled. Damn. Bitch was gonna cry.

'What's up witchu? You heard me. Time to get busy.'

'I ain't had nothin' to eat all day but dick, baby. I need me some bread.' She sniffed.

'You need bread, huh?' Carmine looked at her. 'Then go fuck a baker. *Vamos!*'

She got out the car and he hit the gas, laughing his handsome ass off.

Shit, he was sharp as a tack too-day.

'Go fuck a baker' – ho, ho, ho!

Shit, did he just say 'ho ho ho'?

Man he was *double* sharp!

He spent the rest of the morning collecting from Cards and going to the kind of places he knew Risquée went to – nail parlours, hair salons, boutiques and a few bars she liked to drink rum and Coke in.

He did the cop thing as good as any Jack Lord or Kojak motherfucker. He'd walk in someplace, go up to someone working there, flash his badge and introduce himself as 'Officer Bentley, Miami PD'. He'd ask his questions. He'd get headshakes and, 'No, ain't seen no one like that.' It was disappointing and might have been a real unproductive way of spending a day, if it hadn't been for the vibe he got off the people he was questioning. They all kind of *wilted* when they saw his badge, got a scared look in their eye, started trembling. These cats – some of them big overgrown stone-cold niggas and bitches with monuments of attitude – were intimidated by little old him and his big shiny shield. He liked the way that felt. He felt good, powerful, running things, badass. Damned if it didn't even get his dick a little hard. Cops must've got that way too, when they started out. All that *power* over people. Hell, maybe he should've been a cop instead of a pimp. Sure, the money was shit if you played it by the book, but there were perks a-plenty in what it did for your manhood and self-esteem.

He stopped at a hair salon called Proud Heads, on North West 52nd, near Olinda Park.

Carmine walked inside. A receptionist was opposite the front door, behind her a silhouette of a black woman with a huge afro. The place was full of potentials. Damn! Great late discovery of the day *deux*: he should be fishin' in *this* pussy stream, hittin' all-a those places only women went. No way would they suspect what he was. Shit, he could even pretend to be some fag needing a manicure or his hair relaxed. Nothin' some bitches liked more than a fag for a best friend, some guy to go cry over movies and talk lipstick with. It wasn't zactly too late in the day to change up his plan. Maybe he'd do that at his dude ranch in Nevada. OK, the faggot thing bothered him a lot, but hey, business was business.

The receptionist looked up from the *Ebony* magazine she

was flipping through. Girl had a plain face, no older than nineteen. Radio was on. The Pointer Sisters singing 'Betcha Got a Chick on the Side'. He'd always liked that one.

'Good mo'nin',' he said with a smile.

'Can I help you?'

'Officer Bentley, Miami PD.' He showed her his badge. 'Lookin' for a girl mighta been here. Busted-up face. Goes by the name of Risquée.'

'Risss-*kayyy*?' the girl said. 'Kinda name's that?'

'Kinda name her momma gave her,' Carmine said. 'What name yo' momma give you?'

The girl turned around and yelled out over the hairdryers, radio and general chit-chat in the salon.

'Janet! Poh-lice here to see you.'

Everything stopped a beat in the salon – even the radio, it seemed, though it was still playing – and Carmine felt all eyes turn his way.

He got an uneasy feeling deep in his gut, but he tightened his jaw and stared back at the chicks.

A woman came out from the end, drying her hands. She was short, dark, worried-looking.

'This about Timothy?' she asked.

'No, this ain't about no Timothy,' Carmine said. 'This 'bout somethin' different.'

'So he's cool?'

'This ain't 'bout Timothy. I'm here on different bidniss.'

She frowned and looked at him in a new way that made him uneasy, like she was trying to work out something about him.

'What *bizzz*-ness?' She pronounced it slowly and carefully, taking Carmine in from his shoes to his hair. Bitch musta been one of them mommas beat their kids over table manners and shit. No wonder Timothy was givin' her problems. Those who got treated the harshest rebelled the hardest, Carmine remembered sumshit he'd heard on TV or the radio or read on a wall somewhere.

'I'm lookin' for a girl mighta come in here. Had a busted-up mouth.'

'Her mouth busted-up she'd need a *dentist* not a hair-dresser.'

'Yeah, I hear that,' Carmine said. The bitch was standing there with hands on her hips. Hips were wide too. He knew tricks who liked that shit though. 'Only she mighta come by get her hair done *after* her mouth got patched up, you know? Make herself feel better.'

'You got a picture?'

'No.'

'You a *cop* lookin' for someone and you ain't got a *picture*?'

Damn! He swore this Janet knew he wasn't for real.

'What does she look like – apart from the mouth?'

'She about your height, slimmer, built.'

She scowled at him angrily now. Damn! Musta been conscious 'bout her weight too. One of them bitches ate when she had problems. He smiled, did the nice one all bitches with kids told him was sweet. Made her madder. She musta thought he was laughing at her.

This was going real wrong.

'What did you say your name was?'

'Officer Bentley.' He held out his badge. She took it from him.

'Badge says Detective.'

'Huh?'

'You ain't an Officer if you're a Detective.' She pointed at the shield.

'Oh, right, yeah, see I just got promoted. Still gettin' my head around the title.' He smiled, but he was nervous as a motherfucker, heart beating crazy voodoo all up in his chest.

'*Shaniqua?!!*' Janet hollered out over her shoulder. 'I need you up here a second.'

Gottdayum if Shaniqua wasn't a straight up Diamond. Tall, long legs, café with a little au lait in her complexion, short hair. Black jeans and a blouse tied in a knot over her bare flat middle.

Janet talked to Shaniqua in a whisper. The receptionist was listening in and kept on looking over at him, smiling more and more. Shaniqua was looking at him too, looking harder at his face.

Carmine started to sweat, hairline leaking and running to his jaw. Time to go, time to *go*, he thought, but he couldn't make himself move. Couldn't do nothing. The fuck was wrong with him. The fuck was wrong with *this*?

The receptionist looked straight at him squirming in his shitty wingtips and giggled.

'I do somethin' to make you ha ha?' he said aggressively.

The receptionist was going to answer when hotass Shaniqua spoke to him, 'You after Risquée?'

'You know where she at?'

'You know a virgin called Mary?' Shaniqua answered. She had a deep voice, close to a man's imitating a woman.

'Tell me.'

'Pay me.'

'*What?*'

'Pay me.' Shaniqua came up to him, hand out.

Damn!

'How I know we talkin' 'bout the same Risquée?'

'We are. Now pay me.'

OK, defuse. Cops paid snitches all the time.

'How much?'

'Two hundred.'

'Two *hunnret*? How 'bout I give you *one*?'

'How 'bout you kiss my black ass?'

'I know men pay good money to do just that.' Carmine smiled. She got angry. 'OK, OK. Be cool. I'll pay you.' Carmine turned his back on her and took out his roll. Peeled off four fifties, turned back and held them up folded between his fingers.

'Tell me.'

'Uh-uh.' She held her hand out, rubbing her fingers together. 'You pay to play.'

'You a slot machine?' He handed her the money, which she took and passed to the receptionist. He noticed Janet had disappeared.

He looked for her in the salon. He saw her at the end, talking to a man sitting in a chair with a towel around his shoulders.

The man looked over in his direction, took off the towel, got out of the chair and started walking up.

The man was tall and black.

The man was a cop in uniform.

Shit!

'I help you, sir?' the cop said to Carmine.

'No, I was . . .'

'Impersonatin' a police officer?' the cop said. He was holding Carmine's badge. How the fuck did he get that? Shit! He'd handed it to Janet.

'This is as phoney as a three-dollar bill. And you are under –'

Carmine noticed the cop wasn't wearing his gun belt.

The cop reached out to grab him, but Carmine took a step back and pulled out his piece. The receptionist screamed.

'ID's fake. This ain't. Now back the fuck up!' He pointed the gun at the cop's chest.

The cop didn't move.

'I *ain't* playin'!' He cocked the gun, but his hand was shaking.

'Do like he says, Timothy!' Janet pleaded behind him.

The cop moved back a step.

'Hey – *all* the way!' Carmine said. The cop didn't look scared, but the bitches did. That turned him on a little.

'Toss me that ID.'

The cop flicked it at him.

The gold glint of the badge caught his eye.

Next thing he knew the cop had grabbed his gun arm and was twisting it like he wanted to snap it.

Carmine pulled the trigger.

The cop screamed loudly and fell flat on his back. There were screams all over the salon. The bitches got down on the ground.

There was blood on the floor and a hole in the cop's foot where the bullet had hit. The sole of his shoe looked like a dripping red rose, the leather splayed and twisted in a whorl, blood was pumping out of the hole in the middle.

The cop wasn't holding his foot though; he was shaking, going into convulsions.

Carmine grabbed the ID and ran out of the salon.

35

'You want to tell me what's behind the long face?' Sandra asked Max.

'Work,' he said.

'I figured *that*. You want to tell me about it?'

Max shook his head. It was the day after he and Joe had been to Ruth Cajuste's house. He hadn't stopped thinking about the way Neptune and Crystal's fingers were inter-twined. He'd heard the paramedics had had to use a saw to separate them.

They were sitting in Dino's off Flagler, a diner with tables outside and two long rows of wide booths with crimson leather seats inside. There were pictures and posters of Dean Martin through the ages on the wall, from young drunk to old drunk, comedian to cowboy to crooner, and a working Wurlitzer jukebox filled with his records.

Sandra was eating a flaked tuna-steak sandwich on rye with fresh orange juice. Max hadn't been able to eat anything since the previous day, so he was sticking to cigarettes and coffee.

'Not even a general idea?'

'You really don't wanna know, Sandra. Trust me,' he said, nodding to her food.

She pushed her plate aside. 'What if I do?'

'I'm still not gonna tell you,' he said, but he wished he could talk to her. She looked and sounded like she wanted to know, and her big, steady, attentive eyes showed she was a natural listener; the sort who thought about what the speaker was saying instead of waiting to speak herself, the sort who never missed a thing.

'Is this the way it is with cops? Silence over dialogue?'

'I guess, some, yeah. We got a way higher than national average divorce rate in the force.'

'And you think that's an OK way to be?'

'No, but that's the way it is.'

'Pretty vacant,' she said.

'I can't argue with that.' He shrugged.

'You ever talk about your work to any of your exes?'

'No, never. I figured if I did they wouldn't wanna be around me.'

'Looks like they didn't anyway,' Sandra said.

'You're funny.' Max smiled.

'I have my moments.' She winked mischievously, which made him laugh. He was glad she'd called him earlier that morning and glad he'd come out to meet her. Even though he hadn't been in the mood for small talk and the polite pretences of fledgling courtship, this was turning into their easiest and most relaxed meeting so far. His guard was down and he was letting her take a look at him as he really was instead of throwing up diversions and detours.

Sandra was in her office clothes: a short-sleeved pale blue blouse, undone at the neck, a brown knee-length pinstriped skirt and brown high-heeled shoes with rows of small blue flowers on the sides. She wore a thin white-gold chain around her neck and small white-gold crucifix earrings. It was a conservative look, but a stylish one too, and, judging from the shoes, Max thought, one she'd tweaked to suit her more than her superiors. She was wearing very little make-up, but still looked stunning. In fact, she seemed to get more beautiful every time he saw her.

'There, see, you've lightened up. You know a person uses less muscles smiling than frowning.'

'Is that right?'

'That's what I read.'

'You read a lot?'

'Yeah, I do. I'm one of those people who, when they get

interested in something go out and find out everything there is to know about it. Do you read at all?'

'No. Well, outside police stuff and the papers, I don't get a lot of time, you know. Besides books ain't really my kind of thing, tell you the truth.'

'So, d'you follow sports?'

'I ain't a ball games kinda guy, but I keep up with boxing. I told you I used to box, right?'

'Yeah, I looked you up.'

'No shit?'

'No shit.' She smiled, and told him his entire Golden Gloves record, significant titles he'd won and the dates of his first and last fights. He was impressed.

'You like boxing?' he asked.

'Not much. But I've seen *Rocky* and *Rocky 2.*'

'That wasn't boxing, that was ballet.'

'What about *Raging Bull*? Did you see that?'

'Nah.' Max shook his head. He'd heard about it but hadn't been curious enough to check it out. 'That's the one where De Niro got himself all fat for the part, right?'

'It's a great movie. Sad and disturbing.'

'You should see a real fight,' Max said. 'They're always sad and disturbing – for the loser.'

'Would you take me to one?'

'Any time.' He smiled, realizing he had an opening, the perfect opportunity to ask her out on a proper date.

But before he could suggest anything, she looked at her watch.

'I've gotta go,' she said.

'Too bad,' Max said. 'We never give each other enough time, do we?'

She looked at him and held his stare. Some women he'd gone out with had told him they couldn't handle the look in his eyes, which they'd said, was somewhere between piercing and accusing and something like getting a light shone into their souls. He'd made them feel like they'd done something wrong. Cop's eyes, in short. Sandra didn't seem to have that problem.

'When do you finish today?'

''Bout six.'

'You got any plans for the evening?'

Sure, Max thought. Going back to the garage and talking things through with Joe – zombies, missing babies and a guy called Solomon – and asking himself where this investigation of theirs was going, and how long they could hope to keep it a secret.

'Want to get a drink? You look like you could use one,' she suggested.

'Sure,' he said.

'I know a great spot – great drinks, great food, great music.'

'Where?'

'Little Havana, real close to *mi casa*.'

L'Alegría on South West 11th Avenue was a bar-restaurant with a nightclub downstairs. Max had driven past it many times but had never gone in, hadn't even been tempted. The outside looked unprepossessing, the kind of place which probably framed its health code violations in the kitchen. But the interior proved far classier – dark wood floorboards, tables draped with spotless white tablecloths, laid out with sparkling silverware, napkins in rings and, in the middle, a blue or orange lantern.

He let Sandra do the talking and asked the kind of questions which prompted her to give long answers. She gave him the Passnotes guide to what she did. She talked about her office, about her bosses and co-workers, the different clique, and their power plays. She told him about how she was going to have to fire someone in her team soon and how she was dreading it. Max thought about Joe. Then he thought about Tanner Bradley and how he hadn't wanted to kill him. Then he chased the image away by looking over at a couple sitting, as they were, side by side at a table, holding hands, but he saw again Neptune and Crystal's final frozen clasp.

Sandra noticed the change in his face.

'Are you OK?' she asked him.

'I'm good,' he lied. 'You?'

'Do you dance?'

'Like a gringo,' he said.

'Racist!' She laughed.

They went down to the club. It was very dark and packed solid with moving bodies, everyone doing that damn Casino Dance to that damn saldisco music. Max rolled his eyes and shook his head. Sandra grabbed his hand and tried to teach him some moves, but he could barely master more than the initial steps and was drunker than he'd realized, because he quickly forgot what he was supposed to be doing and had to start all over again.

'You're right,' she yelled over the galloping bass and ear-shredding horns coming out of the speakers. 'You *do* dance like a gringo.'

Then the music slowed as the DJ spun a Spanish-language ballad which reminded him of Julio Iglesias, like every Latin crooner did. Sandra draped her arms around him and pulled him into her and they began to dance together, close, body to body, eyes locked. He felt the heat of her on his skin as they moved – her gracefully, him swaying in lugubrious time. She held him by the neck and stroked his nape and smiled. He held her loosely by the waist, telling his hands to keep off her ass. It would have been the perfect moment for a kiss, but as he started to lean towards her the DJ turned up the beat and another saldisco classic announced itself with a shriek of horns and gate-crashed their moment like a drunken relative desperate for attention.

'You wanna get out of here?' she offered.

'Please,' he said.

Sandra lived in a two-bedroom condo in the pink and blue San Roman building on South West 9th Street. It was the tidiest place Max had ever been in. She paid a cleaner to keep it that way.

They went into her living room, which was painted and carpeted in beige and smelled faintly of incense and peppermint. The right-hand wall was lined with books; atlases and encyclopedias on the top shelf, travel guides, biographies and history books on the next two down, and the rest was given over to fiction. On the other walls were a large map of Cuba and a painting of two women and some kind of upside-down fish, which Max thought so amateurish he assumed it was something she'd done in tenth grade art class.

Sandra went out to the kitchen to make coffee and told him to put on some music.

Max flicked through her albums. There was a lot of Latin music, none of which he knew, and some classical stuff, which he didn't know either, but she had Diana Ross's Chic-produced *Diana*, plus *Bad Girls*, *Innervisions*, *Songs in the Key of Life*, *Let's Get It On*, some Bill Withers and Grover Washington records, Barry White's *Greatest Hits* . . .

She came back in, carrying two white mugs on a tray. She'd changed into faded jeans and a baggy white T-shirt, which made her skin seem a shade darker.

'Probably not your kind of music, huh?' she said, setting the tray down on a table opposite the couch.

'What do you think I'm into?'

'Gringo music: Springsteen, Zeppelin, the Stones – stuff like that?'

'Nah. And don't *ever* talk to me about Brucey baby. My partner's in love with him, plays that shit all the time.

Drives me nuts. You got any Miles? *Kind of Blue, Sketches of Spain*?'

'I forgot. Your jazz genes. No, sorry, I don't. Do you think I should?'

'Everyone who likes music should have at least one Miles Davis album in their collection. Better still, ten,' Max said. 'And, seein' as you're into Grover, you should be lookin' into John Coltrane too. People say Charlie Parker was the corner stone of jazz, but nearly everyone who's ever picked up a sax from '65 onwards sounds more like 'Trane.'

He carried on looking. He found just what he wanted at the end – Al Green's *Greatest Hits*.

'This OK?' He held up the sleeve.

'The Reverend Al? Sure.'

Max went over and sat next to her on the sofa as 'Let's Stay Together' kicked in. They looked at each other for a moment and there was silence between them, not the kind of uncomfortable, embarrassing void that opens up between people who've run out of ways to hide the fact that they have nothing to say, but a natural pause in dialogue.

Max looked at the painting behind her.

'You do that at school?'

'I wish,' she said, turning around. 'It's *El Balcón* – The Balcony – by Amelia Peláez. She was an avant garde Cuban artist. She was famous in her homeland for murals.'

'Sorry,' Max said, 'I don't know too much about art.'

'It's all right. At least you don't pretend to.'

Max heard a hint of recrimination in her voice and guessed then she'd been lied to by someone close to her, maybe a boyfriend who'd cheated on her or had led her on pretending to be something he wasn't – in other words, by someone a little like him.

Although they were sitting real close on her couch in the dead of night, there was an element of the forbidding about her. He decided to hold back, be the passenger, take every-thing at her pace. He sensed that was the way she wanted things and that was fine by him.

'Do you remember all the cases you worked?' Sandra asked, putting down her cup on the table.

'Sure.' Max nodded.

'Raffaela Smalls?'

'Yeah.' He sighed. 'That poor poor kid.'

It had been in 1975. A black, twelve-year-old girl, fished out of the Miami River, naked, arms and feet bound, a bag over her head. She'd been raped and then hung.

'Don't tell me you looked all my cases up too? Same way you did my boxin'.'

'Sort of. I remember when it happened,' she said. 'I remembered your name coming up and thinking you were black on account of it.'

'It's a common misconception,' Max said.

'You never gave up on that case, did you?'

'Took two and a half years, yeah.'

'That's unusual in this city, in this state, a white cop being *that* dedicated to solving a black kid's murder.'

'I was just doin' my job. Me and Joe got handed the case. Me and Joe solved it. There's criminals, there's crime, and we're cops. We do what we do. That's all there was to it.'

'The family said how nice you were to them, how you promised to catch the guy.'

'They were decent people who'd had a child taken away. Ain't no black and white in that, Sandra. Just right and wrong. They deserved justice, and they got it.'

'Her uncle did it.'

'Piece of shit called Levi Simmons.'

'He claimed you and your partner roughed him up bad.'

'He also claimed he didn't do it.'

'He looked pretty beat up in his mugshots.'

Max didn't say anything.

'*Did* you rough him up?'

'He tried to make a move,' Max lied. 'We stopped him.'

'Innocent till proven guilty,' Sandra said.

'He was makin' a *move*,' Max insisted, looking her right in the eye, just as he had Simmons' defence lawyer in court when he'd thrown up the same accusation. 'We did what we had to do in the circumstances.' Max needed a break from examining his career history. 'Can I go and smoke on your balcony?'

'Be my guest.'

She came outside with him. The air was still warm, and a limpid breeze shook the leaves of nearby trees. She didn't have much of a view – more apartment buildings, mostly dark, directly opposite – and then Calle Ocho behind, almost deserted. It was still way quieter than Ocean Drive, where no one ever seemed to sleep if there was an argument to be had or a fight to be fought.

'You know, every day when I leave my home I know there's some poor bastard doin' the same thing, only they won't be comin' back,' Max said. 'They'll get caught in crossfire between rival posses of cocaine cowboys, or else some young kid'll roll up on 'em and blast 'em just to watch 'em fly in the air. That's the way it's gettin' around here now – thrill kills, killing for kicks and braggin' rights. And that's a family they've left behind who'll look to me for answers, who'll look to me to put things right. And that's my job. What I signed up for. Makin' things right.

'I know I ain't ever gonna make much of a difference in the grand scheme of things. I'm past that rookie idealism. Crime goes up, not down. Guns get bigger, more powerful, hold more bullets, kill more people. But in the end, if I can bring a little peace of mind to some dead person's wife or husband, if their kids can grow up knowing that the scumbag who killed their mommy or daddy's dead or in jail for life, then it's worth it. And that's what keeps me goin', no matter how jaded I sometimes get. That's what keeps me goin' every second of every day.'

She didn't say anything. She just moved a little closer to him and leant her head on his shoulder and they stood there together in silence while he finished his cigarette.

They went back inside and carried on talking. Personal stuff, trivial stuff. They joked and laughed a lot. With Sandra, Max felt happier and more relaxed and comfortable than he'd been since he could remember.

And then she asked him what had been bugging him over lunch.

He thought about it for a second, how he'd never brought his job into his private life, how he'd refused to talk about any of it with any of the women he'd been involved with. He'd kept it to himself and in the end it was all they'd left him with – the stuff that never got mentioned. He decided then that more than anything, he wanted Sandra in his life and he wanted her to stay.

'Yesterday me and Joe got a call about a multiple homicide in Overtown. Whole family had been shot. Six bodies. But there was this young couple, boyfriend and girlfriend. They were holding hands. And from the way they were, I could see the girl had got shot first and the guy had lain down right next to her and taken hold of her hand. And that's how he died.'

'He couldn't live without her,' Sandra said.

'That's what I thought too. He musta *really* loved her. Literally the love of his life. And I *also* thought –' but he stopped talking, realizing how sick the words he was about to say might sound.

'What?'

'You don't wanna know'.

'Max,' Sandra took his hand, 'we're both adults and we both know what's happening here. If we're gonna have any kind of relationship it's got to be about sharing and honesty and openness. You'll tell me about your day, I'll tell you about mine. I don't want you keeping anything from me.'

'My part's gonna be difficult, Sandra.'

'Why?'

'There's things about me you'd be best off not knowing.'

'Past stuff?'

'Yeah.' Max nodded.

'You a dirty cop?'

'I don't think I am. But I've gone through bad to get to good. Sometimes you have to in this job. Sometimes you got no choice. Well, you do. You can walk away. But I ain't the kind that walks away.'

'I figured that,' she said.

'OK.' He took a deep breath, as though he was getting ready for a high dive into a bottomless pool. 'I'll tell you what I thought when I saw that couple. I thought that coulda been you and me down there. That I woulda done the same as the guy.'

'That's a sweet thought,' she said.

'That's a *sick* thought,' he corrected her.

'It's a bit *gothic*, I agree.' She smiled. 'And you barely know me.'

'Cop's instinct,' he said.

'I thought that just worked on bad guys.'

'When I'm off-duty it works the other way.'

She laughed and put her arms around him. They hugged and then they kissed.

'You taste like an ashtray.'

'Who told you to lick 'em?'

She burst out laughing. Her laughter filled the room and drowned out the music. Her laughter made him laugh too.

When they'd recovered she leant her head against his shoulder and took his hand. They stayed there like that, staring into space together. The music stopped without them noticing.

He realized she'd dozed off. He listened to her breathing in his ear, felt her gently rise and fall against his arm. He smelled her hair and his nose filled with faint traces of perfume and coconut.

At around 4 a.m. he fell asleep himself.

36

When he woke up two hours later he heard the shower going. After she was done she made them both breakfast of *tostada* and *café con leche*, which they ate at the living-room table. Max imagined every day being like this with her.

An hour later they walked back to where they'd parked their cars on South West 8th. They'd exchanged numbers. Max wanted to see her again that same night, but he knew he couldn't because he'd lost time on the Moyez case.

Before they parted she kissed him on the lips. Like the first time, he watched her pull away before getting into his car. And like the first time, he had the same stupid smile on his face.

He had an hour or two before he was due to punch in. He thought of going over to the garage, but he needed a shower and a change of clothes and he wanted to stay in this special moment and savour it for a while longer.

As he headed down Calle Ocho he turned on the radio and got the news. A cop had been killed in Overtown the day before. Police were looking for a tall, light-skinned black man in a white Crown Victoria.

Back at his apartment, Max had just finished getting dressed when the phone rang. It was Raquel.

'That sample you gave me yesterday. We located our mystery bean.'

'Shoot,' Max said, riffling through his notepad for a clean page.

'It's a calabar bean.' She spelled it for him. 'Two uses: one good, one bad. It produces an alkaloid called physostigmine, which is used to treat glaucoma and is found in over-the-counter eyedrops.

'The bean on its own is highly toxic. It was used to expose those suspected of witchcraft, when it was commonly known as the Ordeal Bean. The person under suspicion would be forced to eat half a bean. If the person vomited, he or she was deemed to be innocent because their bodies had rejected it. If the person died then they were guilty. Most people died.

'The bean depresses the nervous system and causes muscular weakness. It slows the pulse to a crawl but increases blood pressure too.'

'How long does a person live after they've swallowed one?' Max asked.

'One, two hours at the most, depending on the person and the dose.'

Max thought about this for a moment. Lacour and Assad had killed people in different places and at different times.

'Is there an antidote?' Max asked.

'I was getting to that,' Raquel said. 'We found traces of atropine in the shooter's bladder. Atropine's an alkaloid derived from belladonna – deadly nightshade. It counteracts the effects of physostigmine. But, as it was in the bladder, I think he got the antidote some time before he stepped into that courtroom.'

'How long before?'

'Atropine takes a while for the body to completely eliminate. Again, it depends on the person. Three to six weeks.'

Max understood what had happened. After his trial run of murders in Overtown, Assad had been given atropine to keep him alive for the main event.

'I'll tell you this,' Raquel said. 'The levels of physostigmine in the shooter's liver were so high, he was basically a dead man walking before a bullet ever hit him.'

37

'Solomon? That all you got?' Trish Estevez asked Joe.

'Yeah. That's all I got. Sorry.'

'Don't apologize to me. You're the one who's gonna have to do the work.'

Trish was the Miami PD's computer database manager. She'd started out in dispatch in 1967 and then taken computer classes in the evening and gone on to become an expert in the things before they were introduced into the department in 1971, when next to no one knew how to use them. Now she had two people working for her, who she'd trained from scratch. They were transferring all the paper records to floppy disc, an arduous process which would have been easier with more manpower and machines, but the budget was minimal. The dot-matrix printer made up the heart of the computer room. It was about as long and as wide as an upright piano, and stood on two tables which had been pushed together to support it. Trish sat at a desk at the end of the room, watching over her people working at their Compaq machines, each at a desk on either side of the room, near the door, their backs to each other; their fingers hitting the keyboards the only sound. The machines they were working on – VDUs which looked like small portable black and white TVs – couldn't help but remind Joe of something archaic, like the set in his parents' house he and his brothers used to put red or blue strips of plastic over to pretend it was colour, or the small set he'd had in the first apartment he'd lived in when he'd left home.

'Gonna be a big old list. First name, family name, middle name, street name, nickname.' Trish's parents had immigrated from Ireland to Boston when she was seven, and a broad brogue still held fast to her accent.

'I'll start off with first names.'

'Wise choice,' she said and spun her chair to face the grey wall-to-wall cabinet behind her, where rows of 5¼ and 3½ inch floppy discs were lined up in alphabetical order. The former were housed in cardboard sleeves which made Joe think of the old 10-inch 78s his granddad used to play.

She took out seven of the bigger discs and fed them into the computer on her desk. The machine purred and made an accelerated clicking sound before a menu came up on the screen. She hit a few keys.

'Seven hundred and fifty-three entries under first name Solomon,' she said.

'How up to date are they?'

'Last entry was in November.'

'That'll do,' said Joe.

'Come back around four for the paper.'

'Thanks.'

'You guys could make my life a lot easier if you knew how to use one of these.'

'Then you'd be out of work,' Joe said.

'That's why man invented machines.' Trish smiled.

In the library, Max went through a botany book until he found what he was looking for: Calabar bean – seed of *Physostigma venenosum*, a climbing leguminous plant found in West Africa. The seed is half an inch in diameter and of a dark brown colour.

The short piece went on to describe the bean's toxic and medicinal properties, as well as its use in witchcraft.

He turned the page and found a colour photograph of the bean. He recognized it from somewhere. The next photograph down was of the plant it grew from. Green leaves and deep pink-coloured flowers.

Green, he thought. A green suit, matching green eyes.

He looked at the bean again.

And it came back to him: the pimp he'd beaten up outside Al & Shirley's diner on 5th Street, the stuff he'd confiscated and put in his Mustang.

'*Shit!*'

He found the silver cigar tube at the back of the glove compartment. He opened it and shook out the contents into his hand. Five calabar beans.

38

When Joe took off Pip Frino's blindfold and he saw he wasn't in a police station like he expected to be, but in a room with boarded windows, faded, damp-stained yellow wallpaper and ripped flowery lino on the floor, he looked worried.

'What is this place? Where am I?'

'Purgatory,' Max said, 'limboland.'

Max and Joe were sitting opposite him at a wooden table with a one kilo bag of 93 per cent pure Medellín cartel cocaine in between them.

'What am I doin' *here*?' Frino spoke in a rough, growly voice and a heavy Australian accent which gave it gravitas. He was short and thickset, with medium-length lank blond hair and a full beard. The whiteness of his teeth was accentuated by the golden tan of someone who worked outdoors.

They were in an MTF safehouse in Opa Locka. It was early Tuesday morning. Dawn was breaking outside; the birdsong just about filtering through the walls. Frino and his whole crew had been arrested on the Miami River, close to Biscayne Bay, right in the middle of a drop-off in a joint operation between MTF and the Coastguard. The Coastguard got to keep 75 per cent of the drugs, the boats, the crew and all the credit in exchange for handing Frino over to MTF. It had been a smooth operation. No shots fired; a simple swarm and seize.

Max and Joe had gone to Frino's harbour-front penthouse, where they'd found a loaded silver Beretta 92 in a bedside cabinet and a safe with $200,000 cash and Swiss,

Italian, German, British, Australian and New Zealand passports under various names.

Max was looking through the passports without saying a word. Joe sat back in his chair with his arms crossed, angrily eyeballing Frino.

'These yours?' Max held up a few of the passports.

'Yes.'

'That's five to ten years right there. You got a licence for the gun?' Max asked.

'No.'

'Another five to ten. And this morning's bust puts you away for life everlasting. You're thirty-eight. You ever been to jail?'

Frino shook his head.

'You'll go to a maximum security facility. That's hell on earth. Everyone'll try and kill you or fuck you or both. Guy like you won't get old in there,' Max said. Frino eyeballed him back. No emotion. 'You got anything to say?'

'Lawyer,' Frino answered.

'You're not under arrest,' Max said, 'we haven't charged you.'

'Otherwise I'd be in a police station instead of this crab shack,' Frino said.

'You catch on quick,' Joe said. 'Pip a girl's name?'

'Who are you people?'

'Who we are is of no importance to you right now. What we can do to you is,' Max said.

'*Lawyer!*' Frino shouted.

'You're *not* under arrest,' Max repeated.

'Then this is kidnapping.'

'Call it what you want, I don't give a shit,' Max said. 'You run drugs in go-fast boats out of the Bahamas into here. Who for?'

'I freelance. I get green for running white. Whoever's payin'.'

323

'Who was payin' this time?'

'What's this about?' Frino asked.

'We'll come to that,' Max said. 'Answer my question.'

'Is this about cuttin' some kind of deal?'

'Answer my man's question,' Joe said.

'It was a guy called Benito Casares. Colombian. He's a middle-man for a cartel. One of many. I never met the main guys; you never do.'

'Who's the main guy and what's the cartel?'

'Medellín cartel. That's Medellín in Colombia. Main guy – well, there's two, one in Colombia, one in the Bahamas. Pablo Escobar in Colombia, Carlos Lehder in the Bahamas. Norman's Cay. Virtually fuckin' runs the place. But I guess you know that already?'

Max just about stopped himself from looking at Joe.

'So you never met Lehder?'

'No.'

'Where d'you meet Casares?'

'Here. In Miami. Where we always meet.'

'How was that set up?'

'There's a carwash in Little Havana. I'd go there, tell the guys I want to talk to their boss and leave a number. Casares'd call and fix up a meet. I'd turn up.'

'How many times you worked for him?' Max asked.

'Seven in the last two years.'

'So he trusts you?'

'I guess.'

'OK,' Max said. 'Here's the deal. And, so as you know from the off, it's non-negotiable. Our way or jail.'

'I figured that. What do I get out of it?'

'You don't go to jail and you leave the country. And don't come back. Ever,' Max said.

'What do I have to do?'

'I'm gonna tell you something that happened and you're gonna repeat it into a tape recorder downtown with your lawyer present. That will become a statement. You will then have to repeat the statement in court,' Max said. 'You try to fuck us at any stage between now and for ever, and you will reap almighty hell. You understand?'

'In every language,' Frino said and smiled sardonically, showing a set of gleaming white teeth, perfect in every way but for two overlong, vampiric incisors.

'Do we have a deal?'

'What do you want me to say?'

Max told him: Frino was paid by Benito Casares to transport the Moyez shooter from Norman's Cay, and that once they got to Miami, he handed him over to Octavio Grossfeld.

'So I implicate myself in that courtroom shooting?' Frino smiled. 'What kind of fuckin' cops are you?'

Neither Max nor Joe said anything to that. They couldn't. They had no replies, no comebacks, just a deep sense of shame. Frino seemed to pick up on this and sat back in his chair with his arms crossed and his legs splayed, smug and haughty, enjoying himself.

'You guys work on the Kennedy assassination too?' Frino asked.

'Will you do it?' Max responded.

'Sure. Anything to help you boys out, seein' as we're virtually on the same team.'

Jed Powers was sitting in the kitchen with Valdeon, Harris and Brennan, drinking take-out coffee.

'Well?' he asked Max when he came in.

'When he gives his statement he'll say that he ferried in the Moyez shooter from Norman's Cay,' Max said. 'But there's a little more: his real life middle-man happens to work for Carlos Lehder. All Frino has to do is make a call and he'll deliver the guy to us.'

Jed Powers stood up and clapped. The other three followed suit.

'Great police work!' Powers shouted and spun his fist in the air.

Max wanted to be sick.

39

Twenty-nine straight hours later, Max and Joe were sitting on the couch in the Overtown garage, drinking weak coffee and staring at the thick pale green rectangle that was Trish Estevez's list. They hadn't slept at all. They were both drained. The last thing either wanted to do was more work.

Plans had been changed in mid-air. First they'd taken Frino to MTF to walk him through his statement, but once there they'd had word from Eldon that their captive needed to spill more names before any deal could be made. Eldon wanted everyone Frino had ever worked for – especially in Miami. Frino refused to give anything up until he'd talked to his lawyer and ratified the original deal he'd been offered. Max and Joe tried persuasion and then threats, but Frino knew he had the upper hand, so he just sat back with his arms crossed and smirking fangs fully bared.

They talked to Eldon. Burns spent fifteen minutes alone in an interrogation room with Frino. When he came out Frino had given up his every employer.

He was formally charged with multiple counts of drug trafficking and possession with intent to go global and given his phone call. At around midday his lawyer, Ida Basil, walked in and demanded to see the dope they'd allegedly caught her client with. Joe stalled her while Max made calls to the coastguard asking for the 300 kilos of coke they had logged into evidence and claimed as their bust to be brought to MTF. Two hours later the coke came in under armed escort.

The following deal was done: Frino would make a statement implicating Casares and Carlos Lehder in the

Moyez shooting and testify against them in court. He would also help MTF capture Casares. In return he'd be granted full immunity and get deported as soon as he'd given evidence.

Just after 6 p.m., Frino, wearing a wire, walked into Lázaro's Carwash on North West 3rd Street and told them he needed to speak to the boss. He gave them the number of his harbourside pad. He drove back there and waited for the call with Max, Joe, Powers and Valdeon. Casares called him an hour later, screaming about how his load hadn't turned up in Chicago and asking where the fuck it was? Frino calmly told him there'd been complications mid-sea transit, that they'd almost got busted and had had to divert the load to a safehouse in North Miami. Frino said he suspected a leak in the organization and needed to meet Casares in person to tell him about it. Casares said he'd meet him at the house the next day, Tuesday 11 February at 11 a.m.

He was punctual. MTF was waiting for him. They arrested him, his three bodyguards and driver.

Casares was taken to a basement in Jackson Avenue, Coconut Grove, where Eldon was waiting. He said he'd take it from here and sent them home for the rest of the day.

'You know,' Joe tapped his foot on the list, 'we could both make our lives easier by just forgettin' all about this shit and goin' on home.'

'True,' Max nodded, sparking up his Zippo to light a cigarette, 'but then we wouldn't be police at all.'

'True.' Joe nodded and yawned.

'This shit pisses me off. Here we are, doin' *real* police work on the sly and *fake* police work out in the open. This is *not* what I signed up for.'

'I hear that.'

'I'm fucken' *sick* of this shit, Joe. It ain't *right*, you know?'

'So whatchu sayin', man?'

'I'm sayin' I've had enough.'

'You wanna quit?'

'Right now, yeah.' Max sipped his coffee and pulled deep on his Marlboro, holding the smoke in his lungs for a few seconds and then exhaling slowly. 'We could put a stop to Eldon's way of doin' things, you and me.'

'How?' Joe sat up.

'Crack this case – the *real* case – and go public with it. Expose this Moyez bullshit for the sham it is.'

'You wanna take Eldon down?' Joe asked.

'It ain't only 'bout him. It's about the way he *does* things. Would you back me?'

'Hell, yeah!' Joe's big voice filled the confined space and echoed back at them metallically, like a gunshot.

'The only thing that'd stop me – that *will* stop me, I guess – is that if *he* goes down, *we* go down. And I wouldn't wanna be an ex-cop in prison. Would you?'

'We *could* cut a deal,' Joe suggested.

'*You* could, maybe; you got nothin' to hide,' Max said bitterly. 'The only deal they'd give me is life without. That's *if* we lived long enough to make any fucken' deal. Eldon's got his hooks in everyone everywhere.'

'Maybe we could go to the press?'

'We'd still go down. Hell, we'd go down *harder* if we went that route. Police hate bein' the last to know when it concerns their own. You know that.'

Joe didn't say anything, just stared straight ahead of him at the list then at nothing. False dawn. He was still on his own on this. Max wouldn't go along with him. He was right. He had too much to lose. His sense of self-preservation outweighed his principles.

Max extinguished his cigarette in his coffee. The whole time he'd been thinking of Sandra, and the life they could have together, and what she'd said about sharing and openness. He didn't want to lie to her about what it was he did. He thought about requesting a transfer, maybe to Miami Beach PD, if there was an opening.

'Let's make a start on that list,' Max said finally.

They split the list evenly. Joe had the beginning to middle of the alphabet, Max the remainder.

The list was broken down into name, felony details and a capital letter, either C – conviction, W – wanted, A – accomplice, A/S – accomplice suspect and S/I – informant placing suspect at a crime scene. This was followed by a basic physical description and last-known location.

They worked through them in near silence, starring things of importance. Max chain smoked. When it got too much for Joe he opened up the garage to let the tobacco fog out.

Max was finding no trace of a master criminal in his section. All the names so far were mostly petty criminals – home invaders, muggers, cheque forgers, non-fatal stick-up kids, car thieves – plus a few manslaughters and one-off murderers.

When he reached the first name at 'O', he did a double-take and burst out laughing.

'Solomon O'Boogie,' he read out.

'What's he in for?' Joe looked up.

'S/I. Murder in a club on Washington. Informant named him as a major-league drug supplier.'

'Yeah?'

'White male, six foot, grey hair.'

'Solomon O'Boogie, huh?' Joe said, then flipped back a couple of pages. 'I got a Solomon *Boogie* here. Named as an A/S for the shooting of a drug dealer in Little Havana. This one's described as Hispanic, nineteen to twenty-five – female.'

'*Female?*' Max frowned. 'What's the date?'

'2.13.77.'

'Yeah?' Max showed Joe. 'I got the same date.'

Remembering how Charles de Villeneuve was said to have had the power to change his appearance, Max looked across at the picture of the King of Swords.

'Joe, why d'you keep turnin' it around?'

'Shit was creepin' me out,' he said.

'Pussy!' Max chuckled. 'You sleep with the light on too?'

They carried on looking through their lists.

Solomon O'Boogie had four more A/S and S/I entries, two for drug-related murders, one for drug trafficking, one for prostitution, all in the same year, 1977. Every listing gave a different appearance, age and gender. O'Boogie was an old white man, a young white man of 'Jewish appearance', an old black woman with a ginger afro wig and an Asian male, approximately five feet tall, mid-thirties.

'Now this is some *seriously* strange shit here.' Joe turned over the pages rapidly. 'There must be over a hundred listings for this one guy – Solomon Bookman.'

Boukman – the Haitian witchdoctor slave who'd inspired the de Villeneuve cards.

'*What* did you just say?' Max looked up.

'Bookman.'

'Let me see.'

Max looked down the list.

'Bookman, Solomon,' he read. He turned the pages. Joe was right. The list went on and on.

Then he came to the right spelling. Boukman, Solomon. And read on.

The list detailed A/S and S/I reports on murders (most of them drug-related – dealers, gangleaders, suppliers, all shot or stabbed), drugs, prostitution, extortion, all taking place between 1974 and 1980. Bookman/Boukman's appearance changed every time. Male, female, old, young, black, white, Hispanic, Asian, Native American. Spoke with a Spanish, French, Russian, German accent. Had long and short hair, an afro, cornrows, plaits, dreadlocks, was bald. Had blue eyes, brown eyes, black eyes, green eyes, grey eyes.

'That's our guy,' Max said. 'Solomon Boukman.'

'Which one?' Joe asked.

'All of 'em and none of 'em,' Max said. 'My guess is no one knows what he really looks like because they've never seen him. He uses decoys.'

'Then maybe Boukman ain't even his real name. Why go through all that trouble to hide your appearance when you're using your real name?'

'Maybe. Or maybe he *wants* people to know his name. Cause his name ain't gonna turn up anywhere. Nowhere official. No record, no driving licence, no IRS, no utility bills. Man as myth.'

Joe took a deep breath.

'It's just you and me on this, right? If this guy's *that* organized we don't stand a chance.'

'Way it always was.'

'We're talkin' someone with *serious* juice here, Max. Connected like the city grid, friends in high places.'

'We'll take it as far as we can on our own, Joe. Then we'll look at our options.'

40

Back home Max called up the Department of the Interior for a list of Florida-based calabar-bean importers. He identified himself by name, badge number and date of birth and explained what a calabar bean was. He was told to hold.

He held for fifteen minutes. Then he was put through to the plants division.

The list was short enough to read out over the phone. There were three importers – Mount Sinai Medical Center, Miami University School of Medicine and Haiti Mystique – proprietor Sam Ismael.

Next, Max called Drake Henderson. They fixed a meet in the coffee shop in Burdine's department store on Flagler.

Max shaved, showered, swallowed some bennies with coffee and headed out.

'I need the lowdown on three people – two I got names for, one I haven't,' Max said after he'd ordered coffee. They were sitting back to back. Drake had come in after Max, wearing golfing clothes – brown check pants and matching cap, black and white Oxford wingtips, a pale yellow polo neck and a pink pullover tied around his neck. Beside him was a bag of golf clubs. He was eating bright yellow scrambled eggs on rye with a slice of ham and a glass of orange juice.

'First name – Solomon Boukman.' Max spelled it for him.

'I heard that name around the way,' Drake said.

'Where?'

'Around. In passin'.'

'Next, Sam Ismael.' Max's coffee came. He lit a cigarette.

'Now, the third guy is a pimp with green eyes. He's about six feet tall, slim build, light-skinned black, freckles, sharp dresser. Not pimp clothes, more the businessman type. Drives a dark blue Mercedes coupé. Now, this ain't your average pimp. He doesn't strike me as the kind out there on the track, tryin' to knock other pimps for their girls. This one's organized. Recruits 'em workin' in cafés, bars, restaurants. He's got cards printed up with phony names. Poses as a photographer, music producer, film producer.'

'Corporate pimp, huh?' Drake snickered. 'I'll see what I can do. Call me in three days.'

'What do you need?'

'I'm lookin' to rid myself of some competition – the entrepreneurial kind,' Drake whispered. 'I'm gettin' my ass undercut by these two guys outta LA. Ebony 'n' ivory team. The nigga goes by the name o' T-Rex, or Tampa Rex. Real name's Reggie Carroll. The cracker's name is Micky Goss. His streetname's Big Sur, 'cause that's where he came up. Used to be some kinda pro-surfer.

'What they been doin' is sellin' this shit they're callin' freejack – it's like poorman's base. Rock cocaine. They sellin' this shit for fiddy cents a pop, an' people be linin' up all day to get some. They say it's fiddy times the hit of snort, intense like you dunwannaknow. And that shit bin *killin'* my damn bidniss. No one wants a little toot and a toke no mo', they wanna smoke theyselves some freejack. We talkin' them college kids and fashion types I usually do my bidniss wit'.

'Anyways, should you go lookin' in Apartment 302 in the Flamingo buildings out by the Palmetto Expressway in the a.m., you will catch yourselves two lil' chemists and stop a whole new drug epidemic.'

'I'm sure the DEA will be real interested,' Max said. 'You're a model citizen, Drake.'

'I like to help out any way I can. You know me,' Drake

mumbled while scrunching his toast. 'Say, if there's *any* way you can find out how they be makin' that shit, lemme know, right?'

41

Eva Desamours gasped in shock and fear when she walked into the bathroom to give Carmine his bath and saw him standing by the steaming tub in his robe, looking every inch like her worst nightmare come true. She thought her son had been turned into a *zombi*, sent to kill her.

Then she saw he still had eyebrows and her surprise turned quickly into anger.

'What have you done? To your *HAIR*?!!?' she shouted.

'I – I wanted to see – to see what it looked like,' Carmine stammered.

He'd shaved his hair off earlier that afternoon.

Bad move not asking her first, he knew, but there'd been no time.

She pushed the door closed and glowered at him, her face going from disbelief to belligerent ferocity in a blink. She strode across the floor, shoulders hunched, head tilted slightly forward, fists clenched, neckchains making a loud timpani under her plain blue dress.

Oh no, he thought, here comes a ShitFit.

Carmine took a few steps back. She was an enraged bull and he was the penned-in matador, out of tricks, his balls in his mouth.

After he'd shot that cop in the foot, he'd burnt the car and the clothes he'd been wearing and tossed the gun in the sea. Then he'd completely changed his whole look. He was dressing down now in jeans, T-shirts, sneakers and mirror-lens Ray-Ban Aviators, which were too big for his skinny face and hung slightly crooked on his nose. He didn't care. The priority was keeping on the downlow until this situation blew over. He'd heard how the cop had gone and died and that had seriously fucked him up. He was wanted for *murder*. How can you die of a gunshot to the *foot*? Had to be something else happened to him on the way to the emergency room. Maybe the medics had given him the wrong type of blood or sumshit.

The last thing to go had been his hair. Some fag over in Coral Gables had shaved it and waxed his head after. Damn if the faggot hadn't been sweet on his ass too, stroking his scalp and even tickling his fuckin' ear lobes. Couldn't blame him though. Even bald as Kojak he was a handsome motherfu—

'*WHY* didn't you ask my permission?!' His mother was standing so close to him, their bodies were almost touching. Her eyes – small dry hard black beads of anger and poison – were drilling into his.

'Permission f-for what?' He hadn't told his mother about the cop any more than he'd told her about his hair.

'For *THAT*!' She reached up and slapped the back of his head so quick he didn't even see her move.

'I – I – dunno. I – I – just thought it up and went ahead and did it,' Carmine said, his voice scaling up and up, his words coming out in whimpers and bleats.

'You just "thought it up" and "went ahead and did it?" She mimicked his voice, then roared, 'You don't *just* think OR do *anything* without asking my PERMISSION FIRST!'

She punched him in the chest, but the robe's collar absorbed most of the hit so it came through to him like a weak tap. This emboldened him. Mentally he was suddenly back out on the street, and she was some impertinent Card, mouthing off at him.

'The fuck you sayin'!' he shouted, bringing his voice back to normal. 'It ain't yo' damn hair!'

She backed away a couple of steps, astonished, confused.

This inspired him some more.

'I'm twenny-nyynne motherfuckin' years old! You can't tell *me* to *do* a damn motherfuckin' thang – MOTHER!' he yelled. 'An – an – an – an anyways – YOU BALD TOO!'

Now, *why the fuck* hadn't he stood up fo' hisself like this *years* ago? he thought.

She stood, hands on hips, looking him up and down, mouth agape, incredulous. He swore he even saw her wig move a little.

Yeah, he thought. You stand there and stare all you want, like this is some *Star Trek* shit you witnessin', but you *ain't* never washin' my *ass* no mo'. *Fuck* this, fuck Solomon, and *FUCK YOU!*

Fixing his eyes on the door, he started walking forward.

Damn! He was pleased with himself! All it took was to stand up to her and –

Then he hit an obstacle that stopped him dead in his tracks. More precisely, the palm of her hand pushing hard into his chest, right where his heart was.

'*WHAT* did you just say to me, *boy!*' she yelled.

Her voice deafened him and drowned out the sound of his own thoughts. And just as easily as he'd slipped into his street persona, he fell back into being a scared little kid again; her towering over him, threatening to bring the whole world as he knew it down on his head.

He could hear his heart pounding, and he was sure she could feel it too. His mouth dried up all the way down to his throat. And damn if his legs weren't trembling. His will to resist snapped. His bravado fled from his bones like a bird escaping out of an open cage.

'I – I said – I'm – I'm—'

'YOU *WHAT*?!'

'I – I – I . . .'

'You *dare* raise your voice at *me*, boy! *Who* do you think you *are*?'

'I – I'm – I'm s-s-*sorry*,' he blurted.

'STRIP!' she snapped.

He did as he was told and took off his robe and dropped it on the floor.

She looked at it.

He picked it up and went over to the wall to hang it up, then padded back to where he'd been standing.

She looked him up and down, naked and shaking, her eyes stopping on his dick, now all shrivelled up. She came up close to him and grabbed him by the jaw, digging her nails deep into his cheeks, forcing his lips apart.

'Never raise your voice at me again, boy! You hear? *Never!*'

He tried to say yes, but her fingers had clamped his teeth so tight he was scared her nails would tear his skin. He tried to nod his assent, capitulation and surrender, but he couldn't move his head, so fast was her grip.

'You trying to be *independent* now, is that it, boy? Want to be a *MAN*?' she bellowed. 'You're not a man. You were NEVER a man!' She kept on burying her fingers into his skin, her face contorted, mad and merciless. Carmine was utterly terrified. He'd never seen her like this before. 'And you'll never BE a man. NEVER! You're WEAK! A WEAK PIECE OF SHIT like your coward FATHER!

'Now get on your knees,' she commanded, letting go of him.

'What?' He hadn't heard or understood.

'Get. On. Your. FUCKING KNEES!'

Carmine quickly did as he was told.

She kicked off her bathroom slippers and stepped around him. Behind him he heard her lockets bumping together, the chains scraping against them.

The first blow to his head was so hard it made everything inside it shake – his brains, eyes, teeth and tongue all shuddered. She hit him even harder the second time. He cried out and snot flew out of his nose. She kept on whacking the back and top of his head. She was using one of the slippers. They were rubber and plastic, but so solid and thick they might as well have been wood.

He didn't turn around.

She hit him again and again and again. A few stray shots struck his face and ears. A few blows landed on his neck and hurt like fuck, making him groan in agony.

The blows stung and burnt and bit and smarted. She was an accurate hitter too, got him in the exact same spot near the top of his head three times and made him yelp with each strike. Now he knew where he got his shooting skills from. He'd hoped it was from his dad. But they'd come from her.

His scalp felt scalded and raw. He wished he hadn't shaved off his hair. Then he understood the punishment. She would have done this to him no matter what.

He didn't know how many times she beat him, but there was no let up and she didn't get tired. When one blow landed more softly than the last, the next was a hundred times harder.

After a while, his mind went blank. He focused on the door in front of him, the tiles in-between. He looked at his shadow. Eventually, he thought, this *will* stop.

It did occur to him, when she caught him right behind his ear and it hurt so much he thought she'd burned him, that he could always turn himself in to the cops. But he knew Solomon had his hooks all the way into their souls via their wallets. They'd cut him loose and he'd be the star attraction at the next SNBC. They wouldn't have to bother shaving his head.

The pain leaked through his cranium. His head began to hurt like he had an almighty hangover; pressure began to build up in his brow. Every blow made white stars explode in front of his eyes. His nose started to bleed. He couldn't even feel the blows any more.

Eventually he heard her drop the slipper on the floor.

'Now get in the fucking bath!'

He thought she'd have been spent from all that beating, but she scrubbed him harder than ever, really ripping chunks out of his back and legs. The bathwater even had a mild tinge of pink to it.

He stared at the wall of fish in front. That dumb beautiful shoal. They had it so damn easy, nothing better to do all day but swim, eat, look pretty and die.

He thought of his father and Lucita. They'd loved him, he knew, and he'd been happy then. Things would've turned out so differently if they were still alive. He wished he'd died with them that day.

He began to cry. Silently. He did that sometimes when his mother's humiliations got too much to bear, when she'd found a new soft spot to expose and mock, poke at and stab. His face was already wet so she wouldn't see the tears.

He thought of what had happened, his brief moment of rebellion, her retribution.

She was right. He *wasn't* a man.

Crying relieved him. And with it came another kind of relief. His bladder went too. He pissed a long, uncontrollable jet in the water. He positioned his legs and crouched over a little so his mother wouldn't see and the piss made only the most ambiguous of ripples on the surface.

Thank God for Dettol, he thought, which would kill the germs before they could infect the wounds on his back.

Eva had smelt and tasted the stench of fear on Carmine so strong she'd known the little fuck was bluffing. He didn't have the *balls* to stand up to her. All she had to do was bark and stamp her foot and his spine crumbled.

She saw him pissing himself and trying to hide it. She wanted to laugh.

She smelled the tears running down his face. Tears were

like sea water and fresh water mixed together. When they were sad tears they were heavy on the salt, and that's the way Carmine's were. Crying for his pathetic useless little self. And his daddy. And that bitch whore Lucita. If only he *knew* what had happened to Lucita. She'd show him the pictures one day. Maybe. She'd told his father's killers to make sure they all got a piece of Lucita before they killed her. And they had.

She scrubbed away at his back and shoulders, drawing up a pinkish lather as the blood from the opened cuts mixed in with the froth. She was still mad enough at him to beat him some more. She had half a mind to.

Then she smelled something familiar but totally unexpected coming off the side of his head. She put her nose close to the spot and inhaled deeply, tasting what she'd caught in the back of her throat. Metal, oil, smoke – *guns!* She always smelled it strongly on members of Solomon's crew, sometimes weeks after they'd carried out hits or been in shootouts. What was it doing on this pathetic son of a – son of a lowdown scumbag? She smelt the spot again, breathing in so deep it stung her nostrils. *Definitely* guns. On *Carmine*? Couldn't be!

She rolled the taste around her mouth. She detected a hint of the just curdled milk flavour of confusion.

'Who did you shoot?' she asked him.

The little fucker almost jumped out of the tub, splashing the floor, teary-eyed, lips trembling.

'I – I dinn shoot anyone!'

He was wide-eyed with terror.

She just couldn't imagine him pulling a gun on anyone, let alone pulling the trigger. He didn't have the nerve. You needed steel in your soul to kill. He had nothing but shit in his.

'I smell guns on you. *Why?* And don't even think of lying to me, boy!'

Lies smelled like the sweetest perfume but tasted like shit, and the odour was coming off him.

She glowered at him. He was petrified and she liked it – liked having him here, all wrecked, in the palm of her hand, a fish skewered on her hook.

'I – I was messin' around with one of Sam's guns and – and the thing went off. I *swear* thass what happened.'

'So, if I call Sam he'll tell me that?'

'Yeah, sure.'

'Get out of the bath.'

He was too broken up inside to hit the streets that night. Besides, his head was so bruised and swollen it looked like he had most of his hair back.

He lay down on his bed and closed his eyes.

He wished he'd never wake to see another day again.

But he did wake up. And when he did his mother was standing over him.

'Who's Risquée?' she asked.

42

'Don't be angry, be thankful,' Sam said.

'*Thankful!* You damn well sole me the fuck out, man!' Carmine shouted and slammed his palm on the marble cutting slab, his voice echoing around the basement.

'It wasn't like that. She knew something was up.' Sam stayed calm. Eva had called him in the early hours of the morning, asking him why her son smelt of gun smoke and panic. Sam had told her about Risquée and the shooting near the shop and said the whole situation had probably been preying on Carmine's mind.

'She knew something was up,' Sam continued. 'You know that gift she has. If you'd just let me take care of it from the start, none of this would've happened. But you had to go play the big man. See where that got you? Anyway, the problem's solved. She's put Bonbon on it. Who did you tell her Risquée was?'

'Some bitch I tried to turn, freaked out on me.'

'Exactly what I said to her,' Sam said.

'For real?'

'Absolutely,' Sam said. 'We must've had telepathy. Or else been really lucky.'

Sam had, of course, told Eva the truth about Risquée, and Eva had laughed.

'What if Risquée talks to Bonbon?'

'That animal won't let her. And, say she manages to say something, he won't listen. Listening's not his thing,' Sam said, almost feeling sorry for the poor bitch when Solomon's hitman caught up with her. And he would, for sure. Bonbon had never once failed his masters.

'Did you tell my mother 'bout our thang?'

'No.' Sam shook his head. 'Of course not.'

'You sure?' Carmine was searching his face.

'Positive,' Sam said. 'We're both alive, aren't we?'

'Yeah, kinda.' Carmine nodded sadly. He was wearing a baseball cap to hide the damage to his cranium, but he couldn't do much about the cuts and grazes on his hands and face. He had small deep slashes to his cheeks, forehead and a thick cut on the bridge of his nose, all raw and burning. And there was a buzzing noise in his head that wouldn't go away, like he had an angry wasp in there.

'What in the hell did she do to you?'

'Beat me fo' lyin' to her. Beat me wit' my favourite belt. You know that Gucci gator-hide one, gold buckle? She beat me wit' dat, beat me *bad*. I tole her I was shootin' off some rounds witchu.'

'That's a *big* buckle,' Sam said, looking pityingly at Carmine's wounded hands, slashed so viciously the cuts looked like defensive knife wounds.

'Damn thing *broke off* when she was beatin' me too. She went fuckin' *loco* on me, man. It was bad 'nuff lass night, but this mornin' she hauled me outta bed and made me give her the belt from my pants. My damn *pants*! Look at what she done to me!'

Carmine removed his cap, wincing as it came off.

'*Christ!*' Sam gasped.

There were scores of cuts and gouges all over Carmine's black and blue cranium – savage slashes and gouges turned crimson-brown where the blood had clotted and scabs started to form – plus dozens of small lumps and swellings, so much so that the top of his head looked like he had at least a dozen molehills sprouting up under his skin.

'You need to get to a hospital,' Sam said.

'No way.' Carmine shook his head. 'What'm I gonna say? My mamma went all Bates Motel on my ass?'

'Say you got beaten up or somethin'.'

Carmine shook his head sadly.

'Let me get the First Aid kit.'

But before he could, Lulu came down the stairs.

'There's a customer asking questions,' she said in Kreyol.

'Who?' Sam asked.

'White man.'

'I'll be right back,' Sam said to Carmine.

'Good morning. Welcome to Haiti Mystique. I'm Sam Ismael, the manager.'

'How you doin'?' the man said. He was close to six feet tall, solid, broad-shouldered and stern-looking. He had short brown hair, blue eyes and a smile that didn't really suit his mouth.

'Can I help you with anything?'

'Just lookin', thanks,' the man replied.

'I'll be over here if you need me,' Sam said, as he went and stood behind the counter and pretended to be busy checking the stocklist.

The man hadn't identified himself as such, but Sam knew he was a cop: his way of standing – straight, but with his shoulders slightly forward, feet apart like a boxer, in a state of anticipatory aggression; his typically bad clothes – the catalogue-inspired, utility formal look – houndstooth sports coat, black slacks, wingtips, open-necked white Oxford shirt; and then his eyes – cold, piercing, steady, all-seeing, all-appraising, taking everything in and breaking it all down, a spark of savagery about them.

Sam felt panic skim down his spine.

The cop looked at the dolls, the black religious icons, the crosses, the mounted monkey heads, the skulls, the candles. He studied the noticeboard where the witchdoctors advertised their services. Eva's card was up there too. He moved over to the houmfor drums on the floor and tapped one, getting a deep undulating sound which planed out into a hum and lingered for a few seconds before fading away into the ether.

He looked at the shelves of herbs, seeds, roots and weeds.

'You from outta town?' Sam asked.

'Orlando,' the cop said. 'Say, do you sell calabar beans here?'

Sam felt his mouth dry up.

'I occasionally import them for customers. On request. Why? Do you want some?'

'Say I did, could you deliver or would I have to come here to collect them?'

'Whatever's most convenient for you. What do you need them for?'

'I'm doing a paper on herbal cures,' the cop said.

'I see,' Sam said. 'You with Miami University?'

'Yeah.' The cop nodded.

'Probably work out cheaper for you if you ordered through the university,' Sam said. 'I add on import duties, storage and handling charges.'

'Budget's all used up,' the cop said, looking Sam straight in the eye, making him feel like he'd done something wrong. 'What kinda money are we talkin' about?'

'Depends on the quantity. But I usually add on $200 for storage and handling, paperwork too.'

'Must be some classy storage,' the cop quipped. 'What about the beans themselves? How much do they cost?'

'$10 each.'

'I'll think about it,' the cop said. He went over to the tarot-card stand in the middle of the store and slowly rotated it. 'These take me back.'

'Do you read?'

'Not me, no. An ex-girlfriend of mine did,' he said, looking at the decks. 'She used this weird deck though. Not common. French name.'

347

'Marseilles?'

'No . . . it was the – the . . .' He flicked his fingers, searching the air for an answer. 'The de Villeneuve deck. You sell that one?'

'Not here,' Sam said. He could feel his heart beating real fast now, and the tips of his fingers had gone cold. What the hell was this guy doing here? He thought Solomon had all the cops in his pocket. 'They're expensive *and* hard to come by.'

'My ex was real rich – and connected.' The cop laughed and carried on looking around the store. 'Well, thanks for your time,' he said, finally.

'You don't want the beans?'

'Sorry. My pockets ain't that deep.'

Then the back door opened a crack. Sam turned, thinking he'd see Lulu there, but it was Carmine, quickly peering through a gap before suddenly disappearing.

The cop had noticed. He stared at the door, then back at Sam. He nodded to him and left the store.

Moments later Carmine came out, looking scared.

'That guy's a cop! He's the same fucker beat me up in April. Took the beans offa me too – remember?'

Sam picked his telephone up off the floor and started dialling.

'Who you callin'?'

'Your mother.'

43

'He make you?' Joe asked when Max got back in the car, parked four blocks up from the store.

'Yeah,' Max said as he flipped out his notebook and started scribbling. 'He looked real worried.'

'What you get?'

Max showed him.

'Eva Desamours,' Joe read out.

'Only fortune teller he had up on his noticeboard. Otherwise it was all exorcisms, healings, spell-makings, spell-breakings and so on. Eva Desamour's on my list of fortune tellers who use the de Villeneuve cards. In fact, she's the *only* reader in Miami who does. My list didn't have a contact number. Now I got one.'

'What about Ismael?' Joe started the car.

'He ain't our guy, but he works for him,' Max said. 'Ismael's the front man. He owns most of Lemon City. After Preval Lacour killed the Cuestas, he took over the redevelopment contracts. Ismael supplied the calabar beans and tarot cards that ended up in Assad and Lacour's stomachs. We're gonna need to take a closer look inside the store. It's got a basement.'

'How you gonna get a warrant?'

Max looked at Joe and saw he was joking.

44

'Congratulations! You've won!' Sandra said, handing Max a silver envelope. She'd invited him to dinner at Joe's Stone Crabs in Washington Avenue. Despite living in the neighbourhood, Max had never eaten there because the place was always full; it was one of Miami's oldest restaurants and featured prominently in every tourist guide. They didn't do reservations, but Sandra's firm handled their accounts, so she got a table.

'Won what?'

'Take a look!'

Max opened the envelope and burst out laughing. It was six Casino Dance lessons at a studio off Flagler.

'That's real sweet and thoughtful of you,' he said sarcastically. 'This is so I don't embarrass you out in Calle Ocho?'

'You don't embarrass me,' she replied. 'The studio's just around the corner from your building. We can go after your ten to six shift.'

'My colleagues found out I was takin' dancin' lessons, I'd never live it down.' Max laughed.

'You'll be going with me,' she said.

'Won't make a difference.'

'Then don't tell anyone.'

'Won't make a difference either, Sandra. Cops find out everything eventually – especially when it's about one of their own.'

'You *are* coming,' she repeated. ''Cause I'm not going alone.'

'*You* don't need to learn. You move like an angel.'

'Angels don't dance.'

'But if they did, they'd move like you,' Max said.

They looked each other in the eyes for a moment and everything around them seemed to stop.

'It's good to see you,' he said, breaking the spell.

'And you too.'

They leant across the table and kissed.

'Does that mean you'll do it?' she asked.

'God, you're impossible!' He laughed. 'Just let me clear this case I'm workin' on first, all right? Then, yeah, I'll do it.'

'You'll love it.'

'I doubt it.'

'You'll learn to like it.'

'That's what my trainer said when I got my ribs separated in the ring one time.'

'And you carried on, right?'

'I sure did,' Max said.

'There you go.'

Their food arrived. They had ten jumbo crab claws, served with mustard-mayo sauce and melted butter, which gave the vaguely sweet but generally mild-tasting white meat an added kick. They also had a large plate of fried green tomatoes and the biggest hash browns Max had ever seen – the size of a loaf of bread and served in slices.

After dinner they went to the cinema on Lincoln Road to see *Fort Apache, the Bronx*. Sandra had picked the film. Max would've opted for something else, like going to a bar, because the last thing he wanted to do was sit through a cop film, especially one which had been praised for 'gritty authenticity'; it would mean adding another two more hours to his working day. But he'd got more interested when Sandra had told him Pam Grier was in it. He'd seen all her seventies films, which were, without exception, terrible – especially the ones where she kept her clothes on, but, luckily for him, she'd made very few of those.

The cinema was next to empty. They sat towards the front with their Cokes.

The film starred Paul Newman as a middle-aged, by-the-book cop working in one of the worst, most run-down parts of the south Bronx. There were plenty of lingering shots of urban wasteland, which, had they upped the temperature, added sunshine and palm trees, could have been half of Miami.

Fifteen minutes in Max was bored stiff. The plot was meandering and Pam was nowhere in sight. He needed a cigarette and a drink. Paul Newman and his partner tried to talk a transvestite out of throwing himself off a roof. Paul Newman – in his fifties and looking it – started an affair with a young Latina junkie. He yawned and looked at Sandra, who was engrossed. He didn't know why. Maybe he was missing something deep. He remembered the liquor store close to the cinema. He thought of going out to get himself a quart of bourbon and have a smoke. Then Pam appeared and he briefly forgot about his needs. She looked rough in this, because she was playing a psycho-junkie hooker who kills two of Paul Newman's corrupt colleagues. He'd never paid attention to her acting talent before, but he had to admit she was pretty scary, killing people with razor blades hidden in her mouth (she'd used the razor blade in mouth trick in *Foxy Brown*, but that was to free herself), and oozing cold-eyed menace. She killed a couple of corrupt cops and disappeared. He waited for her to come back for a good while, but realized she probably wouldn't be taking her clothes off and decided to slip out.

At the liquor store he bought a quart of bourbon and smoked a Marlboro outside the cinema.

When he sat back down next to Sandra he tipped some of the bourbon into the cup. He offered Sandra some. She shook her head and looked at him with a mixture of disgust and worry.

After the film was finished she insisted on driving his Mustang. He could see she was pissed off with him.

'Did you enjoy the film?' he said as they went down Alton Road.

'How much do you drink?' she asked.

'I'm sorry about that –'

'How much do you drink, Max?'

'On and off, some days more than others.'

'So you drink every day?'

'Yeah.'

'Why?'

'All kindsa reasons: unwinding, socializing, something bad's happened. And 'cause I like it,' he said. 'A lotta cops drink.'

'Why did you drink in the cinema?'

'I thought the film was boring. I needed a break.'

'You were with me.' She sounded hurt.

'You weren't up on the screen,' he quipped.

'Do you have a drink problem?'

'I don't think so, no.'

''Cause I'll tell you this now, I am *not* having a relationship with an alcoholic. There'll be four of us in the same room: you and me, the person you turn into when you're loaded *and* the bottle. I am *not* going to live like that. No way.' She was angry.

'Jeez, Sandra, I'm sorry, all right?'

She was having none of it.

'I had an uncle who was an alcoholic. He died of cirrhosis. He was in a lot of pain at the end, puking blood, scratching his skin raw. I don't want to have to go through that with you, if I can help it.'

They turned on to 15th Street. Max lit a cigarette.

'And *that's* something else that's going to have to go.'

'Damn, Sandra!'

'Kissing you's about as close as I can get to licking a dirty ashtray. You ever licked an ashtray, Max?'

'I *like* smoking,' Max protested.

'No, you don't. You're just hooked. A junkie like Pam Grier was in the movie.'

'A *junkie*? *Me*? Get outta here!'

'Have you tried to quit?'

'No.'

'Bet you can't imagine life without one, huh?'

'I wasn't born with a cigarette in my mouth,' Max said. 'Have you ever smoked?'

'I tried it once and thought it was disgusting. Which it is. And it's dangerous too.'

'So's livin' in Miami.' Max chuckled. 'Besides, cigarettes go great with coffee, drink, after sex, after a meal –'

'They don't go great with life.' Sandra cut him off. 'Are you going to be one of those guys you see, aged sixty, wheeling an oxygen tank around with tubes in their nose 'cause they've got emphysema and can't breathe? Or one of those people with a hole in his throat and a battery-operated voicebox?'

'You're assuming a lot,' Max said.

'Like what?'

'Like we're going to be together that long. I mean, we haven't even – you know – *slept* together.'

'You haven't asked.'

'I have to *ask* you?'

'I'm an old-fashioned girl,' Sandra said.

'I thought you wanted to take it slow.'

'You haven't even made a *move* in – in what's it been? – a month?'

'I didn't wanna scare you off. But since you're offerin' – your place or mine?'

'We're going to yours,' she said.

'I warn you, it's a tip.'

'I figured that,' she replied. 'Besides, my mama always told me to beware of a man with a tidy house. He's either *loco* or a *maricon*.'

45

In his apartment in South Miami Heights, Joe put on his favourite sad song – Bruce Springsteen's 'The Promise' and sat back in his armchair with a glass of red wine.

Lina had just cleared away the plates and blown out the candles from their dinner. It should have been a happy occasion for him – a quiet confirmation of his love for the woman he wanted to marry. But instead, Joe felt bad. He couldn't slip away from the shadows in his mind and let go the heaviness in his heart.

'The Promise' was an unreleased song from the *Darkness on the Edge of Town* sessions, which Bruce had played sporadically on his 1978 tour. It was a tortured, tragic dirge about betrayal and broken dreams, a loser's lament played solo on piano. The recording wasn't the best, taped at a Seattle gig by a member of the audience, but you couldn't hear another sound in the building, save that of someone who's reached the end of the rainbow and found absolutely nothing there but a cold open road to nowhere. To Joe it was the greatest, most moving song Bruce had ever written, and one whose words were coming to mean more and more to him every day.

Joe could have done with a joint right now, to go with the booze and the music. It would have been nice to get his head up a little. He'd always smoked grass with Max, and they'd always ended up laughing hysterically about stupid shit. Like the time they'd played the only white rock record Max owned – a 12 inch single of the Rolling Stones' 'Miss You' – about fifty times over, taking it in turns to imitate Jagger's mid-song rap about Puerto Rican girls that was juss daaahyunnn ta meeetchooo. Eventually, when the high had worn off and they'd got sick of the song, Max had taken the record off and they'd gone down to the beach and played frisbee with it. The thought that he'd have to betray his friend and turn all those good memories to shit was killing him and poisoning everything in the process.

'Bad day?' Lina came into the room and sat down next to him. She still looked every bit as good to him as when he'd spotted her in church across from the altar: petite, dark-skinned, with short hair, high cheekbones, slightly slanted eyes and the kind of smile that could pull him out of the deepest darkest hole, but she wasn't smiling now. She was sharing his troubles.

'Forgot what a good one is.' Joe sighed, gulping down half his wine. He'd told her some of what was happening, how MTF was really run and how he was going to get transferred to public relations after the Moyez case was over. And that would be soon: Casares had given up most of his contacts, including Carlos Lehder, and they were planning swoops on the major players. After that would begin the long process of bringing the 'guilty' to trial, but Joe would be out of the picture way before then, possibly as soon as August. And he hated August in Miami the most. It was always way too hot, people went way too crazy and hurricanes were always one wrong breath away.

'You been goin' to church?' she asked.

He shook his head.

'You should.'

'What in the hell would God say to me about what I'm doin'?' Joe asked bitterly. 'I'm schemin' to betray my partner and best friend, the guy who's had my back and been nothin' but loyal to me ever since we hooked up. It was only 'cause o' him I made Detective.'

'You're doing what's right for you, Joe. And sometimes doing the right thing is the hardest thing of all.' She spoke tenderly but firmly, like he imagined her doing to one of the kids she taught. 'Sooner or later MTF will get exposed. Bad will always out. And you don't want to be there when that storm breaks, because it always rains on the little people the hardest.'

'Yeah, right.' Joe looked in the distance, but saw only the framed, fully autographed *Born to Run* sleeve on his wall.

'The buck's gotta stop somewhere, Joe. Those people you two put away might not have been upstanding citizens, they might even have been monsters, but you, Mingus, Sixdeep and MTF had no right to do what you did. You all broke the law.'

'So whatchu' doin with me then?' Joe asked, searching her eyes.

'Because I believe you can change. And I believe you *want* to change. And I believe the good in you is sick of all this bad stuff you've done.' She took his hand as she spoke. 'You've got integrity, decency and self-respect, Joe Liston.'

'You think so?' Joe sneered with self-disgust. 'You wanna know why I went along with this shit, Lina? Huh? You wanna know? 'Cause I wasn't *meant* to make Detective. I was just a simple doughnuts and coffee Patrol cop, roustin' hookers and pushers ten to twelve hours a day. I was the guy old ladies called out to get their cats off the roof. I was the guy kept the crowds back at homicide scenes. I was a uniform, not a brain.

'See, it didn't matter that I saw things the dicks missed. Didn't matter that I talked to witnesses they didn't bother with. Didn't matter that a lotta the time I had a good idea who the perps were. 'Cause in the Miami PD it don't matter how clever you are, or how good you are, or what good you *could* do if only someone gave you the chance, opened that door up a little to let you in. No, sir! It's down to the colour of your skin. Sure, they just love to say they employ plenty of black folk, but what they don't tell you is what they employ them *as*: Dispatch, Records, Patrol, Front Desk, Lock-up. That's all we ever get. Sure, you'll find one or two black Detectives, but it's a damn small number. So, when I got that shield, it felt good – hell, *I* felt good. *Proud* of myself. I'd *achieved* somethin'.

'And it was all thanks to Max. He didn't owe me squat. He was the golden boy with the predestined future. I was supposed to show him the ropes, help him up his street IQ then fade away. He didn't let it happen. He took me with him. He damn well refused to work with anyone else. You hear that, Lina? He *refused*. He told Sixdeep he'd rather stay in Patrol than work with some cracker who was gonna cut corners on a case so he could go watch a ballgame or ball some hooker. You talk about integrity and decency, that motherfucker's got it in spades!

'You say it's about doin' what's right for me?' he continued as the song ended and the needle left the vinyl and went back to its cradle. 'But it ain't just about that. See, every day in Miami innocent black folks get pulled over by a white or Latino cop. Sometimes it's for a genuine reason, sometimes it's because the cops just want someone they can fuck with. Black man starts to protest, they arrest him for assaulting a police officer, resisting arrest and disturbing the peace. He gets hauled up before a judge, and all the jury see is the colour of his skin. If they're lucky they go to jail. If they're not they end up like McDuffie. And you know what? I hadn'a been a cop, that could've been me takin' that shit, just because of havin' the misfortune of bein' born the wrong colour in this so-called civilized society of ours. Sixdeep, MTF, the way they do things – *we* do things – they're all part of the problem, and a big part of the problem. And yeah, you're right, Lina, I'm sick of it. Sick to my stomach. And they gotta be stopped. Simple as that. And that's what I'm gonna do. But Max is gonna go down with 'em.'

'Because he's part of the same problem you've been talking about,' she said.

'I suppose so,' Joe answered and finished his wine.

'I want to meet him,' Lina said.

'Who? *Max?*'

'Yeah, Max. Your partner.'

'Why?'

'I want to put a face to him. I want to look him in the eye. I want to see what kind of person he is.'

'I've told you.'

'You have. But I want to know for myself.'

'I don't think that's a great idea,' Joe said. 'I'm gonna fuck this guy's life up, and you wanna make *nice?*'

'It's about being sure. Because I'm going to go through this with you too.'

'I'll think about it,' Joe said. And right then a big part of him saw a chance that somehow he could find a way of accepting his well-paid desk job and paper over the humiliation with the material comforts a bigger salary would bring; that he wouldn't have to take the hard option, that he could let it all pass. Lina might like Max as much as he did. Lina might talk him out of it for Max's sake. But then, what about their case? He felt they were getting closer to cracking it every day. It wouldn't be long now before the truth started to show itself.

PART FIVE
June–July 1981

46

'Guess you're gonna have to go get yourself some whole new voodoo, Solomon, 'cause there ain't no cops investigatin' you,' Eldon said without turning around, but keeping his eyes on the dark outline in his rearview mirror.

Solomon didn't answer.

It was after 10.00 p.m., and Eldon was parked in a side road facing his house. The lights were on. He was beat. He'd had a long old day. He needed a hot bath and his bed. Instead he had this: Boukman doing his pop-up act in the back of his car for one of their talks. Eldon hated their 'talks' because talking wasn't one of the nigra's strengths. He had this thing for silence, for saying nothing, for being a conversational black hole. It pissed Eldon off and also made him ill at ease.

Boukman was unique in that way. A lot of the people Eldon had done business with in the past had been talkative as hell. Some you just couldn't shut up. The spics and guineas were the worst offenders; talked the whole fucken' time, like they considered silence a personal affront. Niggers could talk some too – not that they talked properly, no they *jived* in that shouty sing-song way they had, like they was all trying to be James Brown. He'd stopped doing business with Jamaicans because of the way they talked – he couldn't understand a single word they said, and when he got himself an interpreter, he couldn't understand a word *he* said.

The cop Boukman had asked him to look into was some guy who'd walked into Sam Ismael's store a week ago, asking about calabar beans and the de Villeneuve tarot cards. The guy had claimed to be a researcher from the university and hadn't given his name. Even if he had, it would've been a false one. Any cop investigating something on the sly wouldn't exactly go and give out his *real* name, would he?

All he had to go on was a description – short brown hair, blue eyes, under six feet tall, big build, 190–200 pounds, mid thirties – which narrowed it down to about 3,000 people, including Max and Brennan.

Not that anyone was investigating Boukman. Eldon had checked, double-checked and triple-checked every department. The Feds too. It had taken four days – days when he'd been swamped with work because of all the planning and backstage politicking that was going on with the Moyez case. They were in limbo because the Turd Fairy was discussing the potential fall out of busting a major Colombian drug ring with his people in Washington. Some players weren't comfortable arresting so many spics all in one go. Spics had that strange way of suddenly bonding together because they spoke the same lingo. And spies had too much political clout, so they had to be managed with care.

Anyway, it was bullshit. Even if someone was looking into Boukman they wouldn't get far. There wasn't a single picture or accurate description of him on file. No criminal record, no social security number, no immigration documents. *Nada*, as the spics would say. Boukman didn't officially exist. Some of this was down to Eldon erasing all and every trace of him, beginning with his one and only arrest in 1969 for cutting a nigra's Adam's apple out (charges were dropped due to lack of evidence), and continuing to this day, destroying any eye witness reports for anything remotely close to a positive ID and then letting Boukman know the source. But most of the Boukman myth was created by the nigra himself, and, Eldon had to admit, it was a masterstroke of pure fucked up ruthless genius. Boukman used 'doubles' who didn't remotely look like him – out of work actors and actresses, mostly, recruited through small ads – to impersonate him at meetings, and if anyone outside his tight inner circle clapped eyes on him he had them killed. Misinformation is the same as no information, and the dead don't talk.

'Maybe it's someone you don't know about,' Boukman said, finally, in that toneless, emotionless, slightly French voice of his.

'Highly unlikely,' Eldon replied. 'Nothing gets investigated in this city without me knowing about it well in advance. How did Ismael know it was even a cop?'

'It's in the cards,' Solomon answered.

Oh, then it *must* be true, thought Eldon. He yawned and stretched theatrically to let the damn nigra know his voodoo paranoia was boring him. Shit, if those things are so damned accurate why can't you predict who'll win the World Series and make yourselves some nice, easy, legal money instead? Because those things are horseshit – that's why.

'You're takin' this mumbo-jumbo crap way too seriously, you know that?' Eldon said.

Solomon didn't reply, so they sat in a silence which dragged towards the uncomfortable – for Eldon at least. He wondered what Boukman was like with other people, the rest of his voodoo mob, or his woman – if he had one. He didn't care exactly, but he was curious, wouldn't have minded a little genuine insight into the man. In the thirteen years they'd done business they'd never had much in the way of small talk. Actually, they'd had none. The miniscule scraps of what passed for conversation between them involved big subjects, like drugs, delivery, money and death.

The street outside was still. No cars in the road, no people walking around. The neighbourhood was just great that way. An oasis of tranquillity; everything bad happened to someone else, somewhere else, never here. Here it was safe, middle class and very white. If you saw a spic or a nigra they were delivering your mail or moving your furniture in or out.

Eldon started humming Frank's 'Last Night When We Were Young'.

'Only a fool mocks what he doesn't understand,' Solomon interrupted him.

Eldon turned around at that, expecting to see Boukman behind him, but his guest had moved to the left – noiselessly as always – so he was close to the door, a form moulded out of darkness.

'You know what I understand? I understand you're born, you live, you die. With the livin' part you do the best you can, for as long as you can and then you're gone. Worm food or ash. That's *it*. Simple.'

No response.

Jesus! thought Eldon, we could be here all night. He broke into a few bars of 'In the Wee Small Hours of the Morning'. Frank had a tune for every asshole situation.

'I want the photographs and names of every cop in Miami.'

'Excuse me?'

'If the cop's from Miami, Sam can pick him out.'

'Have you been listening to a word I said?' Eldon was angry now. 'There ain't – any body – investigatin' – you.'

Boukman didn't reply, so more silence. Eldon peered into the darkness behind him, trying to see him, wanting to switch on the damn light, go eyeball to eyeball with this piece of shit. Eldon was mad. He wasn't going to show Boukman his files. That was police business – *his* turf.

He couldn't see Boukman at all. He turned around, frustrated, crossed his arms and faced the windscreen, looking longingly at the warm yellow lights in his house.

'Things have changed,' Boukman said, his voice now almost in Eldon's ear, making him jerk in shock. The fucker had moved again, right behind him. He'd felt his breath on his neck, the brush of ice-cold feathers.

'Yeah? How so?' Eldon snapped. Christ, was he pissed! Boukman had given him a *fright* – *him!*

'We have a new supplier.'

'Who? Baby Doc?' Eldon laughed.

'No. His father-in-law, Ernest Bennett. He's bought Air Haiti and taken over trafficking from the Haitian army, which means no more Cessnas with small loads every two days. Now we'll be using proper cargo planes – DC3s. That means five or six times the volume.'

'How many plane loads?' Eldon asked. His heart rate was up.

'Two a day to begin with.'

'Starting when?'

'Next Wednesday.'

Eldon thought about it. This was a serious step up. Solomon Boukman would become the single biggest importer and distributor of coke in Miami. Bigger than the Colombians and Cubans. It would mean a *lot* more money. Way more risk too. Risk everywhere. The Colombians and Cubans wouldn't exactly like the competition. There'd be another war, far worse than the one going on now with Griselda Blanco's people. Then there was the government. The Haitian link would eventually get found out and Reagan would probably hit them hard – topple Baby Doc, bomb or invade the country. But that was later. He'd be long gone before the first storm cloud rolled in. For now he'd make as much damn money as he could. DC3s! *Jesus!*

'Why didn't you mention this first?'

'The photographs are a priority,' Solomon replied.

Sure they are, thought Eldon. I know you now. You're nothing special. You scare like the worst of them. The stakes get higher so you get more paranoid, more suspicious. A predictable cycle. You can never be too cautious, true, but there was a fine line between caution and shooting your own shadow. He knew how this was likely to go. Boukman was one of those guys who killed their entire crews over a hunch. Trouble is, behaving like that only made them even *more* mistrustful than before because they were suddenly surrounded by people they didn't know, didn't go back with. The end was just around the corner.

Still, there was business to attend to and in business there was always a little give involved before you took.

'OK. I'll get you what you want,' Eldon said, after a suitably studied moment where he'd controlled the silence. 'Not that it'll do you any good,' he added.

A taxi pulled up outside Eldon's house. Leanne got out and walked up to the front door, stopping to wave as the cab pulled away.

Boukman leant forward. Eldon felt his icy breath on the side of his neck again. He didn't move. He could feel Boukman studying his daughter, taking her in. He didn't like it one darn bit, didn't like what he knew was going through the nigra's brain. Leanne was a beautiful girl. She turned a lot of guys' heads. He wanted to yell at her to hurry the fuck up, find her keys in her bag and get in the house. He could hear Solomon breathing through his nose, the air sounding like something heavy being dragged up the passages.

Leanne went inside and closed the door.

Eldon let out a sigh of relief he was sure Boukman heard.

'Bring me the pictures in three days,' Boukman said, opening the car door.

Eldon sat in the car long after Boukman had ridden off in the Mercedes that had been parked behind them. He couldn't believe it – the creep had actually unnerved him. This wasn't good. This wasn't good at all.

47

'Solomon Boukman – man or myth?' Drake mumbled as he looked around his tower of Babel – a sandwich so big it could have fed a small elephant: six solid inches of pastrami, beef and turkey inter-layered with pickles, sauerkraut, onions, lettuce and piercingly bright yellow mustard, the whole structure topped and tailed with a thin slice of rye bread and held together by a long wooden skewer. Max had a Cuban coffee and his cigarettes.

They were facing opposite directions in adjacent end-of-aisle booths in Woolfies on Collins Avenue, a vast diner with mirrored columns, plush red leather seats, art deco lamps, and a beige and brown tiled floor.

'Word is he's the crime lord of Miami. Got his finger in absolutely everything there's a law against. Dope, prostitution, extortion, gamblin', numbers, auto theft, etcetera, etcetera.' Drake took the tower apart and partitioned it into five smaller sections, but his meal still looked daunting.

'So how come I never heard of him before?' Max asked. Today his informant had come dressed as a Brazilian soccer player – yellow and green shirt, blue shorts, white tube socks. He had the boots and a ball by his side.

'Thass juss it. Dependin' on who you talk to, Boukman either exists or he don't. Some folks are sayin' the Haitians made him up so they could scare off the niggas that was preyin' on 'em – kinda like a criminal scarecrow or sumshit. The Haitians say he's for real. At least them simple ones straight off the boats do. The rich ones I deal with in Kendall think it's all bullshit too.'

'What about you? What do you think?'

'I ain't the cop here, Mingus. I juss tell you what I hear an' see. But if you want me to take a worthless guess – a guy like that? – you'd-a had to have some paper on him by now. No one that big goes undetected. Leaves a trail.'

'True,' Max said, chasing his sweet, thick black coffee with a pull on his Marlboro.

'Strange thing is, the people who say he's real don't know what he looks like. Or they do, but all the descriptions is different. Some of 'em say he's white, some say he's black, some say he's Latino – and there was this one ole girl tole me he was Chinesey lookin'. And then no one can agree if he's really a he or a she. Or an it. Or an evil genius midget man chile. I even heard he's got two tongues. Can you believe *that*?'

'Two tongues?' Max laughed quietly. 'The ladies must love him.'

'What I thought.' Drake shovelled a wedge of mixed meat and sauerkraut into his mouth.

'So, all this you heard is just word-of-mouth stuff? Nothing concrete?'

'All porch talk. Other thing I found out is that Boukman's got hisself a gang. They call theyselves the Saturday Night Barons Club. The SNBC. You heard of 'em?'

Max shook his head.

'You know why that is? 'Cause they don't exist neither.'

'Right.' Max sighed heavily through a cloud of smoke.

'They ain't like the gangs we got here, or like you seen in *The Warriors*, or them Crips and Bloods in LA, feudin' over colours and area codes. The SNBC don't have no identification, no territories, none o' that. But, you can't miss 'em if you see 'em 'cause they supposed to be twelve feet tall.'

'This is all soundin' like you sat around a campfire listenin' to a bunch of stoners who watch too many horror movies.' Max chuckled as he spoke, but his patience was wearing thin. The information was ridiculous, even if there were parallels with what he and Joe had found in the files.

'I'm tellin' you what I heard, Mingus.' Drake glanced at him sharply, looking genuinely affronted, mustard bracketing the ends of his mouth.

'OK. Go on,' Max said. 'Why's it called the Saturday Night Barons Club?'

'You ever see that James Bond flick – *Live and Let Die*?'

'With Gloria Hendry out of *Black Caesar*? Yeah, I saw that.'

'You remember that guy at the back of the train at the end – big ole brother in whiteface, top hat and tails – laughin' his ass off?'

'Uh-huh.'

'That's Baron Samedi, voodoo god of death who only comes out at night. Samedi means Saturday night in French.'

'So Boukman's gang meet up on Saturday nights, like a Mormon prayer group or something?'

'I don't know when they meet up,' Drake chew-spoke. 'But they supposed to have these ceremonies where they worship Baron Samedi. Human sacrifices take place. Only – OK, I know you gonna laugh – the people they kill, they don't really die. I mean they do, but they come back as – erm – zombies.'

Drake paused, waiting for Max to ridicule him.

'Anyone mention the courtroom shooting in April? The name Jean Assad?' Max asked.

'S'matter o' fact people did, yeah – said he was the guy done the shootin'. They said *he* was a zombie.'

'Were the SNBC behind that?'

'Yup. Assad stole smack from Boukman and wound up gettin' sacrificed and zombified. He popped that Colombian in the courtroom, right?'

Max ignored the question.

'Tell me what else you heard about the gang.'

'Way I hear it, the whole gang's Haitian – at least the principals are. They got a lot of like subcontractors workin' for 'em. Cubans, Colombians, Jamaicans, blacks and whites, Jews – damn near ev'ry one. Only the subcontractors ain't actual members. They do one job or ten, get paid, bye bye.'

'They know who they're workin' for?'

'Only if they fuck up or flip.'

'What about names?'

'Only heard the one: Carmine Desamours. He's Haitian.'

Max immediately thought of Eva Desamours.

'He's that green-eyed pimp you as'd about. Guy runs the best hos in Miami. Got 'em divided up into playin' card suits – based on looks and earnin' potential. Hearts are cream, Spades blue cheese – street meat, y'know? – and the in-betweens are milk and yoghurt. All Carmine's girls got a small tattoo on the inside of their thigh to identify whatever suit they from. If a girl starts out a Diamond and ends up a Club, she has a new tattoo put next to the old one, and the old one gets crossed out.'

'Like a cattle brand,' Max commented, more to himself.

'Carmine ain't like *The Mack* – all fur coats, diamonds 'n' gold 'n' all that pizzazz,' Drake continued. 'He's low key, dresses like a bidniss man and don't drive around in no pimpmobile. Fact, you'd never know him fo' a pimp if you saw him. You'd think he be workin' in a bank or sumshit. Smooth motherfucker, pretty boy too, what I hear. But all them other pimps on the track be scared o' him 'cause he got this guy, this enforcer he uses. Big fat motherfucker goes by the name of Bonbon, on account o' how he eats candy the whole time. Bonbon ain't got no teeth neither. He's got these sharp dentures. Bites people's faces off. Pimps see Carmine comin', they run. Carmine wants to knock they best-lookin' hos, they gots to give 'em up. They give him any static, that Bonbon dude come by an' kill 'em. Right there on the street. He don't give a fuck. Way it is out on the track now, pimps won't even put no pretty girls out on the street no mo' 'cause they know Carmine's just gonna come by and knock 'em.'

'Bonbon got another name?'

'Bonbon's all he go by.'

'What else did you hear about him?'

'Nuttin' much, 'cept he's one scary, fearless motherfucker. Rides around wit' these two dykes. Fine-ass bitches, but they be as bad as him. They his security.'

'Get their names?'

'No. Say, you remember Cook Gunnels?'

'Sure,' Max said. Back in the early seventies, Cook Gunnels had had over a hundred hookers working for him. He called himself the King of Pimps and sometimes you used to see him riding around in a pink open-top caddy with a real gold crown on his head and an ermine cape. Gunnels was a nasty sack of shit. He had a reputation for pouring drain cleaner or battery acid down his girls' throats if they held out on him. He had even filmed himself doing it so he could show his new recruits what he was capable of.

'You know how he juss disappeared one day?' Drake said. 'Everybody thought the mob had put concrete boots on him and dumped him out in the ocean. Now I'm hearin' it weren't the mob, but the SNBC killed him. Did him the way he used to do his girls too. 'Cause straight after he went Carmine came on the scene, took over Cook's bidniss.'

'Interesting,' Max said. 'I've seen this Carmine around though. And he ain't twelve feet tall.'

'Yeah, I hear that.' Drake licked the mustard off the sides of his mouth. 'Figured that part for bullshit anyways.'

'Maybe not. The gang could all be standin' on stilts – like in the circus,' Max joked. 'The name Eva Desamours come up in any of your conversations?'

'Yeah. That's his moms. Badass bitch, the way they tell it.

Her and Carmine used to live over in Pork 'n' Beans. People around there still talk about the beatin's she gave him – right there on the street, front o' everybody, like he was some kinda dog done wrong. No one said nuttin' to her 'cause they was scared to. She was supposed to be some kinda voodoo priestess. She told people's fortunes, and she used to do all the abortions in the area, plus she could cure the clap. Thass how she got to know all the hos.'

'Did Boukman know 'em?'

'He musta done, 'cause he came up in Pork 'n' Beans too. He had his gang even then. People was scared o' him too – at least all the non-Haitians was. He looked after his own. You so much as *touched* a Haitian in the projects, Boukman and his crew would come after you.'

'Noble,' Max commented sarcastically. 'Bet the Haitians paid a lot for his services. Tell me about Sam Ismael.'

'He's good people – legit – far as I can tell.' Drake leant back and belched quietly between mouthfuls. 'Comes from a rich Haitian family. Owns most of Lemon City, runs this voodoo store out on North West 54th.'

'No SNBC/Boukman/Desamours ties?'

'None I heard about.' Drake shook his head. 'Most people seem to like him. They say he's gonna redevelop Lemon City into a Haitian quarter, like Little Havana.'

'What's he gonna call it? "Little Haiti"?'

'Has a nice ring to it, don't it?' Drake smiled. He'd now eaten half his Tower of Babel. 'Maybe you should go by an' tell him.'

'Maybe I just might.' Max checked the time. Just gone 9.15. He thought through the information Drake had given him, what best to start working on first. Eva. He'd traced the number he'd taken down in Haiti Mystique to a house in north Miami.

'What can I do for you?' he asked Drake.

'Put this one here in my favour bank an' let it grow. You

374

did right by me with them Palmetto Expressway mother-fuckers.'

'It was a pleasure,' Max said.

'You find out their secret formula?'

'They're still working on it in forensics,' Max lied as he got up to leave.

'Prolly some complex shit,' Drake said, shoving another layer of meat and pickles into his mouth. The formula was actually simple – 50 per cent cocaine, 50 per cent bicarbonate of soda, water, heat, stir until solid, then break off into small quantities and sell cheaply. Anyone could make it and soon everyone who wanted to would. McCalister at the DEA had told Max this new way of smoking coke had already started taking off in the ghettoes of LA, New York and Chicago, and that if it went nationwide it would be an epidemic.

'No way niggas would get hooked on somethin' that fast there wasn't some Einstein shit behind it,' Drake said. 'No way.'

48

Max went to the garage. He found Joe sharing the couch with a thick stack of papers. He'd been there a good while. He'd gone through five large cups of McDonald's take-out coffee and two cans of Coke. He looked beat – bags under bloodshot eyes, face sagging, a downward slope to his shoulders – and there were large sweat stains under the armpits of his powder-blue shirt and damp patches on the front too.

'You sleep here?'

'As good as.' Joe yawned.

'What you got there?' Max asked.

'Revelations,' Joe said. 'I saw Jack Quiñones over the weekend.'

'Yeah? How is he?' Max smiled fondly. Jack was a whole bunch of very rare things – a Fed he liked, a Fed he trusted, a Fed he could work with and a Fed with a sense of humour. They'd frequently cooperated when he'd been stationed in Miami – another rarity, because while police departments grudgingly shared information and resources, getting more than a straight refusal from a G-Man was like getting Mount Rushmore to crack a smile. Feds looked down on ordinary cops; liked them to know they not only had more power, better resources, better training and bigger brains, but that they could walk on water too, as and when duty called. Jack was the exception. He was more interested in solving crimes and saving lives than in winning bureaucratic pissing contests. Since the previous September, he'd been in Atlanta, trying to catch the killer who'd so far claimed the lives of twenty black children.

'He called me up for some intel on those two Aryan Brotherhood pricks we took down in '79.'

'Lund and Wydell?'

'Remember the uncle, Dennis Kreis? Jack thinks Kreis might have something to do with Atlanta – or at least know the button man. He wanted copies of our files on Kreis. So I traded up for some Fed intel on Boukman.'

'That's *some* intel.' Max glanced over at the block of paper cratering the couch.

'There's at least three dead trees of bullshit there – you know, the usual rumour and conjecture stuff, the guy changin' appearance, the guy bein' in five places at once, the guy havin' two tongues – *but* someone has accurately IDed Boukman.'

'As what? A blonde three-legged midget?' Max laughed.

'No.' Joe shook his head. 'There were photographs.'

'*Were* photographs . . . ?'

'Yeah, they're gone,' Joe said. 'What happened was this: December the fifth last year, the Feds arrested a nineteen-year-old Haitian called Pierre-Jerome Matisse for sellin' coke to frat kids. They'd had him under surveillance for four months. He was gettin' his shit from Haiti. Best quality – high 80s, low 90s. A Pan Am pilot was bringin' it in for him, a kee at a time. The pilot was workin' for the Feds.

'Once they get him in custody Pierre calls his dad in Haiti. Daddy is Legrand Matisse, a colonel in the Haitian army. Daddy has been importin' coke into Miami from Haiti for the past three years. Daddy calls his lawyer, the late Coleman Crabbe of Winesap, McIntosh, Crabbe and Milton.'

'Moyez's lawyer?' Max asked as a cold feeling passed into his stomach.

'The very same.' Joe nodded. 'Up until two years ago, the Feds, the DEA and the Coastguard all thought most of the coke coming into Miami was gettin' in via the Colombians – go-fast boats and light aircraft. It is, but that ain't the main route. A *lot* of the shit we've been gettin' here is comin' in from Haiti.

'They already had intel that Solomon Boukman was a player in the Haitian drug connection, only it wasn't until Matisse that they realized the magnitude of what the guy is actually doin'. I mean, he *is* the Haitian connection.

'The Feds originally thought Boukman was a link in the chain – just another small fish workin' for the Colombians, or maybe workin' with the Cubans. But Boukman ain't just collectin' from point A and deliverin' to point B. They've now established that the motherfucker buys from the Colombians direct, flies it over to Haiti and from Haiti to here. *Then* he sells and distributes. I mean, all he needs to do now is find some place to grow coca leaves and he'll be a one-man industry.'

'How did they know all this?'

'Colonel Matisse. He was workin' for Boukman. According to the report, half the Haitian officer corps are. Matisse was in charge of the pick-up from Colombia to Haiti and the Haiti–Miami drop-off.' Joe wiped his sweaty brow with his hand. 'Matisse cut a deal with the Feds. He'd give 'em Boukman and his entire Haitian operation in exchange for his son's freedom. Crabbe negotiated the whole thing.

'But the Feds have the same problem we do. Who exactly *is* Boukman? What does he *look* like? There's nothin' official on him – no social security number, no immigration papers, no criminal record. *Nada.*'

'Maybe he's an illegal who's been real lucky,' Max said.

'Maybe.' Joe nodded. 'But the Feds know Boukman's got himself some serious juice in high places. I'll come to that.'

Max lit a cigarette and looked in the fridge for some water. There was only beer. He'd promised Sandra he wouldn't have any alcohol until after 7 p.m., and only every other day, and never when they were together – unless it was wine with a meal. Only he didn't drink wine because it gave him an acid stomach and a headache in quick succession. He closed the fridge.

'You ain't havin' a brew?' Joe frowned at his partner with surprise.

'Too early,' Max said.

Joe gave him a knowing look. 'Must be love.'

'Carry on.' Max smiled.

'She gets you to quit the cancer sticks, I'll kiss her feet one toe at a time.'

'Carry *on*,' Max repeated, his smile getting broader.

'OK. So the Feds needed an ID. Matisse told Crabbe he had photographs of Boukman. He said he'd had 'em taken in secret, the last time they met face to face, in 1978. As insurance. Now, it was definitely Boukman, because they went way back. Had mutual friends or – no, that was it – they shared a fortune teller.'

'Who?' Max asked. 'Eva Desamours?'

'I don't know. Or maybe it was in his deposition. Crabbe flew out to Haiti before Christmas and took a full deposition from Matisse. Matisse also gave him the photographs. Crabbe then called the Feds to let them know Matisse hadn't just given up all the Haitian cocaine high command, but he'd also given him his contacts in Customs, the Miami PD, the DEA and the FBI.'

'*Christ!*' Max sat down. 'And Crabbe gave that stuff to his secretary, Nora Wong, right?'

'Yeah.' Joe nodded slowly and heavily, remembering the NYPD's crime scene report and the photographs. 'The Feds never got to see any of it because they didn't free Pierre-Jerome. They wanted to change the terms of the deal. They said they'd have no way of knowing if Matisse wasn't making the whole thing up, so they'd only let the kid go home *after* they had people in custody. And they wanted Matisse to testify against Boukman in open court. Matisse said no dice. Crabbe was in the middle of renegotiating when he got gunned down with Moyez.'

'So Moyez was never the target: Crabbe was.'

'That's right.' Joe nodded.

'*Shit*. Didn't he make any fucken' copies of the deposition?'

'If he did, they ain't turned up. My guess is they're gone,' Joe said.

'What about Matisse?'

'He's dead. On the morning of May the fourth – the same day as the Moyez trial – Matisse, his wife and their two other children were all shot dead as they ate breakfast at their home in Port-au-Prince.'

'And Pierre-Jerome?'

'Found dead in his cell.'

'Wasn't he in solitary?'

'Yeah. Someone put ground glass in his oatmeal. It's an old trick.'

'Mother-*FUCKER*!' Max yelled, getting up. 'How in the fuck did Boukman pull this shit off?'

'Everyone has a price, Max, and everything can be bought. Those drug guys have got a *lot* of money.'

'So Boukman hit *everyone* on the same fucken' day – in *two* countries!'

'Yup.' Joe sighed.

'But think of that! That's high-level counter-intel! That takes meticulous planning! You can't get shit like that together in what? – a *week*!'

'Well, he did it,' Joe said wearily, as Max paced back and forth across the garage. 'Boukman must've had a guy close to Matisse. It's the only explanation.'

'What are the Feds doing now?' Max asked.

'They're tryin' to plug their leak. Then they've gotta start on Boukman all over again. Their last report said Boukman has recruited himself a brand new employee – Ernest

Bennett, father-in-law to Baby Doc Duvalier, the president of Haiti himself.'

'Wouldn't surprise me if it was true, wouldn't surprise me if it was bullshit,' Max said gloomily. He crushed out his cigarette and lit another.

Joe knew Max's angers: there was the cold, speechless kind that was always the prelude to physical violence; frustrations and other people's fuck-ups would make him yell and shout; hitting a brick wall in a case would make him do the same – until he went and sat in a church and got his head together. Joe had seen him close to tears when they'd found the bodies of missing kids – but they weren't tears of sorrow, they were tears of rage. Now he was mad as hell all right, yet there was a worry about his anger, almost a fearful tone to his venting. Joe knew what he was going through. He'd been there this morning, feeling so stunted by the length of Boukman's reach he'd wanted to quit the case. He'd got as far as starting to dial Max's number from a nearby payphone to wake him up and tell him, but then he'd thought of the reasons he'd started this whole thing in the first place and put the receiver down.

Max stopped pacing. He thought of Sandra. He saw again her smiling face on his pillow last night when he'd told her he loved her. He saw her sitting at his kitchen table yesterday morning, dressed in one of his shirts, reading the paper. He'd stood in the doorway just looking at her without her noticing, thinking how beautiful she was and how he was the luckiest guy in the world right then. If they carried on with this case the way they were, he'd be putting her in danger. But he couldn't let Joe down.

Max sat on the couch and looked at the black, sticky oil-stained floor. Outside he heard the rumble of thunder.

49

Carmine parked the dark green Ford pickup in the lot of the Hervis Family Supermarket on South West 8th Avenue and discreetly checked himself out in a mirror. He was delighted with the results. He'd always wished he'd been born with straight hair, like his dad's, and now he'd fulfilled his wish. OK, so it *was* a wig, but it wasn't an *obvious* wig like some of the spades wore, or those ridiculous, blow-away-in-a-breeze toupees those white old timers in South Beach wore, this one was *subtle* – a short straight head of real black hair, parted in the middle with a little fringe falling over his right brow. He looked bona fide *Cubano* now.

It wasn't the first time he'd had straight hair. A few years back he'd had it 'chemically relaxed'. That was a nice moment, driving down Biscayne Bay in his coupé, sea wind blowing back his hair; it even had a little *bounce* to it when he walked – just like white folks in shampoo commercials. Things had of course gone critically wrong when he'd gone home for his bath that evening. His mother had freaked out and hacked it all off with a pair of kitchen scissors – damn near *ripped* it out, when she couldn't work those shears fast enough – and then she'd stuffed it in his mouth and tried to make him swallow it. He'd almost choked to death. But, still, looking back at the momentary happiness he'd felt that afternoon, it had somehow been worth it. She'd never be able to take that away from him, no matter what she did.

Carmine had made other changes to himself too – a whole new disguise. He was pretending to be a house painter, after seeing a bunch of them driving by Haiti Mystique to go and work on the houses Sam was renovating on the corner of

62nd Street and North East 2nd Avenue, close to the Dupuis Building. Carmine had bought a pickup second hand, eight gallons of white and yellow paint, brushes and floor sheets to put in the back; and then, to complete his transformation, he'd got himself a set of khaki overalls and steel-capped boots, which he'd dripped multicoloured paint on for that 'used look'. When Sam had seen him he'd told him he looked like he'd stepped out of a Jackson Pollock exhibition. He'd tried his disguise out on a couple of Clubs. He'd solicited them in español. They'd taken one look at him and said they weren't no soup kitchen pussy. He hadn't blown his cover. He'd just turned, walked out and punched the air in triumph. No one looked twice at a painter – not even hos – so this way he'd be safe from the cops. Not that he'd actually heard anything more about the guy in the salon on the news, but that didn't mean they weren't looking for him.

He checked his watch: 2.37 p.m. Good, he thought, she'd be right in the middle of her shift. He'd catch her unawares, just sneak right up on her. Julita Leljedal.

He'd been looking for Julita for a year and a half. She skipped town, owing him $1,250. Last week one of his Spades had told him they'd seen her working at the – get this – *meat section* of HFS.

When he'd first seen her, in 1976, Julita had been a stripper over at an upmarket club called Luckies on Le Jeune. Back then he used to go trawling a lot of titty bars for potential Diamonds and Clubs, and the girls were usually real easy pickings.

Julita was one of the prettiest, sexiest girls he'd ever seen – long black hair, blue-green eyes like the ocean, light-bronze skin. She was petite – just over five feet tall and flat chested – but *boy* did she have an ass! Guys used to come from all over to see her dance. She had a routine she did with a silver baton. She'd catch a guy's eye, pout her luscious lips at him and then lick the stick and jerk her hand up and down it, while she ground her hips and wiggled her ass. The guy would shower her with all the money in his wallet every time. She had an uncanny way of knowing exactly which guy to focus on too. The night they'd met she'd done her routine on Carmine and he'd thrown her not the usual five- and ten-dollar bills, but a whole bunch of C-notes.

He'd put her and her cousin Kitty up in an apartment overlooking Maximo Gomez Park. She'd carried on dancing, only now she was taking the richest customers home and fucking them too.

Cousin Kitty didn't start off a ho. She was a trainee nurse and, anyway, she was so damn ugly – bad skin, thick pink-framed glasses and greasy brown hair that looked like the hide of a wet donkey – *no way* could Carmine even have turned her out as a Spade, even if he'd wanted to.

But then one night one of Julita's tricks offered her $1,000 to perform an enema on him. Kitty knew exactly what to do. The next night the guy came round for more of the same.

Sensing a too-good-to-miss opportunity, Carmine set Kitty up in business, servicing medical procedure fetishists. She and Julita dressed up in rubber nurse's uniforms and gave those sick fuckolos the times of their lives. For a year, Carmine made serious bank. But then, in February 1979, it had gone pear-shaped. Kitty gave an enema wrong and ruptured a guy's intestine. He died in the apartment. Carmine took the body away and got rid of it. When he went back, Julita and Kitty had split. They'd taken their clothes and the $1,250 the guy had paid them. He'd been looking for them – specifically Julita – ever since.

He got out of the truck and walked over to the super-market. It was a big sprawling place which didn't just sell food, but clothes, plants, electrical tools, TVs and even minor car parts. Everything was in Spanish, from the signs to the canned music to all the conversation he heard around him.

He headed for the meat section.

It took him a while and two double-takes to recognize Julita, first because her hair was bunched up under white netting, second because of the uniform they had her working in – a shapeless dark blue dress with red and white piping – and third because she'd put on a whole heap of weight. Her hips were broader, her ass bigger, her calves were about the size as his waist and she had the beginnings of a double chin. She couldn't have been more than twenty-five when she was working for him. Now she looked ten years older. Mamacita had lost all her sexiness.

He watched her from a distance, as she stacked plastic trays of juicy red steak on a shelf from an overflowing shopping cart. She finished what she was doing and pushed the cart along a little way and then started filling up the shelves again.

When her back was to him, he walked up and greeted her the way he always had.

'*Hola, chica.*'

She froze in mid-motion. He saw her shoulders expand a little as she took a deep breath before turning around.

It was her all right. Her face had got broader and she looked tired and pale, but those eyes hadn't changed much.

'How d'you find me?' she said. She didn't look worried or scared like he'd expected her to, just looked him up and down from his paint-spattered boots to his hair.

'It's a small world, baby.' He smiled, wondering why she hadn't commented on his appearance, let alone failed to recognize him.

'I ain't workin' for you no more, Carmine,' she said.

'I can see that.' He laughed, nodding at the shopping cart. 'You really landed on your knees, girl! Not that you wasn't already on 'em.'

'It's better than what I used to do,' she said.

'If you say so.'

'What do you want?'

'My $1,250.'

'All the money you make off them stupid hos and you comin' after me for a itty-bitty $1,250?'

'So $1,250's itty bitty, huh? Means you got $1,250 to gi' me.'

'I ain't got no $1,250 to give you,' she said. 'Fact, I ain't even got twelve dollars and fifty cents to give you. An' I ain't got zip to give you no how, 'cause I'm outta that life. You know why I left? It wasn't just 'cause of what happened to that old pervert, it was 'cause I was two months pregnant.'

'*For real?* You keep it?'

'Them.'

'You had twins?'

'Girls.'

'*Dayum!*' Carmine didn't know what else to say. It explained the extra pounds. Now, when and if – it was real rare, because contraception was strictly enforced – Cards got pregnant, they were made to have abortions. Well, the earners were. Spades, or Clubs on the slide to Spadedom, were just cut loose.

'Who's the daddy?'

'I dunno,' she said. 'Some trick.'

'How'd that happen?'

'How d'you think?'

'But what about them pills I got for you?'

'They were making me fat.'

Not as fat as you are now, he thought, but didn't say it.

Truth was, he didn't know what to say. Congratulations, was the way it went, but he'd never congratulated nobody on nothin', 'specially not a ho on havin' no kid.

He was stunned, and a little disappointed. OK, he hadn't really come here for the money. It was sweat of a ho's back to him. Truth was, he'd felt a little hurt when Julita had upped and gone like that. He'd wanted to know why. A little part of him had liked her, because in a certain light, dancing up there, before she started losing her clothes, she'd reminded him a lot of Lucita, his father's girlfriend. All right then, he had been a little sweet on her, sweetest he'd ever been on any ho. He'd had a few good times with her outside business hours. She was fun to be around – great sense of humour, made him laugh; sometimes she did this thing where she stopped talking and just looked at him with those eyes of hers that told him so many sweet things. He loved that. And he loved listenin' to her fuckin' those tricks. She just talked that sweet español – '*Si, papi. Siii, papi. Siii, siiii, mi amor*' – and that got them, and him, all the way off. He'd even come close to fuckin' her himself a couple of times, when they'd had a few drinks and were fooling around, but the prospect of his mother findin' out had pulped his wood. Still, in another life, he probably would've wifed her. And they'd-a had twins too – good-looking ones at that.

On the business side she'd been a great earner. She'd given him every cent she made from fucking. She'd never complained or whined or cried like most of his Cards. He was so impressed with this, he'd let her keep the money she made from dancing.

'You got a man now?' he asked.

'What's it to you?'

'Just a question.'

'What kinda man wants a woman with two kids, Carmine?'

A guy who could love you, he thought, but didn't say. Shit, why was he being this way? She was a ho, he told himself, a ho – *yo*' ho.

He looked at her, this time with his money eyes, figuring what he could still do with her. In her state he wouldn't even have put her out as a Spade. Sure, *someone*'d want to fuck her, but he had standards to maintain. Her tits had gotten bigger, which was a plus, but he was sure they sagged; even with a strict diet she'd have stretch marks on her belly and her ass would never regain its money-making shape. She'd be a Club at best, but not for too long.

Not worth it, he told himself. Leave her be. Say goodbye, then turn and go. Go get another ho.

'I'm sorry,' he said at last. Part of him felt responsible for what had happened to her, part of him wanted suddenly and very desperately to stop what he was doing.

'I'm not,' she said. 'You think I miss that life? I don't. And now I gotta chance to help my kids do better than me.'

An idea began to form in Carmine's mind. He had over $10,000 in the glove compartment. He could give her half of it for her babies, like a – what was it they did in companies when they paid people off? – yeah, that was it – a golden handshake.

But as he was thinking this he saw the expression on her face change quite suddenly. Her eyes widened, her mouth opened a little and she went deathly pale.

She wasn't looking at him but over to his right.

Carmine heard slow, heavy and very familiar footsteps coming up and stopping right beside him.

'Well, ain't this nice?' a soft wheezing, lisping voice said in his ear.

Carmine smelt sugared almonds and the stench of rotting meat. It was Bonbon.

'What you doin' here?' Carmine turned to look at him.

'Yo' moms sent me.' Bonbon was sucking on a piece of candy as usual.

Carmine didn't know how or why, dressed the way he was, the fat fuck wasn't sweating bullets. He was wearing a black fedora with a black band, a knee-length coat, black, dark grey wool trousers, a white dress shirt and a bright yellow and red striped waistcoat. His gleaming patent-leather loafers bulged at the sides.

'Why?'

'To run things.'

'Run what?'

'Yo' bidniss.'

'*What?*'

'Sam needs you to cover for him at the store for a couple-a weeks, 'cause he gots bidniss o' the important kind to handle,' Bonbon said. He had standard teeth in – small, gleaming white squares that made his mouth look like an open zipper.

'But I got bidniss o' my *own* important kind. I can't mind no *store*,' Carmine said. Bonbon must've been following him all day although he couldn't remember seeing his car. Then again, he hadn't exactly been paying attention to the possibility of being tailed, so absorbed had he been with his new hair.

'You wanna take it up wit' yo' moms, she's out back in the car.'

Carmine didn't answer. He felt suddenly humiliated, cut down to three feet tall. He looked at Julita, who hadn't moved. She was gawping at Bonbon with pure terror, like he was an oncoming truck and she was nailed to the road.

Bonbon checked Carmine out, head to toe. They were about the same height, but Bonbon's hat gave him an extra few inches, his girth a few extra people.

'Dressed like you been in a paint fight. And whass up with that wack-ass *wig*, man? Look like a dead bat fell on you and liked it.'

Carmine wanted to say something to that, something about him bein' a fat toothless stinking-mouth psycho fuck, but he saw the pearl handles of one of the two Smith & Wesson .44 Magnums Bonbon wore on either hip, jutting out from under his coat.

Bonbon turned to Julita.

'Whatchu' still standin' there fo'?' he hissed sharply, like venom hitting a hot frying pan. 'You owe $1,250. An' you gonna repay it – wit' two hundred po'cent interest.'

'Mister, I ain't got no money,' Julita pleaded.

'I can see *that*,' Bonbon sneered. 'But you gon' go an' get me some.'

'How?' she said, her eyes tearing up. She knew what was coming next and that she couldn't refuse.

'As o' today you got a new job. Corner of 63rd Street. Call it a prom-*ho*-shun.' Bonbon chuckled.

'But – but I got kids – babies . . .' The tears were pouring down her face.

'Sad, sad, too fuckin' bad.' Bonbon shook his head. 'Now go get outta that clown suit and come right back here.'

'Carmine . . . please . . .' Julita cried.

'Carmine ain't gonna help you.' Bonbon got closer to her. 'Go on get yo' things, walk out and get in the black Merc you see outside. Ain't but one. An' don'tchu be tryin' nuttin' like tellin' the manager or callin' the cops, 'cause you *know* what I'ma do to you *and* yo' *bebés*.'

Carmine looked at her sorrowfully.

'Sixty-third Street's in Liberty City,' she said, her voice trembling.

'Thass right. The brothers love theyselves some Cuban pussy, specially them white-lookin' ones like you. You gon' *be* on that track and you gon' *stay* on that track till you settle yo' debt.'

She opened her mouth and tried to speak, but nothing came out of her lips moving soundlessly liked a beached, dying fish.

'Hustle *bitch*!' Bonbon hissed.

She walked away, off to the back of the store, head down, shoulders slumped, unsteady on her feet.

'Now *thass* how you handle hos, Carmine,' Bonbon said, turning back to him with a smile.

'Don't tell me how to do my job!' Carmine snapped. 'I *built* this damn bidniss.'

'Yo' moms and Solomon built dis bidniss,' Bonbon corrected him. 'An' I made sure thangs was runnin' right. You done the next best thang to shit. Pimp always gotta have a whip in one hand and a leash in tha other. All you ever had in yo' hand Carmine was yo' dick. Why this is *mines* now.'

Carmine knew then that his mother had demoted him for good. Bonbon had never disrespected him like this, never talked down to him. He hadn't dared.

Carmine was too stunned to think straight.

He turned around and left the supermarket.

Outside he saw the black Mercedes with the tinted windows parked alongside his truck. He could sense he was being watched from the car. He thought he even heard women's laughter inside as he passed. He didn't look at the Merc. He got in the truck and drove out of the lot, heading for Haiti Mystique.

What the fuck was going on? Why had they done this to him? Sure, his mother hated his guts, but he'd always brought her a steady stream of top-class girls – earners. And he was damn good at finding and recruiting talent. No one could charm a bitch like him – no one – and certainly not *Bonbon*. It made no sense. No sense at all.

Then he thought of Julita, but instead he saw Lucita. Stupid he hadn't realized this before, but even their names were similar. Julita and Lucita.

His heart grew heavy, his throat tightened and an over-whelming sense of hopelessness swallowed him. He couldn't do wrong *or* right without somehow fucking both up.

Without the pimping he was useless, good for absolutely *nothing*.

He saw his mother, imagined how she'd taunt him tonight in the bathroom, rub his failure in his face until he choked on it.

Julita wouldn't last long on 63rd Street. The Spades down there would give her hell 'cause she was the new girl on the block – and a *white* girl at that. Didn't matter she was Cuban.

That'd make it even worse for her. The gangster kids would run trains on her at five bucks a pop. No way would she ever earn back that $1,250. She'd be used up in two months. Bonbon knew this. It was his way of punishing her for stealing off them. Carmine wished he hadn't gone to see her, then none of this would've happened. He'd gone and ruined not just her life, but her little girls' too.

He tried to gee himself up, think of brighter things.

What did they say 'bout hittin' rock bottom? The only way was up.

There was Nevada to look forward to. What about all that money he'd stashed away? That was something to hold on to. All wasn't lost. There was still hope.

Yeah, right!

Who the fuck was he foolin'?

It was just him in here, on his own, cold light of day.

He might've been at the bottom of wherever he'd been kicked to now, but he sensed there was further to fall.

This was the start of the end.

50

The number Max had taken down in Haiti Mystique was for a house on North East 128th Street, North Miami Beach. Both house and phone were registered to Eva Desamours.

Early on Wednesday morning Max and Joe drove out to North Miami Beach in a blue '78 Ford Ranchero they'd got from the car pool. The car ran fine, but outwardly it looked like a piece of shit – rusted fenders, scratches and chipped paint on the bodywork, dents in the hood and side – ideal camouflage for the area, where every vehicle was a third generation hand-me-down.

North Miami Beach wasn't quite the worst the city had to offer, but it was a million miles from the best. Its main tourist attractions were the St Bernard de Clairvaux Church off the West Dixie Highway – a medieval Spanish monastery William Randolph Hearst had bought in Europe and had had dismantled and shipped, down to the last brick, all the way over to the States – and a nudist beach at Haulover Park, across the Intercoastal Waterway, which was the target of regular protests by Christian fundamentalists. In-between the two was a drab area of working- and welfare-class homes, ugly-looking condos and cheapo stores where half the shelves were empty. Crime was high here, most of it comparatively petty and tame by Miami's current standards – burglaries, home invasions, domestic violence, rapes and murders – but there was still too much of it for the under-staffed and over-extended local police to deal with, so they were forced to prioritize. Violence against the very young or the very old got their full attention. Anyone in-between was out of luck.

They found the house – a small pale pink bungalow with a screened porch and a palm tree growing to its left. It was set back from the road and surrounded by a well-tended lawn with a flower-lined brick path leading to the front door, easily the best-looking home in a street filled with dismal bungalows struggling to stay upright, losing the battle against their own decrepitude. Although some owners had erected barbed-wire fences around them, put bars on the windows and left various breeds of attack dogs out in their front yards, gang graffiti still adorned two-thirds of the homes.

They rolled a little further down the road and parked behind a dusty, brown Pontiac, opposite the house. It was 8.05 a.m.

Joe turned on the radio. The Rolling Stones' 'Start Me Up' was playing. The song was all over the airwaves and racing up the charts. Joe nodded his head along with the beat and drummed his fingers on the steering wheel. Max looked out of the window, first at the light grey sky, then at the matching tone of the street, wishing his partner had better taste in music.

Forty minutes later a gleaming black Mercedes 300D with tinted windows, eight-spoke silver rims and whitewall tyres stopped in front of the house. Max took out a Nikon FM camera fitted with a 50 mm lens and started snapping.

A tall, fat, dark-skinned man, wearing a long black coat, white gloves and a fedora stepped out and opened the passenger door. A woman with short black hair and the same complexion as the driver emerged. She was dressed in an elegant brown trouser suit and pumps and carried an alligator-skin purse. She talked to the man for a moment. Next to him she looked starved and frail, but Max could see from the cowed expression on his face that she commanded his absolute respect.

The woman walked briskly up to the house, unlocked the door and went inside. The man got back in the car.

'The driver looks like Fatty Arbuckle's shadow,' Joe quipped.

'Guessing from his appearance, that'll be Bonbon,' Max said, putting the camera down on his lap. 'And the royalty's Eva Desamours.'

At 9.08 a silver Porsche Turbo pulled up behind the Mercedes and a tall, slim, blonde woman got out. She was dressed expensively – tailor-made blue silk suit, gold jewellery on her wrists, hands, neck and ears – and long hair coiffed in a bouffant mane which didn't move at all as she clicked her way along the sidewalk and up the path to the house with the well-drilled grace of a catwalk model. She was beautiful, but it was beauty cut in ice – all the aloofness money could buy. Max knew who she was.

'She must be loaded. That's a brand new Turtle.' Joe nodded at the Porsche 911.

'Don't you recognize her?' Max asked.

'Sure, that's Cheryl Tiegs,' his partner joked.

'Bunny Mason.'

'As in Pitch Mason's wife?'

'Uh-huh.'

Pitch Mason was a major cocaine distributor who had slipped two elaborate DEA stings, because, it was widely rumoured, he'd been tipped off by someone on the inside. During the past year, Mason had become a society-page regular because of the stables and stud farms he owned and because of his wife – a former swimsuit model – who he referred to openly as his 'favourite filly'.

An hour later, Eva Desamours came out with Bunny Mason, walked her to her car, air-kissed her on both cheeks and waved goodbye as she roared off down the road.

The next visitor arrived in a red Ferrari 308 at 10.25. Latina, older, shorter and far stouter than her predecessor.

She had a round, hard face, black hair in a short ponytail and a huge pair of sunglasses that reminded both Max and Joe of the kind of outlandish specs Elton John wore. She was dressed in a black velour tracksuit with diamanté trim and matching slippers. She strode quickly up to the door with all the grace of a pissed-off pitbull.

'Know *her*?' Joe asked.

'No, but counting the Turtle, we've got the drug dealer's automobile trifecta here,' Max said as he photographed the woman disappearing into the house. Mercedes, Porsches and Ferraris had become so popular with Miami's *coco-riche* that car dealers had virtually run out of them and waiting lists were eight months long.

As before Eva came out to the sidewalk with her client and stayed until she'd left the street.

Two more visits followed – a black woman in a Mercedes Benz 450SEL 6.9, a redhead in another Porsche, both in their late twenties/early thirties, both wearing their money, both staying roughly an hour apiece.

'That's a high-end client base. She must be good,' Max remarked.

'Or a good bullshitter,' Joe said.

'Same coin,' Max said. 'You ever had your fortune read?'

'Nah,' Joe said. 'That shit creeps me out.'

'So you believe in it?'

'Sure. There's something in it. But outside of this job, I don't wanna know what's round the corner. Kinda defeats the object of living.'

When she'd seen off her last customer, Bonbon emerged from the car and opened the passenger door. Eva Desam-ours got in and they pulled away. As they did so, Max noticed a line of small pieces of paper lying in the gutter where the Mercedes had been parked.

He went over to take a look. There were at least twenty red and white striped candy wrappers lying there – identical to the one he'd found in the Lacour house. He scooped them up in his handkerchief.

They tailed the Mercedes back to Haiti Mystique. Eva walked into the store at 3.15. Five minutes later Sam Ismael pulled up in an orange Honda and went inside.

They left together after five, each going in separate directions – Ismael east, Eva west.

Max photographed the comings and goings.

'When are we gonna look in there?' Joe asked as they drove past the store, following the Mercedes.

'Tomorrow night,' Max said.

Eva Desamours lived in an imposing coral-rock house in a wide, leafy residential road off Bayshore Drive; only the top tier and roof of her home were visible behind the high wall surrounding it and the palm, banyon and mango trees growing in its grounds.

The Mercedes stopped outside a spiked iron gate, which opened automatically from the inside. The car went in.

'Very flashy,' Joe commented.

'What did you expect? Dopers get high, dealers get to live in a piece of heaven,' Max said.

A few minutes later the gate opened again and the Mercedes came out.

At 5.45 a white Ford pickup truck went through the gate. Max recognized Carmine at the wheel.

'That ain't a pimp mobile,' Joe said.

'Maybe he's been demoted.'

Max got a picture of the plates.

No one came out of the house. When it started going dark, at around 8.30, spotlights went on in the trees, bathing what they could see of the house in a deep green, shadow-splashed pall, making it look like it was covered in camouflage netting. A light went on in one of the top-floor rooms, but they couldn't see inside because the curtains were closed.

They waited another two hours, by which time the light upstairs had gone out.

Max and Joe called it a day.

It was close to midnight when Max got to Sandra's place. They'd decided to spend alternate weeks in each other's apartments as a prelude to buying a home together. Yes, they both agreed things were moving fast, that maybe they should be taking longer, factoring in pauses, checking each other out, looking for fatal flaws, but it just felt right between them. No point in delaying the inevitable.

Before letting himself in, Max sat down on the steps and lit up a cigarette. The atmosphere was hot, humid and oppressive, with no wind and the smell of a downpour heavy in the air. Not that anyone seemed to notice or care. Little Havana was alive with its usual sounds – multiple parties trying to drown each other out with live salsa, car horns, firecrackers, arguments – good natured and angry. He smelled barbecues and Cuban cooking. He really wanted a drink, a shot and a cool brew – that'd be real nice. But Sandra would smell it on him and he'd promised her. He hoped he'd get used to not drinking, that he wouldn't be one of those secret sippers who used mouthwash after every transgression.

Solomon watched the white pig sitting on the steps of the apartment building, smoking his cigarette. He was sat in the back of the yellow cab he'd been following the cop in ever since he and his partner had left Eva's house.

'He's not Cuban,' Solomon said to Bonbon, who was at the wheel. 'His woman must live there.'

'Want me to take him?'

'Not yet,' Solomon said. 'Tomorrow I'll know everything about him.'

The cop flicked his cigarette out into the middle of the street, got up and went into the apartment.

Solomon got out of the cab and walked over to where the cigarette was still smouldering. He put it out with his foot, slipped the butt into a clear ziplock plastic bag and went back to the cab.

Every time it rained in Miami, it was like God was trying to wash the city into the sea. Today He was trying extra hard.

Rain, wind, lightning *and* thunder.

Carmine was getting his tic like crazy, his left cheek snapping back and forth every couple of seconds like a rubber band in the hands of a hyperactive child. He'd slap himself hard to correct it, but it would just get worse, his nervous spasm feeding off his anger and frustration and yanking up half his face, completely closing his eye.

He was stood behind the counter of Haiti Mystique, watching the deluge come down in slanted sheets, relentless in its intensity, transforming the street into a wide, fast-flowing stream. The drains were choked and spilling their dark brown guts; solitary passing cars were throwing up knee-high waves, which would crash on the sidewalk, splash walls and windows and ooze under doorways.

Bad day to do ho bidniss, the sorry state o' my sorry ass, thought Carmine, before remembering, with something close to relief, that he'd been demoted to store manager. That was some kind of joke. There wasn't anything to manage. In all the time he'd been in his 'new job', he hadn't served a single customer. In fact, the only people to come through the door outside of him and Lulu had been Sam and Eva, when they'd had their meeting downstairs yesterday.

Sam had been on the TV news and in the papers, standing in front of a row of derelict buildings on North East 2nd Avenue, talking about how he was going to renovate and reinvigorate the area, how he was going to turn it into a Haitian-themed neighbourhood, and how he was already talking to city officials about renaming the place 'Little Haiti'. The press were already referring to him as 'the Haitian George Merrick', after the man who'd transformed Coral Gables out of orange groves. Same concept, different fruit. Tonight Sam was going to be at a big gala dinner at the Fontainebleau Hotel to formally launch the project.

So Sam was a busy man – too busy to talk to Carmine. Carmine was wondering how much Sam knew about Bonbon taking over the pimping. Had he known about it in advance? Maybe, maybe not. Why would they have told him? It had nothing to do with him. But Carmine couldn't be sure. Just like he couldn't be sure that Sam hadn't told his mother about Nevada.

Nevada? Well, that was all fucked anyway. Wasn't going to happen. He didn't have the heart or guts or balls *or* mind to do that any more – not after what had happened to Julita. He'd spent yesterday night seeing as many of his sideline Cards as he could find, telling them he was cutting them loose. A few had cried, asked him what they were going to do. Some had asked him what *he* was going to do. Most had taken it with a shrug and a see-ya.

He was still getting out of Miami though, and getting out soon – out of the city, out of his mother's clutches, and out of this sad, bad, broken-down existence.

He'd be gone next Wednesday. He was just about ready.

He'd moved all his money to a locker at the airport. He'd stashed the key at home, deep in his jar of coffee. On Departure Day he'd leave like he was going to work, but he'd go to Miami International instead and get on a plane. He wouldn't tell a soul. Not even Sam. And definitely not his mother.

Where would he go?

He'd first thought of Phoenix, because of that Isaac Hayes song – an old favourite of his – where a man leaves a cheating wife for the last time. But he'd dismissed that as a bad idea because the guy in the song never gets there, and, besides, Sam or someone would probably work it out. So he'd gone through the names of American towns he'd stored up in his mind, names of places he'd heard and never forgotten. He'd dismissed the familiar ones, the landmark cities, until he'd come up with Buffalo. Perfect. Who the fuck would think of looking for him in Buffalo?

What he'd do when he got there, he didn't know, but it would be better than this shit.

The rain let up in the early afternoon and the thunder stopped completely. Carmine left Lulu to mind the store and took a drive over to 63rd Street. He was still using the pickup.

The Spades were all out on the sidewalk, some under umbrellas, others in short and shiny plastic raincoats with nothing but their underwear on. They stood near the kerbs in their twos, three and fours, eyeballing every car that passed, sometimes waving and calling out to the drivers they locked eyes with.

He finally saw Julita, off on her own, near the end of the street. She was wearing a red dress that barely covered her crotch, black spike heels and a transparent windcheater. She looked scared, sad and tired. When she saw the pickup slowing she dipped her eyes to the ground. She hadn't even seen him. He thought of stopping and giving her a ride, but he knew he couldn't take her anywhere, so instead he drove on.

He arrived at Haiti Mystique right after 4.00 p.m and sent Lulu home. No point in keeping her around. Besides, he wanted to be alone, give himself space to think.

He looked around for something to keep him busy for the last half hour of his day and saw that the drum collection needed wiping down.

Blondie's 'Rapture' was playing on the radio. He turned it up a little. The song made him laugh, that white girl trying to be the Sugar Hill Gang. She really didn't have the first clue about rapping, thought it was just talking like she was going over speed bumps – and that crap she was spouting about eating cars and bars and men from Mars. Jesus! Still, that bitch *was* fine-looking, a straight-up Heart.

He corrected himself. He had to stop thinking that way, breaking women down into Suits, into how much he could get for them. That day was done. Fact of the matter was – if he was truthful to himself – he never had been a *real* pimp. Not exactly. All he'd actually done was seduce, recruit and collect. The creative side. He'd never actually set up the business. That had all been his mother. All right, so he'd had his Secret Suit. But that wasn't exactly his fault. What else could he do for money? It was all he knew. He was a – what was it those defence lawyers were always saying? – yeah, 'a product of his environment'. That was it! That's what he was. It was all his mother's fault. She'd started it, virtually as soon as they'd moved into Pork 'n' Beans. She'd pimped out their neighbour, a Dominican called Fabiana. Fabiana had borrowed money off her and couldn't repay it. She'd made Fabiana turn tricks in her house. Carmine would hear her getting fucked through her wall. Then she'd hear her crying after the johns had left. One night Fabiana took a dive in front of a speeding car. His mother didn't give a shit, didn't show a hint of remorse. No, what she did was take over Fabiana's house and move another woman in there. Business as usual.

He cleaned the dust off the voodoo drums and started on the aged Rastafarian ones.

The door open behind him.

He turned around.

It took him a few moments to recognize the person standing there.

'*What?* You think you seein' a *ghost*, muthafukka?' Risquée snarled. 'Well you *ain't*. Yo' peckerwood hitman *fucked up*!'

Carmine stood up slowly, looking at her, dumbstruck and utterly shocked. She'd changed quite a bit. She was a lot shorter because she was in Converse sneakers instead of high heels. Her wig had been replaced with cornrows, her hoop earrings with small gold studs, her short dresses with baggy black army pants and a loose black T-shirt. She had no make-up on. She'd lost a lot of weight. Her face was lean and tight. And she was missing her front teeth.

'Why you ain't sayin' nuttin' Kahmynne – *huh*?'

'I – I – I didn't send no one to kill you, baby,' he offered weakly, his voice shredded with fear.

'Yeah – *right*! An' I'm Nancy-fuckin'-Reagan – BABY!' she shouted.

Standing the way she was – straight and tense, eyes gleaming with rage – he couldn't help but think of a cobra right before it strikes.

'I *swear* it wasn't me,' he pleaded. 'I – I had your money. I was gonna give it you.'

'*Boollshit!*'

'I can get you yo' money,' he said.

'I don' wannit!' She started coming towards him.

'What?' He started to panic.

'I . . . don' . . . wannit! That's English fo' "fuck dat shit"!'

'But it's – $50,000!'

'I said *fuck dat shit*! I don't want yo' money no mo'. We pass dat stage, *bitch*!' She reached into her pocket and pulled something out. He couldn't see what. He couldn't move.

'So – what d'you want? Why d'you come back? You know there's – there's people out lookin' fo' you.'

'Who?'

'Bonbon.'

She stopped in her tracks. Even she was scared of Bonbon.

He saw her think things through for a second – but just a second.

'An' you gonna stand there an' tell me you never sent someone ta kill me? You a *DUMBASS MUTHA-FUKKA*, Kahmyyne! You know dat? Good thang yo' dumbness ain't contagious else tha whole world an' its momma be a *DUMBASS MUTHAFUKKA* too!'

He heard the metallic click of a switchblade opening.

'What are you doin'?' he whimpered.

'Killin' yo' sorry ass!'

Risquée swiped hard at his face, missing his head by a fraction. Then she lunged at him like a fencer, but he side-stepped and slipped behind her.

She spun around and slashed at him again, missing by a broader margin.

'Stop this shit!' he yelled.

'*Fuck dat!* An' FUCK YOU!'

She crouched down a little, her gaze dancing wildly all over his face. She feinted, made him move to the left, and then jabbed at his chest. Carmine turned away just in time and the edge of the razor-sharp blade nicked his forearm. He cried out.

She charged at him with a loud scream.

Carmine punched her straight in the face. It wasn't a hard punch but she ran headlong into his fist and it staggered her. She stood still for an instant, swaying on the balls of her feet, blinking.

Carmine rushed her. He grabbed her hard by the wrists and yanked up her arms. He squeezed hard, trying to get her to drop the knife.

'MUTHAFUKKA!' she yelled and started kneeing him in the balls.

He pushed her back.

She kicked out.

He pushed her harder.

She lost her balance and they both went down, him on top of her.

Risquée's head hit the top of a display case and shattered the glass. The knife fell out of her hand and clattered to the floor. Carmine got off her and grabbed the weapon.

'Game over!' he yelled at her triumphantly, brandishing her switchblade. 'Now get the fuck outta here!'

She didn't move. Her body was draped over the case, limp like a scarf, her feet twisted off at odd angles, her arms floppy at her sides.

Holding the knife tight in his fist, in case she was trying to trick him, he looked into the case. Risquée was staring up at him with pitch-black eyes, her mouth wide open. The case held shrivelled, greyish, mummified hands – all sizes, both genders, fingers bent like sharp roots, skin the texture of prunes. They were said to be able to open any lock.

'I said game over! Get out!' Carmine snapped at her.

Then he noticed something else in the case. His mouth dried and a cold heavy weight crashed into the pit of his stomach.

There was a fast-blooming halo of blood around Risquée's head.

'No!' he whispered.

She was dead.

He dropped the knife and lifted up her head and saw a three inch sliver of glass sticking out of the top of her neck, right below the curve of the skull. Her warm blood pumped over his hands and dribbled onto the floorboards.

He looked out of the window and checked the street. No one around. He lowered her gently to the ground, wiped his hands on her trousers, locked the door and turned off the light.

He had to move her. And fast. But all he could do was stare at her body lying there, blood seeping out of it in a thick puddle, wondering what the fuck he was going to do.

He could drive her out to the Glades and leave her for the gators. No one would miss her. But that was too far a trek in the pickup. And he couldn't go now because he was due back home for his bath soon.

He looked at her face. He didn't feel bad about her being dead – she'd come to kill him. It was self-defence: he hadn't meant to kill her. Just like he hadn't meant to kill that cop in the salon.

He thought of calling his mother, telling her what had happened. She could send someone to clean it up. She needed the store.

No, that might fuck up his escape plans. He had to be smart about this.

He looked at Risquée again, as if she could tell him what to do. With her eyes all black and somehow still mad, and her mouth open like that, despite her missing teeth, she couldn't help but remind him of one of those dried gator heads they sold to tourists out in the Glades. The resemblance was almost uncanny.

He had to be smart about this. *Very* smart.

52

The first thing Max and Joe noticed when they broke into Haiti Mystique was the intense smell of bleach. The fumes saturated the air and made their eyes run.

They switched on their flashlights and almost immediately saw a smashed display case and the dried hands heaped up in a small pile on top of the case to its left. Max moved his beam down the stand and noticed a few drops of blood on the wood, then a large rough sandy-coloured circle on the floorboards, much lighter than the greyish-brown tone of the rest of the floor. The smell of bleach was strongest here.

Max touched one of the blood drops on the stand with his gloved index finger. It was dark and sticky and left a smudge. It was three to four hours fresh.

He looked inside the case and saw the whole of the inside was stained pink. He noted the fine upward arterial spray at the back of the case, and on the remaining shards of glass.

Joe examined the hands and noted the bloodstains on some of them.

'Someone took a bad fall here,' Max whispered. 'And very recently.'

They looked around the rest of the store. Joe checked behind the counter. He found a sales ledger and a metal cashbox. There were only five pages of entries in the ledger going back to February 1977. He added up the sales figures for each year and laughed.

'Ismael sure didn't get rich here,' he said. 'Guy made all of $2,900 last year, $2,455 the year before that. His most successful year was 1979. He made a total of $3,233.'

Max studied a shelf of belljars – hands, fingers, tongues, testicles, brains, eyeballs of various colours, feet, human hearts, livers, a brain – all pickled in formaldehyde. The prices were drawn on the jars in marker pen. A hundred dollars bought you an Adam's apple, $200 a tongue, $300 a pair of blue eyes. Below were a range of foetuses in various stages of development, most of them black. These went from $750 for the smallest to $3,000 for the biggest. On the last shelf were chicken eggs, some part hatched with a small beak or part of a head protruding.

Joe came from behind the counter, treading on a loose floorboard which creaked loudly. He looked at the masks and drums, the books of spells and curses, the candles, the statues of saints, the skulls, and the roots and bunches of herbs and twigs hanging down from the ceiling like twisted baubles.

Max's beam landed on the back door. He tried it. It was unlocked.

Downstairs they found themselves in a hot, dimly lit room staring at two long rows of cages of various types and sizes, with a wide gap in between them. It stank of animal shit, and the air buzzed with the clucking of chickens, the flapping of agitated wings and the sound of bodies moving against the metal grilles that held them.

Max saw three mountain goats with long black fur and magnificent horns, which rose a foot above their heads and branched off into sharp points; he saw a chained vulture, a sleeping fox, a brown monkey, and, at the far end, where the cages ended, three chicken coops, and a tank filled with toads.

Beyond that were bales of hay and burlap sacks stuffed, Max guessed, with feed. Although they marked the end of the room, he sensed he hadn't seen everything, that there was more to discover. He moved his flashlight over the hay.

'Max!' Joe whispered from the stairs. 'Come see.'

Behind the stairs Joe was standing near an open trapdoor.

'The fuck is this place?' Joe asked, when the strip lights came on and they found themselves standing in an all-white tiled, cold and sterile space.

Again the smell of bleach saturated the air, far stronger than in the store.

'Operating theatre?' Max suggested, looking from the marble slab and the sluice drain that ran alongside it to the trolley of glinting, stainless-steel surgical instruments he was standing next to.

'Or a torture chamber,' Joe said, pointing to the meathooks hanging from the metal railing running across the ceiling. He went over to the nearby showerhead, which was still dripping. He looked at the plughole, then took one of the scalpels and scraped the blade around the opening. He showed it to Max. 'There's blood here too.'

They walked over to the six large rectangular freezers at the end of the room and each opened one.

They were empty.

They moved on to the next two. Also empty.

But the final pair were filled to capacity with alligator parts, all wrapped in clear ziplock bags, tails in the first freezer, headless torsos in the next.

'That's a lotta luggage,' Max quipped as he hefted one of the carcasses out and placed it on the floor. He took it out of the bag and turned it over. There was a long vertical slash all the way down the animal's trunk, where its insides had been removed. Apart from its tail and head – both removed with precise cuts – it was also missing its legs.

'Got the belts, wallets and pimp shoes right here,' Joe said, cradling a three-foot-long, deep-frozen tail.

They began emptying the freezer's contents and laying

them out on the floor. The tails and torsos varied in length and weight – some so long they'd been sawn in half.

It was Max who found the first human body part – a right arm, black, definitely female, about halfway down.

He showed it to Joe, who, just then, was looking at a black woman's torso, wedged in-between two tails.

Max recovered the left arm and both legs. The head was at the very bottom of Joe's freezer.

They removed the remains from the plastic. They were only partially frozen.

They took them over to the slab and laid them out in order.

Like the gators the body had been cut straight down the middle and all of its internal organs removed.

'How'd she die?' Joe asked.

Other than the clean amputations, there were no marks on the torso, arms and legs. Max inspected the head. When he turned it over he saw the deep gash in the skin below the cranium. He got some tongs and prised back the flesh. Something was imbedded deep in the wound. He reached in with the tongs and pulled out an inch of bloody glass.

'Severed medulla,' he said. 'She was dead before she knew it. My guess is she fell backwards on the glass. Someone was either on top of her, or else they grabbed her head and pushed it down on the glass. So it was either an accident or a murder. And I'm guessing it's murder. Why else would you carve her up?'

'What d'you wanna do?' Joe asked.

'Go get the print kit and the camera.' Max looked at his watch: 10.35 p.m. 'Then we'll go and see Ismael. He should still be at the Fontainebleau. He's hosting that fundraiser there.'

They'd spent most of the day following Sam Ismael around, as he'd gone from one publicity junket to the next around Lemon City. It was culminating tonight in a black-tie dinner at one of Miami's most exclusive hotels.

'But he didn't do this,' Joe said.

'No, he didn't,' Max agreed. 'But this is still his store.'

'When do you wanna call it in?' Joe asked.

'Before we go talk to him.'

53

The cop who'd beaten him up and stolen his money and the beans had come back. Carmine watched him from the gap in the feed sacks praying he wouldn't come all the way over here and discover him crouching there with the bag full of Risquée's insides.

The cop was looking at the cages now, taking in the white chickens, the black roosters, the fox, the vultures, the goats, getting closer.

He'd been coming up the stairs when he'd heard feet on the floorboards. He'd thought his mother had sent people to look for him after he'd missed his bath. So he'd hidden. The animals already knew him as the person who fed them, so they'd made a ruckus.

He wished he'd worked faster when he'd cut up Risquée, but there had been so much to do. Now he knew how humans were different from gators. It was in the guts. Risquée had had miles of them. And they'd stunk. He'd had to stop what he was doing to puke. Four times. Then, for some stupid reason, when it had come to taking off her head he'd cried like a fucking baby.

The cop was real close to finding him now. The last two cages were empty. He was real thorough this one. He was looking at each of the animals, inspecting them. Black chinos, black guayabera shirt, black Converse Allstars. Dressed just like Risquée had been. Except for the piece at his hip. And the tattoos inside his forearms.

What would he do when he got caught sitting next to a bag of human offal? It would look like murder. Maybe he could cop a plea, do a deal, sell out the SNBC and go into witness protection.

'Max?' That was the cop's partner, the big black guy, calling from behind the stairs, where the trapdoor was. 'Come see.'

The white cop went over to look.

A minute later they'd gone downstairs.

Carmine came out of his hiding place and crept up to the ground floor, leaving the rest of Risquée behind.

He drove straight home. The lights were all out in the house. His mother had gone to sleep.

He was bringing his plans forward. He was leaving town now. He'd change his clothes, grab his locker key and go.

In his room he stripped off his bloody clothes, bundled them up into his laundry bag and changed. He got out his finest navy blue Halston suit, Pierre Cardin underwear and silk socks, Gucci shoes, his tailored powder-blue Oxford shirt. He had to look his best now that he was starting his new life – even if he would be entering it in a pickup.

When he was dressed, he gave himself a quick inspection in the mirror and winked at his reflection. He was still a handsome sonofabitch.

Time to go. He looked across the room at the coffee jar.

His mother walked into the room.

'Who did you just kill?' she asked him.

54

Standing on the balcony of his top-floor suite at the Fontainebleau, in his tux and hand-crafted black shoes, Sam Ismael felt like he was nearly there. He could almost taste victory. He was looking out at Miami Beach, transformed by nightfall from a flaking grey tourist trap, to an attainable galaxy of glittering, iridescent neon, a bejewelled lava which appeared to be moving, very slowly, in an unspecified direction. The streets were lit up like luminous veins, traffic flowing white one way, red the other, entering and fleeing. The summer breeze carried stray music up from the clubs, mixed in with the smells of sea and city.

Twenty minutes earlier, a dozen floors below in the ballroom where the Lemon City Regeneration Project was sating itself on fine food and wine at $500 a plate, he'd had unofficial word from the mayor's office that they would approve his proposal to officially change the area's name to Little Haiti. This was due to extensive lobbying on his part, as well as sizeable donations to various interest groups' campaign chests and preferred charities; there was never progress without corruption.

He felt good about what he was doing, good about what it would mean to and for Haitians. They would finally have a place of their own in Miami, a place to come to and settle in, a place where they could rebuild their lives. He didn't care that it was Solomon's drug money funding it. The Colombians and Cubans were doing the same thing, buying up miles of real estate and building condos to rent out to rich folk. They were helping themselves. Sam was helping others.

Only one thing spoiled this moment – well, four in fact

– Solomon Boukman, Bonbon and his two skanky dyke sidekicks – Danielle and Jane – were inside, waiting for a delivery of photographs he had to go through. He hoped it wouldn't take long.

Behind him the window slid open.

'We're ready,' Solomon said.

Sam drained his tumbler of neat Barbancourt rum and walked back into the suite. The lights had all been turned off except for a reading lamp by an armchair. A thick pile of black and white Miami PD headshots was waiting for him on the chair.

Sam sat down and went through them.

Ten minutes later he recognized the man who'd come into his store.

'That's him,' Sam said, holding up the picture.

Solomon's hand reached out from behind him and took it. He turned the picture over.

'Max Mingus. Detective Sergeant. Badge Number 8934054472. Date of Birth 8 March 1950,' he read out. And then, after a short pause, and with a hint of laughter. 'Miami Task Force.

'You can go,' Solomon said to Sam, as he began punching telephone keys.

Before rejoining his guests at the function, Sam went to the restroom to wash his hands and face and get back into schmoozing mode.

He barely registered the two men who came in while he was by the sink, a split second's glance telling him they were nobody he had to bother with.

'Mr Ismael?' the big black man asked him in a tone that sounded official, that sounded like how a cop would speak.

'Yes?' He looked up from the sink, in time to see the other man coming up behind him.

He felt a heavy blow on the back of his neck.

55

They drove Sam Ismael to the MTF condo in Coral Springs, two hours out of Miami.

They dragged him inside and cuffed his right arm to a metal chair welded to the floor of a windowless room with whitewashed walls, a single lightbulb and a table, also bolted down.

Ismael was still groggy from the blow Max had dealt to his neck with a lead-shot-filled beavertail sap. Joe threw a bucket of cold water over him and he came to with a gasp and a start, blinking rapidly, panicked yellowy-brown eyes darting from Joe to the ceiling, to the table, to the door and then to Max, where they stopped and settled.

'Where am I?' he asked Max.

'Well, it ain't the Fontainebleau.'

'Where *am* I?' Ismael banged the table with his free hand.

'I don't believe I correctly identified myself, the last time we met – in your store, remember?' Max looked at him and saw that he did. 'I am Detective Sergeant Mingus of the Miami Task Force. That over there' – motioning his head to Joe, stood against the wall with his hands in his pockets and a plastic carrier bag at his feet – 'is Detective Liston. And you, Sam Ismael, are officially fucked.

'Now, let me clarify just what 'officially fucked' means. It means fuck your lawyer, fuck your civil rights, fuck your human rights, fuck the rights we didn't read you and, most of all, fuck you. And it also means that your life, as you knew it, is officially fucken' over. Do you understand?'

'What do you *want*?'

Max held up a Polaroid photograph of the severed head and placed it in the middle of the table.

'Who is she?'

'How should I know?'

'You *should* know.' Max lined up half a dozen pictures of the girl's body, laid out in loose order on the floor, with inch-wide gaps between the amputated parts. 'That's the basement of your store. And that's what we found in your freezers.'

Ismael looked at the photographs. He went pale.

'I don't know *anything* about this,' he said.

'No?' Max dropped three clear bags of surgical instruments one by one on the table, where they each landed with a bang. 'These have your prints all over them. And forensics will also find blood, tissue and hair samples that match the victim's. Do the math. Prints, plus tissue, plus hair, plus blood equals *you*.'

'But I didn't *do* it!' Sam shouted. 'And you haven't even *got* my prints on those.' Ismael pointed at the instruments. 'We sterilize them after use.'

'Your prints are on there, trust me.' Max smiled. '*Every* digit.'

'Then you *put* them there when I was out cold!' Sam yelled. 'This is an *outrage*!'

Max ignored him.

'OK, let's just say, for the sake of argument, you *are* innocent. You're *still* gonna be charged, and you're *still* gonna have to stand trial. Now, the press will have themselves a field day. Think about it. All that shit you've got in your store, all those body parts, religious icons, candles, masks –'

'Don't forget the chickens,' Joe prompted.

'*And* the chickens too. Can you imagine the headlines? "Prominent Miami Businessman in Human Sacrifice Deep-Freeze Voodoo Death Riddle." This'll be our very own Black Dahlia.

'So it doesn't *matter* if you're innocent, you'll *look* guilty. And that's all that counts. Appearance is *everything* in this country: if you look the part, you get the part.'

'I didn't do it,' Ismael repeated, but quietly, looking at the photographs, horrified.

'Who's this "we"?' Max asked. 'As in *we* sterilize our tools after use? You got an accomplice? Or are you thinkin' of pleading temporary insanity?'

Ismael shook his head.

'Charge me or release me. But if you charge me I'll beat it. And then I'll sue. False arrest. Loss of earnings. Loss of reputation. Psychological damage.'

Max looked him in the eye.

'You forgot police brutality.'

Ismael couldn't stare Max down.

'What's Florida famous for – apart from gators, sunshine, Disney, girls in bikinis and a skyhigh body count?' Max asked.

'I don't know.' Ismael looked puzzled.

'It's not a trick question,' Max said. 'Think.'

Ismael did. Sweat had massed on his forehead and was trickling down his temples and large parrot-beak nose.

'Oranges?' he offered.

'Exactly,' Max said. 'Oranges. They're very good for you. Great source of vitamin C. Which I'm sure you know. You eat oranges?'

'Sometimes.' Ismael shrugged.

'I *love* oranges,' Max said. 'In fact we've got some right here.' Joe handed him the carrier bag. Max took out the contents, one by one – eight large, ripe Florida oranges. He placed one over each photograph and held on to the last.

'What the doctors don't tell you about oranges is that they can also be very fucken' bad for you. There's eight of them there. If I put them back in the bag' – he replaced the fruit in the bag one by one and did it very slowly – 'I have

419

myself a lethal weapon. You've heard about the phone-book trick cops use in interrogation? Hit you in the torso, maximum pain, no external bruising? Real convenient. Same principle with oranges, except there's a twist.' Max knotted the bag. 'A phone book just *hurts* you inside. If I hit you – *hard* – with a bag of Florida's finest, your insides will be a medically irreparable mess. Kidneys, liver, spleen, stomach, bladder all haemorrhaging. It'll take you *days* to die. Long, drawn out, *painful* days. You'll piss, shit *and* puke blood. Very nasty. Wouldn't wish it on anyone – except the twisted fuck who sawed that girl apart.'

Max got off the table and motioned Joe over.

Joe undid Ismael's cuffs, grabbed him by the shoulders and lifted him to his feet like he was made of string. He held him steady.

Max walked up to him.

'*Please!*' Ismael screamed.

Max swung the bag and – deliberately – narrowly missed Ismael's torso's.

'Shit!' Max said. 'Old age.'

He measured Ismael. Stared hard at his stomach like he was taking aim, took a step back, arm extended, all set to swing –

'*Let me see the photo again!*'

'Sit him back down,' Max told Joe, who shoved Ismael towards the table.

Ismael picked up the head shot and studied it closely. His eyes widened and shock spread over his face.

'You know her?' Max asked.

'That's – that's Risquée. I – I – I didn't recognize her . . . immediately,' he stammered. 'She's a – a – a girl. Look, I *didn't* do this. I *swear*.'

'Who did?' Max asked again.

Ismael took a deep breath and stared at Max with the eyes of a man who has just heard the ground starting to give way beneath his feet and the roof caving in above him.

'Carmine,' he said very quietly, the name coming out of him reluctantly. 'It was most likely Carmine. He's been working in the store.'

'Carmine, as in Carmine Desamours?' Max prompted.

'That's right.' Ismael sighed.

'Eva Desamours' son?'

Ismael nodded.

'I thought he was a pimp. What's he doin' in your store?' Max asked.

'He – he changed jobs.'

'What? He get *promoted*?' Joe laughed.

'No. The opposite.'

'And this Risquée – was she one of his girls?' Max tapped the head pic.

'Yeah. He owed her money.'

'*He* owed *her* money. What kind of pimp is *that*?' Max laughed.

'Carmine isn't any more a pimp than I am,' Sam said bitterly. 'And he isn't a killer. It was probably an accident and he panicked.'

'No accident about a dismembered corpse,' Max said, putting the bag of oranges down and looking at Joe. They'd talked tactics in the car, on the way over. All was going to plan. Bamboozle Ismael, push him to give them a name, then *really* push him for what they wanted to know. Joe nodded slightly to Max: Ismael had cracked, now he was ready to break.

But he beat them to it. The panic and fear suddenly left his face. He sat back and smiled at Max.

'Something funny?' Max asked.

'What were you doing in my store?'

Max didn't miss a beat. He'd been ready for this.

'I wanted to see what Solomon Boukman's money

launderer looked like. And I was very interested – *we*' – he motioned to Joe – 'were very interested in the person who supplied some of the ingredients found in the stomachs of Preval Lacour and Jean Assad. Calabar beans and a *very* expensive tarot card – the King of Swords from the de Villeneuve deck – both of which came from your store.'

The smile didn't leave Ismael's face.

'I suppose you're going to offer me a deal. Witness protection and a new identity if I tell you everything? Life or death? Something like that?'

'Something like that,' Max said.

Ismael's smile turned into a smirk.

'You think your witness protection's going to protect me from *Solomon Boukman*?' Ismael said to Max. 'He can reach through any wall and close anyone's eyes. Doesn't matter where or who they are. And he'll kill my whole family too – even if they're completely ignorant of my affairs – because that's what he does.'

'You're assuming we won't get him first,' Max said.

'You're assuming you will. You know he has a – how should I say? – guardian angel?' Ismael pointed upwards with his free hand.

'Who?' Max asked. 'Lucifer?'

'Before you knocked me out in the bathroom, you know where I was? I was with Solomon on the top floor of the Fontainebleau. Suite 467. He won't be there now. You know what I was doing? I was looking at another set of photographs. Headshots. From the Miami police personnel files, trying to identify the plainclothes cop who'd walked into my store. And I did: Detective Sergeant *Max* Mingus. He knows who you are. That makes us both dead men talking.'

Max went numb inside. He looked at Joe and saw surprise and a lot of worry on his partner's face.

Then he looked at Ismael – his smirk, his thin, sweaty

face, his small eyes, his huge curved nose – and he was lost for words. An icy cloud settled on the middle of his back and its chill travelled the length of his spine and then went into his bones. He saw Sandra. He thought of losing her. And he shuddered.

'Where d'he get his information?' Joe asked.

'I don't know. And if it's none of my business, I don't want to know. I launder Solomon's money and front his construction schemes. That's it,' Ismael said. 'But I did overhear him talk about a contact once – a while ago – with Eva. No names mentioned, but she referred to him as the Emperor. As in the tarot card. So I knew this was someone important, someone big, someone whose name they didn't want to broadcast.'

'The Emperor's in the Major Arcana. The dominant cards, the deciders in the deck,' Max said, taking his cigarettes out of his pockets and lighting one. The Emperor didn't signify a person, but a desire to control one's circumstances or surroundings, have dominion over them, influence fate.

'That's right. This isn't just anybody. Like every major drug player in Miami, Solomon's got plenty of cops on his payroll, but the Emperor's in a different league. Either he's an equal partner or he's Solomon's boss. And he's *very* powerful. He's the one who wipes Solomon's prints off everything.'

'Tell me about that conversation you overheard. What was said exactly?' Max asked.

'It was something to do with an FBI operation Solomon had heard about. Eva said "Talk to the Emperor, he'll make it go away,"' Ismael replied.

'Did it?'

'Of course. Everything's always gone away. Solomon operates like an invisible man in the kingdom of the blind. You know he got arrested for murder in 1969? He hacked somebody up with a machete. The police photographed and fingerprinted him. So he had a record. But he never went to trial because the evidence vanished, along with three eyewitnesses. And when Solomon started making serious moves, every record relating to him vanished too – immigration, social security, police files.'

'How do you know?' Joe asked.

'Carmine said they had a ceremonial burning of the files – his and everyone else in his gang. They ceased to exist. They went off radar. Permanently.'

'When was this?'

'Early seventies.'

'And the Emperor was helping him then?'

'I assume so,' Ismael said. 'So what this means is, your offer of protection is nominal at best. If you charge me for Risquée, I'm dead in days. If we cut a deal, I'm dead in a week, maybe two, if I'm lucky. And . . . my family in Haiti? They die the day I do. That's how Solomon does things,' Ismael said, matter-of-factly, like a jaded doctor delivering bad news to his millionth terminally ill patient.

'Then what've you got to lose by tellin' me about the man who's gonna kill you? We can stop him.' Max took a long pull on his Marlboro. 'We're not ordinary police. The city set up our unit because it couldn't trust the PD. Too many leaks, too many people on the cocaine payroll. We operate independently. No one outside MTF knows about this place, or any of our places. And we've got 'em all over Florida. You *will* be safe with us.'

'And what about my family?'

'We can't guarantee their safety from here,' Max said. 'But we can get them moved to the US Embassy in Haiti. They'll be under military guard.'

Ismael sat back in his chair and looked at the ceiling, thinking.

'You have no idea who you're dealing with. If this was the Colombians or the Cubans, I'd say "Where do I sign and how loud do you want me to sing?" But this isn't them. Do you know how Solomon's bringing his coke in here now? He used to work with a group of Haitian army officers. Now he deals with just the one person in Haiti. Ernest Bennett, Baby Doc Duvalier's father-in-law. He's the new news. He owns Air Haiti. He's flying coke into Miami every day by the ton.

'Now, consider this: the Duvalier dictatorship is funded and supported by the US government, and always has been. They're Cold War allies. Cuba's next to Haiti,' Ismael explained. 'The CIA knows *exactly* what's going on with Bennett and they really don't care. You know why? Because they're making money out of this. And lots of it. It's helping fund the Latin-American front in the war on communism.'

'So, you mean, *Boukman's* workin' for the CIA?' Max smirked.

'Yes.'

'Bullshit! Listen to yourself: a *Haitian* drug dealer, selling coke on American streets *for the CIA*?! That's fucken' ridiculous!'

'Solomon isn't working for them directly. But I think the man who's protecting him is.'

'*Right*,' Max said sarcastically. 'I've heard all this kind of shit before. Commie conspiracy theories. We're the richest country in the world. The CIA doesn't *need* money.'

'Not for their legal operations – the state-approved, above board stuff, no, they don't. But there's things your government can't be seen doing. Black ops. Counter-revolutionary work. Funding right-wing paramilitaries to massacre villages and blow up school buses in Nicaragua, Honduras and El Salvador.

'Do you know where I send all the money Solomon brings me? The BCCI bank in Panama City. I didn't set up those accounts. They were there before I got involved with him. You need a reference to open one. You know who Solomon had? General Manuel Noriega. A seriously big cheese. And Noriega has been working for the CIA since the 1950s,' Ismael explained.

Max didn't say anything.

'How did he know Noriega?'

'I doubt they've ever met. The Emperor set that account up for him. I know you don't believe me, but look at the facts: Solomon makes anywhere between five to ten million dollars a month profit from his coke enterprise. Then he's also involved in prostitution, gambling, loansharking, protection, car theft. That nets him another million a month. Plus he's killed *hundreds* of people – or had them killed. He performs human sacrifices. All of that and he's never been so much as questioned by the police, never been put under surveillance, never turned up on any wanted list. The Feds and the DEA *know* who the cocaine cowboys are. They know everything about them. But they know nothing about Solomon. Why?'

'I've seen his name in police files,' Max said.

'Have you seen any accurate physical descriptions? A photograph?'

'No two descriptions are ever the same.'

'Solomon never does anything in person. He uses subcontractors, hired through middle-men, themselves hired by his inner circle. No one outside that circle ever meets him. They think they do, but he sends doubles his place. Usually out of work actors, the kind who can't get waiting jobs. That way if anything goes wrong, no one can ever identify him. And also, it helps perpetuate the myth that he can be in more than one place at the same time. Do you know he once set up meetings with four chapters of the LA Crips at different locations, on the same day, at the same time? They all think they met someone called Solomon Boukman. But they didn't. It was an illusion.'

'What about the doubles? What happens to them?'

'Once the deal's done they're done. He specializes in choosing people who won't be missed. Single people, newly arrived in town, down on their luck.'

'Shit,' Max said.

'And I think the Emperor helps stoke the myth too. He feeds a lot of counter-intel into the system. Those reports you mentioned? Plants. Misinformation. Misinformation is as powerful as information.'

'So what does Boukman actually look like?' Max asked.

'I've never seen him clearly. Whenever I meet him it's in a very dark room, or else he sits behind me. I've heard he's had radical plastic surgery. And you're not going to believe this, but he's got a split tongue. Sort of like a lizard's.'

'You've seen this?'

'No. But Carmine has. Eva Desamours did it. Carmine told me. In Haiti, Eva was a *mambo* – a voodoo priestess – the most powerful one on the island; Solomon was her apprentice. In fact Boukman isn't even his family name. I don't know what it was originally. Eva changed it after she had a vision of the spirit of the slave who led the first uprising against Haiti's colonial masters. He was called Boukman. In her vision he told her to move to America, that Solomon would become a great power there if he took his name – the name of Boukman – and had the tongue of a snake. So the next day, Eva took a knife and sliced Solomon's tongue in two down the middle. Carmine saw it happen. He said Solomon didn't so much as *wince*.'

'Christ!' Joe gasped.

'He wore a metal divider in his mouth to keep the two parts of the tongue apart, until it stayed that way,' Ismael continued. 'And then they all came over here and the prophecy came true.'

'How old was Boukman?'

'Ten or eleven. Him and Carmine are about the same age.'

'Do you believe in that voodoo stuff?' Max asked.

'No, but I believe in Eva. She's the real deal.'

'How?'

'She's not one of those phoney palm readers, those Madame Zora cross my palm with silver types. And she's not like any of the genuine ones, the ones with foresight. She sees *behind* the future – the things that influence fate, the spirits who decide things,' Ismael said. 'Like I said: I don't believe in God, but I believe in Eva.'

Max and Joe exchanged a quick look. Joe shook his head as if to say 'Don't go there yet.'

'What's the rest of Boukman look like?'

'From the little I've seen, normal. Black – dark skin. About your height, but a thinner build. If you saw him in the street he wouldn't look like much. But if you spend time in his company, alone – as I have – you feel this presence as though there's more than one person in the room. It's the best way I can describe it.'

Max looked at Joe, who shrugged. Max could accept the black magic, but he couldn't buy the CIA connection. He was sure Boukman had a mole – or several moles – in the police, but he couldn't imagine it went much higher. Best stick to the hard evidence, the stuff that would stand up in court.

'OK, Sam,' Max said. 'So far you've given us voodoo spirits, faked moon landings and how aliens killed the Kennedys. What we need from you now are concrete facts. The clock is ticking. Boukman most likely knows you're missing. So what's it to be?'

'I'll tell you everything I know. But I'm not going to go on the record until my family's safe.'

'I understand,' Max said. 'But we're gonna get details from you now. Specifics, stuff I can take to my CO, and that my CO can take to the DA. You talk to us now, I'll go and see him as soon as we're done. Your family could be in protective custody in a matter of hours.'

Ismael stared at Max, and then at Joe, and then back at Max.

'I won't sign anything until I hear from my family, that they're safe in the embassy.'

'Fine.'

'And my lawyer approves everything.'

'Fine again.'

'Then you have yourselves a deal.'

Joe went and got a tape recorder. Max made coffee.

And then they started.

Ismael talked for four hours, telling them everything he knew, he didn't hold back – how the Lemon City deal was put together, Preval Lacour, Moyez, the SNBC structure and how it functioned, their connections to every major crime syndicate in North America, the names of everyone he knew about, the human sacrifices, the potions; he told them about the Haitian drug connections, the millions he laundered; he talked shell companies, legitimate businesses, plus hotels, nightclubs and thousands of acres of real estate.

By 5.03 a.m. they were done.

Max and Joe stepped outside and went into another room.

'We've got to tell Eldon now,' Max said.

'You're gonna tell *Eldon*!' Joe was furious.

'Who else?'

'*Shit!*'

'What? We can *not* do this on our own any more, Joe.'

'There's got to be another way – someone else. How about Jack, the Feds?'

'The Feds!' Max stared him up and down. 'MTF lined up a bunch of patsies for the Moyez killing – patsies *I* helped find. An innocent man's dead. Murdered right in front of us. And there's innocent people in custody right now. We go to the Feds with this, we're *all* fucked. No way! We fix this in-house.'

'What if it's Eldon . . . ?'

'What if *what's* Eldon?' Max frowned.

'Working with Boukman?'

'Who? The "Emperor"? Get the fuck outta here, Joe!'

'You don't know.'

'I *do* know,' Max said. 'I've known Eldon Burns half my life. Yeah, there's never been a corner he hasn't cut, but he's *never* done business with criminals. *Never!* He *hates* them. He *hates* what they're doing to this city.' Max searched his friend's face and understood what was behind his protests. 'I know you don't like him, Joe, but don't let that blind you. This ain't about you and him. It never was.' Joe was silent for a moment. Max could see his brain working behind his knotted brow, trying to come up with another solution. When he couldn't find one, his face loosened up dejectedly and he gave his assent with a slight nod.

'He ain't gonna like it, us sneaking behind his back. Me in particular,' Joe said.

'That's the least of our worries. Anyway, I'll take the rap. Fuck it. I'll say the whole thing was my idea. OK?'

'Yeah,' Joe said.

By 5.13 Max was on his way back to Miami.

56

Eldon Burns was pissed – raging, fuming, fucking hopping-mad *pissed*.

He wasn't sure what was worse, Max going behind his back, or Boukman laughing at him when he'd told him their operations were being investigated by an MTF cop – one of his own, right under his nose. That motherfucker had had the temerity to *laugh* at him – ha, ha, ha.

He'd got the call as he was leaving his office late the previous night. He'd stayed put. He'd been there ever since, thinking, working out what to do. Now it was morning and he still didn't have the first fucking clue.

Oh, and in-between his worries and woes, Boukman had called again. He wasn't laughing this time. Sam Ismael had disappeared. He hadn't gone back to the dinner at the Fontainebleau, he wasn't at home and there was a dead girl in the basement of his store – a dissected, semi-frozen dead girl. Carmine – who'd killed her and carved her up – said Max and his black partner had broken into the store. They'd almost caught him too.

Jesus!

Eldon had called the Fontainebleau and talked to the head of security. Ismael had been seen walking out with two men – one tall and black, the other white. Not exactly walking out either, but *walked* out, like he was drunk and needed air. Which was what one of the men – the white one – had said to the doorman: 'He's a bit wasted, needs to clear his head.'

So Max and Liston had broken into Haiti Mystique, discovered the body and arrested Ismael.

Where had they taken him? If they'd gone behind his back, they wouldn't have him stashed in an MTF safehouse.

How much did they know now? How much had Ismael told them?

Ismael could easily implicate Boukman in both drug trafficking and the Lacour and Moyez killings. But did he know the name Eldon Burns? He was far from stupid. He'd probably guessed that Boukman had heavy protection – but had Boukman told him *how* heavy?

And what was Max going to do with the information? Who was he going to go to? He and Liston couldn't take on Boukman alone. They were disloyal, double-dealing scumbags, but they weren't suicidal.

Max wouldn't go to the Feds or the DEA. Both had more leaks in them than the St Valentine's Day Massacre.

And why the fuck had Max gone behind his motherfucking *back*?!

Christ, that didn't just piss him off – it plain fucking *hurt*. He'd known Max more than half his life. Sixteen years they went back! He'd treated him like a son, like his blood, like fucking FAMILY! He'd saved him from a life of crime. He'd looked out for him. He'd cleaned up his messes – all those brutality and intimidation complaints, the suspects he'd beaten up, the evidence he'd planted, and those three men he'd killed out in the Everglades – all of that gone, swept away, as good as vanished. Hell, he'd even given *Liston* a job – against his better fucking instincts.

All of that he'd done for Max, all of that, and that disloyal cocksucker had gone behind his back!

Or maybe it was Liston who'd instigated this shit? Mr By-The-Book. Mr Righteous. Mr Never-Cut-A-Corner. Liston had probably sensed he was getting demoted. Those nigras were always paranoid, had a persecution complex in every gene.

Mother – *Fucker*!

What was he going to do?

If they dared go up against him he'd turn them to dust. They'd know that.

At exactly 6.30, Helga knocked on his door, like she always did after she'd settled down at her desk and turned on the computer, regular as Rolex.

She opened the door and saw him sitting there slumped in his chair, hand on chin, seething.

'Are you OK, Eldon?' she asked.

'When Mingus and Liston get in, send them up here straightaway,' Eldon growled.

She knew him, knew his moods, knew when to talk, when to keep quiet. She nodded and closed the door.

Shit!

This was all happening at the wrong fucking time. The Turd Fairy had mentioned some experiments his people were doing on some kind of cheap version of freebase – so simple you could make it in your kitchen. A couple of guys had roadtested it out in Liberty City recently, but then out of the blue, the DEA had busted them. The project was now temporarily on hold. The drug had a few glitches that needed refining: the high lasted too long and wasn't intense enough. Exciting, pioneering times were just around the corner. If the cheapbase took off they'd have an epidemic on their hands in the ghettos. That would mean more crime, and more crime would mean more police – tough, no-nonsense police too. Police like him. The Turd Fairy was going to wave his wand and get him made Chief. Chief with sweeping powers, Chief with a mandate to reform the Miami police, Chief of this city he loved so much.

But this thing Max was doing could fuck the whole thing up. They needed Boukman's Haitian connection, and they'd need Boukman's distribution to get the cheapbase out there in the inner cities.

If Max and Liston didn't turn up at MTF at 8.30, when

they were due, he'd have to consider sending people out to look for them.

His phone rang. Helga.

'Yeah?'

'Mr Marko's here to see you,' Helga said.

The Turd Fairy! What the fuck did *he* want?

Eldon straightened his tie and put on his jacket.

'Send him in.'

57

Up on the roof, with the sun rising and the sky turning shades of bruised violet and deep pink, Max told Eldon everything they'd found out about Boukman and the SNBC.

He'd planned what he was going to say, in what order.

He started with an apology for going behind Eldon's back. He explained how, during a routine conversation with an informant, the informant had IDed the courtroom shooter as Jean Assad. He and Joe had looked into Assad, simply to tie up a loose end before it tripped up the official MTF investigation and made the division look bad – or worse.

Then Max told him most of the rest – everything he'd found out about Boukman, the SNBC, Eva and Carmine Desamours, Bonbon, Sam Ismael and the Lemon City project; he went into minor detail about the tarot card, major detail about the potions, zombies and calabar beans; he talked about the Haitian cocaine connection, mentioned Ernest Bennett, Baby Doc and money laundering; and he told Eldon about Solomon's protector, the Emperor, and a possible CIA link to the whole thing. He didn't mention the photographs, nor the fact that Boukman knew who he was. He'd got Sandra out of harm's way. The rest he'd handle himself. He was a cop and that kind of shit came with the territory.

He talked for a good ten minutes. He'd expected Eldon to explode, but he didn't. His boss stayed very calm and very attentive. No interruptions. His tell-tale wart stayed its neutral-brown colour.

'We're gonna have to move quickly on this one,' Eldon

said finally. 'I'm going to send a team over to Coral Springs to relieve Liston and babysit Ismael. Then I'm going to talk to the DA. Bringing this Boukman down ain't gonna be a problem, but this thing with Lemon City is political. Ismael touched a lot of big hands with dirty money, if you catch my drift.'

'This could get ugly,' Max said.

'Maybe, maybe not.'

'What about Ismael's family?'

'Leave that to me.'

'Thanks, Eldon.'

'No. Thank *you*, Max.' Eldon put his hand on his shoulder. 'This is *exemplary* police work.'

Max went to his desk and called Sandra. He told her to get out of town, stay with friends, and not to tell her family where she was going. She asked him what the hell was going on. He gave her an edited version of what had happened, and the danger she was in. He told her to call him from wherever she'd gone to.

58

Eldon sat back at his desk and began planning.

The Turd Fairy had waved his magic wand.

It was open season on Haitians.

A week ago two men had been arrested for raping a German tourist. Turned out they were Haitian workmen from the Lemon City project, and illegals too. The *Herald* had got hold of the story and gone digging. They'd interviewed more workers and discovered that more than three-quarters of Ismael's workforce were illegals. They'd been smuggled over from Port-au-Prince in the hold of a cargo ship owned by Sam Ismael. Now the *Herald* was starting to look into Ismael's affairs.

The Turd Fairy's people were letting it happen.

But that wasn't the only thing. Word of the Lemon City project had spread all over Haiti, and there had been a 100 per cent increase in Haitian immigration to Miami. They were coming over in makeshift boats and rafts. Many were drowning and washing up on the coast. Now, Cubans were one thing – they were refugees from the tyranny of communism who could easily be assimilated into a city so steeped in Latin culture it was virtually a home from home – but Haitians were another. They were black, spoke neither English nor Spanish, and had no political reasons for being here – Haiti wasn't a communist country and, for now, Baby Doc was a friend of the US.

The Haitian armada would have to be turned back.

Let them drown in their junkyard rafts. Just not in US waters.

Lemon City's current redevelopment would be shut down.

Meanwhile Ismael would be indicted on a million counts of money laundering, fraud and corruption. Then he'd turn state's and give up Boukman and the SNBC. MTF would move in and shut them down.

Eldon couldn't help but smile. He'd never liked the voodoo nigra, never liked him at all.

He'd need a new team in place to handle the Haitian connection. Couldn't let all that coke fall into the wrong hands. Cassares and Frino – they'd do. They had the experience and he had the goods on them.

He picked up the phone and began dialling.

59

Eva turned over the first two cards in Solomon's spread. The King of Swords was in the upright, enquirer position and, crossing it, the Emperor. In all the other readings she'd ever done for him, the Emperor had always been separate, usually above or behind, but never ever touching the King of Swords. It meant only one thing: the future was no longer theirs to determine.

The Emperor was depicted as a small, stout, man; he was cloaked in ermine, sitting on top of a mountain, surveying his surroundings – a dwarfed city stretching all the way to the rising sun. A raven was perched on his shoulder, a serpent coiled around his leg. On the ground at his feet were an upended cup, a sword, a glowing gold coin and a wand. In the de Villeneuve deck, the Emperor controlled all four suits in the Minor Arcana, all four mortal elements; he was life and death and everything in-between to those under him.

To Eva and Solomon, the Emperor was Eldon Burns. She saw his face there.

She'd first met Eldon in the summer of 1968, although she'd seen him coming in her cards and visions for the last nine years. *He* was the King of Swords then. The spirits had spoken of the white man who would elevate her to great heights, but warned he could bring her down just as fast.

He'd come knocking on her door in Liberty Square one morning, said he wanted some 'dark meat' for a party he was throwing for his fighters. He'd heard all about her brothels from the cops she was paying off. She remembered him then – a powerfully built, sour-faced man with a contemptuous look in his brown eyes and a sardonic curl to his mouth, like he was on the verge of spitting out an unpleasant taste. She'd drunk in his potpourri of foul smells – the rank sweat of ambition, the vinegar of greed, the splintered wood of violence, the maggoty apple of corruption – but noted too the dew of compassion tempering his extremes. He didn't add up at all, but he made sense in his own twisted way; a man at ease with his diametric contradictions – a dirty cop with morals, a turncoat with principles, a redneck with black friends. In short he was an opportunist of the purest kind. Over the years she'd tried to penetrate him, tried to find out what spirits were driving and guiding him, who he took his orders from, but she didn't get far. He had forces around him she was useless against. She'd more than met her match.

Like her, Burns had a refined nose but his seemed only to pick up the scent of money. While he was talking to her that day he'd sniffed out the bricks of Colombian marijuana she had stored in the back of her house; it was how the gang made its money in the early days. She'd read his mind and offered him a deal. He'd told her he wasn't interested in ganja, but in something else that was just starting to come into Miami from Colombia.

She knew what he meant. Over the past six months, her supplier had been slipping single kilo packages into her load – 'Something to try out'. Cocaine – jetset fuel, the Coconut Grove of drugs, popular with the so-called Weekend Warriors, the well-off white collar crowd who partied solidly from Friday night to Sunday morn; the only ones who could afford it.

Burns told her to get him twenty kilos.

And so it began. And so they all got very very rich.

'What do you see?' Solomon asked. He was opposite her, out of range of all light. Behind him stood the spirit of Boukman, watching the reading unfold with an impassive stare.

Eva turned over the four cards surrounding the enquirer. Above was the Moon – deception, hidden enemies plotting and scheming in the dark – the planet was shown in the upper centre of the card as a blue-eyed man scowling down at a runaway slave bathing his feet in a stream. The slave is oblivious to his surroundings – a barking hound to his right, a tree to his left with a noose hanging from one of its branches, and, sneaking up behind him, an armed mob.

The card below was the Five of Swords – defeat, loss, a reversal of fortune – a downcast man with three battered swords slung over his arm, bending down to pick up the shattered pieces of two more from a scorched and bloody earth.

The next card behind the enquirer, representing the recent past, was the Two of Swords – a blindfolded woman sitting with her back to a river, her arms crossed over her heart, a sword in each hand – a warning to keep one's eyes open and to be on the defensive. Except that the position of the card meant that this warning had come too late, or gone unheeded.

The final card in this part of the spread, to the right of the enquirer, symbolized the near future – now to tomorrow: the Knight of Swords, charging, armour bloody, sword raised. Eva saw the face of Max Mingus in the card. She'd extracted his essence from the cigarette butt Solomon had brought her. At first she'd thought Solomon had made a mistake, that it couldn't possibly belong to the same person. The smell was overpoweringly sweet – the cloying honey stench of love, so fresh she'd tasted it to the very pollen. Then she'd seen Mingus and the woman he loved and was loved by. She'd dug deep into the delirium of his early passion – the idiotic infatuation, the blind worship, the shrill excitement, the insatiable lust, all virtually indistinguishable from a teenager who's just lost his cherry – and found the fear trickling through the heart of it like a hidden stream;

fear of something happening to his woman, fear of dragging her down with him. When she'd followed his fear she'd found his rage. He'd had his balls turned off because of what he'd seen people do to children. He hated people who hurt children, hated them with a vengeance. She'd seen the dozens of suspects he'd beaten confessions out of and planted evidence on; she'd seen the five men he'd killed – two in the line of duty, three off the books – monsters all. She glimpsed too, off into the future, the shapes of the seven more lives he'd take.

'Mingus.' She pointed at the card and looked into the darkness opposite her at the round table, where Solomon sat. 'He won't stop coming.'

'Can't The Emperor call him off?'

She shook her head. She saw Mingus and Burns standing somewhere high up, looking out over the city. She saw Burns with a friendly arm around Mingus's shoulders. She saw Mingus younger, Burns looking down at him with a smile.

'They're in league,' she said. 'They always have been. He protects Mingus. He sees himself in Mingus.' She closed her eyes. 'But he's not seeing things as they are. Mingus isn't like him at all.'

She moved to the vertical line of four cards, symbolizing the future. One by one she turned them over.

Her mouth went dry.

This was a major upheaval.

A disaster.

The King of Pentacles, the Eight of Swords, the Tower, the Ten of Swords.

The images swirled in front of her eyes, the colours of the cards luscious and wet and very bright, as if freshly painted: the gold of the King's robe, the gleaming cruel steel of the swords, the burning flames on the bodies falling from the wrecked tower and the blood flowing from the ten gaping wounds in the stuck body.

Her head went light then heavy.

'What do you see?' Solomon repeated, leaning in towards the table, but only slightly, so all she saw of him were his hands, the white of his fingernails in sharp relief against the darkness of his skin.

She took a deep breath and tried to centre herself, to concentrate on the tickertape of interpretation coming through the cards.

She related what came to her; the unfolding of events.

'They have Ismael.' She placed her hand over the King of Pentacles – sitting on a gold throne, surrounded by money – and then wafted her index finger up to the Eight of Swords, another blindfolded woman, also bound at the hands and feet, encircled by eight inverted swords, suspended in mid-air – the card of imprisonment, captivity. She closed her eyes and focused. 'He's talked to Mingus, told him everything. This has just happened.'

'Where do they have him?' Solomon asked.

'Not in Miami. But not far. When he comes back to Miami, that will set things in motion.'

'What things?'

'They will destroy you,' she said. 'The Emperor will take away what he gave.'

'And if I stop Ismael coming to Miami . . . ?'

'It will only slow down the inevitable.' She stared at the Tower, one of the very worst cards you could possibly get, the card of destruction and ruin, of things being taken away: a lightning bolt striking the roof of a lighthouse and blowing it off; burning bodies falling, ships crashing into rocks.

And then, finally, the ultimate outcome: the Ten of Swords – a body lying face down on the ground, pierced by ten blades – death or imprisonment.

She looked at the spirit of Boukman and asked him why this was happening. He didn't even look at her, just kept staring at the cards on the table. If the spirit didn't answer you it meant your fate was sealed, it was almost meant to be this way. Even bad spirits weren't allowed to lie at moments like these.

Eva smelled a faint trace of dry, burning autumn leaves in the air, and a hint of a cold breeze in the room. She knew it was coming from beyond. It might have been early morning in Miami, but it was summer and there was no such thing as cold.

'How bad does it get?'

She ran her hands over the cards. She saw Solomon in prison.

'They'll cage you,' she said, then she saw the bars being bent back, opening, 'But they won't hold you.'

The spirit of Boukman raised his head. He looked down at Solomon and then back at her. He pointed to the Emperor card and raised his index finger to his lips.

'Except. . . you must say nothing about the Emperor. Keep your mouth shut and doors will open for you,' Eva said.

'What about you?' Solomon asked.

She looked at the spirit again, but he turned his back on her. Solomon repeated his question.

'This is *your* reading,' she answered.

The smell of burning leaves had become stronger.

'What shall I do?' Solomon asked.

She looked at the cards.

She gasped in shock and choked as she tried to draw her next breath.

She looked at the spirit, but he was walking away – away from the table, away from them, diminishing, fading into the darkness.

She looked back at the cards again.

They were now, quite suddenly, completely blank. The lustrous designs were gone, replaced instead by a dull greyish shade of white. She grabbed the rest of the deck and started turning over the cards one by one.

They were all identical – blank, ashy white.

She fanned the remainder out on the table.

All blank.

The smell in her nostrils intensified. Not leaves now, but something else, something metallic.

In the darkness around her she heard the scraping sounds of claws, claws on wood. And then a distant growling, the growling of dogs.

She closed her eyes and tried to focus, tried to listen for another sound, but the clawing and the growling got louder until she could hear the sound of heavy steps, circling her head.

She felt so very old and very tired, and alone, all alone, nothing and no one left to support her.

When she opened her eyes again the cards were still blank, but she could see images – faces, two of them – right there in the grain on the table, fragments peeking through the worthless cardboard rectangles.

She swept the tarots off the table and looked.

Carmine?

No. Of course not. The little shit was alive and downstairs in the basement.

No, it was his diseased prick of a father and that cunt bitch mistress of his. They were looking up at her and smiling. Gloating.

'What shall I do?' Solomon asked again, his voice cutting through her chaos and lodging itself in her heart.

She sat back in her chair, away from the table and the light, and the empty cards devoid of meaning. She pushed herself back so he could no longer see her or the warm wet tears spilling from her broken soul.

'Don't make it easy for them. Hurt them all the way,' she said, thinking of Mingus' woman. 'You're a warrior. Go to war.'

60

At his desk, Max nervously checked his watch: 9.47 a.m. Over three hours since he'd briefed Eldon. He'd heard nothing from him, nothing from Sandra, and nothing from Joe – although an MTF unit had been sent out to relieve him.

Eldon's reaction was bothering him. He'd taken it all way too fucking calmly. Max had gone into Eldon's office expecting fury, or at least some kind of diatribe about conducting private investigations on MTF time, with a strong accent on trust and loyalty, and a whole load of shit about all the years they'd known each other, how far they went back, all they'd been through. But Eldon hadn't seemed surprised. He hadn't even challenged the zombie angle. Had he been swayed by Max's explanation, the excuse he'd given? No, it wasn't that. Eldon saw through bullshit. He'd virtually written the book on it.

Was *Eldon* the Emperor? Like Joe had suggested. The thought *had* crossed his mind too, but he'd kicked it out. Eldon was many things, but he wasn't a criminal. Max knew him well enough for that. Eldon hated criminals, the cocaine traffickers especially. They were killing the city. Impossible.

He stared at his unwanted cup of piss-poor coffee, at the fine layer of oily bean scum floating on the surface.

His phone rang. He grabbed it.

'Miami Task Force. Detective Sergeant Mingus speaking.'

'Max?'

Sandra.

'Hey . . .' He smiled.

'Listen carefully . . .' Something was wrong. There were

tremors in her voice. 'I've been . . . I've been kidnapped.'
She sounded like she couldn't believe it. 'Go to the phonebooths . . . opposite – opposite the courthouse. Go there
now. Wait for the call.'

'Sandra? Listen. Are you –'

The line went dead before he could ask her if she was
OK.

Five minutes later he was at the booth. He sensed he was
being watched but he didn't know from where. He scanned
the street, looking for a stationary car and people who didn't
seem quite right, but all the turmoil in his head fucked with
his faculties.

How the hell had they got Sandra? She'd told him she
was leaving town, going someplace safe. Unless they'd been
watching her apartment all along. Which meant they must
have been following him.

Since when?

Had they hurt her?

The phone rang.

'Sandra . . . ?'

A man spoke to him: deep voice, French accent, level
tone.

Boukman?

'Every morning you go and smoke a cigarette on the
beach. Be at the same place there at midnight. Come alone.
If you don't, you'll never see her alive again.'

'If you hurt her I swear I'll –'

The man hung up.

61

Max got to the beach two hours early. He found his spot, sat down and lit a cigarette. It was a clear night. The stars were twinkling like a spray of rhinestone pinheads and the dense heat was cut in two by a cool breeze coming in from the sea. The air tasted of pure salt and smelt of those rare days when he'd had nothing better to do but lie in the sand and let himself be lulled into an easy half-sleep by the sound of the waves lapping at the shore.

He stared out at the ocean. The crests of the bigger waves reminded him of dead gulls in an oil slick. To his left he could just about make out the outlines of the Collins Avenue hotels, haloed in neon, a light in every window, a life in every room. In the opposite direction he could see a large group of people sitting around a bonfire, singing and laughing as the flames formed an amber tepee. One of their number was playing guitar. They all sounded young and probably were. No one with any sense or good intentions came out here at night: he wished them away, yet he was glad for their company and their innocence.

He'd brought both his guns – hip and ankle – plus two extra clips, but he doubted he'd need them. Boukman didn't want him dead just yet. He wanted him to suffer.

Since that last phone conversation, his day had been one long, fraught, agonizing blur. He'd said nothing to anyone about Sandra's kidnapping. Not to Joe when he'd come back from Coral Springs, and not to Eldon when he'd called them both into his office for a good news/bad news update – the Ismael family had been moved to the US Embassy in Port-au-Prince, but there were 'logistical difficulties' with

448

Sam's deal because both his lawyer and the DA wouldn't be free to start negotiations until tomorrow. At midday he and Joe had gone to the Overtown garage, removed all the boxes of paperwork and brought them back to MTF. Then they'd had a long meeting which everyone in the unit attended. Provisional plans had been drawn up for simultaneous arrests of all the SNBC members Ismael had named. Top of the list were Carmine and Eva Desamours. Max should have felt exhilaration and excitement, the thrill of the impending chase, satisfaction at the way things were coming together and how they'd turned out so far, but all he could think about was Sandra. Sandra and what she was going through, how he hadn't been able to protect her, and how, if she'd never met him, none of this would've happened.

The kids were singing 'California Girls' – except they'd substituted the title state for 'Florida'. No one seemed to know the words to the verses, so they stuck to the chorus. They'd start it, stop it, laugh, giggle, whoop, belch, talk and then start singing again.

Time passed slowly. People drifted around behind him, alone or in twos or threes, but he couldn't see much more than the vaguest smudges of them in the darkness. Max chain-smoked, checked his guns and homed in on the sound of the sea. None of it helped his nerves, which were shot. His pulse was up and his mouth was dry. He remembered how Sandra had come out here with him the morning after the night they'd first made love. They'd watched the sun come up from his spot. They hadn't said much. They hadn't needed to. He teared up.

At a quarter to midnight he stood up.

He listened out for incoming footsteps, scanning right to left, then back again.

Nothing.

He turned around and looked towards Ocean Drive and Lummus Park.

Then, out of the corner of his eye, he saw the campfire had disappeared.

Or so he thought, because, very quickly, he realized someone was standing in his line of sight, blocking the view. The person was coming towards him.

He saw the silhouette of a head and shoulders, then the person moved abruptly to the left and the flames were back in view. The kids were dancing around them in a circle, holding hands.

'Why are you investigating me?' the man addressed him from the darkness. Haitian accent, the tone calm and measured and quiet, a loud whisper. It wasn't the voice from the phone.

'Who are you?' Max tried to position himself in the direction the voice was coming from, but he couldn't get a specific bearing. It was all around him, and seemed close too, almost at his ear.

'You know who I am,' the man answered.

'Boukman?' Max chased the voice, his eyes straining for a face in the darkness, but finding none. 'Where's Sandra?'

'Why are you investigating me?' the man repeated. There was a hint of gravel in his whisper.

Max thought he saw the man standing directly in front of him, his back to the sea. He took a few steps forward.

Big mistake. What sounded like twenty guns were suddenly cocked all around him; the air crackled with hammers snapping back into firing position.

He stopped.

'Why are you investigating me?' the man repeated, no change in his tone, no impatience; someone with the upper hand and all the time in the world to play it.

'Because I'm a fucken' *cop*, genius!' Max snapped. 'Where's Sandra?'

No reply to that. Without moving his head or body, Max quickly glanced about him. Hints of metal and the very slightest outlines of the people holding it, figures in dark relief. He thought he could smell stale sweat, cigarettes and aftershave. He could smell candy too.

'Give me back what's mine and I'll give you your woman.'

This time the man spoke to Max's left. Max didn't turn to follow the sound.

The beach party was carrying on regardless, in splendid isolation. They were mangling 'God Only Knows'.

'You mean Ismael? He's in police custody. I can't bust him out of *that*.'

'He's not in custody,' the man said. 'He's in one of your safehouses. Look –'

'The *Emperor* tell you that?' Max interjected, trying to tilt things his way, lessen the odds.

It didn't work.

'Look in your mailbox,' the man continued in exactly the same smooth, emotionless way, 'you'll find a number there. If you have what I want, call no later than 7.00 p.m. tomorrow. No stalling, no delays or your woman dies.'

'Well, you hear this, Boukman – or whoever the fuck you are,' Max snarled, turning around. 'You hurt a hair on her head, you're a dead man. You, your whole fucken' crew *and* that cocksucker who's been protectin' you all these years – you're all fucken' *dead*!'

He waited for a reaction.

None came. His rage was swallowed in a vacuum, there was just the same controlled silence between them; beyond that, the noise of the world.

And then, one by one, anti-clockwise, he heard guns being de-cocked, then low murmurs in a language he didn't know drifting away from him, dispersing all over the beach in different directions, like a flock of songless birds.

He thought he heard a woman laugh.

Max stayed put and, in his head, counted very slowly to a hundred. When he finished he started again, in reverse.

At zero he took a few tentative steps forward, paused, listened, walked a little further, paused, listened – then ran like a motherfucker back to his apartment building.

62

'You sure she's still alive?' Eldon asked Max as he handed him a tumbler of whisky.

'Yes, I'm sure of it. I can *feel* it. I can feel *her*.' Max took the glass and downed half its contents in one continuous motion.

'Amputees can "feel" lost limbs too, Max.' Eldon frowned.

Max gave him a sharp look. 'Well, in *cold*, practical terms, Eldon, it doesn't make any sense for Boukman to have already killed Sandra. He wants Ismael back.' Max swallowed the rest of the whisky and put the glass down. 'But either which way it's fucked. Say I turn up with Ismael, Boukman might kill the three of us on the spot, or maybe he'll pop Ismael and Sandra, and leave me alive so I can take the rap for springin' a suspect *and* watch Sandra die over and over again in my memory. And if I don't go through with it, he'll kill Sandra anyway. This motherfucker is *not* going to negotiate. It's either his way or no way.'

It was 4.15 in the morning. Max and Joe were sitting at the coffee table in the corner of Eldon's office, flanking their boss, who occupied the couch. It was a full house. Also there were Jed Powers; Emilio Anorga from the DEA – a stout, big-chested, thick-limbed man, whose bushy black horseshoe of a moustache with ends stopping at the edge of his chin had earned him the nickname YMCA, after the Village People; Daryl Loewen – a redheaded ex-Marine with near translucent eyelashes and skin so pale he always wore a hat outdoors to stave off sunburn; and Rico Casados from SWAT, who friends called Chief Firestorm partly because of all the shoot-outs he'd been involved in and because his mother was Seminole.

Max had called Joe first to tell him what had happened. They'd talked tactics for an hour, then Max had called Eldon, who'd told them to come over to his office. They'd assumed it would be just them, but Eldon had summoned a war council.

'You got any ideas?' Eldon looked from Max to Joe and back to Max. His wart was stop-sign red.

'Yeah.' Max finished his drink and lit a cigarette. Eldon slid his marble ashtray over the table to him. 'We've got the names and addresses of the main SNBC players. Boukman has an inner circle, people he trusts. He'll have at least some of those people at the meet, for back-up. We put them under surveillance. Tail them. They'll know where the meet's going down, and they'll be heading there well before me.

'Solomon's going to assume that if I turn up to the meet, I'll have back-up, that this'll be a police operation. So we put that idea out of his head completely. We plant a news story that Ismael's been busted out of custody. We get it out on the radio and TV, we get it out on all the police frequencies. Boukman'll be tuning in somewhere for sure.'

'Like that *Capricorn One* movie where they fake the landing on Mars?' Rico laughed incredulously.

'Something like that, yeah.' Max nodded. 'It'll have to look convincing if it's on TV.'

He looked at Eldon for signs of disapproval, saw none, carried on.

'Now, we've traced the number he left me to a callbox on 73rd Street in Liberty City. I figure Boukman's going to play phone tag with me before he tells me where to meet. When I call I'll be told to go to another phone somewhere else and wait for it to ring. He'll do that a few times. All the while I'm driving around, he'll have me followed to make sure I've got Ismael with me, and that I haven't brought back-up. I can wear a wire. You can have a chopper tail me.'

Eldon smiled.

'We're one step ahead of you 'cause we're sitting on the SNBC right now,' he said.

'How come?' Max looked at him quizzically.

'We talked to Ismael yesterday after Liston left.' Eldon flicked his eyes in Joe's direction. 'We cross-referenced the names he gave you in case he was holding out.'

'Was he?' Max asked.

'No, but he was *very* helpful with additional details – minor points.' Eldon smiled his lupine grin, all gleaming, sated teeth.

'How long's surveillance been up?'

'Since seven yesterday evening.'

'*Seven?* Did you tail anyone to the beach last night?'

'We sure did.'

'So you knew I'd met Boukman?'

'No. We couldn't get close enough without blowing our cover. *Sixteen* people went out there. Twelve were SNBC elite. One was Bonbon, two were these women he always has with him, and there was one other – a man. Must've been Boukman.'

'Did you get visual ID?'

'No. They took photographs, but they didn't get his face.'

'Shit.' Max felt disappointed. They'd almost had Boukman there and then. They could've taken him down. But what would have happened to Sandra?

'We'll run with your plan,' Eldon said. 'I'm going to start making some calls now. Emilio, what can you bring to the party?'

'Twenty or so troops,' Anorga said.

'Rico?'

'Three units,' Casados replied. 'What kind of numbers you anticipating?'

'No idea. He ain't gonna come to this light.'

'Weaponry?'

'Better shit than us. They're criminals,' Eldon said. 'What about you, Daryl?'

'There's one thing we're not considering here.' Loewen leant slightly across the table towards Eldon.

'Yes?'

'Ismael.'

'What about him?' Eldon frowned.

'You're not really taking him to Boukman?'

'That's the idea.'

'You can't do that.' Loewen shook his head.

'Why not?'

'You can't use him as a bargaining chip. He's too valuable.' Loewen had a nasal tone which gave everything he said the irritating, whiny undertone of a mosquito on a sleepless night.

'So what do you suggest?'

'Get a vehicle with tinted windows. Put a dummy in there.'

'A *dummy*?' Eldon looked at him like he was talking shit in a foreign language. His wart went crimson.

'You'll be putting a key witness in a massive criminal conspiracy in the line of fire.'

'So?'

'What about the deal you offered him?'

'What "deal", Daryl? I didn't offer him any "deal",' Eldon said.

'What about the DA, what about his lawyer? Weren't they supposed to be meeting today?'

'Yes, they *were*,' Eldon said, 'but things have changed. Ismael talked. On the record.'

'But what about the investigation?'

'This ain't an investigation any more, Daryl. This is *war*. They touched one of us, so we kill all of them. Miami justice at its simplest and most efficient. *No one* fucks with my crew and lives happily ever after,' Eldon said coldly. 'Consider this piece of shit, Daryl. Ismael is Boukman's money man. Just 'cause he uses a pen and a calculator instead of a gun doesn't make him any less of a scumbag. In fact, it makes him *more* of one. All you ever hear from these little ghetto fucks we roust is how they '"never had no chance, never had no choice". You know that litany – never had no schoolin', never had no dads, never had no mamas, never had no *chance*, never had no *choice* – what else were they supposed to do but hit the highway to crime? A lot of people with liberal stirrings buy into that crap. I don't – even if it is maybe a little bit true. But let's say it's *completely* true. What kind of excuse does Sam Ismael have? None what-so-fucken'-ever! He *had* schoolin', he *had* a daddy, he *had* a momma, he *had* a chance – and he *blew* it – he *had* a choice – and he chose *wrong*. So fuck him!'

'We're deliberately putting a suspect in harm's way,' Loewen insisted.

'It's a bit late in your fucken' day to turn into a paragon of virtue, Daryl!' Eldon roared and Loewen flinched. 'Ismael ain't even a *suspect* now. He's *guilty*. He's confessed. Signed and sealed. That piece of shit helped run a multi-million-dollar drug empire. The Lemon City programme he fronted? He *knew* people had been killed over that! Whole fucken' families – *children*, Daryl, children. And they *took* the fucken' babies. God knows what those voodoo fucks did to 'em! So give me a fucken' break with your pieties! Get your head straight and your code in order!'

Max saw Joe smirking at Eldon and shaking his head.

'Who are you protecting, Daryl? The innocent woman who's been kidnapped, or some asshole cocksucker criminal who's life ain't worth a second of hers? We're here to get her and Max out of this alive. That's *all* you should be thinking of right now. If you're gonna get an attack of ethics then fuck off, we don't need you!' Eldon yelled, his temper gauge deep burgundy.

Eldon and Daryl went eye to eye across the table. Both men's shoulders tensed. Daryl looked like he wanted any excuse to punch Eldon. Eldon looked like he was going to give him one. A heavy anticipatory silence fell around the room.

Eldon broke it.

'Are you with us, Daryl?'

Loewen didn't reply.

'Are – you – with – us? *Daryl?*' Eldon repeated, his bottom lip quivering. Max had never seen him quite so angry before.

'I can commit twenty-five men,' Daryl said weakly and sat back in his chair, pissed off but defeated.

'Thank you, Daryl,' Eldon said sarcastically, staring at him like he'd just tossed him off a plane at high altitude.

'Who's running the op?' Max asked, to refocus the room.

'I am.' Eldon turned to Max.

'*You?* When was the last time you handled tactical ops?'

'About 1881.' Eldon chuckled. 'Jed'll coordinate, but I'll be right next to him. You ain't going through this on your own.'

'That's absolutely right,' Joe said. 'I'm goin' with you, Max.'

'No.' Max shook his head. 'I already stand a good chance of losing one person I care about. I ain't pushing that to two.'

'You're not losing anyone,' Joe countered. 'I got you into this, I'm getting you out.'

'He's right,' Eldon said, without looking at Joe. 'No one goes to hell alone.'

63

Friday morning. Carmine woke up and found Solomon standing at the end of his bed, partly illuminated by the thin spears of light slicing through the gaps in the blinds and falling across his dark blue shirt and parts of his face. Carmine wasn't so much looking at Solomon as at what he was holding – the M21 sniper rifle he'd used to hunt gators with Sam. He'd left it in the store. They must have collected it with Risquée's thawed remains.

'What do you want?'

'Do this one thing and you're free to go.'

'Free . . . ? To go where?' Carmine sat up. He hadn't been out the house in two days. His mother had grounded him. He'd barely left his room, except to eat, piss and have his bath. His mother had hardly spoken to him. She'd seemed preoccupied, worried even. He hadn't dared ask her what was wrong because he knew she'd blame him and probably go into a ShitFit.

Solomon didn't answer his question, simply carried on standing there with the rifle in his hands.

'What's this "thing"?' Carmine asked.

'I'll tell you in the car. Get dressed.'

64

Friday morning, 8 a.m. Wearing his tux and a fresh set of facial bruises, Ismael was brought back to MTF in the back of a mail van. He was put in an interrogation room and left alone. He asked for his lawyer. He didn't get an answer. He asked to see Max or Joe. He was told they were unavailable. He asked for his lawyer again. He still didn't get an answer.

2 p.m. The bogus news story hit the airwaves. TV and radio carried a report about an ambush on three unmarked police cars ferrying murder suspect Sam Ismael back to Miami on the junction of North West 29th Street and Coral Hills Drive. Two security trucks (reported stolen out of Tampa the day before) had blocked the convoy and about eight men wearing monkey masks, black boiler suits and armed with assault weapons had poured out of the back of the trucks and surrounded the cars. The suspect – Sam Ismael – had been abducted and bundled into a green Plymouth Barracuda. Meanwhile the cops had been disarmed, the radios smashed, and their cars shot up. As the attackers were fleeing, one of the officers – Pirro Oviedo – managed to reach his weapon, but had been shot and killed before he could use it. There was now a city- and state-wide manhunt for Ismael and his abductors.

TV news showed repeated images of paramedics stretchering what appeared to be a body in a bag from the scene.

4.30 p.m. Ismael was put in the back of a police cruiser, made to lie down with a blanket thrown over him. He was then driven out of MTF and taken to an underground parking lot near the courthouse across the road, where Max and Joe were waiting for him in a black bulletproof Deville sedan with tinted windows. The car was on loan from the DEA, who'd recovered it in a raid on a drug dealer's house.

'My lawyer's not coming, is he?' Ismael asked Max when he saw him.

'No,' Max said, studying Ismael's swollen nose, black eye and the bruise to his left cheek. They'd worked him over good – more than they needed to. He almost felt like apologizing, but it wasn't the time or place.

Ismael, understanding exactly what was happening, gave Max a bitter, yet resigned smile.

'Is my family safe at least?'

'They've been moved to the embassy,' Max answered. But with the way things were going, he wasn't sure if it was true.

'Then let's go,' Ismael said.

Max opened the passenger door. Ismael got in, followed by Joe.

They headed out towards Little Havana, where Max would make the call to Boukman's number.

4.50 p.m. Max called the number he'd found in his mailbox from a booth on Calle Ocho.

It rang three times before it was answered.

Max heard traffic in the background.

'This is Mingus. I have what you want.'

A man's voice came on the line. According to the surveillance they had on the booth, the man Max was addressing was a skinny, tall, young black male in dungarees and with short dreadlocks. He'd been watching the callbox since the morning.

'Come to the place you're calling,' the man said slowly and mechanically, like he was reading from a piece of paper.

'What?' Max asked.

'The phone you're calling. You a cop. You know where it's at.'

'Who did he kidnap?' Ismael asked as they drove to their next destination.

'My girlfriend,' Max said.

'He'll kill you both, you know – maybe me too – quickly, if I'm lucky.'

'It won't go down that way.'

'You hope.'

'I *know*,' Max corrected him.

'Oh?'

'I wouldn't be here if I thought differently.'

'Is that why you're smoking two cigarettes at once?' Ismael sniggered.

Max looked from the Marlboro burning between his fingers to the ashtray, where another cigarette was smouldering at the halfway mark. He crushed it out.

'If you think you're going to trap him, you're not.' Ismael caught Max's eye in the rearview mirror.

'Hey!' Joe snapped at him. 'Shut the fuck up, will ya? You're ruinin' my good mood.'

Ismael looked out of the window at the clear blue sky, the palm trees passing by like they were on a conveyor belt, the open-topped cars, the people in them heading to the beach in sunglasses and smiles, the whole road drenched in golden afternoon sunlight.

'Shame,' he sighed, 'such a beautiful day.'

65

5.30 p.m. For the past hour and a half, all the tails on the SNBC members had reported the same thing. Six cars carrying between four and five people, and a red transit van, had left various locations in Miami at around the same time, and were all taking the same route: straight up North West 7th Avenue, left down North West 119th Street, up Opa Locka Boulevard, and then right down Unity Boulevard.

Once in Opa Locka, they'd navigated the side roads, until they'd reached a stretch of wasteland right in front of the Biscayne Canal, very close to the airport. Now they were all standing around, stretching their legs, waiting. There was but one building nearby – a derelict, three-floor structure that had once been the offices of the Florida Aviation Camp.

Eldon, Jed Powers, Emilo Anorga and Rico Casados had watched the SNBC's progress in the MTF control room on the second floor. Eight operators manned radios and shouted out locations to a man moving pins across a large road map of Miami and its surrounding area. The air was thick with static crackles, disembodied voices, tense anticipation, cigarette smoke and sweat. The pins were red, orange, yellow, white, pink and black.

'You know why he picked that spot?' Powers pointed to the row of pins lined up next to North West 37th Avenue. 'We can't fly into that airspace, 'cause of the planes. Rules out choppers.'

'No it doesn't.' Eldon studied the map. 'We'll just have to ground all the flights.'

'Shall I tell Max about the meet?'

'Not until he gets his final instructions,' Eldon said,

looking at the blue pin representing Max's car. He was in Overtown, waiting by a phone.

'They're probably holding the girl in the van,' Rico said. 'We could move on 'em in forty minutes, an hour at the most. End this now.'

Eldon shook his head.

'Boukman hasn't arrived yet.'

'How do you know?'

Eldon had made notes of all the physical descriptions of the SNBC members in Opa Locka.

'According to Ismael, Boukman never goes anywhere without his bodyguard, Bonbon. Big fat guy in a hat and long coat. No sign of him yet. When he shows, Boukman'll show.'

Rico nodded, took out a cigar and lit it, moving the end slowly around the flame of his Zippo.

'If that's Cuban, I'll have to arrest you,' Eldon joked, wafting the thick, pungent smoke out of his face.

One of the radio operators shouted out that a dark blue Mercedes had left the Desamours house.

66

Daylight was starting to fade. Carmine panned the area below him, left to right: six cars and a white van parked with their tail ends to the filthy brown-green Biscayne Canal; close to thirty people were hanging around. He recognized a few familiar faces – core SNBC killers, several of them old guard, Solomon's original Liberty City crew. The others were new to him, mostly male, although there was a smattering of women too. They were milling around, talking, joking, laughing in voices which didn't carry. Most of them were in bullet-proof vests, and all were wearing those same piece-of-shit disco-throwback Compuchron watches Solomon had made him put on. He'd seen plenty of heavy artillery being passed around: Uzis, Macs, M16s, AKs, Mossberg pumps, a couple of British SLRs. Everyone had handled the main attraction, the Austrian Steyr AUG rifle, with its translucent magazine and weird design, like something out of that movie, *Day of the Jackal*. Across from them lay a long, wide and flat stretch of ground, brown dirt with tufts of dead or dying grass sticking out, nothing either side of it.

Carmine checked the time: 6.47 flashed up in red on the LED screen at the touch of a button. He'd been here under an hour. He was nervous as hell and sweating like a motherfucker, his shirt sticking to his chest, back and underarms, the crotch of his trousers damp. It was hot up here on the third floor of the crumbling building he was stationed in. The constant sound of planes taking off and landing at the nearby airport wasn't helping his state of mind either – lots of jets and two-seaters, engines farting through the air, tyres squealing on the runway. The heavier ones made the building shake and creak as they landed, dislodging plaster and stirring up dirt, which he'd breathe in and sneeze out. Solomon, his driver Marcus, Bonbon and his two killer dykes – what were their names? – Danielle and Jane – were up here with him too, standing behind him, saying little. Once in a while Bonbon would come over and look through the glassless window, inspecting the troops, communicating with them via walkie-talkie, saying nothing of any importance, most likely getting off on playing General for the day.

In the car on the way over, Solomon had had the radio tuned to the news and turned up loud. Sam Ismael had been sprung from a police convoy by an armed gang. A cop had been killed. That had amused Bonbon no end.

'Mingus must want his bitch back *baaaad* – dumbass pig!' He'd clapped his hands and slapped his big blubbery thighs, laughing in a high-pitched staccato wheeze.

Without anyone needing to tell him, Carmine had understood what they wanted him to do, although no one had actually said anything.

By 8.00 it was getting close to dark. Heavy shades of scarlet, purple and orange-tinged black dominated the sky. The area directly in front of the building had a faint steely-blue glow about it, as if it had soaked up most of the airport's ambient light.

Bonbon came over, his small feet crushing and popping and scratching across the debris-strewn floor, his entry into Carmine's orbit announced by the stench of candy and carrion coming from his mouth and the crackling of his walkie-talkie.

But it was Solomon who spoke to him.

'Max Mingus will arrive here with Sam Ismael between ten and eleven. His girlfriend will be brought out from the van and walked over. They'll meet in the middle there, to the right of you. My man takes two steps back. I want you

466

to shoot her first. In the head. Then count to four and shoot him. Think you can do that?'

'I ain't done this kind of shit before.' Carmine saw Solomon standing against the wall, right next to his rifle, the sparse light catching only his eyes. 'Why don't you get one of your guys instead?'

'You can put a bullet in the eye of a tic on an angel's wing. This has to be *very* precise. You're the man for the job.'

It was true, he was a great shot. Ever since he'd got his hands on a .38 Special his mother had kept around their home in Liberty City, he'd had an affinity with guns. He'd taught Solomon to shoot when they were teenagers. Back then, Solomon couldn't have hit the Freedom Tower if he'd been standing right in front of it. Carmine had showed him how to hold, aim, stand and breathe. Solomon had turned out OK – the right side of competent.

'And after this you'll let me go?' Carmine asked in a near croak. His mouth and throat were dry from fear and the dust in the room.

'That's what I said,' Solomon replied. 'You can take all that money you stole off me and move to Nevada.'

Carmine felt his guts clench. How the fuck had he found out?

'I – I – I didn't steal any money off you!' he stammered.

'No such thing as a half lie, Carmine. You ran hookers on the side. You kept the money. That's not the way we do things.'

Carmine was stunned. How had he found out? Had Sam told him? How long had he known? What was he going to do about it? There was no threat in Solomon's voice, no anger, no emotion. But then there never was.

'Why you lettin' me go? You've killed people for less,' Carmine managed to say.

'If I killed you I'd be doing you a favour. You are and were nothing without me and your mother. She gave you life. I gave you *a* life. I want you to remember that for as long as you live.'

With that Solomon walked away, leaving Carmine to his turmoil, confusion, fear and a hundred unanswered questions.

He picked up his rifle and looked through the sight, checking the vision. He focused the crosshairs on a small rock on the ground. The light was fine. He wouldn't miss.

How the fuck had Solomon found out about his business? He'd been so discreet, so careful . . . It had to be Sam, he thought, because there wasn't any other logical explanation. Sam had told Solomon or his mother or both of them. But why hadn't they done anything sooner? Why hadn't they made an example of him?

He heard crickets in the air. He heard the people talking by the cars. He heard Bonbon, Danielle and Jane whispering. But he didn't hear any more planes.

67

When they reached the stretch of open wasteground they'd been directed to, Max flashed his headlights twice in the direction of the canal. He caught two brief glimpses of the seven vehicles he knew were lined up there, and an even briefer one of the heavily armed platoon crowded behind them.

Joe, in the front passenger seat, looked at the building to their left, a typical Opa Locka structure – 1920s faux-Moorish, with a domed roof, arched entrances and windows – derelict, crumbling and begging for the wrecking ball. Three floors, three windows apiece, too dark to see inside.

A pair of headlights flashed back at them across the plain of dirt.

'We got the signal. Over,' Joe said into the radio and then glanced across at Max, who was staring through the windscreen, his face tight, his expression rigid, giving nothing away.

Powers' voice crackled back: 'Waiting on your word. Be safe. Over and out.'

Be *safe*! Joe thought. He'd never been so damn scared in all his life. Apart from his sidearm, he had three rifles lying across his lap – an Atchisson assault shotgun with a 20-round drum magazine, and two fully automatic M16s each fitted with a taped together pair of 30-round box magazines. His palms were sweating and he couldn't stop blinking.

Suddenly seven pairs of headlights came on, full beam, momentarily dazzling them with an eruption of white, as they lit up the ground – grey-brown, rubble- and trash-strewn, dry as a desert, save a large puddle close to the car.

'You set?' Joe asked his partner.

Max nodded.

Joe handed Max an M16. Max took a deep breath and opened the door.

'Keep the engine running,' he said to Joe and stepped outside.

Joe lowered the driver's door window, lay across the seats and positioned himself so he could get a clear shot at the building. They'd guessed Boukman would be holed up in there, directing operations. He'd have at least one sniper with him too. The trouble was, they didn't know exactly where he was in the building, and Joe couldn't see much of anything beyond the outlines of the windows.

Max began to walk forward, head slightly down, squinting into the beams. The hot air smelled of plane fuel and rank water. He glanced at the building as he moved, scanning it left to right, floor to floor, window to window. He felt eyes on him, tracking him, aiming at him. And he could feel Boukman most of all, the weight of his scrutiny, the same sense of dissection and evaluation, of being broken down into core components, strengths and weaknesses, heart and fear.

'Stop!' a voice yelled out from the glare.

Max complied.

'Where's Ismael?'

'Right here. Where's Sandra?' Max shouted back.

'Show and tell, baby!' a different voice shouted out. There was some laughter.

'Bring her out! Let me see her!'

Max heard a short burst of walkie-talkie static come from the building. He looked across. Definitely the third floor. He didn't know which window, but he was guessing the middle one. Best vantage point. He signalled this to Joe – three fingers of his left hand tapped against the back of his thigh.

Joe saw the sign. He aimed at the middle window. Behind him, in the passenger seat, Ismael was breathing heavily through his mouth and nose. Poor bastard sounded like he was on a respirator.

Max saw someone step out from behind a car and blot out one of the headlights, then both as he began to approach. Max raised his rifle and got the figure in his sights: a tall man, walking slowly – behind someone else. Someone shorter.

Sandra.

At the sight of her, Max's heart started beating hard in his chest and his legs shook, tremors running from his hips to his toes and back like a high-voltage current.

He felt rage and a lot of fear for her safety. He wanted to get her out of there and he wanted to kill the fucker behind her, then he wanted to kill Boukman and his whole crew.

He kept his rifle aimed at the tall man's head, which wasn't hard, because the asshole had given him an optimum target – a bright yellow sweatband around his forehead.

They stopped a few feet away. Sweatband stood off to Sandra's right and pointed a chrome-plated .44 Magnum with a four-inch barrel at her head and cocked it.

Max shot a brief look at Sandra. Their eyes met. She was terror-stricken. She was wearing his denim shirt. She'd hated it on him. He'd loved it on her.

He wanted to say something reassuring, something about how everything was going to be OK, but they both knew that was bullshit. They were in deep deep shit.

He stared at Sweatband – a muscular six feet two in military khakis and desert boots, a bulletproof vest over his chest, black camouflage on his face and bald head.

Fucken' wargame-playin' dumbass, Max thought.

'Here's how it's gonna go,' Max said to him. 'First you lower your weapon.'

'Fuck dat!' Sweatband spat.

'At this range I can put three bullets in your brain faster than you can pull that trigger. You'll be dead before your fingers know it.' Max watched Sweatband's eyes cloud over with doubt and uncertainty. This wasn't in the script.

'Lower your weapon,' Max repeated, slightly louder and more insistently.

Sweatband tried to eyeball him, but he couldn't exactly front convincingly with the muzzle of a high-powered assault rifle pointed at his forehead. So he lowered his gun.

'Good,' Max said. 'Now, she's going to walk to the car. She's going to get in. Then Ismael's going to come out. You got that?'

'Ain't – ain't my call,' Sweatband said.

'You're the guy with the gun in his face. So it *is* your call,' Max answered.

Now Sweatband was *really* lost – freefalling through dense fog. His eyes were straining off to the right, upwards. He wanted orders.

Max looked quickly at Sandra.

Then he saw Sweatband turn, first his head, then his whole body towards the building. He looked up at the middle window.

That was all Max needed.

He rushed between Sweatband and Sandra and pushed her to the ground.

'Go to the car! Crawl! Keep down!' he yelled at her as he got behind Sweatband, hooked his arm around his throat, shoved his knee in his lower back and pulled tight.

Sweatband dropped his gun. He kicked and flailed, trying to get Max off him, gurgling and gasping and spluttering for air through his constricted windpipe.

Max jammed his M16 under Sweatband's armpit and fired straight at the middle window. He heard a cry and a scream.

A shot came from the building and struck Sweatband full in the chest, pushing him and Max to the ground. The fall knocked the rifle from Max's hand. Sweatband went for it. Max pulled out his ankle piece and shot him in the head.

A barrage of automatic fire erupted from behind the headlights and swarm after swarm of bullets cut through the air, smashing into Joe's car, killing the light.

He saw Sandra speed-crawling towards the car.

The window sniper fired at him three times, missing his head by ever decreasing margins. Max pushed Sweatband's body on its side. Two bullets smacked into it. He shot back, emptying his gun into the black space that was the window.

'Shooters on the canal and the third floor! GO! GO! GO! GO!' Joe yelled into his radio and fired a volley at the middle window. 'Stay the fuck down!' he yelled at Ismael as a continuous hail of lead pounded the car, taking out the windscreen and blowing out the front tyres. It sagged. Bullets tore into the roof.

Max got hold of his M16, switched it to fully automatic and fired at the bank of headlights.

Joe didn't hear the passenger door open, nor see Ismael creep out of the car.

Max heard a splash of water behind him and turned to see a dark figure stealing up on him.

Ismael. What the fuck?

Ismael flipped over and fell on his back.

He heard someone yell 'NO!' from the third floor.

At that moment Sandra made it to the side of the car and got in.

Two spotlights simultaneously lit the row of cars and the building.

Max hadn't heard the choppers and neither had Solomon's men.

Twin streams of high-calibre tracer fire came down from the sky, pouring into the upper floors of the building, tearing up the brickwork, ripping through the open windows.

One of the choppers was directly above Max. Spent

casings fell from the sky and clattered and bounced on the ground.

The volleys of bullets stopped coming from the cars as they were pounded by machine-gun fire, first from the chopper then, behind them, from the canal. The headlights died in blocks. Cars started up. One tore out of the line, then swerved and crashed into the building.

Max saw people running towards him, shooting. He fired back. So did Joe, leaning out of the window, pumping rounds out of the Atchisson.

Then Rico's SWAT teams moved in behind Joe and opened fire on the stragglers.

The van blew up.

Solomon's men were cut down. They fell flat on their faces, their sides, or keeled over on their backs.

Some dropped their weapons and started to raise their hands, but they were shot too – from above or from the front, sometimes both.

The firing stopped. One of the choppers took off, flying towards the airport, searchlight fixed on the ground.

Max turned around and looked for Sandra. She was nowhere in sight.

He called out for her.

SWAT moved past him.

'Sandra?' He stood up and went to the car.

She was lying in the back seat with her hands over her ears, shaking.

She screamed and kicked out when Max leant over her. When she saw it was him, she sat up, threw her arms around him and held him tight, sobbing.

'It's OK, baby. It's over,' he said, kissing the top of her head. Then he buried his face in her hair and started crying himself, overwhelmed with relief and by a million prayers all being answered at once. He swore he'd never put her in harm's way again.

Joe got quietly out of the car to give them some privacy. His legs and shoulders were tensed up and tight, and he was getting the beginnings of a nervous headache. He looked at the aftermath of the firefight; the carnage and destruction lit up by the hovering chopper's quivering spotlight. A noxious mist of gun smoke hung in the air, wafting back and forth like wan muslin drapes. SWAT personnel combed the wasteground, checking the still, rounded forms that were the dead, kicking weapons away from the wounded before cuffing them. A team entered the building, torches mounted on their weapons. Soon they were barking 'Clear' multiple times. The van burnt near the canal, its skeleton visible in thin geometrical lines under layers of burning flame. All around him he heard sirens – police, ambulance, fire service. After gunplay, paperwork.

68

Solomon drove carefully. He took the side roads out of Opa Locka, keeping to the speed limit. The maroon Dodge Magnum was perfect cover, something common and anonymous, something that blended in, something that didn't spell drug dealer, something the cops wouldn't be looking for. And they were everywhere – on the roads and in the skies, sirens undercutting every sound, spotlights probing the ether – chasing a shadow through the night.

Carmine and Bonbon were in the back. Carmine was in shock; numb, paralysed, close to complete insentience. Bonbon was laughing hysterically – a hacking squealing cackle, which started with a phlegmy blast that first vibrated up and down in his larynx before breaking free and rocketing up out of his mouth in a pitch suggesting a rubber duck getting mauled by a rabid cat.

'HEEE-YUKKA-YI-HI-*HI!*'

Everything had happened so fucking fast: too quick for Carmine to think and react – too quick for *any* of them to react. He'd had Mingus's woman in his sights, but he hadn't pulled the trigger. When it had come down to it, he couldn't kill an innocent person in cold blood. Simple as that. She didn't deserve to die.

Then the cop had grabbed that stupid fucker in the fatigues and opened up on them. Marcus and Jane had died instantly.

'HEEE-YUKKA-YI-HI-*HI!*'

Bonbon looked down at him, glittering silvery slug-slime lines for eyes, face a big blobby mass of trembling mirth.

His laugh corroded Carmine's shell.

'Fuck you laughin' at?'

'YOU!' Bonbon roared, spraying Carmine with a mass of spit, halitosis and candy; tears running down his cheeks. He had his piranha dentures in. He looked like an obese dog.

'The one friend you had in the world – the one *person* in the world didn't think you was a no good piece of *caca* and you . . . you fuckin' *SHOT* him! You *SHOT HIM* – HEEE-YUKKA-YI-HI-*HI!*'

Carmine had seen Mingus' girlfriend crawling towards their car. Solomon had seen her too. 'Shoot the bitch,' he'd ordered, no emotion or urgency, just cold neutrality, like he'd asked for cream in his coffee.

Carmine had deliberately aimed wide, past her head, and pulled the trigger. But at that precise moment a dark shape had dashed out from nowhere and taken the bullet meant for the girl. Only when he was laid out flat on his back, with his face turned toward the building, had Carmine recognized Sam. Why the fuck had he run out like that into certain death? Maybe that was the way he'd wanted it. Maybe, somewhere, he was grateful it was Carmine who'd killed him. Not that it made it any better.

'"*Nooooooo!*"' Bonbon screeched, high-pitched, flapping his hands on limp wrists. 'Thass what you said up in there when you shot him. "*Nooooooo!*" – like some donkey takin' it up the ass. *Nooooooo!* I shot my boyfwend! *Nooooooooo!* HEEE-YUKKA-YI-HI-*HI!*'

'Shut your mouth, you sick fat fuck!' Carmine snarled.

But Bonbon didn't and his laughter seeped into Carmine's insides and mingled with his hurt and his sorrow and his anger, stirring everything up – all the humiliation he'd ever had to endure in silence, all the shit he'd had to swallow. He wanted this to end – and he wanted it to end *now*.

He hadn't been surprised when the choppers had appeared, because he'd expected something was up when the planes stopped flying. Yet he'd still been completely caught off guard by the *way* they'd showed up – out of thin air, as if by pure magic; the room had suddenly and abruptly filled with the brightest bluey-white light. He'd seen the bullets coming at them like giant fireflies soaked in gasoline. When they'd hit the building they'd blown inch-wide holes clean through the bricks, every one of them letting in a shaft of light, as if God's own angels had teamed up with the cops and were raining spears at them. He'd never felt so cursed, so doomed. His life had been worthless and his death even more so: he was going to die here, fighting for people he hated.

Then Solomon had grabbed him by the ankles and pulled him away from the window and they'd run out of the room and down the stairs. Him, Solomon, Bonbon and Danielle. Bullets tore through walls and came straight at them, blindly yet accurately. Danielle was hit in the side and fell down the stairs. She'd begged Bonbon to help her. He'd shot her in the head and stepped over her.

'HEEE-YUKKA-YI-HI-*HI!*'

They were close to Miami now. Carmine could see the city lights glittering through the windshield, a row of bared diamond and jade teeth, the Freedom Tower a fang.

'Where are we going?' he asked Solomon.

'Get Eva.' Solomon didn't turn around.

Solomon had anticipated an ambush and had made contingency plans. They'd all arrived in Opa Locka in a Mercedes, but they'd abandoned it behind the building as they'd fled. They'd made for the airport. A hole had been cut in the fence around the runway. Once inside the perimeter, they'd followed it round to where another hole had been cut, this one close to a road. That was where the Dodge was parked.

'Simple thang like killin' you cain't even git right! You a straight up fuckin' retarded faggot, Carmine! HEEE-YUKKA-YI-HI-*HI!*'

Bonbon. The fat fuck hadn't even suffered a scratch. The bastard still had his hat on.

Carmine watched him guffawing, his head tilted back, the seat reverberating with his wretched laughter. Bonbon's prodigious gut was sticking all the way out between the flaps of his coat, the gold buttons of his waistcoat looking like they were set to flee the fabric.

Carmine's eyes fell on the handles of Bonbon's silver Magnums.

'Stop laughing,' he said quietly.

'HEEE-YUKKA-YI-HI-*HI!*'

'Stop laughing at me, motherfucker!'

'Or *what . . . ?*' Bonbon sneered. 'Whatchu gonna do, mamma's boy? Huh?'

'FUCK YOU!' Carmine screamed and snatched one of the guns from Bonbon's holster.

He stabbed the barrel into the fat man's chin, sinking the metal deep into a cushion of blubber.

Then he squeezed the trigger.

Bonbon's head erupted as though a grenade had been tossed into a full barrel of red wine. Carmine, the side windows, the back window and parts of the front were saturated in a mixture of blood, dessicated brain, hair, skin and fragmented bone.

Solomon turned around in shock, accidentally swerving the Dodge into the opposite lane. He spun the wheel sharply to right the car, sending Bonbon's near headless corpse toppling over onto Carmine, who caught a warm jet of jugular blood straight in the face. He savagely pushed the body away from him. It fell on the passenger door which sprang open. The body toppled out, colliding with a car coming the opposite way. The car smacked into the side of the Dodge, sending it spinning out across the middle of the lane where it was hit from both sides and at great force by hurtling traffic.

Carmine was thrown from his seat. He heard glass shattering all around him and metal being crushed like paper, then a series of loud thuds, followed by screams. Solomon was slumped over the wheel. The windscreen was gone.

The Dodge was penned in from both sides by smashed and smoking cars. Carmine scrambled over the front seats, crawled out and slid across the hood into the road. He was dazed, his head was spinning, and there was a pain in his neck. He still had Bonbon's gun in his hand. He shoved it down his pants.

Eight cars were piled up in an ungainly heap in the road. He smelled leaking petrol and burnt rubber.

Up ahead of him one part of the road was completely clear. The other was gradually choking up with a line of backed-up traffic. It wouldn't be long before the cops came. He had to get out of here.

He started walking up the road.

'CARMINE!' Solomon shouted at him. He didn't turn around. Even if he'd wanted to, he couldn't because the pain in his neck was extreme and spreading to his shoulders.

'Don't you walk away, Carmine! Don't you *dare* walk away!' Solomon shouted.

But Carmine carried on walking towards the line of stalled traffic. Then he ran. People were getting out of their cars, heading towards him and the crash site.

A short Latino man in a white shirt was waving both hands at him.

'Stop walking, man. You're hurt, man. Stop walking.'

Carmine tried to push past him but the man grabbed his arm. He was strong and Carmine was too weak, shocked and dizzy to put up much resistance.

'You need to sit down. You been in a bad accident. Sit down,' the Latino implored, wincing at the sight of the man he wanted to help soaked in blood.

Carmine saw his chance.

'Lemme . . . Lemme sit down in your car,' he said. 'I hurt my neck real bad. I need support.'

'Sure, sure.' The Latino led him over to the second car in the line – a silver Firebird coupé.

He opened the passenger door and helped Carmine get in.

Carmine checked the keys were in the ignition. They were hanging at the end of a fob with Fidel Castro's face on it, crossed out by a red slash, like a No Smoking sign.

Carmine slammed the passenger door shut and locked it. Then he slid over to the driver's side and did the same.

The Latino started banging on the window. People turned around.

Carmine switched on the ignition and hit the gas. He quickly steered out of the line and into the wide-open lane and sped off.

69

'How the fuck did this happen? How the fuck did he get away?' Max shone his torch at the large rectangular gap in the airport's perimeter fence. 'The building should've been completely surrounded.'

'They must've left before SWAT moved in,' Powers said.

'This was Plan B. In case something went wrong.' Joe pointed his Maglite at the ground near the wire, bent down and picked up half a dozen strips of duct tape.

'He came here in that Mercedes we found at the back of the building,' Powers said. 'Same one we tailed from the Desamours house. Six people came outta the car – the two dead girls, the dead guy in the building, Bonbon, a high-yella-type guy with a rifle and another man.'

'Description?' Max asked.

'Tall. Slim. Didn't get his face.'

'Story of our fucken' life – and his.' Max was very angry and very frustrated. Boukman had been theirs to lose and they'd done just that.

'And surveillance got pulled back just before you went in, right?'

'You know the drill, Max,' Eldon said. He was standing next to him.

'Yeah, and so does Boukman. He's got a guy on the inside, so he would've known how we work the big plays. Air, then ground,' Joe said. 'They bailed as soon as the choppers showed.'

'You were point man on this, right?' Max looked at Powers. 'Why didn't you have nobody at the airport?'

'We had 'em at the exits.' Powers looked at the ground. 'We honestly didn't think he'd get out of that building.'

'Well he fucken' *did*!' Max shouted.

'That's if he was here at all,' Powers suggested.

'He *was* here,' Max insisted, angry and frustrated, 'and he got away. Question is *how*? You had road blocks, right?'

'Major arteries,' Powers said. 'But this area has more outs than a sieve.'

'Maybe he slipped through the road blocks unnoticed,' Joe said. 'He'd have had another car parked around here. Kind of vehicle you wouldn't notice.'

'Could be he's still in the area,' Powers said. 'We're doing a door to door now.'

'Oh yeah? "Knock-knock. Have you seen this man? Sorry we only know what his tongue looks like,"' Max said sarcastically. He looked at Eldon, whose expression was thunderous. 'Anyone at the Desamours house now?'

Eldon shook his head.

'Why the fuck not?'

'Whole division's here,' Eldon said.

'Someone should be at that house – should be there right now. Put two units on it.'

'You really think he'd go back there after *this*? If I was him I'd be in the wind,' Powers said.

'That's why he ain't you. Eva Desamours and Boukman go way back. He was her apprentice. She's probably the closest he has to a mother. We need to get out there now.'

'No, Max.' Joe stepped up to him. '*You* need to be with Sandra. You came for her not Boukman.'

'But he's out there, Joe, right now, gettin' away.'

'We'll find him. We'll flip the guys we caught today. They'll tell us something. We're hitting the SNBC soon. All the addresses Ismael gave us. Closing down all the bank accounts.'

'The fucker's *out* there. And as long as he is, Sandra's not safe. We've seen what he can do.'

'Boukman may be runnin' now, but he's got no place to go. He's exposed. He won't get far,' Joe reassured him. 'But that's for tomorrow. Right now Sandra needs you, Max. Go to her.'

Max stood his ground. He wanted to kill Boukman. He wanted him dead so he couldn't hurt Sandra again.

'He's right, Max. You get outta here. Go be with your girl,' Eldon said. 'That's an order.'

70

His mother's house was dark and felt unusually empty, bereft of her presence and the accompanying sense of dread Carmine always had whenever he walked in. He guessed she had fled. That's what he would have done in her position. Still, just to be sure, he was careful not to make a sound as he crept down to the basement.

In his room, he stripped out of his bloody clothes. His head, neck, arms and hands were caked in sticky brownish blood, and he was giving off a heavy carrion stink. He couldn't go anywhere looking like this. He needed to wash.

He packed a small bag with clean clothes, put on a pair of jeans and chose a shirt to travel in. Then he took the locker key out of the coffee jar and slipped it into his trouser pocket along with the keys to the pickup, which was still parked outside.

He tiptoed up to the bathroom.

He didn't turn on the light. The shadowy indigo glow of the aquarium was enough to see by. He closed the door, filled up the sink with warm water and washed the blood off his skin. Then he washed his stubbly scalp as best he could. He'd pause regularly to listen for signs of movement – his mother's feet on the stairs, the clinking of her necklaces and lockets – and for the sound of police sirens. He heard nothing but his pounding heartbeat.

When he was done he dried himself with two of his mother's white bathtowels, which were soft as a bed of wool and smelled pleasantly of eau de cologne and talcum powder. He got dressed and checked himself in the mirror. He smiled at what he could see. He was still a regular handsome motherfucker. *Plus* he had $365,000 – *all* his.

First thing he'd do when he got to Buffalo would be to buy himself some nice clothes. Then he'd go out and get himself a fly bitch, but one with money and a regular job, going places; and one who appreciated the fine things in life – fine things, like him.

He'd be happy and he'd be free.

The light suddenly went on in the bathroom and Eva was standing there.

Every part of Carmine froze solid. Except his eyelids, which he blinked manically as his vision scrambled to adjust from dark to light.

'Where's Solomon?' she asked.

He couldn't turn his head to look at her because of a vice-like stiffness around the nape and down to his shoulders, so he turned his entire body in her direction. She was standing by the open door, dressed in brown leather sandals and a plain light blue denim dress with wooden buttons up the front.

'What happened?' She looked him over, half naked, then saw the two bloody towels and puddles of reddish water around his feet.

'Cops,' he said quietly. 'Cops ambushed us.'

She looked him up and down slowly, inspecting him, taking all of him in. She didn't appear at all surprised by what he'd said. Maybe she already knew.

'Whose blood is that? Where's Solomon?' she said hurriedly.

He didn't answer. His heart was beating faster. He couldn't help it. He was getting scared.

'I said, *where's Solomon?*'

Until then, she'd been composed, neutral, matter of fact. Now there was a snarl in her voice.

'There was an – an accident,' Carmine managed to say.

'I thought you said you got ambushed.'

'We – we got away,' he said. 'Then there was an accident.'

'Is he hurt?'

'Yeah – I mean, no. I – He was OK when I left him.'

'You LEFT HIM?' she shouted.

'I had to get away,' Carmine pleaded. His mouth was dry and his throat tight. He could clearly see her building up to a ShitFit: her nostrils were flaring and her hard black eyes seemed to be getting smaller.

'Where *is* he?' She took two steps towards him, her eyes leaping from him to the towels and back again.

'There was a pile up. A loada cars crashed into us.'

'*Answer* me, you little prick! Where *is* he?' she barked.

'I – I – I don't know.'

'What do you mean, you don't know?'

'I don't . . .'

She looked over at the tub, where he'd left his bag.

'You snivelling, cowardly PIECE OF SHIT! You LEFT HIM!' she screamed. 'YOU LEFT HIM!'

She came closer to him.

'Yeah. Thass right,' Carmine said. 'Thass right. I *left* him. Maybe the cops've got him now.'

She wasn't listening. She was staring over at the sink, to the shelf, where he'd left Bonbon's gun. He hadn't cleaned it. It was still covered in the fat man's blood.

'What are you doing with Bonbon's gun?'

'Bonbon's dead.'

'Who killed him?'

'*Me.*' Carmine tapped his chest. '*I* did. I shot him. Wit' his own gun.' He couldn't help himself. He smiled. He was *proud* of what he'd done.

'*You* killed him?' She looked like she wanted to laugh and might have done if she didn't have so much on her mind.

'Yeah. *I* killed him,' Carmine said. He felt a little bolder, a little rebellious even. He remembered he had the keys to the locker and the keys to the pickup in his pocket. Everything he needed. All he had to do was walk out. And he could. Physically she'd be no match for him. But could he stand up to her? He didn't know. He was in her world, following her rules, going at her pace.

'Where are you going?' She pointed at his bag without looking at it.

'I'm gettin' the fuck out.'

'You're *what*?'

'Gettin' the fuck out,' he repeated.

She covered the ground between them and slapped him hard across the face.

'Don't you *dare* speak to me like that.'

'FUCK YOU!' Carmine yelled at her.

She raised her hand to backhand him, but Carmine caught her wrist and pushed her away.

He grabbed the gun off the shelf and pointed it at her. She ignored him.

'You're not going *anywhere*,' she said, black eyes boiling with hatred and rage.

'Yes I *am*.' Carmine pointed the gun at her. 'An' you ain't stoppin' me.'

'Run your bath,' she said.

'*What?*'

'Run. Your. Bath.'

'Get outta my way.'

'Run. Your. Bath.'

'I've. Had. A. Wash.' He cocked the gun.

'Run. Your. Bath. And don't you DARE disobey me, boy!' she repeated, her fierce eyes boring into his as she came closer to him.

He wasn't backing down, but somewhere inside he wanted to.

'You're a crazy *FUCKIN' BITCH!*' he screeched.

She laughed at him. He felt tears massing in his eyes. He

knew he was close to breaking down. He knew he was close to letting her have her way. He felt so crushed and small and insignificant by her presence, her personality, her contempt and her hatred for him. He was pointing a loaded gun at her and she wasn't in the least bit scared because she knew he wasn't going to use it on her.

'I'm warning you . . . Get out of my way,' he sobbed.

'Or *what*? You're going to shoot me! Is that it? I don't think so. You wouldn't *dare*. You're a scared little boy. A coward – just like your father! A no-good, weak piece of shit.'

His hand was starting to shake. She noticed. She smiled.

'*See?*' she sneered. 'You're shaking. You're pissing yourself. You don't have the *nerve*! You don't have the balls. You *never* had the *guts* to stand up to me. *Me* – a frail little old woman. You're a *joke*, Carmine. A pathetic weak feeble joke. Your whole life's a *joke*. Weak! *Weak!* WEAK!'

He didn't remember pulling the trigger. It just happened. He'd had enough of her voice, sneering, taunting, screaming in his aching head; tearing at his heart, crushing his soul. He'd wanted it to stop. He'd wanted her to stop. For ever. And his pain and desire translated into the few pounds of pressure he put on the sliver of metal.

His mother toppled over backwards and landed on the floor, spreadeagled, a small, smoking black hole in her chest, a spreading red pool under her back.

Carmine picked up the bag and headed for the door, the blast undulating in his ears.

Before leaving the bathroom, he stopped and looked at her.

She wasn't dead. Her eyes were moving.

They locked stares.

'You taught me well, *Mother*,' Carmine said to her. 'I hate you. I've *always* hated you. And I'll *always* hate you.'

Eva saw his lips move but couldn't hear what he was saying. Her ears were ringing from the pistol shot that had torn through her heart.

She waited for what she knew would come next. She'd seen it and it was beautiful. Moments before the body died and freed the spirit, a comforting, cleansing pure white light gently obliterated all trace of this life and gradually illuminated the way to the next.

It was true: God forgave everyone. Even her. She was only human, after all – for now.

She felt very cold all over. She couldn't feel her legs. The pain in her chest was intense as her heart struggled hard to heal itself and close the fatal rupture.

She was looking forward to the next stage. She'd be able to watch over Solomon and guide him. As for that wretched murderous bastard son of hers – she'd haunt him to his grave, and then she'd make sure his existence beyond it was misery too. There'd be a bath waiting for him in eternity. He wouldn't *ever* escape her.

She wanted to laugh but she couldn't because her muscles weren't working any more. Any time now the beautiful light would come. Any time now.

Then it came.

But not the light.

No.

Not the light.

An inky black smoke – part fume, part liquid – gradually poured into her vision, blotting out her surroundings. And then she heard the sound of dogs again – not scratching and circling as before, but stampeding, rushing towards her at great speed, their paws thunderous, as if they were as big as horses.

The total darkness parted and she saw the great beasts bearing down on her, more terrifying than anything she'd ever seen in her many visions, than anything she could ever have imagined. She wanted to scream but she knew it was pointless. No one would ever hear her again.

Carmine knew he should have already left the house, but he was stuck at the foot of the stairs leading to his mother's forbidden quarters, a hostage to his own curiosity. There was light pouring out of the open door.

Now she was dead he could do what he wanted.

He found himself on a landing, facing four identical doors sunk into alcoves – tall, round-topped, made of heavy, polished dark wood; none had locks or handles, and all had the same moulding – an egg surrounded by a serpent swallowing its tail. There were two doors to his left, one to his right and one directly in front of him.

He didn't have much time. He couldn't see everything. He could only see one thing. He had to make a choice.

It wasn't hard.

He walked forward and pushed the door into his mother's bedroom.

Spacious, cool, musk scented. A library ran along the right wall, broken up by two windows, which faced the street. The shelves were filled with large, heavy, hide-bound antique books of spells and potions, divination, demonology and mediumship, their titles stamped in gold on the spines.

Facing the library was a king-sized bed, made up with dark blue sheets and pillows. His eyes were drawn to a framed black and white photograph on a bedside cabinet. It was a headshot of his mother, the kind actors and models have in their resumés, just the face, set against a dark background. Seeing it made him understand where he got his vanity from.

He looked across to the other side of the bed. There was a photograph there too, in the same style as his mother's, only it was of someone else.

He recognized the face but he didn't know what it was doing there. He went over and picked it up.

Solomon.

All the rumours he'd heard about him having had extensive plastic surgery and his skin bleached were just that – tall tales disseminated by Chinese whispers, the usual misinformation that stoked the myth. Solomon looked slightly older than the years-old memory Carmine had of him – a few wrinkles around the eyes, two deep furrows in his forehead – but other than that he hadn't changed much.

What was his photograph doing at his mother's bedside?

He knew, but didn't fully understand and didn't want to believe.

He sat down on the edge of the bed.

How long had they been together?

The answers were right in front of him, on top of a chest of drawers near the window.

There were half a dozen more photographs – all colour – of Solomon and Eva together in Miami with their arms around each other outside Pork 'n' Beans, sitting close together at a restaurant table, in a locked embrace on the beach, dancing together in a club, posing with a pile of money and staring longingly into each other's eyes on a boat, getting progressively older, richer and more fashion conscious.

They'd *always* been together.

He guessed he should have known, but how could he? He'd never suspected a thing, never witnessed the slightest hint of intimacy between them.

He wasn't just shocked, but disgusted too. Disgusted at Solomon, because he was no better than his mother. They were as one. He wished he'd killed him out there on the road.

What a fool he'd been.

Bitter tears ran down his face.

His first impulse was to trash the room, rip it to shreds, but he didn't have time and the gesture would be meaningless. He had to do something else, something that mattered, something that counted; something that *hurt*.

71

'Think you'll ever catch him – the man with no face?' Sandra asked Max over breakfast.

'I don't know.' Max pushed away his plate and lit his first cigarette of the morning. Sandra had cooked them a shrimp and onion omelette on Cuban bread, which was delicious, but he didn't have too much of an appetite. In the three days that had passed since the Opa Locka shoot-out he'd eaten as sparingly as a piranha in a vegetable patch. 'If I was him, with all this heat, I'd be well out of here by now – out of town, out of state, out of the country. That's what any normal, right-thinking person would do.

'But Boukman ain't that person. He's not just gonna give up and walk away. All that power, all that money, all that control. He's used to it, he's used to having his own way. People like him don't leave their thrones. They die on 'em. He's gonna wanna restore order and hit back. When he does, I hope we'll be ready.'

They were staying in a room on the top floor of Atlantic Towers, a high-security, state-owned building off Flagler, used by visiting politicians and dignitaries, connected celebrities and by cops and Feds to stash star witnesses.

Sandra had been released from hospital two days ago. She'd been treated for shock, dehydration and the minor cuts and bruises she'd got when she'd crawled over to the car. Luckily she'd suffered no serious physical injuries.

A shrink had talked to her for an hour, prescribed a month's supply of Valium, given her a distant date for a follow-up meeting, and a number to call if there were any problems in-between. She refused to take the pills, saying she didn't need them; she was fine, she insisted. And outwardly, to Max, she appeared to be just that. She showed none of the typical signs of trauma: she slept soundly and ate regularly; she wasn't jumpy, stressed, or paranoid. In fact, she was almost exactly as she had been before. Max wasn't sure if this was simply down to innate toughness, or if it wasn't the silent build-up to a delayed reaction. He'd seen it happen in the past to cops involved in shoot-outs. They'd be business-as-usual for a few months and then, suddenly, flip out and go into meltdown.

Although she remembered her ordeal vividly, she couldn't provide much in the way of information. As soon as Max had told her to go into hiding, she'd packed and left her apartment. She was putting her case in the trunk of her car when a black Mercedes had pulled up alongside her. Bonbon was in the front passenger seat. A woman with a gun had stepped out and ordered her to get in. She'd been blindfolded and her mouth, hands and feet taped. When they had come off, she'd found herself alone in a bare, windowless room, with just a mattress on the floor and a pot to piss in. An hour later a man had come in with a telephone. He'd ordered her to tell Max that she'd been kidnapped and to go to the phonebooths outside the courthouse. He'd dialled Max's number and held the receiver in one hand and a gun to her head in the other. She was left on her own until the next morning, when the same man had brought her food and water and taken out her pot. She'd tried talking to him, but he'd ignored her. A few hours later he'd come in and blindfolded her. She'd been led out of the room, up some stairs, walked outside and made to get in a van. The blindfold came off moments before she'd been escorted out across the wasteground at Opa Locka.

After the shoot-out, they'd found Bonbon's body minus most of its head on I95, close to the scene of an eight-car pile-up. Two black men – one covered in blood – had stolen cars and fled the scene. Descriptions of both were vague. Later, in Kendall, the Desamours house had gone up in flames. A woman's body had been found in the remains. She'd been shot in the chest with a .44 at point-blank range. Max guessed it was Eva Desamours, but there was no way of knowing yet – all her skin had been burnt off, and they were still checking dental records.

MTF had issued the media with an artist's impression of Carmine Desamours, along with a photograph of a white pickup truck similar to the one Max and Joe had seen at the Desamours house. A day later the owner of a used-car lot close to the Omni Mall on Biscayne Boulevard reported that Carmine had part-exchanged the truck for an olive-green 1977 Chevy Impala.

As for a description of Solomon, they were nowhere close. The second black man who'd fled the I95 crash had stolen a Mustang, which was found abandoned on Maynada Street, Coral Gables. It had run out of petrol. At 11.45 p.m. a woman in a Volvo 262 reported that she'd been carjacked by a 'nigger with a gun' on nearby Hardee Road.

'How are the interviews going?' Sandra asked.

Along with the six survivors from the shoot-out, MTF had so far arrested twenty-seven SNBC members.

'No one's talking. They're all terrified of Boukman. We've threatened them with the worst we can do – life in prison or the death penalty. You know what this guy said to us yesterday? "You think you're bad? He's *worse*." I mean, what can be worse than life in prison or death, right?' Max laughed.

'The power of myth,' she said. 'If you catch him and bring him in, you'll shatter the myth.'

'You think?' Max asked. 'If we bring him in, no one's gonna believe it's really him. They're gonna say we made it all up.' He took Sandra's hand. 'Anyway, how are you feeling?'

'In a word – scared,' she said.

'You're safe here.'

'Not scared for me. I'm scared for you.'

'I'll be OK.' Max shrugged.

'Will you?' Sandra stared at him. 'You don't want to catch Boukman, do you? You want to kill him.'

'That's true.' Max crushed out his cigarette and lit another.

'That makes you no different to him. And you *are* different, Max. Completely.' Sandra sipped her coffee. 'What do you know about Haiti?'

'Papa Doc, Baby Doc, voodoo, cocaine.' Max counted them off on his fingers.

'I've read about it and I know some Haitians. Out there you're either very rich or very poor. There's no in-between, and 95 per cent of the population is *very* poor. They've got nothing but the dirt they walk on. You've got to understand Boukman, examine what made him the way he is, examine what drives him. He came up in a place where killing's a way of life, where things *you* took for granted when you were a kid, he didn't have.'

'What is this? Sympathy for the devil?' Max let go of her hand and laughed. 'He kidnapped you, Sandra, with the specific intention of killing you, and you're trying to what – *understand* him? There's nothing to understand about the guy. He's a sadistic scumbag.

'You know, most Haitians in Miami are hard-working, honest, law-abiding people. They live in the shittiest conditions this city has to offer, but you don't see them killing people. And they've all come from the same place as Boukman. So don't give me that sociological shit. That's for blackboards and trust-fund liberals.'

'You don't believe that,' she said.

'I do, you know.'

'Then you've had an empathy bypass.'

'No, I have *not*.' Max felt his anger rise. 'I empathize *plenty*.

497

But I empathize with those who *deserve* empathy – the victims of monsters like Boukman. He ordered whole families killed. *Whole families*, Sandra – children – *babies*. *That* ain't about social inequality or global injustice. That's about right and wrong. You wanna examine people like him – do it in the fucken' *morgue*.'

Max looked away from her furiously and stared out of the window. The sky was a dense black, mottled with grey.

He felt bad for shouting at her. He shouldn't even have been angry with her, not after what she'd been through. He turned to apologize, but she cut him off.

'Inside that pissed-off head of yours, there's a compassionate, honourable, decent guy. I know it. I saw it in you the day we met. You've just got to let him out before it's too late,' she said.

'Too late? Too late for who?'

'For you. For us. But mostly for you. There'll always be another Boukman. And another after him. And another. They'll keep coming, long after you're gone. You can't change that, but *can* change yourself.'

The phone rang.

Saved by the bell, Max thought as he got up to answer it.

It was Joe.

'Carmine Desamours checked out of the Palace Motel twenty minutes ago. It's right near the airport. The manager called it in. Saw Desamours on TV. We've alerted the units.'

'Where are you now?' Max asked.

'MTF.'

'Meet me in the garage.'

He went back to Sandra and kissed her on the cheek. 'I gotta go.'

She stood up and hugged him.

He took her face in his hands and looked into her big brown eyes and almost didn't want to leave. He kissed her.

'I love you,' he whispered.

'I love you too,' she said and kissed him again. 'Please be careful.'

'I will.'

72

At 8 a.m. Carmine checked out of the motel he'd been lying low in for three days and hit the road.

His flight to Buffalo didn't leave until 10.45, but he had one more thing to do before he left town.

He drove to 63rd Street and pulled up by the kerb where Julita was standing.

She came over to the window, stick-on smile and eyes criss-crossing the street for cops. It took her a few long seconds to recognize him.

'Get in,' he said.

'Where we goin'?'

'Just get in quick,' he insisted.

They drove off.

'Cops are lookin' for you. You're in the papers. I seen this drawing of you on TV.'

'I seen that too. Didn't look like me.'

'Drawing was better-lookin',' she retorted.

He laughed.

'Bonbon's dead,' he told her. 'You see *that* on TV?'

'No, but I heard he was. I heard you killed him.'

'Who told you?' he asked.

'One of the girls. I figured it for bullshit. Everyone out here figured the same. We think it's just some story Bonbon put out to fuck with our heads. He does that a lot,' she said.

'Well, it's true,' Carmine said. 'Bonbon's dead.'

'So, you back in charge?'

'It's a new day, baby. You're unemployed. I'm takin' you home. Where'd you live?'

'Quit fuckin' wit' me, Carmine.'

'I ain't fuckin' wit' you. I'm for real. But I ain't got no time to convince you, so tell me yo' address.'

'I can't just *leave*.'

'Why not?'

'I got to earn my paper.'

The fat fuck had scared her good, brainwashed her, and the street had done the rest. It hadn't taken long. It never did.

'Bonbon's dead, Julita. DEAD. You don't owe him nuttin'. And you ain't hoin' no mo'. Address? Quick. *Please*.'

She told him.

Fifteen minutes later they were parked outside a sorry-looking orange condo in Little Havana, cracks snaking up the walls, bars on all the windows.

'You know I'm gettin' evicted at the end of this month?' she said. 'It ain't like it was with you. Bonbon took every last cent, gave nothin' back.'

Carmine opened the glove compartment and handed her a large brown envelope.

She looked inside. Her mouth dropped open and her eyes came so far out of their sockets he thought they were going to pop out.

'What's this?'

'What it looks like?'

$100,000. The least he could do. He wished he'd had more so he could have spared more.

'This — *this* is for *me*?' She took out a brick of C-notes. Her hand was shaking.

'Yeah. It's for you.' He nodded.

'Why?'

'Call it a goin' away present,' he said.

'You leavin'?' she asked, without taking her eyes off the money, as if she were afraid to, lest it vanished.

'Yeah.'

'Where you goin'?'

'Far away from here. An' I ain't *never* comin' back.'

She put the money in the envelope and closed her hands tight around the opening. She was shaking.

'Why you doin' this?' She searched his face.

'You know, I never tole you, but – er – in my own fucked-up way, I always kinda liked you, Julita. I always kinda liked you *a lot*. Prolly 'cause you reminded me of this Latin lady who was nice to me way back when,' Carmine said, looking out of the window to hide his embarrassment. He'd never told *any* girl he liked her. 'She was called Lucita. She had long black hair like yours. She used to sing me to sleep on her lap. Best place I ever been.'

'Lucita, huh?' She smiled. 'Maybe it was just my name you liked.'

'Yeah, maybe . . . Or maybe it was more than juss that.' Carmine laughed, remembering the first time he'd seen her dancing up on stage, hypnotizing those drunk drooling assholes with her magic ass and sinuous moves; then he remembered her black and vicious sense of humour, her way with one-liners – put-downs like knock-out punches.

'Who knows? In another life? You and me?' Carmine sighed, looking at her again.

'This life's all we got, Carmine.' She sniffled, as her shock made way for tears, which mingled with her mascara and ran sootily down her face.

'Sucks, don't it? Only gettin' that one shot.' Carmine dabbed at her cheeks with a handkerchief, which he then gave her. He looked at his watch. 'I gotta go.'

She grabbed his hand.

'Let's *all* go. You, me, the kids.'

Carmine shook his head.

'No. First up, I ain't daddy material, Julita. I ain't no one's idea of a good example. And, as long as you wit' me, you ain't gonna be safe. Cops are after me, Solomon's after me. If I ain't dead, I'm in jail.'

'*Then vaya con Dios*, Carmine. I won't forget you.' She threw her arms around him and held him tight. When she pulled away she left her tears cooling on his cheek.

'No, *please* forget me,' he said. 'An' please forgive me for draggin' you into all o' this ... this shit. Take care o' yo' babies. Take care o' yo' self. An' you get outta this place too, you hear? Get well away from here.'

Carmine walked straight past the two cops at the airport entrance without looking at either of them. He had on his gold-rimmed Ray-Bans, a light grey suit and an open-necked white Oxford shirt. He looked inconspicuously respectable, just another businessman with an attaché case in one hand and a suitcase in the other, flying home after a convention.

It was a Friday, so Departures was busy, just as he'd expected. He scoped out the place. Plenty of uniformed police about and plenty of plainclothes too, failing to look like civilians as they scoured faces.

He'd already bought his ticket – under a false name: Ray Washington. He checked his bag in and held on to the attaché case. It was where his money was.

His plane was leaving for New York in forty minutes.

He made his way to the boarding gates.

Up until then he hadn't been nervous, but now, suddenly, he went into panic mode. The noise around him – canned music, flight announcements, conversations – merged into a saw-like buzz. His heart began to pound fast and hard, his mouth dried up and sweat started dribbling down his forehead and temples.

He walked a little faster.

Up ahead of him was the entrance to the boarding gates. Two people were checking tickets behind a desk. Behind them were three cops. They were looking at every face that went through.

He remembered the gun he'd packed in his briefcase.

He'd dumped Bonbon's Magnum and bought himself a .38 snubnose, just in case. He had to get rid of it before he crossed into the boarding area. They had metal detectors. Why hadn't he thought of that?

He regretted not simply driving away. Why hadn't he done that? Just left on the night of the shoot-out? What was he thinking? That it'd all blow over after three days? Why take a fucking *plane*? It wasn't like he was leaving the country?

Why in the hell did he have to be so damn smart only *after* he'd been totally utterly fuckin' *stupid*?

He stopped.

It wasn't too late. He could turn around, walk out, get back in his car ... No, take a cab. What if the driver recognized him?

Shit.

OK. Start again. Turn around, walk out, get in your car, drive the fuck away.

Sweat poured freely down his face, got under his glasses, itched.

He noticed one of the cops behind the desk was now staring at him.

He turned around.

A crowd of people was coming towards him.

Passengers.

He started walking away hurriedly.

He saw someone threading through the crowd, slaloming past the moving bodies, looking at him the whole time.

And then he noticed there were more people winding their way towards him.

Four, no five, no *six* black men ... including Solomon.

He stopped again and turned back to the boarding gates.

The cop who'd been staring at him was looking at a sheet of paper, and then back at him. He said something to the other two cops, who both looked right at him.

Carmine knew he was fucked.

He could surrender right now, or . . . he turned to face Solomon, who was getting closer. He opened the case and took out his gun.

He let the case fall. The money spilt out with a sound close to a splash.

People around him gasped and bumped into each other.

Someone asked him: 'Hey, is that yours . . . ?'

He raised his gun, cocked it and walked towards Solomon. All around him people stopped where they were. He got a bead on Solomon and fired once. Solomon dropped to the ground and rolled away to his left.

Carmine aimed again, but, before he could get another shot off, his torso exploded with pain.

He was surrounded by onlookers, gawping, shaking, crying, blank-faced, curious.

His chest felt crushed. He was finding it hard to breathe. His shirt and jacket were the same bright red.

He was going to die.

He looked for Solomon in his audience.

He saw him, standing there, one of maybe twenty faces, staring at him impassively.

And then there was a new arrival, someone he recognized: that cop who'd beaten him up in the parking lot of Al & Shirley's.

Max Mingus.

Out of breath, red-faced. He had pushed in and was standing right next to Solomon.

Solomon was looking right at him.

Carmine wanted to get up and warn Mingus, but he couldn't. He tried to raise his arm to at least point Solomon out, but it was too heavy. He tried to say something, but his throat was fast filling up with blood.

He decided to use his eyes instead. He looked Mingus in

the eye, locked into him and then moved his eyeballs sharply to the right. Mingus didn't react.

He started to do it again, but his vision blurred and then fogged up, the colours leeching away into the purest white he'd ever seen.

Fuck it, he thought. I *tried*, right?

PART SIX
August–October 1981

73

Max came to haphazardly, rushing in and out of consciousness as if he was sprinting through time zones on winged feet – day to night, to day to night again. Wakefulness was hard to stand: it brought a wild dizziness to his brain and sharp stabbing pains to his neck and shoulders. He tried to fix and focus his eyes on a specific image, but his new environment whirled fast before him like greased carousel horses, defying all purchase and definition. He found it easier simply to close his eyes and sink deep and fast into oblivion, where the pain faded and his head settled and cleared.

The second to last thing he remembered was Carmine Desamours lying on the ground, his torso ripped open and shredded red; a fast-expanding crimson puddle under his back. He'd made eye contact with Max, his green irises registering first recognition, then trying to tell him something. Desamours had flicked his glance sharply to the right, twice. Max had turned and found himself face to face with a dark-skinned man with cuts all over his forehead and a very familiar stare.

As he'd reached for his gun, he'd felt a powerful crack on the nape of his neck.

A small engine whirred at his ear. He opened his eyes again. He was no longer dizzy, just exhausted, worn down to the bone. Things were coming into focus. He was in a vast, bare space with a concrete floor – about the size of a warehouse or an aircraft hangar – with a large, powerful spotlight beaming down on him from the ceiling, warming his exposed flesh. He was stark naked. He'd been shaved clean from ankles to groin, and his skin was gleaming, as if he'd been covered in oil.

How long had he been out?

He moved his head back to look up, but the engine stopped and a pair of rough, strong hands grabbed either side of his skull.

'Keep still,' a man ordered him.

He was sitting in a chair. His arms were tied behind his back and his legs were bound at the ankles. He could only roll on and off. He was as good as trapped.

The whirring resumed. He felt a dull, blunt object moving up along his cranium. Hair tumbled over his forehead and rolled softly and itchily over his face. *Clippers.* His head was being shaved. He thought of death-row inmates getting shorn like sheep before they got the chair; he remembered reading about what they'd done to the girlfriends of Nazi soldiers in Europe after liberation.

'Where's Boukman?' Max asked.

The barber didn't answer, just went about his business, now working on Max's temples, occasionally blowing away loose hair.

'Close your eyes,' the barber growled when he'd finished.

Max complied. He felt the clippers moving across his forehead, his eyebrows crackling between the oscillating metal teeth. Then he heard the snip-snip of scissors.

'*Rinse!*' the barber shouted.

A bucket of cold water was dumped over Max's head. The shock of it so sudden and unexpected it made him scream.

But it completely woke him up too.

He knew what was happening.

Tomorrow – if today was still Friday – was Saturday.

The ceremony.

The SNBC.

He'd first – briefly – regained consciousness in an ambulance. He'd found himself strapped to a gurney and the siren was wailing. The vehicle was shaking. They were moving at high speed. Two men in police uniform were leaning over him, one rolling up a sleeve, the other prepping a syringe.

Before they'd shot him up with stuff that had sent him back to sleep he'd realized Boukman had had phoney cops on the airport concourse. Or were they real cops working for him?

After the drenching, the barber – a tapering hulk of over-developed muscle packed in a sleeveless denim shirt, grey sweatpants and a Hermès headscarf – sprayed the top of Max's head with shaving foam and spread it over his scalp. He produced a cutthroat razor from his pocket and scraped the stubble off Max's dome, wiping the blade residue on a cloth. He did Max's brows last.

'*Rinse!*'

They left him alone, dripping in a big puddle of water.

He looked around. He saw the bright light above him, the concrete ground and a trapdoor approximately twenty feet away. There were reddish-brown markings on the ground around the chair: a cross to his left, a star to his right and a line dividing them; the symbols were framed by the outline of a coffin.

Max raised his legs off the floor. His ankles were bound with a thick tourniquet of packaging tape. He tried moving his hands. He could barely wriggle his fingers.

There was no way out of this. He was going to die the long way.

Boukman would feed him the potion, put a gun in his hand and send him out to murder. He would no longer know who he was, let alone recognize the target. He prayed that target wouldn't be Sandra – and if it *was* her that the potion or a bullet would kill him before he even came *close* to taking her life.

At that moment he felt his captor's gaze on him. He was roving around in the darkness, studying Max from every angle. First from the back, then his profile, then his face. Max didn't bother searching for him. He knew he was there with an unverifiable certainty.

'BOUKMAN' he yelled. 'You hidin' again, you fucken' cocksucker? You fucken' coward! Why don't you show your face, asshole? Come on out! What've you got to lose, huh? I know what you fucken' look like!'

But Boukman didn't come out. Max's words echoed around the empty space, and his anger – his useless rage – hugged the air like cold cordite.

'Hey . . .' Max said after a few moments' reflection, his tone normal, resigned. 'If I don't see you again, hear this . . . *Fuck you!*'

Some time later the barber returned, wheeling a small metal table. Two other men followed behind, carrying a black plastic bucket, which they set down on the floor in front of Max, out of reach of his feet, but close enough for him to see the contents: a putrid-looking milky-green liquid with the viscous consistency of pea soup.

'That the Kool Aid?' Max sneered.

The two men looked first at each other and then at him and then again at one another and chuckled in unison.

The barber positioned the table close to the bucket. On top were a small stack of Dixie cups, a plastic funnel, a spindle of catgut, a matchbox, a soup ladle and a leather case in the shape of a pocketbook.

He wasn't quite scared yet, more apprehensive and nervous.

The barber dipped the ladle into the bucket and filled a cup.

'You can make this easy on yourself and just suck it

down,' he said, as he took the matchbox, slid it open and sprinkled its contents – small coloured squares – into the cup. 'Or else you make us force you. Your choice.'

'Fuck off!' Max shouted.

'Most people get it over with – glug-glug,' the barber suggested calmly.

'Fuck *off*!'

The barber nodded to the two men.

One locked his arm around Max's head, covering his eyes, while the other grabbed Max's legs, straightened them and held them fast.

Strong fingers gripped Max's lower jaw and forced it down, stretching his skin, muscles and ligaments to tearing point, until the whole lower half of his head felt like it was going to snap off.

He struggled about, wriggling and thrashing and rolling his shoulders, but he was too constricted for his movements to count for anything other than a nominal, face-saving resistance.

The chair was tilted and the plastic funnel was jammed into his mouth, the end reaching his back teeth. He bit down on it but the plastic was hard and unyielding.

Then his mouth was flooded with a glacial, slimy, lumpy fluid that tasted rancid and sour – curdled milk cut with vinegar and bleach, coupled with a strong trace of bitter herbs and fresh grass. He tried to constrict his throat to stop it going down but he couldn't. The potion swept past his epiglottis and rushed into his stomach.

The funnel was removed from his mouth.

The man behind him let go of his jaw and uncovered his eyes.

Max could feel the fluid in his stomach, cold and heavy, as if he'd just swallowed a dozen whole ice cubes.

The barber was standing before him, smiling, the funnel dripping greenly on the floor.

'*Bon appetit,*' he said.

'FUCK YOU!' Max shouted. His throat and mouth were raw and coated with grit, his tongue swollen and tender.

'You have a brave mouth, *blanc,*' the barber said as he unzipped the leather case and opened it like a book, revealing two rows of surgical sewing needles, arranged in order of length and thickness, on either side of the case. The barber studied Max's face for a moment and opted for a thick, four-inch-long needle. He cut a length of catgut from the spindle, knotted one end and threaded it through the eye. When he'd finished he nodded to the man standing behind Max.

The man clamped his palms on Max's head and held it firm and still. The barber came over, crouched down and pinched Max's lips tightly together with his fingers. He pushed the needle slowly through the corner of Max's left lower lip. Max screamed and tears ran down his face as the point first punctured the skin and then penetrated the cushion of soft tissue, before bursting out of his upper lip. The pain doubled as the tough catgut slithered bloodily up and out through the hole. The barber wound the slack around his fist and tugged at it hard, dragging Max's mouth up towards his nose, before sticking the needle back through his bottom lip and repeating the process. He sewed carefully and methodically, taking his time, until Max's lips were completely sealed.

When he'd finished, the barber cut another, shorter length of catgut and put a single stitch through Max's nose.

By then Max was in such pain he barely noticed.

The barber wheeled the table away and the men carried off the bucket, leaving Max to his suffering and the poison in his stomach.

He could feel the potion moving subtly, incrementally in his gut, like a living thing, finding its way around inside of him, familiarizing itself with him, slowly taking over.

He sensed himself becoming weaker, strength trickling out of him, away from his legs and arms, dissipating out into the air through the ends of fingers and toes. Tiredness was creeping through him, shutting him down, switch by switch.

The ceremony began.

First, he was encircled by people on stilts – all exactly the same height, all identically dressed in top hats, tailcoats, pinstriped trousers, ruffled shirts and black gloves; all with their faces heavily made-up in pancake white from forehead to nose and black for the remainder. They stood, steady and unwavering, their hands folded in front of them and their eyes fixed on him, human totems dwarfing the sacrificial offering.

Then the light on him grew brighter and hotter and a circle of drums began to pound. The stiltmen joined hands and began to move around him, slowly, anti-clockwise, one giant step at a time.

The drums were joined by mass chanting, the sound of a hundred or more voices, reciting words he couldn't understand in a prayer-like cadence, delivered in the lowest register.

Max could no longer feel much of his body. His eyes and ears were still working, his nose just about, and his guts too, channelling the potion, breaking it down, dispatching its lethal components into his bloodstream.

He couldn't move his mouth or jaw. Breathing was difficult, mere whispers of air getting through the narrow gaps in his nostrils. He tried – reflexively, again and again – to inhale through his mouth, but his mouth was as good as gone. He'd suck in and get absolutely nothing.

He was no longer brave or defiant.

He was terrified – a little for himself, but mostly for Sandra and of what he'd be made to do to her. Boukman would send him to accomplish what he'd failed to achieve in Opa Locka.

The drum beats picked up, faster and faster they went, and the stiltmen moved with them, gaining speed, quickening their pace until their colours began to fragment and bleed into each other before his eyes, the monochrome contrasts merging into a single unbroken circle of grey – the tone of graphite strokes on paper and overcast Miami summer mornings and decades old prison barbed wire.

The chanting was no longer a verse, but a single word, one he recognized, shouted in unison, loudly, very loudly:

SSSSO-LO-*MON*
SSSSO-LO-*MON*
SSSSO-LO-*MON*
SSSSO-LO-*MON*

Now the drums were being beaten so fast they sounded like propellers, and the stiltmen were orbiting him with centrifugal force, emitting a faint cooling breeze that wafted his way.

SSSSO-LO-*MON*
SSSSO-LO-*MON*

Then the trapdoor dropped open and a shaft of blood-red light came out of the ground.

SSSSO-LO-*MON*
SSSSO-LO-*MON*

A man rose up from the floor – a man dressed and made-up as the stiltmen were, except he was all in white.

He stepped out of the light and took two paces towards Max. He folded his arms, reached inside his coat and pulled out two long gleaming samurai swords, which caught the light and dazzled Max. He closed his eyes, very briefly.

When he opened them again the man was standing a few feet away from him, twirling the swords at high speed as if they were batons. The kaleidoscopic bolts of light were shooting from the blades – red, pink, orange, violet, yellow and blue splattered Max's eyeballs and blinded him to his surroundings.

He found himself thinking of sunsets. Sunsets on the beach opposite his home; watching the sun dripping down behind the darkening ocean like a drop of burning honey. Every day ended at sunset.

74

'Don't blame yourself,' Eldon mumbled to Joe as they stood together on the MTF roof at dawn on Sunday, sunlight starting to dissolve the night away from Miami's flat city-scape, giving it the biliousness of unearthed bones.

Both men were exhausted – physically and mentally – and their nerves were frayed from a combination of non-stop anxiety, missed sleep and way too much coffee. They'd been up close to forty-eight hours looking for Max. No result.

The last time Joe had seen his partner was when they'd split up outside the airport. Then he'd watched security camera footage of two fake cops dragging him out of the concourse, a shadowy man with an indiscernible face at their side, unchallenged by the dozens of officers trying to keep control of the hysterical, panicked crowd in the building.

'Max was like kin to me,' Eldon continued, following a flock of seagulls making for the ocean.

'*Was* . . . ?' Joe said.

'Come on, you gotta be realistic at times like these, prepare for the worst. Max's dead. Boukman's finished what he tried to do in Opa Locka.'

'That's straight-up cold,' Joe said.

'It is what it is,' Eldon said. 'You think this is *easy* for me? You think this ain't *hurtin'* me? I'm *dyin'* in here.' Eldon pointed to the middle of his chest. He had tears in his eyes. 'Max was damn *family*.'

'The son you never had, right?' Joe said, with a trace of sarcasm.

'Yeah.' Eldon missed it. 'Something like that. We were

real close, you know? He came to me about everything. *Everything.*'

'He didn't come to you about Boukman,' Joe reminded him.

'Well, he *should* have. If he had, he'd-a still been alive.'

'Yeah, *right*.' Joe chuckled grimly. 'Like it was that easy.'

'What are you saying?' Eldon frowned and narrowed his eyes.

'You know why he never told you nothin' 'bout Boukman? It was 'cause you woulda done nothin'. You were too busy puttin' the Moyez case on a bunch of guys didn't have nothin' to do with it. You didn't give a shit who the *real* perps were. It's all about lookin' good on TV and pleasin' them politicians you hobnob with.

'The *real* Moyez investigation was *our* thing – *our* case. Not yours, not MTF's – *ours*. Me and Max did it in our time, on our own dollar. That's 'cause Max is and always will be what you, Mr Burns, are not. And that is a *real* cop. You just wear the uniform. Underneath it, you're just a mercenary. A soldier of political fortune. A gun for hire. And *this* – MTF – your unit, your *creation* – ain't nothin' but a bunch of thugs with a licence to kill. You're runnin' a crew of straight-up gangsters. Just like Boukman.'

Eldon was open-mouthed and speechless, his stare criss-crossing Joe's face in every direction, as if he was trying to be certain Joe had actually just spoken the words he'd heard. His wart was a weak tint of pink.

'So, no, I *don't* blame myself. I blame *you*, Mr Burns. You're responsible for this. You and this fucked up paramilitary outfit you run. And if Max turns up dead, you'll have his blood on your hands, same as Boukman,' Joe said. He was angry and bitter, but calm with it. He hadn't raised his voice at all.

His boss was still mute, in a whole new terrain with no map and no get-out clause.

'After I bring Boukman in, I want to transfer out of here – but only *after* I bring Boukman in,' Joe continued, ''cause you know what? I don't like the way you do things, *Mister* Burns. And, most of all, I *really* don't like *you*.'

Eldon glanced out at the city, and then back at the sea, bewildered. He looked at Joe and found his subordinate appeared to have grown a few inches taller in his moment of rectitude. Eldon had to look *up* at him. It was humiliating, but it was just the two of them up here, so no one could see it.

'Do you know why I brought you up here, Liston, you dumbfuck loser?' Eldon mustered his voice, but it was hollow, without its usual booming, crushing authority.

'Somethin' to do with dividin' up the scarlet robes?' Joe asked.

'*Huh?*' Eldon frowned.

'You read The Bible, Mr Burns?'

'Is *that* what this is about? You a Jesus freak?'

'No.' Joe smiled wryly. 'I'm just big on right and wrong.'

'Fine!' Eldon snorted. 'Bring Boukman in and you'll get your wish. In *spades*.'

Joe let the racial insult go. He truly didn't give a fuck.

He turned and started walking towards the steps, then stopped.

'Oh, and one more lil' detail – 'bout my forthcoming transfer. I *ain't* gonna be no grinnin' house nigger in Public Relations. You can tear up *that* plan.'

Joe was heading out of Eldon's office when the phone rang. He hoped – and dreaded – that the call might be about Max, so he decided to hang around and listen.

Eldon came in quickly through the side door and grabbed the phone.

'*Yeah?*' he snarled, back in his game. '*What!*' He looked at Joe. '*When?*' He opened a drawer, took out a .38, checked

the cylinder and placed it on the desk. 'Where is he? . . .
fuck!'

He hung up.

'You are *not* gonna believe—'

He didn't have time to finish because the door opened
and Max walked in.

'What the *fuck* . . . ?' Joe gasped.

Max was completely bald, missing his eyebrows and his
mouth was swollen, bruised and encrusted with dried blood.
His eyes were glazed and fixed straight ahead, seeing without
recognition. He was wearing a long black raincoat Joe had
never seen him in.

'Max?' Joe started walking towards him.

Max reached into his coat and pulled out a MAC11.

'BURNS! GET DOWN!' Joe yelled and took a dive to
the right, hitting the carpet as Max opened fire in the direction of Eldon's desk, pulverizing the glass display case
behind it with a single sustained burst of .380 ACP rounds,
flying out at 950 feet per second; the small weapon jiggling
in his hands as he drained the magazine, bullets flying wide
and crooked, smashing all the windows, splitting chairs,
blowing chunks out of the walls and side door and strafing
the top of the mahogany desk until it looked like porcupine
hide.

Max emptied the MAC11 in seconds, dropped it and
reached for his service pistol.

At that very instant Eldon, who'd crawled around the
desk with his .38, took aim at his would-be assassin and
fired.

Joe got up and ran at Max, slamming his shoulder into
Max's hip and bringing him down easily.

Eldon's bullet missed them both by a close, hot whistle.

Joe took the automatic out of Max's holster and tossed
it. He did the same with Max's ankle piece.

'Is he dead?' Eldon asked.

'No.' Joe looked at his partner, whose eyes were on Eldon. 'Get a medic!'

Eldon looked for the phone and found it – the casing completely blown off, a busted mess of coils, springs and twisted metal.

Max, meanwhile, reached for his hip holster grabbed at air and brought his empty hand up in Eldon's direction and pulled in his index finger a few times, before dropping his arm.

'GET A FUCKIN' MEDIC, NOW!' Joe shouted at Eldon, who was standing dazed, looking around his ruined office.

75

Monday mornings were when Gemma Harlan liked to teach her interns something new about autopsies. New week, new lesson was her motto. Today she'd be demonstrating the art and practice of organ removal. She had an ideal cadaver to work on, cause of death known – the police shooting at the airport – so no suspicious circumstances, therefore no detailed medical report to write up, just the basics, and perfect material to try out her new recruit on.

For the last two weeks a young man called Darius Vincenzio had been learning the ropes. Darius, who they all called 'V' around the morgue, was a quick study; he only needed to be told and shown something once to get the hang of it. Gemma was highly impressed with him and was even considering offering him a job at the end of his internship. The only thing that worried her was that he hadn't yet DNPed – dashed and puked. Most interns did that at their first or second sight of viscera – she had – but, so far, he hadn't betrayed so much as the slightest hint of discomfort around the dead. She hoped he wasn't holding back and damming up until something really gruesome came along, and that he wasn't a nutjob.

The body was fetched out of the Burger King refrigerated truck and wheeled into the morgue, where it was taken out of its bag, identified, measured and weighed.

Carmine Desamours. Sex: male. Race: black. Hair: black. Eyes: green. Height: 179 cm. Weight 154 lbs. Birthmarks: a mole to the left of the navel. Scars: extensive and historical.

The wounds were examined – two clean entry wounds on either side of the spine, consistent with .38 calibre bullets, the skin was indented and singed black with gunpowder. The exit wounds in the chest were larger – the size of quarters.

After Darius and Martin had washed the body and placed it on the slab, Gemma told her intern to make the cuts, as she hit play on the cassette deck and Bacharach and orchestra's 'Raindrops Keep Fallin' On My Head' came out of the speakers.

Darius made the Y-incision behind the ears and down the sides of the neck to the breastbone. Then he made the T-incision across the shoulders and down the trunk to the pubic bone. He concluded with a vertical cut across the middle of the neck. The openings were textbook perfect, as usual.

Gemma pulled back the flaps of skin and exposed the chest plate. She then took an electric saw and cut through the ribs to the side of the chest cavity, before very carefully lifting off the sternum and its appended ribs, exposing the heart and lungs.

Gemma went to work, explaining every cut and the importance of doing it in order as she worked the scalpel through the tissue, starting with the heart, and then moving on to the punctured lungs. She removed the left lung and then let Darius test out his new knowledge on the right. He was a natural, excising it perfectly.

They moved on to the first part of the digestive system – small intestine, oesophagus, pancreas, stomach, duodenum and spleen – a more delicate extraction procedure, which she preferred to demonstrate in full a couple of times, before letting her interns loose on it – even the most gifted ones like Darius.

After she'd removed the corpse's stomach, she handed it over to Darius to place on the scales.

He took it from her. And then he frowned.

'Somethin' don't feel right here,' he said, palpating a corner of the organ.

'What?'

'It's got like – something inside.'

'Probably food.'

'Don't feel like food,' he said. 'This is – like – *hard*.'

'Could be a bullet,' Martin said from across the slab. 'You'd be surprised where those things end up. One time, this guy who'd got shot in the head? We found the slug in his rectum.'

'This ain't a bullet. Less he got shot with a golfball.' Darius felt the floppy stomach some more.

'Hand it over.' Gemma stuck her hands out impatiently.

The stomach had a small round object inside it, like an egg.

'OK. Weigh it first, then we'll open it up.'

76

'Have some fruit.' Sandra plucked at the bunch of grapes at Max's bedside.

'I want a smoke,' Max said through lips so swollen they looked like they'd been transplanted from a cartoon trout.

'You want to infect your mouth? You heard the doctor. No cigarettes till you're healed.'

'I *need* a smoke.'

'You've had enough poison. Go on, eat some fruit. It'll do you good.'

'Later.' Max sat himself up on the hospital bed and took a sip from a glass of water.

'How are you feeling?' she asked.

'Hungry.' He started to smile, but pain tore into his lips as his skin stretched, so he let his mouth droop.

Yesterday morning he'd been rushed from Eldon's office to Jackson Memorial Hospital, where they'd pumped his stomach. While this was happening, Joe had contacted Raquel Fajima about working up an antidote to the poison that had already got into Max's system. She'd quickly given him a list of things to ask the doctors for and had rushed over to help them prepare it.

When the anaesthetic had worn off, Max had come to screaming, thinking he was still in the middle of the ceremony. He'd been restrained and shot up with a sedative that had knocked him out until the early evening. When he'd next opened his eyes it was to Eldon, Joe and Sandra all standing around his bedside.

A doctor had examined him and told him he'd have to

stay in hospital for at least a week to undergo tests, assessments and evaluations.

After she'd left, Joe told him what had happened. Max was shocked and bewildered. He had no recollection of anything beyond thinking of the sunset.

'Looks like we both gave each other a fright,' Max said.

'Hopefully one cancels out the other.' Sandra took his hand. 'And we can get on with our lives.'

'I'm sorry.'

'You've got nothing to apologize for, baby.' She kissed him on the forehead and ran her hand softly over his bald dome and smiled. 'Except for this. It's not a good look, Mr Kojak.'

Max laughed, accidentally smiled and then winced in pain.

'You remember anything else?' she asked him.

'No, but . . . I had this dream this morning. It was like a continuation of the last thought I had at the ceremony, before everything went blank – bein' on the beach watching the sunset.' He took her hand. He thought hard about what he was about to tell her, and how he was going to have to explain it. He could, of course, keep it from her. It would have been the easiest thing to do, to lie with omission, but it was something she needed to know about him.

'In my dream, I'm not on the beach any more. I've moved on. I'm in this room. This dark room, no windows or doors. The kind you can't ever enter or leave. And I'm floatin' above this table, and there's these three men sat around it. They've all got bullet holes in their chests. And they're all lookin' up at me. No expression, just lookin'. Only their eyes are as dead as they are. No light, no blood, no soul. Nothing inside. And then one of them pulls out a spare chair and pats it, as in – "Come, join us". And I'm hovering there, above them, not moving. And I don't know what to do. And that lasted all through the rest of the dream, until I woke up.'

'Who were the men?'

And so he told her about the people he'd taken out to the Everglades. He explained what they'd done, told her about how MTF sometimes worked, and what he'd felt he had to do in the circumstances. She listened carefully and silently, her reactions minimal.

When he'd finished he told her the truth about MTF and the Moyez killing, and how he and Joe had found out about Boukman.

'I guessed as much – about those . . . those three men – from the things you said on our first night together,' Sandra said at the end. 'Do you still agree with what you did?'

'No, I don't,' Max replied. 'I don't think it's wrong they're dead. Only *how*. And why. But I had no choice.'

'So, if you could do it again – would you do or undo?'

'I'd look for another way,' he said. 'If there was one.'

'And if there wasn't?'

'I'd *try* to find one. And I'd try *real* hard.'

She came over to him and they hugged and kissed.

Then there was a single knock at the door and Joe walked in, out of breath and sweating.

'Hey, Max, hey, Sandra. How you doin', partner?'

'I'm doin' OK,' Max replied.

'That's good. Listen, I can't stay,' Joe said. 'I was on my way over here and I got a message 'bout a lead just turned up.'

'Where?'

'In the morgue.'

'Wait up,' Max said, 'I'm comin'.'

77

'THE MOST WANTED MAN IN MIAMI' screamed the front-page headline of Wednesday's *Herald*. Printed below, dead centre, across three columns was Solomon Boukman's photograph. Stripped of its myths and connotations – and the $150,000 reward for information resulting in capture – his physiognomy was unremarkable, bereft of a single defining locus, one that could easily be mistaken for a hundred others: dark and thin, clean shaven, short hair, blank eyes, a hint of a smile about the lips.

A sidebar gave Boukman's particulars:

Race: Black/Haitian

Height: 5 ft 10 in

Build: Medium

Age: 30–35

Distinguishing features: Split/forked tongue

Very likely armed and highly dangerous. Do not approach. Call 911.

There was, of course, no mention of how the police had come by the photograph. It had been found in a condom in Carmine Desamours' stomach, neatly cut up into numerous squares, each with a number on the back for quick assembly.

That same morning Max met Drake in Al & Shirley's on 5th Street. Or what had been Al & Shirley's. It was now under new ownership and called Espléndido. The decor hadn't changed, but it was dirtier and the windows were starting to get filmed with grease. The prices were lower and the menu was exclusively in Spanish.

Drake had come to breakfast dressed like a boxer in

training – Everlast boots, grey sweatpants and a matching hooded sweatshirt with cut-off sleeves. His hands were wrapped and he had a leather jump rope draped around his shoulders. Max wanted to laugh at his informant's latest athletic get-up: with his willowy frame, stringy arms, long neck and prominent jaw, Drake looked about as convincing a fighter as Elvis had in *Kid Galahad*.

'Boukman's holed up in Lemon City,' Drake mumbled through mouthfuls of scrambled eggs and diced ham.

'Anywhere specific?'

'He's movin' around,' Drake said. 'Stupid place to be, you ask me. It's *real* hot there right now.'

It sure was. Max had seen it all on the news and heard about it from the cops, who were now on tactical alert in case things kicked off and they had another McDuffie on their hands. On Monday, raids had been carried out all over Lemon City. Dozens of illegal Haitian immigrants had been arrested and taken to a detention centre close to the Port of Miami, where they were being held and interviewed before being shipped back to their homeland. It was like Mariel in reverse.

The raids were met with almost immediate hostility – police cars and trucks had been stoned and people had been beaten by police as they'd either resisted arrest or tried to intervene to stop their relatives and friends being taken away. Then, yesterday night, a forty-year-old taxi driver called Evans Ducolas had died of a heart attack in the back of a police car after being hauled away as a suspected illegal. It turned out that Ducolas wasn't an illegal at all: the previous month he'd received his Green Card. Community leaders had organized a street protest for this afternoon.

'I heard Boukman kidnapped some cop's old lady – and fucked the cop up real bad. Wasn't you, was it?'

'No,' Max said. 'I had a fight with a barber, fell down some stairs and cut myself shaving. All at once.'

'What you shave with? Chopper blades?' Drake laughed.

78

'Why in the fuck would he hide out here? First place he'd know we'd look for him, right?' Max said as they cruised slowly around the red-roofed buildings of Edison Courts between North West 62nd and 67th Streets.

'Maybe he's dumb,' Joe suggested.

'He *ain't* dumb.'

'Think he's one of those guys *wants* to get caught?'

'Nah.' Max shook his head. 'Boukman wanted to get caught he'd walk right into MTF and put his hands in the air. If he's here, he's here for a reason.'

An hour before they'd set out the summer rain had come down in a hard and heavy burst, but now the sun was back out, intense and blazing, and the water was evaporating into a fine mist which wafted over the street, a spectral veil tinged with rainbow colours.

There were plenty of people around, all streaming out of their homes and heading towards the demonstration now gathering on North West 54th Street. They stopped to look inside the black Chevy Monte Carlo Max and Joe were driving, instantly recognizing them as cops, collective curiosity giving way to worry and hostility.

So far they'd had no luck whatsoever asking random bystanders if they'd seen Boukman. They'd been met with blank stares, shakes of the head, firm 'Nos' and straight-up 'Fuck yous'.

'Know what this reminds me of?' Max asked.

'Uh-huh.'

Liberty City the previous year, right before the not guilty verdict came in, the entire neighbourhood on lockdown as people – already expecting injustice to prevail – got set to explode. There was the same edgy stillness in the air now, of anger massing on a hair-trigger.

Max and Joe were both wearing bulletproof vests. Max had a pair of loaded Remington combat shotguns across his lap. The police were on tactical alert and a chopper was circling the area.

'Can't say I blame 'em,' Joe said. 'Haitians have had a bum rap in this city from the minute they got here. Cubans? We fish 'em out the water, give 'em a towel and a tow, a pat on the back and a Green Card. Haitians – we send right back. Ain't right. Ain't fair. Haitians have got it *as* hard, if not harder in their homeland than they do in Cuba. *Except* Baby Doc's a *fascist* dictator instead of a commie, so our government supports him. And you know what makes the way we treat Haitians all the more fucked up? Haiti helped America out in the War of Independence.'

'Yeah?'

'Absolute truth.'

'How do you know this?'

'I read about it.' Joe looked across at him. 'You should read some too, Max. Educate yourself. These are *all* your people – our people – out here, in this city. The ones we signed up to protect and serve. You've got to know where they've been to understand where they're coming from.'

'You sound like Sandra.' Max sighed.

'As in intelligent and informed?'

'As in gettin' on my case.'

'She's right to. You're clever, but you don't know shit. If ignorance is bliss, you're just about the smiliest motherfucker I know,' Joe said.

Two men were lying dead in Leogane Hardware on North East 2nd Avenue. The first – dressed in khakis and a white T-shirt – was bundled up on his side in a corner close to the entrance. A part of his head was oozing thickly down the middle of the door. There was a gun down his waistband and a black leather sports bag at his feet. The other man – substantially older – was lying behind the store counter, a chrome .44 Magnum in his hand and a fresh, still seeping bullet wound in his chest.

'Robber popped the owner at point-blank range, probably after he got what he was looking for,' Officer Alonzo Penabaz said, matter-of-factly, as he looked from the old man to the open and empty register. 'Only he didn't put him all the way away, 'cause the owner had time to get the big payback.'

Penabaz had heard the shots. He and his partner Otis Mandel had been stationed in a prowler at the juncture of 54th Street, watching the demonstration growing ever bigger like a giant simmering amoeba. They were a nominal, deliberately low-key presence meant to project due sensitivity and respect to the community, after the barrage of press criticism over the death of Evans Ducolas. Yet there were two choppers overhead, riot units positioned on Lemon City's boundaries and the National Guard was on standby, ready to move in at a moment's notice if the protest turned violent.

'What was the take?' Penabaz asked Mandel, who was gawping into the open sports bag like he usually gawped at hot tail – mouth open, lower jaw slightly trembling, tongue licking the back of his lower lip.

Mandel took out two bricks of money.

'That ain't all of it. Must be at least ten to fifteen Gs in here. Hundreds and twenties,' Mandel said, riffling through the contents.

Penabaz wolf-whistled and grinned.

'What do you wanna do, Officer?' he asked Mandel.

'Book it into evidence – *of course.*'

'After you.' Penabaz grinned.

'What about this?' Mandel waved a finger over the carnage.

'We'll call it in when we get back to the car. They won't send no one out here till this blows over or . . . blows up. Let's roll.'

They walked out of the store, both already making plans for what they were going to do with the money. Mandel was thinking of that seriously *sweet* pussy a G would buy – maybe some nice clothes too, for the occasion; Penabaz would square his two bookies and lay some new bets.

It was sunny but the clouds were stealing the blueness back out of the sky again. Miami in the summer was always like this: overbearing heat and then overbearing rain that did nothing whatsoever to clear the air, simply made it worse.

Up ahead of them a lot of people were streaming into 54th Street, and a few too many were gathered around their empty prowler, but both men's sense of danger – imminent or imagined – was doused by their mutual and individual money-spending daydreams.

'*Hey!*'

A woman's voice behind them registered, but they didn't turn around.

'*Hey! Police!* Over here! Over here!'

They stopped and turned around.

A big woman in a bright yellow dress was running towards them, waving both her arms in the air.

'Roro's dead! Roro's dead! Boulette shot him! I saw the whole thing! I saw the whole thing!' she blurted out, panting and agitated, when she reached them.

'*Who* got shot, ma'm?' Penabaz asked her.

'*Roro!*' the woman screamed. She was in her twenties, light-skinned, flushed red, eyes bugging out, close to hysterical. 'Back there in that hardware store! You've gotta come *now!*'

'Who's Ro-ro?'

'Roro – the store manager. My boss! He's dead! He got shot!'

'Which store, mam?' Penabaz spoke slowly and calmly, giving himself time and space to think – only he was fresh out of ideas and points of reference: this kind of thing hadn't happened before. They'd always got away clean.

'Back up there!' The woman pointed up the road.

'Someone was shot, you say?' Penabaz asked.

'YES!' She grabbed his arm. 'Come quick!'

Penabaz disengaged his arm and gave her a stern look. The woman wilted a little.

People were suddenly appearing out of nowhere, coming from houses and parked cars, coming down the street, all slowing and then stopping to see what was going on, gradually congealing into an audience.

'We can't do that right now, mam,' Penabaz said. 'We've got to watch 54th.'

'You can't . . . *what?*'

'Orders, mam, sorry. But we'll call it in and some officers will be over to assist you.'

'You mean . . . you ain't even gonna come *look!*'

The woman was almost in tears.

'Orders, mam. I'm very sorry.' Penabaz laid a comforting paw on her shoulder. He took a notebook out of his breast pocket. 'What's your name?'

'Garcelle,' the woman said. 'Garcelle Tomas – no "H".'

'What's the name of the store?'

'Orders my ass!' a man grumbled loudly from within the thick semi-circle of people standing around watching. A few people laughed.

Penabaz didn't catch what Garcelle said, but he scribbled nonsense on his pad.

'You just don't give a fuck!' someone else accused, louder, bolder.

'One less nigger to worry about!' yelled another.

'Right on! Tell it, brother, tell it!'

Penabaz looked at the crowd and tried to project authority, but the size of it – close to thirty people now – shocked and shook him. He glanced at Mandel and saw fear all over his partner's face.

'We're gonna call it in right now, mam, don't worry,' Penabaz said to Garcelle, as firmly as he could manage against the anxiety fast flooding into him.

He started heading for the car, Mandel following.

'HEY!' Garcelle shouted, coming after them, the crowd following. 'What, what's *that*?'

The cops pretended they hadn't heard her and carried on walking, but faster.

'Let's get the fuck outta here,' Mandel whispered to Penabaz.

Garcelle grabbed Mandel's arm and stopped him in his tracks.

'THAT'S RORO'S BAG YOU CARRYIN'!' she shouted.

'Wa-hat . . . th-th-this?' Mandel stammered, pointing at the bag.

'Yeah – THAT! *That* is money for when he retired. He was gonna build himself a place back home in Haiti! Boulette came in and robbed him. Only Roro shot him before he could get away. Now *you* the thieves!'

The crowd fanned out and encircled the three of them.

'You're m-m-mistaken,' Mandel said. 'It's mine.'

'You paint a little white monkey under your bag, *Officer*?'

'Wah-what?'

'Roro did. A little white monkey. Bet if you turn that bag over there'll be a little white monkey on there. It was Roro's mark, on account of how he was always eatin' bananas. Go on and show me under the bag. If the monkey ain't there, you can go on your way. If it *is* there, then you a thief – *Officer*. Show me the bag. Come on!'

Mandel looked to Penabaz for a lifeline.

'SHOW ME THE BAG!' Garcelle shouted.

Shaking, Mandel lifted up the bag.

On the underside was a small painting of a chimp in profile, eating a banana under a palm tree.

'*Thief*!' Garcelle spat at him. 'Gimme that bag!'

Then Penabaz intervened, holding up his hands.

'This isn't the way it looks at all, mam. We were taking this bag away for safekeeping.'

'Safekeepin' my ass! You just about the *keepin'* part! You just told me – and everyone else here – you didn't even *go* to the store!' And without letting go of Mandel's arm, she turned to the crowd. 'Didn't y'all hear him say that?'

'YES, WE DID!' the crowd hollered back.

'DIDN'T. Y'ALL. HEAR. HIM. SAY THAT!'

'YES WE DID!'

'You lyin'-ass thievin'-ass corrupt cop!' Garcelle said to Mandel.

'Let's kick they asses!' a man yelled.

'Give this back!' The woman grabbed at the bag's handle, but the cop held on. They struggled. Garcelle, urged on by the onlookers, was getting the upper hand while Mandel was losing his grip and with it his nerve.

Penabaz saw this and knew it was time for drastic action. He drew his gun and pointed it at Garcelle.

'Let go and step away NOW!'

She didn't. He cocked the hammer to emphasize his intent.

The crowd backed off a little.

Garcelle let go of the bag but didn't move away. She stood where she was with her hands by her sides, terrified, incredulous and above all angry. There were tears in her eyes.

'Roro worked all his goddamned life for that money,' she said. 'And you – you just *steal* it offa him.'

The cops began to back away.

'You should be *ashamed* of yourselves!' Garcelle yelled after them. 'And I got your *names* too! Penabaz and Mandel. I'm gonna *report* your thievin' asses!'

Mandel stopped walking.

'Fuck this,' he whispered.

'What are you doing?' Penabaz asked.

'I'm giving it back.'

'The fuck you are!'

'We're busted. I ain't goin' to jail –'

Behind them, the cops heard an almighty crash. They turned and saw their car being beat to shit by a mob with bats, clubs and metal poles. The back window had been staved in, the tyres slashed and a couple of kids were on the roof, kicking out the lights.

And it was worse: a mass of people were moving up towards them from 54th Street.

From Garcelle's end, people were doing the same.

The two cops looked at each other. They knew they were fucked.

A bottle flew through the air and caught Penabaz on the side of the head. He went down, dropping his gun.

The crowds charged at them.

Mandel was struck in the back by a brick. He let go of the bag and went for his gun, but was brought down by a blow to the legs and then, almost immediately, people swarmed around him, kicking and punching him.

He blacked out.

Meanwhile, Penabaz, dazed, his head bleeding profusely, managed to slither away, unnoticed in the violence and confusion.

He stumbled up North East 2nd Avenue. At first he was lost, like he'd woken up from a deep sleep to find himself dumped back in a dream. Then, as the sheer terror of his situation sunk in, his senses overrode his pain and dizziness and he began to find his legs and run.

Missiles began to follow him. Then a tattoo of pursuing feet.

He ran faster. And faster.

He got onto 56th Street, praying he'd see police cars there, but it was empty of all traffic.

He carried on running. But he wasn't going fast enough, he knew, and sooner or later someone was going to catch up with him and take him down.

He began to pray as he ran.

'Don't let them kill me, God. Don't let them kill me. Please.'

And then a miracle.

A solitary yellow cab turned into the road and started heading his way.

He ran into the lane, towards the cab, waving his arms in the air. The cab slowed and then stopped.

'Thank you, God!' Penabaz looked up into the heavens as he went over to the vehicle.

'Get me outta here, man!' Penabaz said to the black driver, as he tried to open the passenger door. It was locked.

'Come on, man! They're gonna fucken' kill me. Open the fucken' door!'

The driver looked very calmly at the road up ahead and at the mob spilling out of North East 2nd Avenue and heading towards them.

'Come on! *Please!*'

When the driver looked back at Penabaz, the cop suddenly recognized him.

He reached for his holster, but remembered, mid-motion, that he'd dropped his gun in the street. The driver reached over slightly towards the door and Penabaz thought he was going to open it. But, instead, the driver lifted a sawn-off shotgun from the seat and blew the cop's face clean off to the bone.

Max and Joe were coming down 56th Street when they saw the cop get shot by the cab driver. The cab sped away before the cop's body hit the ground, screeching past them in a blur.

'Officer down! Officer down! North East 56th Street! North East 56th Street!' Max shouted into the radio as Joe hit the brakes and got out to check on the fallen cop.

'Please state your intentions,' the dispatcher's voice crackled back.

Max looked through the windshield. Joe shook his head. The cop was dead.

'In pursuit of suspect. Suspect is driving a yellow cab. Heading east on 56th. Request back-up.'

They chased the cab through Lemon City and watched as violence began to erupt all over the area like ripe, diseased sores.

On street after street, cars were being broken into, stores were being looted, windows smashed, people were being beaten up or fleeing for their lives, rocks, bottles and sticks were flying in volleys through the air.

Back-up was nowhere in sight. The radio crackled with emergency calls, requests for help, requests for ambulances, reports of cops being dragged out of their vehicles, reports of shots being fired.

Max had his pistol in one hand, his rifle in the other. Their Chevy was stoned or people ran alongside it and tried to smash the windows whenever they slowed down or stopped to avoid hitting pedestrians.

Petrol was siphoned out of cars and into bottles. First buildings went up in flames, then mounds of tyres, then the cars themselves. Thick acrid smoke began to fill the streets.

The cab got onto North East 3rd Avenue, which was comparatively clear, and started tearing up the road. Max and Joe were close on its tail. Max leant out of the window and tried to shoot out the tyres, but the driver was zigzagging left and right, so he couldn't get a clear aim.

Suddenly three prowlers and a riot truck came zooming towards them. The cab swerved and skidded into the opposite lane and then tore back up the road, passing the Chevy.

Joe reversed and spun the car around, in time to see the back of the cab disappearing down a side street.

They came out on North East 55th Terrace. The road was choked with people running away from a line of cars which had been rolled across the road and set ablaze.

They saw the cab. It was in the middle of the road, at an angle, all four doors wide open, being pushed by a group of people.

Max searched the crowd.

Then, on the right sidewalk, he saw a man standing quite calmly in the chaos, looking right at them. He was wearing jeans, a black sweatshirt, white sneakers and a black do-rag. He had a sawn-off shotgun in his hand.

'There! That's him!' Max pointed out Do-rag and opened the door.

Do-rag turned and started walking off down the road, quite calmly, once in a while looking over his shoulder back at them.

'WHERE YOU FUCKIN' GOIN'!' screamed Joe.

'We can't drive through this.'

Rifle in hand, Max got out and started running down the sidewalk.

When Do-rag saw him coming he broke from saunter to lightning sprint in a fraction of a second.

Joe stated his position to the dispatcher, requested back-up again and, cursing his partner's recklessness, got out of the car.

Max chased the man through crowds of panicked, angry people. Do-rag slipped around them like an expert skier negotiating a slalom course, moving with the agility of a gazelle on speed. Max – jacked up on adrenaline, but fresh out of hospital, weighed down by his bulletproof vest, 190 pounds of sluggish muscle, painkillers and blinded by the sweat streaming down his face – hit the crowd like a wrecking ball, crashing, pushing, toppling and stamping on whoever didn't get out of his way fast enough. People tried to get at him, the lone white face in that seething cauldron of black rage, fists and kicks were thrown, but he ducked, or sidestepped, or smashed his rifle butt into stomachs and faces, or fired shots above their heads. When a man came running up behind Max with a meat cleaver, Joe shot him in the shoulder without hesitation and moved on.

Do-rag zipped across the sidewalk like it was made of ice. He ran across the street, through a crowd carrying furniture out of a store. Max followed him, toppling an old man who was being carried high up above the chaos in an armchair.

Do-rag ran around a brown three-storey building. Max reached the corner in time to see him scooting up the fire escape, three steps at a time. When he reached the top floor, he went over to the window nearest the stairs, opened it from below and slipped inside.

He didn't close the window behind him.

Max was about to take the fire escape when he saw Joe coming.

'He's on the third floor. Second room on the right. He's left the window open,' Max said. 'Take the front.'

Joe nodded and headed for the building's entrance, while Max stole quietly and quickly up the stairs to the window.

He looked inside. He'd expected to see a small, cramped, low-rent apartment, but found himself staring into a long bare space with unvarnished wooden floors and white-washed walls painted with yellow and black voodoo symbols – snakes coiled around candles, coffins marked with crosses, hands gripping a cracked skull. The opposite wall was covered in a mural of Baron Samedi walking through a village, collecting bones.

Do-rag was sitting on the floor with his back turned, and the shotgun by his side. He was facing a large black painted cross with a purple cloth draped around the beams.

He was alone.

Max gingerly crept into the room and tiptoed towards the man, his gun trained on his head.

'Freeze, asshole! Police!'

The man didn't move.

'Face down on the floor with your hands behind your head!'

The man still didn't move.

Max kicked the shotgun away and then put his foot on the man's back and sent him toppling on his front.

He was about to frisk him when there were several heavy bangs on the door, followed by a huge crash. Part of the mural came away as Joe came bursting in.

Max turned Do-rag over.

He didn't immediately realize who it was. The face was plain, a photofit of a black Everyman.

But there was something about his stare, and mostly the hint of the smile, the mouth's not quite muffled mirth.

Boukman.

The shock hit him and he felt himself retreat a step or two, dazed, stung by a phantom punch.

Boukman lay quite still, arms spread out, palms out, and his eyes on Max, beaming recognition.

Max was speechless.

So was Joe.

They stood him up, dragged him against the wall and frisked him.

'Open your mouth and stick your tongue out,' Joe ordered.

Boukman affected a yawn and rolled out his split tongue

– pale pink, except for the ends, which diverged and were pointed and red.

Both Joe and Max winced at the sight of it.

'Put it away,' Max mumbled disgustedly.

Keeping his rifle trained on Boukman's head, the barrel inches away, Max sized him up. They were about the same height, but Boukman was of a much slighter build, an almost insignificant presence. Only his eyes – which never once left Max's – hinted at innate strength, at a will and ability to do what others wouldn't.

'Solomon Boukman: you are under arrest, motherfucker,' Max began. 'You have the right to remain silent. Anything you say can and *will* be used against you as evidence. You have the right to a lawyer. If you can't afford one, the state will provide one.'

Max looked around for a chair to sit Boukman down in so they could question him about his high-level protector. He couldn't see one anywhere. He noticed how the place had once been four separate apartments, but the walls had been knocked out. Outside he saw columns of dark smoke rising up into the sky and a Miami PD chopper flying low across roofs. They couldn't take Boukman in until the riot was over. Their car would probably be burning now.

'And you also have the right . . .'

Max thought about what he'd been through, the needle through his lips, almost killing Eldon and Joe. Then he thought of Sandra. And how Boukman had kidnapped her.

'. . . to file a complaint against me . . .'

And the small, fragile restraint separating man from beast snapped.

'. . . for police brutality.'

Max swung his rifle butt hard at Boukman's face. The wood connected flush with the bone and Boukman went down with a quiet plop. He spat blood and started pushing himself up, but Max grabbed him by the shoulders and threw him against the wall. He pounded him like a heavy bag, slamming his fists into his head and torso. Boukman collapsed under the fusillade of punches, but Max didn't stop. Screaming and snarling he kicked and stamped on his prone body.

Boukman stopped moving, but Max, in a blind vengeful rage, didn't notice, didn't even care.

He grabbed Boukman's head and started banging it on the floor.

Joe, who'd stood by, knowing this would happen, decided to intervene. He gripped his partner in a bear hug and dragged him off.

'He's had enough now, Max! And so have you! That's it!'

Max lunged forward but Joe pushed him back against the wall. Max struggled, but Joe penned him in using his bulk.

'Cool it now, Max! Come on! Come on now . . .'

Joe kept him there until he saw the mad fury begin to dim in his partner's eyes; the violence give way to the possibility of reason.

'Let's do the right thing. By the book. OK?'

Max took deep breaths. Joe could see him calming himself inside, standing down.

Max looked at him, clear-eyed, and nodded.

Joe stepped away from him, but as he did so, Max saw Boukman had stood up and was staring at them – specifically at Max. His eyes were swollen almost shut, his nose and mouth were bloody, and his left cheek was a bloated, protuberant lump, and yet there was amusement etched through all the damage.

Then, before either cop could fully react, Boukman spun around and bolted for the window at an almost unnatural speed, as if he'd been whisked across the room by a hidden hand. He leapt feet first through the glass, taking most of the window frame with him. He missed the fire escape gangway and fell through thin air.

Max and Joe rushed over and looked down at the ground. They saw only shattered glass and splintered wood below.

Boukman was already up on his feet and running away from the building, making for the streets.

They bundled down the fire escape.

There was blood all over the debris where Boukman had landed, and a trail of thick wet red splashes mapped the direction he'd taken.

They followed the blood markers down the sidewalk and across the street. The riot squads had moved in. Choppers were sweeping the sky, which had darkened considerably, storm clouds mingling with the towers of black smoke rising from incinerated buildings and cars, as a hot dirty wind fanned the flames and blew tear gas and gasoline fumes into their faces.

They kept their watering eyes to the ground, following Boukman's spoor, the blood making bigger and bigger marks. Max guessed Boukman had opened an artery. The faster he was running the more blood he was losing. He didn't have long and neither did they, if they wanted to get him alive.

They negotiated scenes of chaos: full-scale battles between helmeted, baton-wielding cops and rioters on one street; a car being rammed into the front of a laundromat in another; a near empty supermarket being looted; a man running through the streets with an aquarium; a woman pushing a cartload of golfclubs; groups of people making petrol bombs.

The blood splashes began to diminish in size. They began to note bloody handprints on walls and whatever windows were still intact.

They came to 54th Street, which was now completely deserted and strewn with trash and detritus. They looked for blood up and down the sidewalk and on the road, but saw none.

They crossed over the road and looked on the other side. Nothing.

Max looked back to the opposite side and noticed a store on the very corner of the street. They'd had their backs to it and hadn't seen it.

The front was completely covered with thick steel shutters. On the side of the shutters, close to a narrow passageway dividing the store from a barbershop, was a bloody handprint.

They crossed the road again and went down the passageway, crouching, Max in front.

The back door of the store was wide open, hanging a little off its hinges and smeared with fresh blood.

They crept towards it and flattened themselves against the wall.

Max looked in. It was empty and dark, except for thin slivers of light coming through gaps in the shutters.

Boukman was lying in the middle of the floor, on his side, motionless.

Max went over to him carefully. He prodded him on his back with his foot.

Boukman unravelled, his limbs flopping out softly, like lifeless tentacles.

Max checked his vital signs. The pulse was faint, and his skin already had the coolness of death.

He stared at Boukman for a second, watching the life drain out of him with every fading heartbeat. It was tempting to let him die here, alone, except for his enemies, in the darkness and dirt. He deserved no better. It even made a kind of sense, but it wasn't right. And, ultimately, it was no kind of justice.

Joe sensed what Max was thinking, as good as knew it.

'What do you want to do with him, Max?'

Max thought about it a little more. He knew the way things worked in the city. The police would get blamed for the riot that was still raging outside – even if it wasn't their fault. Boukman might even get off.

'He killed a cop, Max, and we saw him do it,' Joe said. 'He started this shit. Not us.'

'Let's take this motherfucker in,' Max said to Joe.

Max cut open Boukman's trouser leg, located the wound – a long deep gash in the side of his thigh – and used his belt as a tourniquet to stop the bleeding.

Then, as he was bending down to pick Boukman up, he saw a flicker in the Haitian's swollen eyes and saw he was looking at him.

Boukman whispered something to him in the faintest, slightest breath, the words making the sound of a knife being sharpened on a whetstone.

Max bent down to hear.

He didn't catch it all. But he made out one word, clearly. 'Live.'

He waited in case Boukman repeated himself, or said something else, but he didn't.

Max hoisted Boukman up on his shoulders and carried him from the store and back into the street.

On the first Tuesday in October, Eldon Burns made the trip from Miami to Raiford Prison in Union County, to see Solomon Boukman. According to the warden, Boukman – now fully recovered after losing almost four pints of blood on the day of his arrest – had said next to nothing to anyone after he'd arrived. He answered questions in monosyllables, affirmative or negative grunts, or nods or shakes of the head. Only at night, in his sleep, did they hear him speak, but then in words no one in the prison could understand. He used a multitude of voices, none of them English. They'd bugged his cell and sent the recordings to language experts, who'd identified eighteenth century French, Haitian Kreyol and two West African dialects. The translations were identical. Solomon said the same thing in every language.

'You give me reason to live.'

'Your lawyer won't be coming any more,' Eldon announced after the guards had left him alone with Boukman in the interview room. 'Conflict of interest.'

Eldon sat down at the wooden table across from Boukman and observed him for a moment. He'd lost weight, to the extent that he resembled an anorexic teenager dressing tough in his standard-issue prison denim. His face was gaunt, his eyes baggy and his skin had the cold tone of burnt-out matchsticks, coupled with the sickly pallor common to prisoners with limited access to daylight and fresh air. He didn't look like much, but looks were deceiving. All the inmates at Raiford were terrified of him.

Boukman hadn't had advance warning of Eldon's visit,

but he wasn't remotely surprised to see him. Or else he'd mastered the inmate's theatre of complete indifference to perfection: in prison you learnt to blend in with the walls.

Eldon reached into the padded envelope he'd brought with him and placed its contents on the table in front of Boukman. Three TDK C90 cassette tapes – black, grey and clear – each with dates written on the labels. Boukman glanced at them briefly, his expression unchanged.

'Think I didn't know you taped our conversations? Two copies for you' – Eldon pointed to the grey and clear tapes – 'and one for Pruitt McGreevy – or, as we call him, Mr McGrievance. How much did you know about your lawyer, exactly?'

Eldon waited for Boukman to answer. He didn't. He merely sat back in his chair and folded his arms. Eldon noted he'd done up all the buttons of his shirt-front, collar and cuffs.

'All those high and mighty liberal principles of his,' Eldon continued. 'The man defends nigras pro bono, and all along he's got a *pro-boner* for under-age girls. Scandal like that – if it came out – would kill his career. He didn't want to be disbarred. I'm sure you understand. It wasn't personal.'

Boukman stared at Eldon, their eyes locking for the first time in broad daylight for many years. Eldon had almost forgotten those unique brown eyes with their bottomless stare, empty as skull sockets and filled with the same darkness. They were eyes old before their time, eyes that had lost their power to be surprised by anything life had to show them, no matter how shocking, cruel or atrocious. It took most criminals – even the hardest cases – years to perfect that inscrutability, that coldness and remove, but none of them even came close to matching Boukman.

'Even *with* the tapes, he couldn't have helped you. Cause you ain't gonna be tried for the drugs or the kidnapping or all that killing – those fucked-up voodoo sacrifices, all that shit you did. We don't care about that. You people kill each other every day. It's no story.

'But killing a cop, now that *is* a story. And *that's* what you're goin' down for. It's open and shut. Two highly decorated officers saw you do it. Your prints are on the murder weapon. Ballistics match. Done deal. The best lawyer in the world couldn't get you out of that. It's a straight-up death-row bounce. You'll get the chair.'

Boukman smiled very slightly at that, the ends of his mouth betraying the same hint of private amusement seen in his newspaper picture and mugshot. Then he leant forward and spoke, his voice no more than a murmur, 'Your "two highly decorated officers" – Max Mingus and Joe Liston – they were after me, but they never actually *caught* me. They caught a random taxi driver who killed a cop. If they're the best you've got, you might as well hand the city over to the criminals. But what am I saying? The city's *already* in the hands of criminals.' Boukman tilted his head at Eldon. 'Does Mingus know him and me were on the same team?'

'You've got nothin' left, Boukman.' Eldon ignored the taunt, but its boldness rankled. Why hadn't they killed this fucker in Lemon City? Why hadn't they let him bleed out? 'We've got it *all* – *all* your people, *all* your property, *all* your money. And your Haitian connections? *I've* got *all* those.'

'Enjoy . . . while it lasts. Because nothing that good lasts for ever.' Boukman's eyes glinted with knowing mockery.

Eldon snorted contemptuously and shook his head.

'What I don't get . . . You *knew* the jig was up in Opa Locka. You could've run. Split town. Split the country. Why d'you stay? Why d'you go to Lemon City – of *all* the other places you could've gone to?'

'I know my destiny.'

'Eva's bullshit again!' Eldon chuckled.

Boukman lost his smirk at the mention of Eva's name.

'Destiny can't be changed, any more than a bullet can be recalled.'

'So you knew it was comin' and you did nothin' to change it? You Haitians are a bunch of fucken' losers, you know that?' Eldon laughed.

'You don't know *how* this ends,' Boukman replied.

'Oh, I *do*,' Eldon said. 'It ends with you frying in an electric chair a year or two from now: your insides boiling, your flesh burning like paper and your eyes popping out of your skull.'

'It doesn't end that way at all for me,' Boukman replied. 'You'll cage me, but you'll *never* kill me.'

'You sure of that?'

Boukman nodded and sat back in his chair and folded his arms.

'Why?'

'Everything has come to pass. Everything has come true. To the letter. Right down to your betrayal.'

'Yeah?' Eldon was incredulous. 'Then why did you fucken' do business with me?'

'Destiny and bullets,' Boukman replied.

'Eva did some job on you.' Eldon laughed. 'Turned you into a permanent fucken' zombie! Did she know she was going to burn to death in her own house?'

'She didn't die in the fire,' Boukman said, with a slight touch of emotion. 'She was dead when I found her.'

'Carmine kill her?'

Boukman didn't answer. He crossed his arms tighter.

'Don't make no difference anyway. Case is closed. Good riddance.' Eldon thought he saw a shadow of hurt darken Boukman's eyes, but it was gone so quickly it might have been wishful thinking on his part.

'Why did you come here?' Boukman asked.

Eldon had ostensibly come to tell Boukman that his

insurance policy – the tapes he'd been planning to use against him – had expired. But he'd really come to show that dumb nigger just how powerful and all-knowing he was.

But it hadn't really worked out that way. Boukman's attitude – his resignation to his fate and the certainty, his cast-iron faith that he'd escape the inevitable – had unnerved and even undone him. He was suddenly conscious of the sweat running down his temples, of the uncomfortable feeling in his gut that maybe – just maybe, in some impossible way – Boukman might even be right about the way things were going to turn out.

Eldon felt beaten. Powerless. Insignificant.

Without saying a word to the prisoner, he put the tapes back in the envelope, stood up and banged on the door for the guard.

'I thought so,' Boukman said, his voice suddenly at his ear.

Eldon turned around sharply, expecting to see him standing right behind him, but he hadn't moved from the table. He was smiling broadly at Eldon, showing a set of strong white teeth and, between them, the curled, pointed tips of his splayed tongue.

As the door opened and Eldon stepped out of the room he heard Boukman laugh behind him. It wasn't a loud laugh, more a snigger, but a hard, contemptuous one which reminded him of hailstones on a tin roof.

The laughter stayed with him, not in his ears, but in his brain, embedded in his memory, swirling around and around in his head as it followed him out of the prison and into his car. It was with him as he drove to Gainesville Regional Airport and caught the flight back to Miami. And then, once he was airborne, it got marginally louder and significantly harsher, especially when he tried to concentrate on the business he had before him that evening – a meeting with the Mayor, to discuss his imminent promotion to Deputy Chief, and how he was going to help clean up the police force and make Miami great again.

EPILOGUE
5 November 1982

'How did it go?' Sandra asked Max after he'd sat down next to her on the sand. It was early evening and the sun was going down, bathing the beach in a deep coppery glow. The holidaymakers were all packing up and drifting away back to their hotels, while the gulls were circling the trash they'd left behind like vultures. Soon the junkies and the homeless bums would be marking out their turf for the night.

'It went,' he said. It had been his third and final day on the witness stand in the trial of Solomon Boukman, and he was dead beat, drained to the last dregs, good for nothing but some idle small talk, a couple of hours of mindless TV and a good long sleep.

'His lawyer chew you up today?'

'No.' Max shook his head. 'He left his teeth at home. Again.'

Boukman's public defender was one of the worst lawyers he'd ever encountered – if not the worst. Or should that be the best? A half-decent lawyer would have at least tried to cast a shadow of doubt over his and Joe's testimony: they never actually saw *who* pulled the trigger on the cop, never positively IDed *Boukman* behind the wheel of the cab (which was never recovered after the riot); they could, theoretically, have been chasing the wrong man. And then there were all those injuries Boukman had sustained – three broken ribs, a busted nose, a fractured cheek and a dislocated jaw – which Max didn't even get cross-examined about. Not that the predominantly white jury would have bought into Boukman's innocence anyway: the press had already blamed him for starting what was now known as the 'Little Haiti

Riot' when he'd killed Otis Mandel, an honest, hard-working patrol cop who'd left behind a wife and daughter; and no lawyer could argue with forensics and fingerprint evidence. Boukman was going down. No doubt about it.

'So why are you upset?'

'I'm not.' Max smiled at her. 'I'm just tired.'

'Something's bugging you. Something's got under your skin.' Sandra looked at him with her big brown eyes that saw everything.

'Can I tell you later?'

'Nothing wrong with now.'

'Everything's wrong with now.' He looked out at the sea and the family in front of them – a couple and their two young children, a boy and a girl in matching yellow floppy hats.

Sandra was frowning at him. 'I insist.'

'I've . . . I've decided to leave the force. I'm not gonna be a cop any more. I don't *wanna* be a cop any more. Not this way.'

He thought she'd be pleasantly shocked, but she was merely pleased.

'I knew you weren't happy there,' she said.

'Why?'

'After you brought Boukman in, you just stopped caring.'

'You noticed?'

'Oh yeah.'

Yeah, he *had* stopped caring, but it had nothing to do with Boukman.

First Joe had left last October. He'd transferred out to Vice. Half the girls he'd busted in his first six months on the job had once worked for Carmine and Eva Desamours.

Then Eldon had been made Deputy Chief, to much press fanfare. He was hailed, in some papers, as 'Miami's best shot at salvation'. He'd immediately expanded and reorganized MTF into individual units, all reporting to him.

Max got promoted to Lieutenant and put in charge of MTF's Robbery and Homicide division. He hated it. MTF may have been reorganized, but that simply meant it had become more proficient at doing what it had done before. Evidence was still planted, people were still framed or killed, and judges and juries lied to: the wrong bad guys got convicted and the right ones walked. 'Make it fit and make it stick' became MTF's unofficial motto. There was no point in talking to Eldon about it, because it was the way Eldon had always done things, and the way he'd *always* do things.

And as for Max, he could either put up or pack up.

He'd lived that way, one foot out of the door, one foot in, right up until the start of the Boukman trial.

When he'd been called to the witness stand and placed his hand on the Bible to give his oath, he'd remembered his swearing-in ceremony, when he'd first joined the police. He'd really believed in what he was doing then, really believed that he could make a difference. And then he'd remembered how he and Joe had tracked Boukman, on their own, working out of that garage in Overtown. It all seemed to have happened to someone else.

And that was when he'd made his decision.

'I don't know what I'll do,' Max concluded.

'We'll think of something. Don't worry. It'll be all right. It'll be *more* than all right. You'll see.'

'You think?'

'I *know*. What does your gut tell you?'

'If I stay it'll just get worse,' Max answered. 'But if I leave, it can only get better. Me and Eldon may have history, but this is about the future.'

'There you go,' she said. 'I never did like Eldon. Those brief times we met, in the hospital, and when you made Lieutenant . . . something about him wasn't right. Something didn't fit and didn't stick.'

'Anything specific?'

'Instinct.' Sandra shrugged.

'That's what you get from livin' with a cop. A little of our sixth sense rubs off.'

'Oh, I've *always* had it, baby.'

'Then you should've been a cop.'

They laughed and after the laughter they let the sound of the waves take over for a while.

Sandra watched the family in front of them. The father was holding the girl up and making her squeal with laughter as he pulled faces and growled. This made Sandra smile, the way Max had noticed she always did when she saw happy children – or children generally. It was her private, daydreaming smile, the one she never shared with him; the one she had when she was seeing her hopes and dreams being projected through others.

She put her arm around him and leant her head on his shoulder.

'You know,' she sighed, 'I'm really looking forward to spending the rest of my life with you.'

He smiled at that. He thought of something appropriate to say in return, and the words came to him quickly.

But as he opened his mouth to speak he felt a sudden chill shoot down his spine and his body spasmed and shook.

Sandra sat up and looked at him worriedly.

'What is it? Are you OK?'

She ran her fingers along his forearm and felt goosepimples.

'I'm fine.' He nodded, suddenly warm again, like nothing had happened.

She rubbed his arm and looked up at the sky and its dwindling light.

'We best be going in,' she said. 'It'll be dark soon.'

'Yeah,' Max replied with an unknowing certainty, 'I know.'

NICK STONE

MR CLARINET

**Winner of the CWA Ian Fleming Steel Dagger
for Best Thriller of the Year**

Winner of the International Thriller Writers' Best Debut Novel

Winner of the Macavity Award for Best First Novel

The job: find a rich man's kidnapped son in Haiti

The reward: $10 million to bring the boy back alive

The man: Max Mingus, ex-cop, ex-PI and now ex-con

The stakes: his predecessors haven't just failed, they've been
destroyed …

Max Mingus knows the price of a bad risk, but he takes the Haiti job
because no one else will. A lawless island of voodoo and black magic
where each man must face his personal demons, Haiti is also home
to a monster they call Mr Clarinet – infamous for spiriting countless
children away from their families.

In searching for the boy – alive or dead – Max has only his life to lose.
But in Haiti, there are fates far worse than death …

'A triumphant debut' *Observer*

'An intriguing plot, believable characters and thrills and spills to keep
you turning the pages eagerly. A rollicking read' *Big Issue*

MICHAEL MORLEY

SPIDER

> *'For a second she thinks she is dead,*
> *then she opens her eyes and wishes she was.'*

The press call him the Black River Killer and his stats are shocking: 16 murders; not captured in 20 years; the FBI's best profiler – Jack King – burned out and beaten, his career shattered.

Jack and his wife now run a hotel in Tuscany. And though he still gets nightmares, rural Italy is a whole world away from BRK's brutal crime scenes in South Carolina. Or so Jack thought …

As Italian cops discover the body of a young woman – her remains mutilated like BRK's victims – a gruesome package arrives at the FBI, twin events that conspire to lure the profiler back into the hunt.

But this time, who is the spider and who is the fly?

'A terrifying read that will keep you hooked' Simon Kernick

'*Spider* chillingly captures the harsh realities of a deteriorated mind' Lynda La Plante

'A chillingly vivid thriller. Don't read it alone in the middle of the night' Steven Bochco

CHRIS MOONEY

THE SECRET FRIEND

Two dead girls in the river
Two tiny statues of the Virgin Mary concealed in their clothing
One CSI on the hunt for their killer

When Judith Chen is found floating in Boston's harbour, links are made with the murder of Emma Hale, a student who vanished without trace, only for her body to wash up months later.

CSI Darby McCormick is assigned to the case and uncovers a piece of overlooked evidence from the Hale investigation – which brings her into contact with Malcolm Fletcher, a former FBI agent now on the Most Wanted list after a string of bloody murders. And when a third student goes missing, Darby is led into a dangerous game of cat-and-mouse with deadly links to the past – and a man who speaks to the Blessed Virgin. A man who wants to be a secret friend to the girls he abducts …

'Masterful … dark and disturbing' Linda Fairstein

'Chris Mooney is a wonderful writer' Michael Connelly

He just wanted a decent book to read ...

Not too much to ask, is it? It was in 1935 when Allen Lane, Managing Director of Bodley Head Publishers, stood on a platform at Exeter railway station looking for something good to read on his journey back to London. His choice was limited to popular magazines and poor-quality paperbacks – the same choice faced every day by the vast majority of readers, few of whom could afford hardbacks. Lane's disappointment and subsequent anger at the range of books generally available led him to found a company – and change the world.

'We believed in the existence in this country of a vast reading public for intelligent books at a low price, and staked everything on it'
Sir Allen Lane, 1902–1970, founder of Penguin Books

The quality paperback had arrived – and not just in bookshops. Lane was adamant that his Penguins should appear in chain stores and tobacconists, and should cost no more than a packet of cigarettes.

Reading habits (and cigarette prices) have changed since 1935, but Penguin still believes in publishing the best books for everybody to enjoy. We still believe that good design costs no more than bad design, and we still believe that quality books published passionately and responsibly make the world a better place.

So wherever you see the little bird – whether it's on a piece of prize-winning literary fiction or a celebrity autobiography, political tour de force or historical masterpiece, a serial-killer thriller, reference book, world classic or a piece of pure escapism – you can bet that it represents the very best that the genre has to offer.

Whatever you like to read – trust Penguin.